The Saga Begins

In a time before the Dragon Wars consumed Tarmor, the Dragonsouls ruled over the five races. Then, during the destruction of the Cataclysm that followed the wars, the Dragonsouls disappeared. Most wizards thought them destroyed forever, and a great peace settled over the land, each of the five races finding its place, decimated and hidden as it may be.

But the winds of Chaos blow eternal, and peace can never last. Secrets thought hidden are oft discovered. Though magic only remains in the hands of a few, and the Paladins of Balance are vanishing, some may still stand against the coming storm. Those who will rise have yet to prove themselves, and who stokes the tempest is yet to be known.

"A Balance Broken" is the first tale of The Dragonsoul Saga, a story to span an epic horizon, yet enters the hidden recesses of the human heart, even if that heart is not so human.

The Dragonsoul Saga

by
J.T. Hartke

Book One
A Balance Broken

Dragonsoul Saga Short Stories

about 100 years before Book One
A Healer's Lesson

Follow the Saga at
www.dragonsoulsaga.com

J. T. Hartke

A Balance Broken

Book One of the Dragonsoul Saga

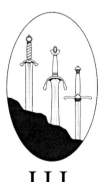

I.I.I.
fantasy

THIS BOOK IS PUBLISHED BY
IMAGINED INTERPRISES, INC.

Content Editor - Maxwell Alexander Drake
Line Editor - Jo Wilkins
Line Editor/Proof Editor - Rob Smith
Proof Editor - Lorraine Stalians

Published in the United States by
Imagined Interprises, Inc.,
6955 N. Durango Dr. Suite. 1115-717
Las Vegas, NV 89149
I.I.I. fantasy is a registered trademark of
Imagined Interprises, Inc.
The Dragonsoul Saga is a registered trademark of
J.T. Hartke

www.dragonsoulsaga.com

www.imaginedinterprises.com

ISBN: 978-1-936525-60-7 (Hardback Edition)

Hardback Edition: July 2012
Printed in the United States of America

The startlement at seeing your first words in print notwithstanding, I should take a page to thank those who made this possible.

First, let me thank Drake, Rob, Jo, and Lorraine, who found a rusty blade and polished it as best they could. I hope the steel they found underneath reaches our readers. I also want to thank Brie, Brian, and the rest of the staff at I.I.I. for being eternally patient and committed to the Dragonsoul project.

I also want to thank Amy, Colby, Kari, and Joe, who actually took the time to read the drafts before I learned to write (better). I appreciate the undeserved compliments. And to my family and friends who never doubted – thanks so much for the support.

And mostly, thanks to Julie, who makes it all possible just by being who she is. I would never have thought myself an "artist" until she dared to let me think so.

JTH

 # Table Of Contents

For Julie, my love and my muse, without whom this would never have happened.

DRAGONSCLAW

Dragons Feet

Dragonscale
Mountains

HIGHSPUR

LONE SEA

The
Wastes

GALLOND RIVER

THE ROCK

Iron
Hills

FREE
CITIES

KIRATH

STONEBOURNE
FORK

IRONFORT

LOST KINGDOM
OF
LOND

NOVON

DADRIC

RIVER ROAD

DERN

GAVANOR

KERRIGEIR

Red
Hills

Blue Mountains

RUINS OF
DAITHMOR

RAPPENRON RIVER

TALEGEIR

BROKEN
BAY

Avari
Plain

Gray
Mountains

TARMOR
492 A.R. (AFTER RETURN)

-LEAGUES-

25 50 75 100 125 150

WILDARA

GRAYWATCH
CASTLE

LONGCLIFF

Fallen Hils

TAMADON

KALNESS

SOTH MOEL

FELARA

THREEFORTS

DAREESH

SARI
SEA

SARINAN RIVER

GA' LIC

Yadush
Highlands

VAR' US

PARADUS

SARIA

SHAZREL

"*The Balance shifts as the Balance will. Its opposing forces wax and wane. However, the Balance itself always exists. No matter how Chaos may reign in one place or time, Order will hold its sway elsewhere. Be it across the world, or across the Universe.*"

— *Volastarun Mardus, "Writings on Opposition", 414 B.C. (Before Cataclysm)*

pROLOGUE

"Arise, oh people of the Northlands, children of the bristling boar. Arise and seek the fiery stars."
— Boar Clan traditional

Slar watched the cold, ebon water of the Galesh River churn past. Its dark hue matched his mood.

His humor held far less cheer than it did a week ago, before the Boar Clan patrol marched out from under the solid gates of Blackstone. Slar had thought this a final foray into clan territory before the Winter Gathering—a pleasant trot through the late autumn countryside. Continuing the journey, however, brought a solid knot of worry into his gut. It burned deep within, an anxiety he had never felt before, even at the approach of battle.

Put away your worry, old woman! Neither Bear nor Wolf would raid this far south during this season. His thoughts turned toward his sons. *I will see them soon enough—when the clan seeks shelter at Blackstone.* His eyes searched the leaden sky, seeing only a horizon that matched his heart. *Looks like we will have a long winter together as it is.*

"Storm gathering behind us, Captain," Sergeant Radgred grumbled in a low tone as he walked past Slar. The veteran stalked toward the tight circle of warriors resting nearby. "Up, you dogs! We're on to Sourbay!"

The squad gathered within moments, the squeak and clink of leather on metal the only sounds they made. With a wave of Radgred's arm, the patrol set off again. Their mail rang with the rhythm of their march as they exited the small copse of trees in which they had taken their afternoon rest.

After about a mile, Slar leapt atop a lichen-crusted boulder, his nail-shod boots scrambling for purchase against the stone. Looking back to scan the westward horizon, the burning knot in his gut sank even further. He squinted against the wind that howled along the northern slopes of the Dragonscale Mountains. The last of the sun hid behind purplish clouds, heavy with the first snow of winter. They hugged the rocky, conifer-covered slopes, hiding the eternal white of impassable peaks.

Slar signaled to the column some distance down the worn, ancient road. "We had better make double time, Sergeant!"

Radgred looked back. "Aye, Captain!" For a fraction of a second, the sergeant's face sank at the sight of the storm. His expression shifted to grim determination before he smacked the shoulder of one of the warriors. "You heard the Captain. *Move!*"

Slar scanned the landscape from his perch. Ahead, a small stream trickled down from the Dragonscales, its clear flow carving a narrow gorge before it tumbled into the Galesh. He jumped down from the boulder, wincing at a creak in his knees that had not been there a year ago. He ignored the protesting cartilage and the sourness lingering in his stomach and sprinted to the front of his patrol.

"With me, lads!" he shouted, passing them with a steady gait. "There is cover ahead." The troops picked up speed to match that of their captain. Radgred followed at the rear, scowling each time he glanced over his shoulder.

His eyes alert, Slar watched the fir trees that spread down the mountains. They began to sway as the first flakes of snow whipped about the squad. By the time he led his warriors down a dry gully toward the gorge, white powder had gathered within the crevasses. Reaching the bottom, Slar ordered Radgred to unroll the heavy, oiled mammoth skin the sergeant carried on his stout back, and the entire patrol huddled beneath it.

Forcing cheer into his voice, Slar wrapped an arm around the warrior next to him. "We can't build a fire, but if we gather together we can save our warmth from draining away." He shouted against the storm that now raged beyond the shaggy tarp. "Huddle close, lads! This is going to be a long night."

His dreams were fitful. Gloomy images flitted through his mind, calling to him from a great distance. Slar searched his dream for the source of the summons, but before it ended, it was he who fled from a dark hunter.

Morning broke outside their dome of snow and flesh. Slar crawled from cover and blinked at the sunshine glittering off a blanket of white. The snow had piled deep, even within the relative cover of the gorge. The thump of drifts settling under the new sun echoed from the cleft in the rock.

After a breakfast of hardtack and snowmelt, he led his men out of the gorge and back onto the road, hidden by a few inches of swiftly melting whiteness. *I know this land like I know the veins tracking the back of my fists. It is as if this land's very soil and water flow within my blood as well. I pray to the Fires that my sons may roam it as long as I have.* The frown on his face deepened. *I fear they will not.* "Back to it, lads." He waved a hand forward, shooing away his dark thoughts. "We can be in Sourbay by nightfall if we press hard."

He shifted the scimitar on his hip, caressing its worn handle. *This sword travelled the road long before I ever did.* The knot of anxiety still tore at his gut, unrelieved by the storm's passing or his morning movement. He struggled to keep a grimace of pain from his face. Shaking off his discomfort, he jogged to the front of his men. He set a fast pace that would test their stamina. *Perhaps I can shake loose this pain, and my useless worry.*

It was still there, though, when he led his men into the outskirts of Kragnek, a small village that was the last settlement before Sourbay. Mud brick huts with thatched roofs huddled on a small knoll overlooking the Galesh. A few goats milled through the recently harvested barley fields. Slar smiled. *Barley bread is our staple, but barley beer keeps us alive!*

He marched his men to the open-aired bar serving the small community. "A round of beer for my men, who run like heroes," he said to the barkeep. "With a fresh loaf for each – and yogurt as well." Slar dug into his pouch, past the gold to the copper underneath. *The glitter of real gold will cause a riot in a town as poor as this.*

"To the captain!" Radgred hoisted his brew and quaffed it down.

A cheer rang out before the rest of the squad followed their sergeant's lead. The beer mugs emptied well before the bread disappeared.

While the men ate, Slar pulled his sergeant aside. "I have a feeling of unease," he whispered, "greater than any I have had since you first led me on this trail nigh twenty years ago." He glanced toward the warriors, who paid them no mind, and continued in an even lower tone. "Something unnatural haunts our steps. Not just raiders from another clan. Something more…powerful. I know not what it is."

Radgred raised an eyebrow, matching Slar's clandestine tone. "You are the one with the Old Blood. That is why you are captain, and I am still sergeant. Even though you never sought to become Boar chieftain like your father once did, you still sense things that others do not." He narrowed his eyes. "Your whole family has this ability. I trust your lead, as I once did your father's." The sergeant clapped Slar on the back. "As I will some day follow your sons."

Slar watched Radgred while the sergeant gathered the squad once more. They grabbed what sustenance still lay on the table and jumped into line behind their captain. Slar trotted the first few miles. Running his warriors on a full stomach would waste the food he had just bought them.

The beer he had consumed did nothing to ease the fire in his stomach. Before long, Slar doubled their pace. *The faster we reach Sourbay, the sooner we return to Blackstone.* Slar frowned at his sergeant, whose focus remained upon the surrounding woods.

Talk of my sons has set them on my mind. Grindar should arrive at Blackstone any day. I bet he found another wife this summer. He smiled at the memory of his youngest son. *Sharrog won Victor status at his first Clanhold this year! Perhaps he might even be home from his Victor's Hunt when we return!*

The knot in Slar's gut loosened somewhat with thoughts of his sons and home. He knew that before long, the days in the Northlands would last only a few hours, and a winter storm might last for days. Blackstone, however, would be warm with the fires of Slar's people. The meat from their hunts would fill bellies throughout the long, dark season.

His pace never slackening, Slar ran his squad into the early autumn evening. Dusk hung in the air when the squad jogged into a sharp cleft cut into the rocky hillside.

"Weren't these carved by the shamans of our people in the Elder Days?" Warrior Lishnak asked under his breath.

"It is true," Slar said to the new recruit. "They wielded great power. That was in a time of greater glory for the Clans." *Before the Dragon Wars left us broken. Before the Clans began to turn on one another.*

Gossamer threads of twilight sifted through the tree limbs, casting an eerie glow upon the unblemished snow as Slar followed the coiled road through the cleft. The sour knot in Slar's gut tightened into the fiery ball he knew from the moment before battle. Looking over his shoulder, he saw the sun had left the sky purple.

Stars pricked the firmament, until sudden darkness, deeper than the night, blackened them out as it flew overhead.

"Spread out!" Slar drew his family sword and dove to the ground. The pace of his heart quickened. "Take cover!" He held his breath while Radgred and the others scrambled into the brush along the road.

Slar crept forward on all fours. The cold snow bit his knuckles, but the feeling remained distant. His mind focused outside his body, becoming one with the world around him.

The black shadow darted overhead again and crashed to the earth. The concussion threw Slar backward along with chunks of stone and earth. He slammed into the ground, breath fleeing from his lungs.

Forcing his chest to heave again, he shook his head to clear the ringing in his ears. He scrambled to his feet, ignoring the crimson that seeped from scrapes on his elbows and the pain throbbing through his cheek. He shook his head to clear his senses. His heart pounded furiously, though it was not from the fear of any enemy. Awe and respect for the power that radiated before him coursed through his being. Anticipation and trepidation filled his heart at the sight of it.

The swirling shape seeped upward from the blast crater, forming itself with more purpose than simple smoke. It spread a deep shadow across the snow, turning it black rather than just hiding the light. A roiling, vaporous figure coalesced above Slar. The shadow morphed into a serpentine face. Two sparkling points of silver opened before him.

A voice like the breaking of an ancient, rusty hinge screeched into the night. *Come forth, Slar, Captain of the Boar Clan!*

The silver light of the eyes bore down on Slar. The pain that had tightened his gut throughout their march faded, slipping away from his perception, much like his sword that clattered to the ground. He dismissed it all, as his entire being focused only on the form billowing before him in the windless night.

Bathed in the light, Slar raised his green-tinted claws into the sky in exaltation. Even though his conscious mind did not completely comprehend, his warrior's heart recognized the colossal power of the spirit hovering before him. The blood red irises of his eyes beamed with adoration as the grating thunder of the voice continued.

I am Galdreth, ancient master of your people. Dismiss your fears for them. My prison weakens at long last! You are my Chosen, and I shall raise you to become Warchief of the united Orc clans.

Slar barely noticed the gasps of startled fear that escaped his warriors. Radgred shuffling up behind him only scraped his conscious mind. He took another tentative step toward the presence towering over him, ignoring the tiny screams of pain from his lacerated hands and knees. The fear in his heart had disappeared, replaced by a sense of joy and wild freedom.

The voice howled again, echoing over Slar, his men, and the empty countryside.

You must find the vessel I have chosen, so that I may break free of my prison. Then I shall remake the history of the Dragon Wars and return the Orc clans to their ancient glory!

5

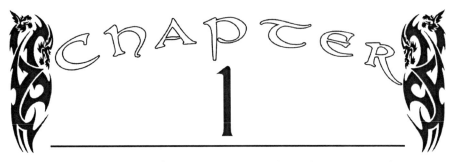

CHAPTER 1

Before the foundation of the Western Realm, the inn now known as The Sleeping Gryphon was an outpost of the Bluecloaks, far outside the border of the kingdom. However, as the west became more civilized, this structure became a waystop not just for soldiers, but for nearly every trader or pioneer passing along the westward trail. Rebuilt at the expense of the king after the Gavanor Rebellion, it has become one of the finest inns in the entire kingdom.
– "Second History of Gannon, Vol. III" by Elyn Bravano

Tallen Westar stretched his hand back under the old stove and scrubbed the horsehair brush back and forth with vigor. The grime he targeted came free at last, though not without a good scrape of his knuckle on iron. He cursed and sucked a small dot of blood welling up on his finger. Tallen despised this job, but his arms were the only ones in the family long enough to reach that spot.

"Cleaning is half of cooking," his father used to tell him. His memories of the old man were few, but still clear – most of them revolving around the kitchen where the innkeeper taught his youngest son the cooking part of the family trade. The thought saddened Tallen, bringing back memories of Lloyd Westar's death in the Bloody Flux nearly a decade ago. *With Mother gone to the cabin most of the year, it's left to me to keep this kitchen running. Dad would have wanted it that way.*

"Have you finished in there yet?" his middle brother called from the open, three-storied great room. Glynn offered a friendlier countenance with the customers, if not his younger brother, and usually took on the duties behind the bar. "Won't be any more folks eating tonight, and Linsay went home. I need your help out here with the drinkers."

Tallen tossed his brush into the bucket of wash water, splashing gray suds onto the tile floor. Most of the black came off his hands with a hardy wipe on a towel. He stepped through the swinging half-door and approached the washbasin behind the bar. "You just want to get everyone out tonight so you can go home to *her*. The new hasn't yet rubbed off your nuptial bed."

Glynn tossed a white rag at Tallen to replace the dirtied one he had thrown over his shoulder. "Get rid of that grime under your nails before you serve any of my customers." Glynn's frown split into a wide grin, as he leaned over to whisper, "Actually, Linsay can't keep her hands off me. You'll understand if you can ever ask Jennette to marry you."

Tallen laughed in spite of his doubt, the comment about his fingernails irking him more than the one about his sometime girlfriend. *Father would never have abided dirty hands in the Gryphon, and neither will I!*

He bent over the washbasin and scrubbed the fine, sheepswool brush over his hands. His umbrage at the thoughtless comment from his brother washed away with the grease.

Glynn stood at the other end of the bar, fists on his hips and an odd look on his face.

He knows he's too hard on me, but he doesn't have the guts to admit it. I know he's had a lot on his shoulders since Dad died, Mom left, and Jaerd joined the army. I can give him the space to be himself. I just wish he could do the same for me.

"Truth is," Glynn said, now in a more fraternal tone, "and don't tell mother in any of your letters to her up north…" He looked over his shoulder as if Kaylyn might appear at any time. "But I think Linsay may already be…" his grin doubled in width, "…with child!"

Bursting with a hearty laugh, Tallen wrapped his arms around his older, smaller brother. Glynn returned the gesture, first tentative, then slapping Tallen on the back.

"You must keep it quiet," he whispered into Tallen's ear. "For now, at least."

Although a few patrons called for more ale, the crowd inside the Gryphon remained sparse. As evening wore into night, the clear sky hanging over the inn had filled with clouds carrying the promise of rain. Tallen knew most farmers would work late in their fields to beat the coming storm. *Everyone else is at home saving their coin for the Sowing Festival in three weeks. My own purse is a little lighter than I might like.* Tallen scowled at the few customers haunting the corners of the spacious common room. *Looks like that situation isn't getting any better tonight.*

The last two farmers, both with plenty of sons and grandsons to plow their fields for them, wobbled out. Tallen wiped down their abandoned table. The old men had left a copper each next to their thrice-emptied mugs. Tallen frowned. He could not buy half a mug for himself with the measly tip. He made a foul gesture, little finger flicking his nose toward the closing door, but jumped when it banged open again, caught by a gust of wind.

Lightning crackled through the night, announcing the rain's arrival. Two men stood framed against the flash. One, tall with flowing black hair and a thick mustache, bore a longsword strapped over his shoulder. The other, shorter and rotund, wore a graying goatee beard and carried a dog-headed staff. Both men were clad in the blue cloaks of the Royal Guard of Gannon, though red fringe trimmed the shorter man's cloth.

"Hallo to the inn," called the taller soldier, whose collar held three silver stars. "My men and I seek shelter before this deluge makes our travel impossible. Have you rooms open? We carry the king's coin."

"Absolutely, General," Glynn said with pride from behind the bar. "Always a room in the Sleeping Gryphon for Bluecloaks. It's been that way since the Western Realm was founded."

Tallen pulled chairs out from around a large table near the still glowing central fireplace. "Even before it was founded." He tossed a couple of split hickory logs onto the embers, stoking the flames to warm the room. More heavily armed soldiers followed the first two men through the door, seating themselves with some order around the long table Tallen prepared. A wolfhound the size of a small horse followed close behind them. The dog padded over to a rug near the fireplace, circled twice, and curled up, his snout examining the entire room.

The general cast his eyes about the inn and nodded in approval. "Stew and bread for all of us, if you have any – including a bowl for Brawny here." The wolfhound snorted. "Ale all around." He flipped a fat, Eastern mark in Tallen's direction.

Catching the shiny piece of gold in the air, Tallen examined it for a moment. Stamped upon it glittered the image of Arathan VII, like most coins in the kingdom these days. The Old King, as he was often called, had ruled for nearly seventy years. Few grandfathers could remember a time before his reign.

"I have some of today's stew still warm in the kettle, sir." Tallen nodded his head. "Would you take butter or oil for your bread?"

"Both," grumbled the rotund man with the staff. "And that stew better have hoofed meat in it for the price Boris paid." His gray eyes had not left Tallen since the soldiers entered the inn, and something about the man's stare rattled Tallen's nerves.

"I use beef from a farm just a few miles away sir." His voice remained cool. "I assure you it was fresh when I prepared it this morning. The vegetables are last autumn's store – carrot, onion, and parsnip. However, they keep quite well in our root cellar here."

The man's bushy eyebrows loosened, but the stare continued. Tallen felt it on his neck all the way into the kitchen. *It's not just that he watches me, it's the intensity. I've never felt such a gaze.*

The olive oil glistened a pale green when Tallen poured it into a small bowl. "This comes from a special provider," he called through the service window, "who makes a trip from Gavanor six times a year. He brings me the freshest of his stock from Avaros. My younger sister, Dawne, churns the butter."

Tallen tossed a little more beef stock into the cauldron hung on the heavy iron hook within the fireplace. A little adjustment to his banked fire, and soon the stew bubbled away again. He scooped out enough for half a dozen bowls, placing them on a tray along with the butter and oil. He set a couple loaves of bread next to them and hefted the tray onto his shoulder. Bumping the swinging door with his hip, he returned to the great room.

"Here you go, sirs." Tallen smiled, sliding the tray to the center of the table. "Hope everything meets your needs." He sat a bowl down in front of the dog, who almost had it gobbled down before he turned back to the six soldiers.

"Thank you, lad." The general wiped foam from his coal black mustache with the back of his hand. "If it is half as good as it smells, your stew will be almost as welcome as the ale."

"Hear, hear," said a giant of a man who sat at the captain's right, tearing into a butter-slathered loaf. He tossed a chunk of the bread to Brawny, who caught it in midair. A big, dwarf made battle-axe rested on the empty table behind the soldier. Tallen had seen their craft before, but never one so large. The image in his mind of the huge man wielding it sent a shiver down his spine.

The officer in the red-fringed cloak sniffed his bowl. "Smells like it could use more pepper." He bit into a small, tentative spoonful before the frown faded. "Not bad. Well seasoned, for the most part, but definitely needs more pepper."

Tallen nodded. "I would agree with you for my own palate, sir, but I must keep the locals happy." With haste, he grabbed the grinder from a nearby table and sat it before the man. "They fear spices as if they might melt the stomach."

The older Bluecloak's pale eyes, barely leaving Tallen since their arrival, remained focused on him. "Do you know what this red fringe on my cloak means, boy?"

"Yes sir." Despite his nerves, Tallen fought down his indignation at the mage's assumption of ignorance. "You are one of the Royal Battlemages sworn to the service of His Majesty, King Arathan. It is likely you trained on the Isle of Wizards, and probable that you excel in the Fire Aspect." He paused, but could not hold it all in. "We have books here on the frontier, sir. They read just as easily in small towns as they do in great cities. This inn's own library is quite well stocked, and they are available for use by patrons." *You are far from the first mage to eat from my kitchen. Though it has been a few years.*

The furrow in the mage's brow deepened. "Are you a Dreamer, boy?" he growled.

Shock darted through Tallen. "I'm sorry?" He chose his words with care. "I— I have dreams, like any normal person."

"I mean…*Dreams.*" The Bluecloak mage squeezed his finger and thumb together. "Ones that seem more real than others. Dreams that sometimes come true." The man continued his harsh stare a moment before leaning closer to the taller officer. Even though they both wore three silver stars upon their collar, the mage seemed to defer. "I think I see something in him."

The general shifted his gaze from the stew to Tallen. Eyes that nearly matched the blue of his cloak appraised Tallen with a deft stare. Tallen's gut sank, as if a predator had noticed him.

"You are the judge of power, not I." The general released Tallen from his gaze. "Eat your stew." He pointed his spoon at the mage's bowl, before taking another bite from his own. "We have more to worry about than apprentice hunting right now," he said around the mouthful. The general swallowed with a satisfied smile that crept above the dimple in his chin. "And let the lad do his job. He seems to do it well."

The Battlemage's scowl did not disappear from his face, but he did dip a piece of bread into his bowl. The frown lessened while he chewed. After a second bite, he waved his hand at Tallen in dismissal.

Tallen slipped away, the mage's words filling him with apprehension. Something in the back of his mind warned him to avoid the Bluecloaks as much as possible for the rest of the night, although he knew that was easier said than done.

When Tallen delivered their second round of ale and more bread, the mage sat deep in whispered conversation with his commander. The gruff man seemed to give him no more mind than he might any other waiter. Before Tallen left the table, however, he was certain he overheard the word "Highspur". *The great fortress?*

After the soldiers quaffed their second ale—wooden spoons

clattering into bowls wiped clean with bread— the general rose from his seat.

"That is enough for tonight, fellows," he said. "We must be onward before dawn, rain or not."

The rest of the squad rose with precision. The tallest, four bronze discs upon his collar, picked up the long, dwarven battle-axe when he stood. "You heard the Earl, boys. Get some clean sack time before we wander out into the wilderness."

The other soldiers grabbed their gear and followed the sergeant. Brawny hopped up from his spot near the fire, and trotted after the soldiers.

Tallen moved to gather the empties. The mage ignored him when he stood, though the soldiers nodded thanks, each leaving a silver penny behind on the table.

"Good night, sirs," Tallen said, watching Glynn lead them into the west wing. He stacked the empty bowls on a platter and took them into the kitchen. He stood at the sink washing dishes when Glynn returned through the swinging door.

"They will be off early. Their commander gave me coin for their rooms." Glynn tried to stifle a yawn. "Do you have that gold mark he tossed you?"

Tallen sighed and wiped the dishwater from his hands before reaching into his pocket.

"Keep it." Glynn gave him a confident nod. "You do a fine job. Dad would be proud."

The startled expression that crept onto Tallen's face was unbidden, but obvious.

"Well, you don't have to gawk at me." Glynn filled his voice with feigned hurt. "I can give a compliment." He shrugged. "Once in a while."

Tallen laughed. "Linsay is rubbing off on you. Your baby will be a good one."

Glynn clapped him on the back with a smile before heading off to his own bed. Tallen cleaned every dish and put out the hearth fire before he followed.

Darkness swirled around Tallen. He struggled for orientation. Vaporous clouds of shadow muddled his perception. His stomach turned. Tallen knew he had been here before, and with each visit, he gathered more awareness. He righted himself, though he was certain there could be no up or down here, and fought to gather his senses.

Memories of the one book he found describing this place flittered into his confused consciousness. The wizards called it the Dreamrealm, a thing of magic and the dominion of the Dreamers. He had asked every bookseller and peddler that came west for more information about it. His search had been in vain, for none could further his query.

Tallen looked outward, though he had no real eyes in the Dreamrealm. He thought of walking, and he floated forward, though he had no real legs. A galaxy of starpoints surrounded him, flashing in a blinding rainbow of colors. The more Tallen came here – the more he concentrated on those fascinating twinkles of light – the closer he came to touching them.

Focusing, Tallen reached outward, but no hand moved in the darkness. These visits had increased over the last year while his body and mind matured, and certain lights he recognized now. One of the points glowed dusky white, its beauty captivating him. It called to him beyond his normal senses. His absent heart yearned to touch it.

A sudden stab of fear tore into his peaceful thoughts and ripped the glistening white point from his awareness. Another presence swarmed about him in the darkness, one Tallen had never sensed before. Even though he had no neck in the Dreamrealm, he felt the hairs lift upon the back of it.

Silvery shadows shimmered through the darkness, wafting like smoke rising from the bowl of a pipe. It wrapped around him, caressing – insistent and pervasive all at once. Tallen fought to move. He could not think beyond the coalescing form curled about him. Glowing with a silver light, it condensed. Two pitch-black eyes peered out from the reptilian face that materialized before him.

Tallen's heart would have stopped had he been in his body during that eternal moment. Those liquid drops of blackness captured his eyeless gaze, a black deeper than that of the Dreamrealm. They stared into his soul, ripping it open, leaving it bare.

Like silk sliding along steel, a voice rang out. *Know that they come for you, human!* The thing screamed into the emptiness it now filled. *Know that I am Gan returned! The ancient trap once set for Galdreth and I has at last weakened!*

The spirit softened its tone, but the words still reverberated in Tallen's mind. *Galdreth seeks to escape it, yet I remain held tighter than my counterpart. I may only approach you in this realm for a short time, but Galdreth can once again touch the physical world.*

The form gathered itself, the voice taking on its previous, more strident timbre. *If Galdreth is let loose, the chaos would destroy the world. Do not forget the People of Gan.*

The bright figure and the power that held Tallen breathless blinked out. Only the darkness of the Dreamrealm loomed about him, now far more foreboding. Tallen reached for the waking world like a breathless swimmer scrambling for the surface of a lake.

He woke to the cyan of pre-dawn creeping through his narrow, second story window. His heart raced, and his head thumped. Tossing the sweat-drenched sheets aside, Tallen stumbled to his small, blue-painted dresser. With a sigh of relief, he splashed cool water from the chipped basin onto his face. His heart pounded in rhythm with his head. The all too real dream had rattled him to his core. While the Dreamrealm was something familiar to him, the entity that had spoken there was not. He splashed water again to drive away the ghosts of his encounter, but the memory of the dream still haunted him, even though the words spoken had slipped away.

Outside Tallen heard the hushed calls of men and the jingle and stamp of horses geared for a journey. Quiet whickers and a short whinny broke through the muffled sounds of dawn. The noise of the horses, common to the inn, helped sooth his nerves. Dabbing his face with a towel, Tallen looked out of the window overlooking the courtyard of the inn and watched the Bluecloaks mount in unison. The muscular wolfhound had already cleared the front gate. The mustached general gave a muted call and waved for his soldiers to follow him toward the River Road.

The Bluecloak mage paused, his red fringe shifting about him. That sharp gaze stared up at Tallen's window, though there was no way the man could have seen him in the faint light. Tallen felt those eyes pierce his – a stare meant for him and him alone. The Battlemage nodded once, before turning his horse to follow his companions.

CHAPTER 2

The five Free Cities, once known as the Last Cities, are all that remain of the lost elven kingdom of Lond. They are also the only places in Tarmor where humans, elves, and dwarves live in common community. This not only provides for diverse cities, but for a difficult political and economic atmosphere. By the fourth century A.R. (After Return), only Kerrigier and maybe Novon, could still be called cities. The others remained little more than prairie cow towns.
— "History of Gannon, Appendix C" by Elyn Bravano

Maddrena Conaleon filled her lungs with the crisp night air. She relished the fresh scents of spring hanging on the breeze. Beneath the more pleasant smells hung the pungent scent of urine, something unavoidable in a city, even one so small as Dern. Maddi watched the moon lift into the night, its sizeable curve recently risen. It provided enough light to work by, but not enough to be easily spied.

"The perfect night for a heist," she whispered to the silver crescent.

The soft soles of her calfskin boots allowed her to grip the slate beneath her feet with ease. She climbed to her favorite vantage point on the roof of a former counting house. She kept one of her hideouts here, places where she found refuge when occasion called. Scanning the horizon of the city from the heights, she saw the Earth Temple rising in the distance. Horse-sized sconces lit its ziggurat shape of stacked mud bricks. The townhouse she sought sat on the square within the temple's shadow.

If the old bastard spoke the truth. Maddi tied her glossy black hair into a bun with a leather thong. Taking a deep breath, she made her first leap of the night. When she touched down with grace on the other side of the alley, the slight skitter of her soles on slate forced a tingle of nerves up the back of her thighs. *The first one is always the hardest.*

Steadying herself with another deep breath, she took off at a quick trot. Her nimble frame danced across the rooftops, packed one next to another along the winding, cobblestone streets. Some of the shingles slid under her feet, but she kept herself steady. At one point, she was forced to shimmy down a gutter pipe, dash across a quiet avenue, and use her rope and grapnel to scale back up the wall of an abandoned tannery. Once there, she felt back in her element, skipping across the low slate roofs of her city.

Soon the townhouse she sought coalesced from the darkness, one story taller than the buildings packed next to it. Maddi tossed her grapnel up and pulled herself along the hempen rope. Scanning the city from her new vantage, she ducked behind the parapet and coiled her line. Only empty streets, dimly lit by the temple sconces, lay before her.

Keeping her crouch low, she scurried across the flat rooftop until she discovered a wooden hatch bound by iron and a heavy padlock. Given time, she knew she could spring the lock, but the rusted hinges on the old portal appeared a far easier target. She squeezed a little olive oil from her pouch onto the hinges before pulling out her toolkit. A little twisting with her pliers and a couple taps of a small hammer and chisel – muffled by a wool cloth – and the corroded hinge-pins came loose. Maddi pushed and the door fell inward, hanging awkwardly from the still-latched padlock.

Dust swirled through the air as she dropped down into the attic. A few old trunks sat strewn about. From the smell, she doubted they held anything more than mothballed clothes, probably long since out of style.

Another hatchway, this one unlocked and with a folding ladder, led her to a floor of empty bedrooms covered in a decade-thick layer of dust. The stairwell leading down to the second floor remained undisturbed, lit through tall windows by the moon. Outside she could see the Earth Temple and the gray, quiet streets of the square.

Once Maddi reached the hallway below, she gasped in surprise. A set of large boot prints trotted up the stairs from the ground floor, entered a side room, and then headed back down the way they had come. She leaned in closer to examine the prints. Only the slightest sprinkling of new dust lay over them.

The old coot's story may be true, then. Drawing a quiet breath, Maddi flitted through the shadows toward the entry, avoiding the tall windows. This locked door was hinged on the inside. *I guess I'll have to do this the hard way.* She pulled a delicate leather pouch from her bag, and fished through the dozens of lock picks it held, each designed in a different size or shape, most made of steel, a few of wood or bone. She avoided the one made of a smoky, glasslike substance, hidden within the pouch that Renna had

15

given to her. *I can't chance using that pick. I might shatter its beauty.*

Another breath steadied her racing heart, before she pulled out two of the simple pieces of steel. After a dip in olive oil, she worked them inside the keyhole for a few moments. The lock clicked open. With a twist of the knob, she pushed the heavy door inward.

A broad oak desk sat in front of two thick-curtained windows, barely visible in the moonlight from the hall. Maddi pulled a clear marble from her shirt pocket, and held it in her open palm. Through pursed lips, she blew a wisp of breath over the small, glass globe. The marble sparked to life with a faint glow, just bright enough to see the sheet covered furnishings within the study. The recent boot prints led to the desk, behind it, and back out the door.

Maddi followed them in absolute silence, frowning with doubt. *He was too drunk when we spoke in the Queen of Wands this evening. He couldn't have known what he was talking about, could he? Although, he did know about the hatch on the roof…*

The linen covered chair had been placed back under the desk, but Maddi saw from the swishing patterns in the dust that the previous entrant had pulled it out. She did the same and ducked under the desk with her glowing marble. One of the floorboards was larger than the others. She found it easy to pry up the plank, and place it aside, careful to make no sound.

An old, folded piece of calfskin had been hidden within the recess. Maddi pulled it out before replacing the floorboard. She unfolded the skin to reveal a rusty tin box with an intricate lock that held it tight.

I'll work on that later in privacy. Leaving the calfskin on the floor, she tucked her prize away and hopped to her feet. She dashed back into the hallway. Another soft breath and the marble blinked out. Up the stairs she trotted, paying less heed then she had during her entrance. She climbed into the attic and hoisted herself onto the roof, excited to examine her prize.

Sinewy arms wrapped around her, hard as old tree roots. She tensed as a cold blade pressed against her throat.

"'Ere now, lassie," the slurred voice grumbled into her ear. "Thought you could pull one over on ol' Jeevsie, did ya?" His breath reeked of the onion the old drunk had been eating like an apple in the tavern. When he hacked to clear his throat, the stench of sour wine and vomit stung her eyes. "Well?" His tremulous hand shook the knife where it touched her slim neck. She felt a tiny prick of pain, followed by the tickle of warmth trickling down her neck. "Seems that whatever you slipped into muh wine didn't last as long as you mighta hoped."

Dip me in the Fires! I know better than to short dose a drunk! Always takes a heavier measure to break through the alcohol already swirling in their brains.

The man pushed his face even closer to hers. "I been watchin' this place since Lord Baelric fired me an' left town. I been waitin' ta hit it since I saw him sneak back in last week. This was *my* score!"

His voice broke, sounding as rusty as the knife felt against her throat. Maddi hoped his reactions might be the same. She focused her mind, knowing that old drunks were often quick drunks.

"Course I knew he lef' somefin'," Jeevsie grumbled in her ear, his slobber dripping onto the nape of her neck. "I heard him curse a woman's greed as he locked the door, empty handed. I got a feeling she wanted what he hid, and he didn't want her to have it." He hacked again, the stench of his breath turning her stomach. "I jus' didn' have the skill to git through the locks. Knew you did though." He hissed. "Stupid to trust a little bitch!"

Damn it! I should have been paying more attention! Maddi moved a fraction, shifting her body closer to his and farther from the knife.

"Oh, think I forgot ye was a lass, did ye?" The hard-handed man grunted. His wiry beard scraped against the skin behind her ear. The hand that clamped over her mouth loosened and shifted downward to grab her breast. Maddi did not struggle, even though her spine curdled with revulsion at the touch. The knife lingered near her throat. She shuddered at the thought of the rusty edge ripping through her windpipe.

"You treat old Jeevsie nice," he cooed, as Maddi's lip curled in revulsion, "an' I might find it easier to let you off this rooftop with your throat still closed."

Maddi nodded in silence, shifting a hand behind her and reaching for the strings of his breeches.

"Tha's muh gal," he mumbled, his knife hand slipping from her neck.

She offered a slight smile, then snarled as she grabbed his crotch fiercely, crushing the shriveled parts she found there.

The old drunk's voice squealed, rising to the pitch of a young girl. He stumbled, almost dropping the knife in his agony.

Spinning on her heel, Maddi smashed the tin treasure box into his face. She heard the satisfying crunch of bone, followed by a wet gurgle.

Jeevsie blindly swung the knife at her, missing by half a yard when she dodged out of his way. He swung again, catching the cuff of her shirt, and cutting off a button that clattered into the night.

Her boiling anger froze, and the ice crept into her voice. "Now you've done it."

She drove the box into his face once more. This time his nose crumpled under her attack. She lost herself in a moment of rage at his touch. Two and three swings later, blood leaked from the ruin of his face onto the rooftop.

Maddi pulled back, bringing her rage under control. A thief she might be, but not a killer.

She wiped the gore-smeared box on Jeevsie's stained jacket. His breathing came in shallow puffs, but the rest of his body remained still. Her voice filled with disgust. "You forced this from me." She rose to her feet and dropped over the side of the building.

Her trip back across town flew by, her mind still in shock from the attack. Slipping inside the old counting house, now used as a flophouse, Maddi frowned at its rundown condition. *It's a safe place to sleep.* She covered her neck with her hand as she passed the proprietor. She smiled, and he returned it. She had paid him double his normal rates for privacy, so he allowed her use of the old safe as a bunk.

Tucked inside its block walls and wrapped in a fine wool blanket, she worked the tricky lock under the flickering light of a candle, until the rusty lid popped up. She pried its bent hinges wide for a better look.

Inside rested a small gold locket hung on a thick chain. It opened to reveal the cameos of two young children, a boy and a girl, both brunette and smiling. Maddi tossed the chain aside and pulled at the satin backing of the box. With a hearty jerk, it came loose. White sparkles greeted her eyes, which returned the gesture. A half dozen diamonds, each nearly a carat in size glittered in the candle glow.

Maddi laughed and fondled the gems. "A woman's greed, eh?" She tucked them into a velvet pouch and curled up with it next to her chest. She blew out the candle, throwing the room into blackness, and picked up the locket before drifting to sleep. Caressing it, she wondered who the children might be.

Maddi shielded her eyes against the midmorning sun, bright with the promise of a warm spring. She skipped over a puddle. The cobblestone streets in this part of town stood in better repair than those near her flophouse, and more businesses occupied the tightly packed buildings. She hefted the bag she carried higher on her shoulder and hopped up the two steps into the apothecary. A familiar bell rang when she opened the door.

The waft of scents greeting her held flavors both exotic and familiar. Last season's herbs hung from the rafters drying, while seedlings covered dozens of trays on the counter. Maddi took a deep breath. The scents of foreign spices crept into her sinuses, mingled with the more astringent smell of curative balms and chemicals. The aromas seasoned the memories of her childhood.

"Well, I'm amazed you remember how to find your way here, it's been so long since you last visited." Renna, the closest thing to a mother Maddi had ever known, entered from the back room. Even though they were really just distant cousins, Renna had taken Maddi in when her father died of the Bloody Flux. Maddi had never known her natural mother. All her father had told her was that she passed during childbirth.

Maddi inclined her head toward her foster mother. "I've been busy."

Renna stepped out from behind the counter. Her mock-disapproving scowl changed to concern when she saw Maddi in the light. She gasped at the red-spotted white gauze Maddi had wrapped around her own neck. "What happened to you this time?"

"I made a mistake that won't happen again."

Renna stepped closer and unwound the bandage with care. The elder woman batted Maddi's hand away when she raised it in protest.

"I've taught you a lot, young lady," Renna said with a firm tone, "but I still know some things you don't." She gasped when she revealed the wound and clucked her tongue when Maddi placed the used bandage on a counter. "You used a good salve, and you wrapped it well, but that will still leave a heavy scar. You are too beautiful to allow that."

Maddi scoffed. "I made the mending balm myself. The scar should be minimal."

"Yes." Renna closed her eyes and reached for Maddi. "But I will leave no scar at all."

Startled by its suddenness, Maddi gave in to the cool, clear tingle of Renna's healing Talent. Its familiar tickle had channeled through her body many times over the course of her life. Yet each instance shocked her anew, like dunking her body into ice water. Renna's Talent crept along her neck. Maddi stopped herself from scratching at the sensation of skin and torn muscle mending

19

together. She cringed at the image of a dozen tiny beetles crawling up her throat. She gasped, and it was gone.

"Have a large lunch." Renna stepped back, her gaze an eternal examination

"I know." Maddi stood there uncomfortably, dreading the subject she had to broach.

Best to be direct about it. "I have to leave town," she blurted out.

Renna's face remained calm. "I prepared myself for this." Maddi had expected a far more heated reaction. "Is it because of *that*?" She pointed an accusatory finger at the crimson-spotted bandage.

"It is related," Maddi admitted. "But it is not the only reason."

Renna looked up at Maddi with sadness in her eyes. "Am I one of those reasons?"

Maddi tried to force her sadness into anger.

Damn it, woman! A fight would have made this much easier. Giving in to her better virtues, Maddi sighed. "You are not one of the reasons. In fact, you are the only one I can think of to stay." She took Renna's hand, fighting back the tears she had sworn would not come during this conversation. "It's this town – the thieves are too thick, and the pickings too thin. I have to move on."

Her foster mother nodded, tears glistening in her eyes. "I knew this day would come – especially once I agreed to teach you about more than just herbs." The older woman wiped her welling tears with a small kerchief. "Do you need anything from me?"

Maddi smiled. "As a matter of fact, I have something for you. Here..."

The diamonds sparkled when Maddi poured them out onto the counter. They tumbled to a stop near the now forgotten bandage.

"By the Waters..." Renna gasped. "No wonder you must leave in a hurry."

"Sell them one at a time—"

Renna raised a weary hand. "I know how to fence a gem. I'm the one who taught you."

Maddi returned a shy smile.

Leaving here is more difficult that I had expected.

Renna spread her hands on the counter in front of her. "If you are leaving forever, then there is something else I must tell you. It is something I have suspected for a long time, but..." She paused, her brow furrowing. "I suppose I haven't found the courage to tell you, because it can be as much a burden as a blessing."

"What are you talking about?" Maddi's voice trembled. "Is this about my mother?"

"No, Maddi," Renna said, "it is about you." She crossed behind the main counter of her shop in silence and pulled out one of the large bags of mixed herbs she sold to travelers. Renna paused, working her mouth. Finally opening the bag, she found the words she sought. "My Talent in healing is limited. That's why I spent so much of my career learning about herbs, potions, and other curative methods – to supplement its weakness." She reached up among the dozens of jars in her personal stash of ingredients, placing several on the counter next to the travel pack. She shook her head, returning one Maddi thought contained saffron to the shelf. Renna replaced it on the counter with a jar holding wormroot. "But the part of my Talent that is somewhat gifted is an ability to see the Talent in others – to see the seed that can bloom with practice and training." Renna picked small samples from each of her chosen jars, wrapped them in waxed parchment, and placed them in a small leather pouch. She looked up from her work to meet Maddi's gaze directly. "You have the Talent, Maddi. I have always suspected – perhaps it is part of why I took you in with such readiness. In recent years, however, I have come to be certain."

Maddi's heart leaped into her throat and her mouth clamped shut. Blood pounded in her ears with the shock of realization. Pieces of her life, moments of empathy and odd sensations, clicked into place and made sense.

Renna spoke, filling the silence. "A Doctor that lived here many years ago opened my Talent for me. I never went to the Doctor's College in Daynon. Perhaps that is why my Talent never bloomed enough for me to mend more than flesh wounds." She looked up again from her packing, and the tears rose once more in her eyes. "If you get that far, you should seek the College out. I don't have the strength to open your Talent myself, or I would have tried to do so long before now."

Maddi's thoughts still swirled about inside her head. *I could be a Talented healer? What does that do for me? Healers can't heal themselves!*

"Will I need to attend this College to use my...my Talent?"

"Not necessarily." Renna pulled the strings tight on the pack. "If you come across a very Talented doctor somewhere else, they might do it for you. But if you want to make certain it is done right, and that it maximizes your potential, you should go to the College." Renna smiled and tossed the pack to Maddi. "Besides, much of the other healing knowledge I have given you, the wisdom of country midwives, is likely still a secret to them. You might be able to teach them a thing or two yourself."

21

Maddi stared at the bulging sack of herbs. A gift of Renna's most precious ingredients was not what she had expected – a fight maybe, or at least an upset argument, but not kindness and acceptance.

I certainly did not expect to be told that I have healing Talent! "I don't know what to say, Renna." Maddi squeezed the words around a sob that ached in her jaw.

"Say you'll consider going to the College." Her foster mother raised a brow of concern. "I know that you have chosen another path for yourself, but that does not have to last forever. A Doctor has a much safer lifestyle than a…" Renna tilted her head toward the stained bandage lying next to the naked diamonds.

With a nod of acquiescence, Maddi folded her arms around the pack of herbs. "I will consider it."

"That is all I can ask." Renna came around the counter and approached her. "You will leave today?"

"Yes." The pressure returned to Maddi's head, and she fought back another sob. "I already purchased a horse."

Renna spread her arms with uncertainty, the tears now winding their way down her cheeks. Maddi collapsed into those arms, her headache draining away when she let the sobs come at last. The two stood there near a minute, the warmth of their embrace and the coolness of their tears the only sensations Maddi felt. "Goodbye, mother," she sobbed at last.

In the end, Renna let go first with a soft caress of Maddi's cheek and a sniffle. Maddi whispered another good-bye and turned for the exit. The final ringing of the little bell brought on the threat of more tears. She closed the door behind her and leaned against it, drawing a deep breath.

The clatter of horse hooves on cobblestone shook her. Maddi dabbed her eyes with her cloak to hide any proof of emotion from the passers-by. With a quiet sniff, she stalked toward the livery stables.

CHAPTER 3

When Benicus Varlan, son of the Emerald Duke, handed his father's head to King Aradon, not only was the Gavanor Rebellion formally ended, but the ducal line of succession remained within the Varlan family. With the line of Princes ended in Gavanor, the son now possessed much of what the father had sought – no liege lord other than a far away king and an entire Realm to rule, rather than just a city.
– "Short History of the Gavanor Rebellion" by Jalianos Sofra

Lieutenant Jaerd Westar struggled to hold his head high while he marched into the great hall of the Citadel of Gavanor. He forced himself to focus on following the emerald green cloak in front of him, ignoring the rainbow of nobility gathered on either side. The bees buzzing in his stomach threatened to bring up the lavish lunch laid out in honor of him and his fellow officers. The food had been rich enough that he might have felt ill despite his nerves.

I've been outnumbered by brigands in a dozen fights. That never had me as shaken as this pomp and circumstance.

A hush covered the throng within the great hall while he and his two companions in burnished armor marched down the long, stone-flagged aisle. Most of the soldiers stood in ranks near the entry. The multicolored coats of the Western Realm baronies huddled in segregated clusters near the dais at the far end, bearing the gold chains and sigils of their houses. Jaerd strode beneath corresponding pennants hung from the high ceiling, the gray stone wall on emerald green of Gavanor at their forefront. Jaerd noticed the golden cougar on maroon of Whitehall Castle drooped in a far corner, its listless manner a match to his spirit. He stared at the long aisle down the middle of the crowd as if it were a path to the hangman's noose.

The two officers he marched behind appeared to hold no such trepidation. They wore beaming, almost absurd smiles. Wolfsgate Captain Loren Baner marched in front of Jaerd, his uniform straining at the belly. The leader of their little procession, General Sandor Vahl, made enough money to have his uniform let out so it did not pull so tight on his even larger gut. Watching the two of them waddle forward sickened Jaerd almost as much as the ceremony. *These men will outrank me forever!*

Duke Aginor Varlan rose from his chair on the lower step of the dais. Above it, on the highest step, sat the black throne that once accommodated the Princes of Gavanor. Jaerd's stomach eased somewhat at the sight of the duke. He knew the man had proven his bravery fifteen years ago in the Border Skirmishes, back when Jaerd had played in the pond near the Sleeping Gryphon.

Aginor waved his men to haste. *It is an honor to serve in his guard.* The other officers did not notice, continuing onward in their stately procession. Jaerd willed the wide men to move faster, but they would not speed their advance down the gauntlet of western nobility.

At last, Captain Baner and General Vahl took their places in front of the duke, Jaerd on their far left. Duke Aginor moved toward Vahl, but at the last moment, turned on his heel and stepped up to Jaerd. The higher-ranking officers shuffled their feet. Even though Jaerd was not an expert on protocol, every fool knew that the duke should recognize the senior officers first.

"Lieutenant Jaerd Westar," Duke Aginor intoned, his voice familiar with how to use the hall's acoustics, "you have proven yourself a valiant soldier of the Gavanor guard. You enlisted ten years ago as a guardsman and have climbed your way up the ranks to become an officer." Jaerd's face shifted into the closest thing to a smile he had worn all day. "Your service was invaluable to my son in wiping out the Miller's Creek Brigands." Jaerd's eye caught a nod from Doran Varlan, a vocal supporter of his promotion into the officer corps. "This…" The duke held up a silver, five-pointed star identical to the one already affixed to Jaerd's collar. "…is well deserved."

Duke Aginor reached up to the emerald green of Jaerd's tunic, and pinned the second star there next to the first. The duke then pulled down on his own matching tunic, the stone wall of Gavanor picked out in thread of silver, and straightened it with formality. He gave a sharp salute, right fist over heart, which Jaerd snapped in return. A familiar twinkle remained in the duke's eye.

"Wolfsgate Captain Jaerd Westar." The duke released his salute. "We welcome you to service."

"With honor!" Jaerd called in a clear voice that rang throughout the hall.

Aginor stepped to the next officer. "Former Wolfsgate Captain Loren Baner," he spoke out, "You have served with honor in your position for a decade, managing the flux of traffic through the

Wolfsgate. You caught many smugglers in your day." The duke paused. Jaerd had never seen him with such a flat expression. "This is why I have decided that rather than make you General of Gates, you shall be transferred to Magdonton as General of Docks there. That position has been empty for many months now. Your skills will be useful against river smugglers."

A soft, almost imperceptible gasp rustled through the crowd. The men dressed in midnight blue of House Magdon smiled begrudgingly. One not much older than Jaerd wore a silver chain with a crescent and stars in gold and diamonds suspended around his neck.

The duke leaned in to pin a third star upon Baner's collar, but the man seemed not to notice. His face remained in a shocked grimace, yet he retained enough sense to return the duke's salute.

Duke Aginor turned to the last and eldest officer. "General of Gates Sandor Vahl, your service began when my father ruled this realm. You served me during the Border Skirmishes as a capable assistant quartermaster." The duke stared into the general's eyes with a commanding presence, his stony jaw locked. "Your retirement will be accepted with regrets. I have commissioned an engineering battalion to build you a fine house along the Stonebourne."

This time the crowd openly muttered. Vahl's relatives barked calls of surprise. The general himself looked as if he could choke. His face reddened, and his fingers clutched into fists.

"My liege," he sputtered, "I was to become your Marshal!"

"Things change, General." The duke shrugged. "I felt it was time to shake things up in *my* army." The duke turned his voice on the crowd that still had not calmed. "We have become complacent! Years of peace and good seasons have left us fat and slow." The duke did not hide his direct stares at the heavyset officers. Jaerd sucked in his solid gut just a bit tighter. "My son Doran will serve as General of Gates until I find an officer worthy of the title. I will serve as my own Marshal of the guard." The duke looked directly at the multihued representatives of his bannermen. "The barons of the realm should do the same. Too long has name and length of service been the major requirement of rank." The duke's voice took on a softer tone, one of a caring lord. "I fear we are too satisfied in our safety. I for one will not let our realm be caught unaware by the inexorable tragedies that come with the future."

The duke walked back toward his dais, while the multitude murmured. Many nodded their heads in agreement, while some, mostly those in the most garish or expensive dress, scowled with disapproval. Doran Varlan joined his father with an outstretched hand of encouragement, as did Baron Chalse Whitehall. The pot-bellied man in maroon heartily nodded his close trimmed, balding scalp. The new General Baner walked over to the men from house Magdon with a hat-in-hand smile. They greeted him with fair nods. The former General Vahl stormed out of the hall with grumbling members of his family. Most of the green-cloaked soldiers smiled and nodded, but the few royal Bluecloaks in attendance watched everything with intensity.

Jaerd was about to slip away to the barracks when Duke Aginor waved his hand. "Captain Westar, please join us."

With a deep breath similar to the one he took before drawing his sword, Jaerd trotted over to the nobles, his well-blackened boots ringing against the stone.

"Congratulations, Captain." Doran Varlan smiled and offered Jaerd his hand. "I knew you were going to make good a long time ago."

"Doesn't surprise me either," Baron Whitehall pronounced. "The Westars are from Dadric, from a long line of old Gannonite stock. They've been out here since Gavanor was little more than a castle on a knob of stone."

"Thank you, sirs." Jaerd bowed his head. "I am honored by your trust."

The duke pointed at him. "You've earned it Captain…as have some others."

Doran chuckled. "Already scouting for my replacement, Father?"

"More so for mine!" Duke Aginor laughed in return. "I look forward to a measure of retirement soon." He gave his son a poke. "It's your generation's turn to take the reins. I want to go hunting."

Jaerd shifted his feet in discomfort.

Doran smiled at his father. "It all depends on how upset House Darilla is over your 'retiring' General Vahl." He laced his voice with sarcasm.

The duke huffed. "We shall deal with Baron Maylar when the time comes. He is not so close to his cousin as the fool might believe."

Baron Whitehall joined Doran in another chuckle.

Staring at the floor, Jaerd listened to the nobles jest with each other. "If you have no more need of me, my lords," he broke in with a bow of respect, "I have new duties at the Wolfsgate."

All three of the nobles laughed aloud.

"Don't overdo it, Westar." The baron clapped Jaerd on the back. "They trust you'll do the job."

Doran shifted his green cloak over one shoulder. "Likely the fellow has sense and wants to spend as little time among noblemen as he can."

Jaerd had fought alongside the ducal heir against the Miller's Creek Brigands enough to know the man had earned those three stars on his tunic.

"Actually, this is the whole point of my speech." Duke Aginor nodded his head with certainty. "The average nobleman's son would have stood here kissing our behinds until we ran him off." He saluted Jaerd again, this time with less formality. Jaerd returned it as if on parade. "You may take your post, Captain, but I want you to understand that you are a part of this restructuring I have proposed. Some of my peers do not entirely approve of it. Your position at Wolfsgate is essential. Keep your eyes open." The duke paused as if considering. "Have you heard of the Earl of Mourne? Do you know his face?"

I believe they served together in the Border Skirmishes. Jaerd nodded. "Yes, sir. Black hair and mustache."

The duke nodded. "We agreed that he would use the Wolfsgate upon his return."

Lifting an eyebrow, Jaerd folded his arms behind his back. "Will he be cloaked in blue?"

"Likely. He travels in the company of other Bluecloaks as well as a Battlemage." Duke Aginor's bronze eyes searched Jaerd. Apparently finding what he sought, a confident smile crossed his face. "It may be several weeks before he arrives. The Earl Boris should ask for the Wolfsgate Captain when he does. Bring him directly to the citadel upon his return." His voice slipped to a near whisper. "Tell none in your command who he is, just for whom to look. Bring him directly here yourself."

"Directly here." Jaerd saluted again. "Yes sir."

Duke Aginor shifted his shoulders into a more relaxed posture. "Well done, Captain Westar." The duke returned the salute. "Dismissed."

Jaerd snapped a turn and marched with purpose from the great hall. Most of the crowd had dispersed. Only a few onlookers lingered. Some gave him an appraising stare, while one or two scowled in his direction. He paid no attention. His heart leapt with unexpected excitement over his new position. Yet his gut sank at the same time with trepidation at its challenges. Jaerd clenched his hands, focused on ideas of how to improve his command.

I'll still be standing at the gate all day, no matter how many stars I wear.

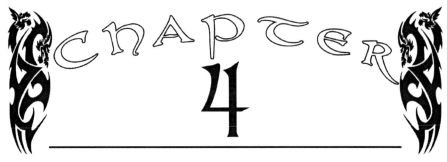

CHAPTER 4

"Fie! Turn me not into a toad!"
– Prince Amadon to the wizard Cannor, "The Mage's Eye" Act II, Scene iii

Dorias Ravenhawke, last of the rogue wizards, sighed while contemplating the trees of Ravenswood. The Gray Mountains loomed in the distance, their white peaks sparkling in the sun. Dorias reveled in the forest hued with the pale green of rising spring. Tumbled black stones lay cast about among the ancient trunks, carved with the ravens that gave the forest its name. Dorias had built the very tower on which he now stood out of similar blocks. *No one owns the stones any longer. Those that carved them died a thousand years before the Dragon Wars began.*

A flutter of black wings drew Dorias from his reverie. The bird was late.

"Merl!" A hefty raven landed on its pinewood perch set into the parapet. Dorias handed him a strip of jerky. "You've had fun on your little 'sabbatical', eh?"

The raven let out a brash caw and rubbed its head on Dorias' cloak. "Ladies!" it called in quite clear Common Tongue.

"Ah, yes." Dorias' laugh carried out over the forest. "I assume there will be a rash of rather large young hatchlings born this year?"

Merl cawed again in the affirmative.

Dorias ran a hand over his close-cropped, salt-and-pepper hair. He knew his own wings held far more silver than Merl's. "But now you are done for the season, true?"

The raven hopped from his perch to Dorias' shoulder. He stretched his wings out to shade the wizard's head from the noonday sun and rubbed his onyx beak on Dorias' collar.

"Good." Pushing the door open, Dorias climbed down the spiral stairwell leading from the roof of his tower. "We have many things to do."

Following the downward curve of the stairwell, Dorias

passed his bedroom. He descended further, ignoring the door to the library. He had crammed it full of carved shelves in a dizzying array of styles, each packed with books, scrolls, and odd items found on his many journeys. Continuing down the wide stone steps, he spiraled past a dozen more doors, some of which opened onto rooms that would confuse the average being. One of them appeared to open out onto a terrace overlooking the Jade Sea from one of the thousands of islands surrounding it. It was an illusion of course, an illusion Dorias had created with a self-sustaining spell of Psoul magic, the Aspect of the Dreamers.

"The Dreamrealm is closed to me, Merl." Dorias shook his head. "I have tried to enter it for the last several nights. It is as if a dark cloud obscures it. I have never felt such a thing."

He touched a carved walnut door near the bottom of the tower, and it swung open on its own. Rosewood paneled the walls inside. An array of shelves tucked into the paneling held his favorite tomes and trophies. A rather simple maplewood desk sat squarely in the middle, while ordinary windows looked out on the Ravenswood forest behind it. He walked over and pulled out the soft, velvet-upholstered chair. He sat in it with a comfortable sigh, the warm velvet ensconcing him. Merl hopped up to perch upon its tall back and turned to clean his wings.

"I hope your presence can help me break into the Dreamrealm," Dorias told the raven, opening one of the side drawers. "This might help as well." He pulled out a creamy crystal almost the size of his thumb. A low reverberation thrummed through the study when he placed it on the desk. The deep hum crawled down his back and settled into his buttocks. "I think this will work…"

The crystal's pitch rose, and a soft glow kindled in its heart. Dorias opened himself to his power and directed an intense beam of Psoul Aspect into the blossom of light. He closed his eyes and made an attempt at connection. His consciousness dived into the crystal.

A cloud still obscured the Dreamrealm. He thrust himself toward it, pushing first with gentle pressure from his mind, then increasing the flow of Psoul Aspect until it neared his limit. The shadow met him like a giant, impenetrable fog, smothering every attempt to enter the place he knew as well as the waking world.

Dorias let the stream of Psoul go. "Burn it in the Flames!" He considered summoning the Earth Aspect to smash the crystal, but a more constructive idea entered his mind. "Come on, Merl." Dorias rose and slipped the crystal into a pouch on his belt. "Let's go for a ride."

Merl cawed a query.

"Well," Dorias said with a smile, "you will fly, of course."

Merl fluttered to Dorias' shoulder, and they left the study. Dorias trotted down the last few twists of the stairs, stopping only long enough to grab an apple from a fruit bowl.

A wide pool covered the entire ground floor of the tower with a maze of stepping stone paths crossing it. Dozens of multihued koi fish swirled the still water, darting back and forth beneath the lily pads and birds of paradise. The soft trickle from a waterfall at the edge of the pool brushed upon Dorias' ears. He stepped toward a patio with a large double door and pushed it open.

A wooded pasture stretched out before him, set in an eternal summer with no rain.

He whistled. "Shade!"

Out from behind a spread oak, a charcoal mare galloped over one of the grass-covered hillocks. She whinnied, stomping with pride once she came close. Merl cawed a greeting to the horse, who snorted in return. She took another step and nudged her diamond spotted forehead into Dorias' shoulder, uttering a soft nicker.

"Hey, there," Dorias said. "Good to see you too." He handed her the apple. The mare's satin-whiskered lips tickled his hand when she popped the apple in one bite, crunching away with a happy shake of her head.

"We need to go for a ride." Dorias stroked the mare's neck while she nuzzled him, seeking another apple. "Maybe after we get back. Come on."

The mare took her light saddle without qualm. Dorias used an old style bridle, one without a bit. *Shade follows my lead by trust, not by force.*

He led her out of the pasture and into the room with the pool. Gathering a small stream of Psoul, Earth, and Water magic, the three Aspects in which he most excelled, Dorias reached out and placed his hand upon the tower wall. The stone blocks folded back on themselves, opening onto the gloomy Ravenswood. Once they passed through, the wall knit itself back together, leaving the unblemished black surface of the tower behind.

"Let's cover some ground." Dorias grunted, swinging into the saddle. Shade gave him a moment to settle, then took off at a quick trot. Merl flew ahead through the trees.

Wrapping his cloak about him to ward off the coolness of the shadows, Dorias rode through the trees. He barely noticed the light underbrush, speckled with white diamond and knickerbreech blossoms. Violets popped up here and there, as did mayapples, short and unopened.

"I bet if we looked in the right spots, we could find some morels," Dorias beamed. Shade took no interest in mushrooms, and Merl had flown out of sight. "Fair enough," he huffed. "I suppose we do have more important things on our plate than mushrooms worth their weight in silver."

The shattered relics of the ancient people of Ravenswood lay scattered between the trees. Gigantic oaks grew over the black stones, some of those trees centuries old themselves. A large mound rose to his left, its rim crowned with tall hickories. The stones carved with ravens lay gathered in large numbers upon its slopes. Merl dropped from the sky and landed on Shade's rump. The raven croaked at the mound, his wings spread wide.

"Don't worry, Merl." Dorias gave the raven a kernel of corn from his vest. "We won't be going back in there. I found what I wanted last time." He patted the milky crystal in his pouch. "Among other things."

The mound receded behind them. Soon the trees opened up, and the stones became larger. Wide foundations remained here, where the people had built their capital. Shade picked her way between the crumbled buildings, Dorias allowing her to choose her own path.

At the top of a rise, marble columns ringed a wide bowl near thirty yards across. The raven people had formed it from a vein of stone so white that after two-dozen centuries, it still blinded the eye. Merl perched upon the tallest column and watched in silence, while Dorias dismounted and walked out into the center of the dish. A small pedestal of the same snow-colored stone rose from the center. Removing the milky crystal from his pouch, he placed it onto the pedestal and stepped back.

The resonance he had felt before returned, this time spreading wider. Dorias bored into the crystal with Psoul magic, increasing the power he used in his study. The air surrounding him vibrated. Shade backed away from the rim of the bowl, and Merl fluttered from the column when it wobbled. A hum shook the elder trees spread around.

Dorias funneled more of the Psoul Aspect into the crystal. He closed his eyes and found the passage to the Dreamrealm. The cloud of shadow remained. It felt murkier, more substantial. He pressed against it with tentative power. His tendrils found small cracks, places in the Dreamrealm where the fog was not so dense. He reached further inside.

This is too easy. Perhaps I should be more cautious with all this power.

With a vengeance, the obstructing cloud snapped back at him, pushing his magic away with a violent thrust. His tendrils of Psoul snapped, ripping out the last of his breath. The dark power tossed his presence from the Dreamrealm like a ragdoll, and Dorias popped back into his body. He found himself airborne from the concussion. He gasped when he struck the rim of the bowl, and then slipped into a dazed stupor.

He woke to a whiskered nudge, followed by soft wetness. Shade whinnied in concern.

"Wake!" the rough call came.

"Shut up, you overgrown crow." Dorias squinted through the pain in his head and rump. He stood, tentative in his movements. "It is obvious that we deal with something far more powerful than I originally thought."

He patted Shade on the nose to reassure her. The mare nudged him again, before stepping back from the edge of the bowl. *She does not like setting hoof on the stone. It took a lot for her to come close enough to wake me.*

With careful steps, Dorias walked back to the center pedestal. The crystal had vaporized, leaving a light scorch on the pristine surface. Not a shard remained.

"Damn."

Dorias mulled through his thoughts during the ride home. Once they arrived at the tower, he removed Shade's saddle and led her out into the illusory pasture. She gave herself a good shake, and he set a whole bowl of apples down next to a trickle of fresh water. She danced around him happily, nudging closer for a scratch.

"We may be leaving on a much longer ride soon," Dorias whispered in her ear as he brushed her neck. "Enjoy your home for now."

Upon entering his study, Dorias collapsed into his velvet chair and sipped on a cup of green tea, steeped with a little willow bark for his headache. *I need to sit here and think. No power has ever stymied my entrance into the Dreamrealm.*

He stared out the window and watched the mountain shadows creep across the forest while the sun dropped behind them. The porcelain cup, long emptied, remained in his hands. His gaze seldom shifted, even as night cast its shadow over the tower.

"What!" Merl croaked at last. The raven remained perched upon Dorias' chair.

32

"I have known what I must do since we arrived back home." His eyes remained fixed on the dark mountains. "I have just been sitting here working up the courage to admit it." He reached to scratch Merl's beak. "We must go to the Isle."

"*What*!" The raven's caw nearly rattled the windowpanes.

"I know." Dorias sighed. "Varana will not be happy to see us."

Merl flapped his wings and warbled a derisive sound.

"Alright," Dorias admitted, "not happy to see *me*. However, I can only hope she will allow me a look at the libraries there. She owes me that much."

I will never forgive Malcolm for forcing me to kill him. Why would he not surrender to her?

Dorias cleared his throat and pushed himself up from the chair. Merl hopped to his shoulder. "Well, let's at least get some good rest tonight." He stretched his arms with a sigh of resignation. "We will be leaving early tomorrow."

The Avari Plain stretched before Dorias when he and Shade rode out from the cover of the Ravenswood. Merl flew ahead, by far the most excited of the three to undertake this journey. Dorias enjoyed the scenery, but dreaded his destination.

They set a quick pace along the Rappenron River where it swung beside the edge of the Avari. For days, they travelled in peace, Merl scouting out ahead while Dorias and Shade followed the river.

As they paused to rest one afternoon, Dorias heard a low rumble from deep within the ground. He remounted Shade in haste and rode her to the peak of a small ridge. A gritty haze hung against the horizon, obscuring a hundred thousand wooly mounds trotting across the landscape. Bison ranged over the plain, spreading like a sea of horn, hoof, and brown fur. Their movement shook the land and left a trail of destruction and dust that hung in the air for some time. Dorias soon spied a dozen wolves trailing the herd. A pride of prairie lions tracked them too, though they stayed well clear of the other predators. Buzzards circled back along the trail, closing the cycle of life behind the passing herd.

Two more days on the trail, and they approached where the

Rappenron River met the Andon. *Once the Rappenron alone fed the Andon, but that was before the Cataclysm – before the Dragonscales climbed into the sky and drove all waters to the Great River.*

The sun dipped toward the west when Dorias came upon the confluence. A tall outcropping of rock hung over the swirling eddies where the cold water of the Rappenron met the warmer flow of the Andon River. Sheltered between the rocks and the water, Dorias made camp and unsaddled Shade to give her rein to graze.

"I'll have a scoop of oats for you later." He scratched her shoulders before wandering down closer to the river. Merl lighted to a tree nearby.

"Let's find dinner, shall we?" Dorias reached out to his power. His strength in the Aspect of Air was not great, but still enough for the task at hand. He stretched a thin tendril of Air out into the water. Near one of the warmer eddies, he found a small school of trout. Dorias wrapped his strand around one of the fish and ripped it up from the river. The silvery creature thrashed against his magic, yet Dorias held it firm.

"Fish!" Merl cawed into the twilight.

Dorias smiled in agreement. "Not so challenging as the old fashioned way, I'll grant, but it is certainly faster."

His strength in the Fire Aspect was no greater than his power in Air, yet he still possessed enough to get a good campfire going faster than flint and steel or even a dwarven match. Dorias scaled the whole fish and placed it over the fire to roast, seasoned with a little salt and herbs he carried in his pack.

After his meal, he leaned back against the rock, his belly full of broiled trout. Merl picked at the bones nearby, and Shade munched on her evening oats.

"Time for a pipe, I say. I believe it would be the perfect dessert."

Dorias had just sparked the bowl with the tiniest burst of Fire, when the skin across the back of his neck began to crawl. With a wild snort, Shade backed away from the campsite, her ears flattened against her head, while Merl leaped into the air, abandoning his fish carcass.

Dorias rose to his feet, teetering on the edge of embracing his power. "Please come out, Ancient One. I know when I am in the presence of one of your kind." His heart raced, awaiting an answer to his call.

The trees rustled. A hulking form heaved from behind the outcrop. The fading sunset danced off golden scales. A long sinewy neck resolved itself, ending in a head with a wide, leonine face. Sharp fangs, inches long, protruded from the upper lip. Its vertical slit eyes focused on him, reflecting gold and green in the last of the dying sunlight. A slightly sulfurous scent wafted into the clearing, hinted with a flavor of cinnamon.

Dorias let go of his power. It could not match a dragon so large at this range. Shade held her ground, but her eyes rolled white, and her hooves stamped the turf. Merl, however, sat perched in a nearby tree, watching.

"I could have burned you and your horse from the sky, had I wanted to, wizard," the great beast rumbled with a slurred accent still quite understandable. "But I have a desire to share words. My mother taught me your resonance before she died. She told me that the wizard known as the Ravenhawke could be trusted above all humans." The dragon scoffed, an ominous sound from so deep a chest. "That is, of course, a relative idea. No humans can truly be trusted. We have learned that hard lesson over the centuries."

With a wave of respect, Dorias bowed near to the ground. "Ancient One, you honor me with your presence. You could only be of the brood of Grannis. She honored me with her trust a long time ago." He flourished his hands again. "I offer you my words and my service if you wish."

The dragon laughed. The bellowing sound cheered Dorias, while at the same time driving fear into his heart. The mix of emotion made him feel almost giddy. "I have no need of your service, human," the dragon returned, "and only precious few of your words." He sat on his haunches. The long digit at the end of his front claw folded the leathery, golden wings back along his forearm. He leaned upon the padded knuckle where it met his thumbclaw. "I am Groovax, the son of Grannis." The creature curved a long, scaled tail around the front of his claws as he sat. "I come to give you a warning."

Dorias stood up straight, thumbing his short goatee. "A warning?"

The dragon paused, his golden eyes piercing into Dorias' soul. He stood there, trapped within the dragon's gaze. He would not have turned from it even if he could have. *I have great respect for this creature. I want him to respect me.*

The dragon pulled a great breath into his nostrils. Most men would have feared that flames might follow, but Dorias knew that it was a sign of respect. *He has accepted my scent.*

"Many of my lesser kin have disappeared." The dragon's lips moved with great dexterity, forming the words clearly. "I believe they flock to the Dragonscales. Whatever call they answer I cannot fathom. The presence hides from me behind a dark cloud." He flicked his long tongue along his upper lip, curling it in a threatening way around his fangs. "Those of my kind who have heard the call are removed by many generations from the Ancient Ones. They are more…primitive. My sire was of the Ancient, as well as my mother."

Dorias raised one eyebrow with hesitation, uncertain the dragon allowed questions in this parley. "Why do you tell me this?"

A ridge above the dragon's own eye lifted. "I tell you because…" The dragon paused again as if considering. "…because there are too few Ancient Ones left among us to stop our kin. Whatever power calls the lesser dragons cannot mean well for those of us who remain beyond its influence." Groovax flicked his tail, his horned brow furrowing. "Most of my brethren have given up on human kind."

"Yes." Dorias tapped his bare upper lip. "That would explain why so few have been seen in recent centuries. Most humans believe dragons to be extinct."

"We nearly are." Groovax held both regret and anger in his voice. "A good portion of that is our own doing, however."

Dorias nodded. Of all humans, he best understood the sad history of the dragons. "There is something I should tell you." The dragon's head popped forward, sending Dorias a half step back. He calmed his heart with a deep breath before continuing. "I believe that I have sensed the same presence you mentioned."

The dragon cocked his head in a quizzical expression. "It forbids me entry into the Dreamrealm," Dorias continued. "It is a dark, shadowy cloud that I cannot penetrate with my mind."

Silence pervaded the clearing. Groovax stared in thought. Shade stamped cautiously. Any other horse would have bolted long before. Merl sat in his perch, for once saying nothing.

"Perhaps…" The dragon cocked his head. "I will not speculate. Your magic is far different from ours." He stepped back and stretched his arms, fanning out the fingers of his golden wings. They caught the firelight and reflected it back like polished bronze. "I know your resonance, human. If you find a way back into your Dreamrealm, you may contact me from there. If I discover anything more, I will find you myself."

Dorias bowed again. "You may be confident in your trust, Lord Dragon. This darkness has spurned me to action already. Our alliance against it honors me."

Groovax laughed once more. It echoed across of the rivers below, masking the rush of their flow. Dorias felt the laughter in his stomach and bones. It made him want to giggle.

"We shall see if this becomes an *alliance*, human." The dragon laughed again, flapped his wings, and leaped into the moonlit sky. Dorias heard another chuckle from a distance as the great beast disappeared into the night. His spirits dipped in sadness at the dragon's parting.

"Flame!" Merl cawed out, startling Dorias.

"At least that flame isn't aimed at us, Merl." He watched a dark shape cross the moon. "For now."

CHAPTER 5

"Blessed are the Fires from which were made. Blessed be the Fires to which we return"
— Boar Clan funerary rites

Slar slumped back into the tall chair of carved ebony, abandoned to him by Boar chieftain Lagdred. A sneering Brother Ortax leaned in close to his ear.

"The Wolves do not deserve to join our holy war," the lead shaman of the Boar Clan whispered. "Send them on their way. They ask too much."

A wave of Slar's hand silenced the shaman. Ortax stepped back with a deferential nod of his head.

"It is the command of Galdreth that I be Warchief of the united clans, not just the Boar and Ram." Slar inclined his head toward the orcs gathered in front of him. "Much as we have this one chair at Blackstone for the chieftain of the Boar, we shall have seven when we build a new fortress at Dragonsclaw."

He heaved himself up, shifting the ancient scimitar of his family that rested on his hip. The representatives of the Wolf Clan fingered their own weapons. "No one is more aware of the long standing feud between Wolf and Boar than you and I, Fargon."

The grizzled captain of the Wolves scowled at him. Slar remembered that face laughing with him many years ago. "You were fostered with my father to seal the peace after our last clanwar. You and I have hunted Boar lands together."

"You made a wife of my cousin," Fargon grumbled in reply.

"And no one misses Naleena more than I!" Slar snapped, more harshly than he intended. "Her death haunts me still, and her son chooses to live among your people."

Fargon lifted a black eyebrow. "He is your son, too."

Slar snorted and waved a hand. "My sons are warriors of the Boar Clan. One has captured Victor status to honor his people."

Fargon remained silent, but his lips curled to show a fang.

Instead, the orc wrapped in a black wolf pelt spoke.

"This discussion is not to the point." The shaman lifted a finger. "This is about the honor of the Wolf Clan. We insist that we not be lackeys to the Boar, unlike the sad Rams." He shot a glance at the one Ram in attendance.

Balthor kept his silence, though rage scudded across his face.

Slar folded his hands behind his back and addressed the room. "The place of the Wolf Clan in this alliance shall be the same as it is for Boar and Ram, for Bear and Snake and all the others once they join. This is the time we have awaited, my fellows. Galdreth has returned to us from the Elder Days." He brought his hands forward into fists. "Do you not understand that this is our opportunity to wipe away all the old clan rivalries? It is our chance to take our rightful place in this land—to drive the humans back into the sea from whence they came."

Fargon's pink eyes fixed on Slar, reminding him of his long dead wife. His heart twinged at the memory of her. He had thought those feelings long since buried. *Those eyes also remind me of Nalan's, though I have not seen him in ten years. If only he had chosen the warrior's path instead of…*

Those thoughts were not for now, and Slar drove them from his mind. He slapped his hands together. "Many of the Boar Clan, under the leadership of my son Grindar, have already begun the journey to Dragonsclaw, while more Boar warriors muster for Chieftain Lagdred. The Ram Clan gathers at Dragonsclaw as well. Galdreth commands that you do the same." Slar did not favor this approach, but felt forced to use it. "Do not forget that our ancient master has returned. Has Galdreth not appeared before Chieftain Valgrar?"

Fargon nodded. "The spirit has shown itself to my uncle. That is the only reason we stand here now." The warrior watched him in silence. Slar was about to renew his argument when Fargon finally continued. "I will return to Craghold. Chieftain Valgrar shall have the final say, but we cannot ignore Galdreth's return." He moved to walk away before he paused and met Slar's gaze squarely. "Even if Valgrar decides not to come, I will meet you at Dragonsclaw. Not because of the return of some ancient spirit that I do not understand, but because of your words, which I grasp quite well." He nodded again, this time with a bit of a bow. "I will greet you again before Midsummer…Warchief."

The Wolf Clan delegation ushered themselves from Blackstone's great hall, Fargon the last to leave. He tapped his fist to his heart in silent farewell before the doors closed behind him.

"Will he bring his clan?" Ortax asked once the bar slammed down.

"It is not the Wolves that I worry about." Slar's eyes remained upon the exit through which Fargon and his men had left. "The Shark will join us when Wolf does. Snake and Bear will come in time. It is the Mammoth who hold my doubts."

Balthor of the Ram grunted his agreement.

Yes. The Ram and Boar founded our friendship fighting the Mammoth Clan.

"Chieftain Sargash will choose to join us when Galdreth comes upon him." Ortax lifted his nose with a confident air. He had been among the first to support alliance once the spirit appeared to him.

Yet you did not support me as Warchief. I will not forget that. Nor will Galdreth. When the rear door squeaked open, Slar turned and his frown for Ortax melted. Radgred came around the corner, a slight smile on his aged face. Behind him strode Sharrog, his face so much like Slar's. *My Midsummer boy, Victor at his first Clanhold!*

"So I see you have returned from your hunt." Slar grinned as wide as propriety allowed in public. "Has the ice cracked yet?"

"It has indeed, father." Sharrog tapped a fist over his heart. The smile, however, shifted to a frown. "There were few mammoths to be found, but the caribou were great in number."

Slar reached out to clasp his son's arm. "Good then. We will have plenty of supplies for our march to Dragonsclaw."

Sharrog frowned and moved as if to speak, but Radgred interrupted. "Perhaps we should get something to eat." The old sergeant growled at the gathered orcs. "The Warchief and son should have a meal of the fresh meat together."

With a nod of understanding, Sharrog walked out the door through which he had entered. Radgred followed close behind him. But before Slar exited, he addressed the assembled orcs. "I thank you all for your attendance." He looked at the Ram chieftain's son. "Especially you, Balthor. This alliance between Ram and Boar will be the core of a new nation for our people." He returned Balthor's nod of agreement. "We begin our journey to Dragonsclaw in three days. It will be an honor to walk on Ram Clan land again."

Balthor dropped into a full bow. "It is our honor, Warchief."

Brother Ortax frowned at the younger orc. "The honor is to serve Galdreth."

"Indeed," Slar added with an air of finality.

The group broke up with a round of nods. Slar had never known a time when his people were so agreeable. *Perhaps the fear that Galdreth brings is the greatest motivator of all. My arguments would never have held sway in normal times.*

Shifting his swordbelt one last time, Slar followed his son and advisor toward the central stairwell leading to his chambers at the top of Blackstone. All the warriors who stood guard in the hall saluted their Warchief, fist over heart when he passed. He returned it to each of them in turn, slowing his progress even more. By the time he reached the stairs, Sharrog and Radgred neared their top. Slar took the steps two at a time, catching the pair as they reached the door to his new chambers.

"Father! Glad you could join us." The younger orc laughed. "The needs of your alliance are tedious. I prefer open battle to the intrigues of the hall myself."

"Ha!" Radgred tipped his chin. "What do you know of real battle, youngling? A dozen years of training and one victory at Clanhold, and you think you know war!" He rubbed an old wound on his shoulder. Slar remembered the battle against the Wolf Clan where Radgred had gained it. "I will take these good meals and warm beds any time."

"Yes, but you are not the one standing with shamans all day." Slar sniffed the air. The scent of fresh kill wafted near his nostrils. "Perhaps you are right about the food, though."

Laid out in the entry hall to his private suite sat raw and rare cuts of meat heaped on silver platters. In the center of the table lay an uncooked mammoth tenderloin the size of Slar's leg. Spread out next to it they found several loins of elk and caribou in various states of doneness. On another platter sat a piece of the mammoth's liver. Other organs lay piled on silver and pewter dishes. A chest-sized saltcellar sat open upon a table, heaped with shiny white, gray, and pink crystals.

"I also brought this." Sharrog pulled a small leather bag from his pack. A pungent scent leaped into Slar's nose. "A pouch of uncle Grimbrad's herbs, from the patch near his lodge."

Radgred eyed the meats. "I will stoke the brazier in the central room."

The three lingered over the meal for the rest of the evening. Dark red wine washed the meat into Slar's belly, while the tasty salts danced on his tongue. He and Sharrog shared the oversized liver without cooking it.

Purple blood ran over Slar's chin. He wiped it on the side of his hand then licked his finger clean. "So you did find at least one mammoth."

Sharrog nodded. He took another tear off the rich, slimy organ. "One alone, and he was young at that."

"I wonder if their orc cousins will be as scarce when the time comes." Radgred held a piece of the tenderloin on an iron rod over the fire. "I do not have Ortax's faith in Chief Sargash."

Slar opened his mouth to speak until he felt the old knot in his gut tighten. He knew the pain had nothing to do with the flood of meat. The knot had been absent throughout the winter, while he and his sons, with Radgred's help, gathered the Boar, Ram, and eventually the Wolf Clans together. Only thrice had he felt the pain – when Galdreth appeared to the other clan chieftains with Slar in his presence. But that dreadful burning flared now.

The dark shadow swirled together in an instant. Galdreth's strength always radiated at its most powerful when it first appeared. The silver eyes glittered from the shadows within the parlor. They shined down upon Slar, who wiped the liver blood from his lips. Radgred and Sharrog dropped to their knees, meats cast aside. Radgred went directly to a prostrate position, while Sharrog eyed the spirit before he followed the older orc.

"My master," Slar whispered, bowing low.

The voice grated like old rust. *Your alliance grows, but not with the alacrity I require. I shall go unto the remaining clans alone. I cannot wait for your feeble bodies to travel there.*

Slar offered another bow. "Yes, my master." His stomach pains lessened. *Let the dark spirit go alone.* He kept his eyes averted. "We will be at Dragonsclaw within two weeks. Over fifty thousand Boar, Ram, and Wolf warriors will gather at your call."

That is not enough!

The knot sharpened, like a knife twisting in Slar's gut.

You must begin the training of new reserves that will join us. The Bear and Snake will have to provide the rest of our strength.

"We will begin gathering new forces at once, master." Slar swallowed against the bile that threatened to rise in his throat with the words.

What of my vessel? I have given you the tracing stones. Have they found him yet?

The longer Slar listened to the voice, the more his agony grew. It grated upon his mind and spirit, as well as his ears. "The first team is preparing to strike, my master. Their orders are clear and specific. More teams move into place."

Very good, Warchief Slar. You will bring the vessel to Dragonsclaw immediately upon his capture.

"I shall, master Galdreth."

The shadowy spirit spiraled in upon itself, disappearing with an audible concussion.

Slar stood erect, shifting his swordbelt to its proper position. Sharrog rose with more ease than Radgred, who huffed and straightened his knees.

"I despise that being," Sharrog spat at the emptiness left behind.

"You should watch your tongue." Radgred pointed at the young warrior. "You are too untried to know what is best for your people."

Slar sighed. *I do not wish to agree with my son, but I do.* He scratched his knuckles on his day-old beard. "Our people have fought among each other for centuries, ever since the humans returned. Trapped in the Northlands, without an outlet for our growth, we waste our lives and resources attacking each other over and over again." Slar reached toward Sharrog. "If we follow Galdreth's lead, we can unite our people and regain a place of power equal to, even surpassing, that of the other races. Without Galdreth's presence, we would never have gotten this far in bringing the clans together." He grabbed his son's shoulders. "What we might do here has not been done in a thousand years."

Sharrog spread his hands. "At what cost, father?"

Slar did not answer. He simply shook his head. "You are too young to understand. I will see that you learn." He took a step back. "You will soon have a taste of the battle you claim to crave. You *will* scream Galdreth's name when you charge into it."

Sharrog tossed the piece of liver he had just bitten into back on the platter. He spit the chunk in his mouth onto the fire, where it hissed and spluttered away. "As you say, father." He wiped his hands and face on a crimson towel. "I shall gather my grunts. We will march toward Dragonsclaw before the night is out. We shall be your eyes and ears along the western Dragonscales."

Slar wanted to protest. He wanted this feast to continue into the night, with more wine and women to join them later. However, the burning in his stomach soured the idea of more food, and his pride prevented him asking Sharrog to stay.

Slar called to his son's back as he stalked toward the stairwell. "You will have a place of honor in the host."

Sharrog turned at the door. "Perhaps. Only I will fight with the ancient warcries of the Boar Clan on my lips." His blood red eyes met Slar's. "And I will die calling out the name of my mother and father." He marched away down the steps.

Radgred tore into a chunk of mammoth loin and licked the grease from his skewer. "He will see reason."

Slar shook his head. "I fear he already does."

CHAPTER 6

Fear not to incorporate the pagan traditions of the people when teaching them of the Balance. It is through our harnessing of their ingrained symbology and calendar that we can more easily spread the Temple's influence to those of all previous faiths.
— Letters of Banelaw the Paladin to the High Elder Caladrion (122 A.R.)

The central dome of the Temple of Balance in Dadric did not spread wide enough to contain all of the townspeople. The situation required dozens of citizens to gather outside the circle of supporting pillars, huddled upon the grassy knoll on which the temple sat. Tallen Westar smelled the burning incense, but he heard only murmurs from the priest. If he stood on tiptoe, he could see the already bald young man swinging the censer. Behind Brother Benard, an older man in pristine black and white robes incanted prayers to the Balance, for good sun and plentiful rains to bless the fields this season.

I've heard it enough times to recite the bloody prayer myself. Tallen sighed. *At least Father Vernin is quiet and kind. We've had worse before.*

While Tallen listened to the priest drone on, most of his attention focused on the azure robed priestess of Water. Her exotic features enchanted him, with her almond eyes and chocolate colored skin. She hailed from the Southern Realm, near the border with Hadon, where Water worship remained quite common. Sister Jelena stopped by the Sleeping Gryphon once every summer to bless the grotto and pool that welled up behind it. She told Tallen once that it was ancient and holy. Alone of all holidays, the priests of Balance allowed the sister to join them in the temple for the Sowing Festival. Superstitious old farmers, whose purses the priests would dip into from time to time, considered it bad luck to ignore the Water Aspect at the Sowing Festival.

If Sister Jelena only knew what the priests said about her after a few drinks in the Gryphon. With a shake of his head, Tallen turned his gaze to the crowd gathered around him. He noticed Jennette standing near the outer edge of the temple with her father, who still wore the flour-dusted apron of his trade.

Maybe I can have a drink with her later. I haven't seen her since last I bought the bread myself. That's been near a week.

A nudge in his ribs jarred him.

"Come on, dummy. It's over." Dawne giggled. "Let's go get a drink on the Mootlawn."

His sister pulled him by the hand through the meandering crowd. The wealthy folk headed for parties at their estates or in private gardens. Most of the working people targeted the honeymead stand set up on the common grounds near the center of town. Some left for the fields. No serious farmer would waste a clear day this time of year if seed rested unsown. *Most will leave the fields early and be at the Gryphon by evening. Then they'll be late to work tomorrow…*

For the afternoon, however, the inn remained closed, and Tallen felt free to join his sister for a few mugs on the Mootlawn.

"Alright," he laughed, relenting and following her lead. "But only a couple. Glynn will need me later." He eyed his little sister. She had never really known their father. "You would be helpful too."

"Why, I would be honored to sing in your inn tonight, Master Westar." Dawne laughed and gave a quick curtsey. She rose and tugged his hand harder, her long, golden locks waving with her excitement. "But only after I have warmed up my instrument with a good libation first."

"That's not exactly what I meant." Tallen shook his head. He could not deny that her mood was infectious. "Perhaps I will join you for a song."

Dawne cackled. "In that case, we had better get several libations in you."

Tallen licked the creamy foam of the sweet mead from his lip. The traditional cow horns kept the frothy head to a perfect height. Before long, Tallen had emptied his twice. Dawne still sipped from her first.

She nodded at his empty horn. "I thought I was the thirsty one."

"I was certain I would see Jennette here today," Tallen said after a scan of the crowd. He recognized a few of the girls there, but the one he sought was nowhere to be found. "I saw her at the temple."

Dawne stood on tiptoes and cast her eyes about. "Don't see her either." She sat again and sipped her mead. "Maybe she doesn't want to be seen."

Tallen shook his head. "Last week when I stopped by the bakery she told me she would find me here."

Dawne shrugged. "Then she will be here."

They both refilled their horns before strolling out toward the center of the Mootlawn, where a huge stack of logs and branches climbed to three times Tallen's considerable height.

He turned to Dawne. "I need to be back at the inn right after they set the bonfire. Glynn and Linsay will both be working, and I think Linsay's sister starts tonight." He gulped from his horn. The scent of pork roasted with herbs and garlic floated across the crowd. "Come on. Let's get a chop. This mead makes me hungry."

Dawne pushed him toward the stand. "You're buying."

The pork snapped between Tallen's teeth, yielding a hot, salty juice that slid over his tongue. They sat together, eating and drinking until the sun began to fade from the sky. Most of the townsfolk, including many of the farmers who worked throughout the day, assembled for the lighting of the bonfire. Deep in the recesses of twilight, he finally saw her. Jennette moved along the edge of the crowd, darting back toward the warehouses at the south end of the Mootlawn.

Tallen leaned toward his sister, eyes following Jennette as she slipped away. "I'm heading back to the inn a little early."

Dawne's eyes popped open in surprise. "You're not staying for the fire?"

Tallen tilted his head toward the warehouses. "Jennette."

Dawne nodded with a knowing smile and a tip of her drinking horn.

As he passed through the gathering crowd, his eyes caught another glimpse of Jennette's long braid bouncing ahead, a pink and spring green ribbon tied around it. Everyone bunched together to watch the fire kindle, and Tallen lost sight of her.

He spied her again as he reached the back of the throng, entering an alleyway between two warehouses. Something odd tickled him at the back of his awareness. *I feel like a dog with his hackles up.* He shook it off and ducked after her, following the many twists and turns in the warren of warehouses. The scent of new cut cedar floated from one or two, but most of the old buildings sat empty.

Tallen squinted down every side alley. *She probably wants to make me jump by hiding around the one corner I won't look.*

He darted down a street that led back to the Sleeping Gryphon, sitting on a hill to the east of town.

A young man's voice rang out from the alleyway ahead. "I want us to be married this summer, earlier if possible." Tallen thought he recognized it, but exactly who it was escaped him.

The voice grew more earnest. "My father can get the Baron to perform the ceremony himself when he returns from Gavanor. I want to have you as my wife. You agreed!"

Tallen ran through faces of local young men, rich ones from his words. He could not place it immediately.

"But I must—"

It took but one word for Tallen to recognize the girl's voice. Three slipped out before he could step around the corner.

"Jennette!"

The young woman stood there, fingers rising to her mouth in shock. Ardric Haesby had his hands on her shoulders, surprise not quite as stark on his features.

"Are you going to marry him?" Tallen could not keep the anger from his quivering voice. His stomach twisted. The mead made his words harsh, but he did not care. "Have the two of you already bedded?"

Jennette gaped. Ardric gathered his fists. Tallen felt himself doing the same.

"You need to watch your mouth," Ardric growled.

Jennette stepped in front of him. "Let me handle this." Her brow knitted in an expression of pain as she turned to Tallen. "I'm sorry, Tallen, I really am. This started as my father's idea. I only saw Ardric to please Father…at first."

Tallen's heart sank. His hands opened and closed. Swirling patterns of color danced in his mind, colors so real he could almost touch them. They slipped away as the anger clouded all else from his brain.

"I see." Tallen's lip curled in rage. "It's the watch captain's son over the son of a dead innkeeper then – a profitable choice." He glared icy daggers at Ardric and frosted his tone. "If you want her…then you can *have* her. I'm done." He turned away and stalked, then ran, all the way the Gryphon where it sat nearly half a mile from the city's eastern gate. Only when he passed through the entrance into the inn's courtyard did he slow. The world spun around him when he stopped and bent over to draw in deep, painful breaths. His hands shook. His legs threatened to collapse. He leaned against the center well and threw his fists in the air. "Damn her to the Flames!"

"Damn who?"

Tallen started, his heart leaping into his throat. He had not noticed Glynn crossing from the stable to the inn when he entered.

"Sorry, brother." Glynn laughed. "Didn't mean to orc-jump you." He laughed even harder.

"Never mind." Tallen sneered. "It's Jennette. She wants to marry Ardric Haesby. I caught them between the warehouses."

His older brother scowled, the laughter dropping from his lips. "Seriously? Last time I saw the two of you together, your lips were so tight I thought I would need a bucket of cold water to tear you apart!"

Tallen folded his arms and glowered even harder at his brother.

Glynn's face turned sheepish. "Alright, so she's a tramp." He clapped Tallen on the shoulder. "Damn her to the Flames, as you say." He pulled him toward the door. "Come on in. I'll buy you a shot of that delicious pear bourbon you make."

Shaking his head, Tallen let his brother guide him inside the Sleeping Gryphon. Linsay and two other serving girls scampered about preparing the inn for the coming crowd. His brother led him to the bar, where he poured two jiggers of the inn's finest reserve batch.

Glynn lifted one glass. "Women…" His eyes flashed to Linsay, who seemed not to notice.

Tallen snorted. "Yeah." Both of them took the shot in one gulp. It burned a little going down, and the fruit hopped up into his nostrils. Tallen's stomach warmed while it soaked through.

"Help me behind the bar tonight." Glynn set down his glass. "We won't be selling much in the way of food."

Tallen nodded. Thoughts of Jennette were already growing numb. He poured another pair of shots. "To family," he said, raising his glass again. "It's really all you've got."

Glynn hoisted his drink. "Family."

The bourbon warmed Tallen's chest, deadening further his turbulent emotions. His legs and hands steadied.

The crowd they greeted after the bonfire threatened to burst through the rafters, gathering on the wide floor and both upper balconies. Eventually Tallen set up a keg outside for Linsay to serve those who waited in line. The reedy sound of dancing music rang out over the prairie.

Tallen focused his mind on his work, pushing all thoughts of Jennette into the background. Virtually every drop of the pear bourbon sold out at a silver penny a glass. Often he got a second penny for his trouble. The brothers kept the drinks flowing until almost midnight, when the crowd at last began to thin.

After a short silence from the band, Tallen heard his sister begin to play her harp and sing *Late to the Night* as her opening tune. A round of cheers greeted it from the locals. Couples danced in the bare spaces left by the exit of already tired patrons. Soon, two local boys joined Dawne with a drum and flute.

"Do you know those musicians?" Glynn carried a suspicious glint in his eyes.

"They're not bad fellows." Tallen shook his head as he wiped a spot on the bar. "Besides, Dawne would stick her fist in their eye if they did anything wrong."

"Just that it sounds like they have practiced together." His brother filled another horn. "That usually happens in private."

Tallen laughed. "It was here, while you were gone on your honeymoon this winter."

"Just keep your eyes open is all I'm saying." Glynn dipped an uncertain nod. "She's your little sister too."

Tallen frowned and reached for a bottle of rye whiskey. "Of course. You need not remind me."

Glynn stopped pouring and met Tallen's gaze. "Sorry. I know you watch out for her."

Dawne and her cohorts played for well over an hour before leaving the stage to well-deserved applause. She disappeared out the back with her friends. Tallen doubted they were up to little more than sharing a flagon and a pipe.

The century-old grandfather clock chimed two in the morning. Tallen looked at Glynn, his face weary.

The elder brother nodded in agreement, and rang the ancient ship's bell sitting behind the counter. "You don't have to go home, but you can't stay here!" He waved away a dozen patrons still holding coin.

Careful not to be too rough, Jik, the stable boy, ushered the crowd out with some urgency. Most of the patrons still carried their horns from the celebration, now filled with Westar family ale. They took the horns with them, toasting to the Gryphon all the way out. Linsay gathered up the house mugs at the door. She allowed the patrons one swallow to finish their drink before they left. The greater part succeeded.

Dawne appeared through the back door. "I will take care of your dishes." She pulled out a chair at a side table. "You sit here. What happened between you and Jennette is already getting around." She placed a bottle of his bourbon on the table next to him. "I found this in my room. You start. I'll drink with you when I'm done."

Glynn shook his head at Tallen's scowl. "I only told my wife!"

Linsay's mouth gaped. "I only told your sister!"

Dawne pushed through the swinging doors to the back. "I only told the musicians."

Tallen shrugged. "Then it will be all over town by morning."

He had filled his stomach with three fingers of the bottle before the others joined him at the table.

Glynn turned a chair around to sit upon. "The inn is as clean as it needs to be tonight. Do you want to talk, or just drink?"

"Drink, then sleep." Tallen gave them a wan smile. "I'm not that crushed," he lied, trying to sound brave for his family. "I don't know that I really loved her. I guess it was just convenient."

His pain threatened to rise up in his chest, and burst forth in the form of tears. He pushed it back down by swallowing the rest of his bourbon. Knowing he might lose control if he remained, he wobbled to his feet and left the others toasting him with another drink before he sought his bed. It was some time before the alcohol overpowered his shredded emotions, and he drifted off to sleep.

His stomach woke him as it tried to hop out and greet the dawn. Vomiting into his chamber pot, Tallen cursed himself for mixing mead and bourbon. His head throbbed with a sharp pain. Nothing more came up, no matter how hard he wretched. He took a sip of water from the glass on his dresser. His belly accepted the liquid, for the moment.

He stumbled down to the kitchen. The fire took its time getting started, but eventually he had tea steeping. Toast with butter and his homemade strawberry preserves helped too.

Dawne trundled in, blinking bleary eyes. "Got some of that for me?"

"Last of the bread." Tallen moved the final bite toward his mouth. At the last moment, he stopped and stuffed it between her lips.

Dawne wolfed it down with a smile. "I'll head over to the bakery to get more for today. Make me a cup of that tea to go first."

"I'll get the bread." Tallen downed his cup. "You make your own tea. And some bacon might be nice when I get back." He walked out the door and took the path down the backside of the hill on which the Gryphon sat.

We'll see if Jennette can look me in the eye today. A happy gait crept into his step as he trotted into town, cutting along the edge of the warehouses where the drama had taken place last night. His head still thumped, and his stomach still rumbled, but neither seemed quite as bad now. *Strange, but I feel free…or at least, better than I did last night.*

The bakery sat not far from the Mootlawn, which still held the refuse of last night's debauchery scattered about it. Tallen skirted the grassy space and trotted toward the overwhelming smell of fresh bread. The doors stood open, the scent wafting out into the town.

"I'll only need five loaves today," Tallen stated to the braided girl behind the counter. When she turned, however, hazel eyes glared at him instead of brown.

"Tallen!" Jennette's younger sister called. "I heard you discovered Ardric and Jennette last night. Dawne's friend told me. I'm sorry it happened that way, and I know she must be too." Her eyes darted back and forth in a nervous twitch. "But the thing is – she never came home. Neither did Ardric from what his parents say."

"Oh, Karana," Tallen scoffed, waving his hand through the yeasty air. "They probably just eloped. They were quite clear to me that they wanted to get married."

Karana's face pinched in anger. "Jennette would never leave without telling someone. You of all people know this is not like her."

Folding his arms, Tallen lifted one eyebrow. "I'm not certain I know her that well at all."

Karana huffed and folded arms back. "If that's all you have for a heart, then no wonder she chose Ardric." She counted five crusty, still-warm loaves, wrapped them in paper, and passed them to him. "I'll put it on the Gryphon's bill," she added with an icy tone.

Her words still stung when Tallen walked out into the cobblestone street. *Jennette is the one who lied to me – who led me on. I have every right to be angry.*

In his distraction, Tallen crossed the open Mootlawn, his thoughts dwelling so much on Jennette that he did not realize it until he passed the still smoldering remains of the bonfire. A few kids hired by the festival council worked at cleaning up the remaining mess. With a shrug, Tallen took the short cut through the warehouses, following the same path he had in pursuit of Jennette.

The streets stood empty, as did most of the buildings. He passed the alley where he had found them. It sat desolate as well. Tallen felt a pull toward the old building across the way. The colors of the rainbow flashed in his head again.

What am I doing here? I need to get back to the inn with this bread.

He ignored the warning of his logical mind. Instead, he followed the invisible call drawing him toward the warehouse. The door leaned open slightly. He stepped inside, almost in a trance.

Shafts of light broke through the upper windows, sparkling off the motes of dust in the air. Two pairs of boot prints shuffled through the old sawdust on the floor. When Tallen dropped the bread loaves, they tumbled across the planks making a scuffed pattern of their own.

The blood ran and pooled where it dripped between the cracks of the boards. Tallen's eyes followed the crimson trail to its source. The bodies of Jennette Morton and Ardric Haesby lay in a gruesome pile. She sprawled face down, a pool of blood gathered at her neck. The long braid that had bounced along in front of him last night was cut and missing. What he saw of her face looked pale and ghastly, drained of any colors save blue and gray. Ardric lay scattered about, chopped to pieces. One of his legs leaned against a wooden pillar, as if waiting for him to come claim it. His head had been smashed with a very heavy blow. The metallic smell of blood mixed in the air with the more acrid scent of spilled bowels. Tallen collapsed to his knees – the bread and tea pouring from his stomach.

"By the Waters!" His senses shattered in a dozen directions. Part of him wanted to pull the bodies back together, while his conscious mind only desired to scream for help.

The conscious part won. "Help!" Leaping to his feet, Tallen dashed out the door. "Help! I need the watch. Someone help!" He ran out of the maze of warehouses, his calls at last catching the attention of a guardsman.

"What's going on here?" A man in maroon livery with a heavy

cudgel and short sword trotted in his direction. "It's early in the day to be shouting so."

"They are dead!" Tallen blurted. "I found their bodies. Hurry!"

The guardsman's face grew more serious, and he motioned for Tallen to lead on.

Drawing a deep breath, he jogged back toward the warehouse. The guardsman followed close behind. Once inside, the man lifted a gauntleted hand over his mouth as he leaned over, retching against the smell and sight. Tallen could not look. He walked back to the door, gasping for fresh air. Dropping to his bottom in the street, tears welled within his eyes.

"Stay right here." The guardsman exited the building, his face pale. "I will bring the watch sergeant."

Tallen sat there in a daze, sobbing. His thoughts tumbled down a dozen avenues. "How could this have happened?"

He did not wait long before the guardsman returned with his sergeant and two other members of the watch. The sergeant walked into the warehouse, gone for only a moment. When he returned, a grim expression filled his face.

"Easy there lad." The man spoke in soft tones, his hand patting Tallen's shoulder. "Did you know them?"

"Yes sir." Tallen cleared his throat and wiped his cheeks with a sleeve. "It is Ardric Haesby and …" Tallen could barely bring himself to say her name. "…Jennette Morton. I'm Tallen Westar. I know them from the inn."

The guardsmen almost choked in shock at Ardric's name.

"Ardric? Are you certain?" The sergeant's voice quivered. At Tallen's nod, he pointed to one of the guardsmen. "Get the captain." The man ran off at top speed. "Lad, you'll have to stay here for the time being."

Eternity passed in those moments while Tallen remained in his seat. His head rested in his hands. He stared at the gravel, tracing every edge of the stone in his mind. He could not accept reality.

"Bring more guards!" Tallen heard a voice shout. "I want this entire district closed off. Where is Westar?" Captain Artur Haesby swung his arms about frantically, sending a half dozen guardsmen in every direction. "I want to see them." He stormed into the warehouse.

Tallen heard the cry of anguish that shrieked from the empty building. One like it echoed in his own heart. The steps sounded swift when they came back out.

The captain's voice strained, a snarl of anger upon his lips. "Take Westar into custody. He had a history with the girl." His velvet gloved finger pointed at Tallen. "He has motive."

Tallen hung his head in his hands, barely noticing the bustle around him. *This is almost fitting. Just when I begin to think being jilted was a good thing…*

He did not struggle at all when the guards took him in hand. His heart grew numb, the walk to the jail a blur to his memory. Only when the cell door slammed behind him did he come to his senses. He collapsed to the dirty straw mattress in the corner.

Evening crept through the window before they allowed Glynn to visit him.

"Burn them in the Flames!" He grabbed Tallen's hand through the bars. "I've been here for hours." A haggard expression hung on his face. "Linsay and Dawne are here too, but they only let me come back here. The family barrister is drawing up a petition for the Baron, but his lordship is in Gavanor." Glynn took a deep breath and clamped Tallen's hand tighter. "We will get you out of here."

"I hope so," Tallen said, tears threatening. "I did not do this, Glynn. You saw me last night at the inn." He squeezed his brother's hand with desperation. "You gave them my alibi, right?"

Glynn reached through with his other hand to grab Tallen's shoulder. "You don't have to tell me. Of course you didn't do this. I told the sergeant at the desk that you were right next to me from before sundown until the wee hours." Glynn looked over his shoulder, brows drawn down in a scowl. "That sergeant even had the guts to admit that he might agree with me, but he has to follow his captain's orders. That bastard should have no jurisdiction. His son is one of the victims!"

Tallen did not sleep throughout the long and lonely night. He remained on the edge of tears. *At least they put me in a solitary cell. Who knows what kind of characters they have in the common lock up?*

When morning slipped through the watch house windows, Tallen's stomach grumbled with ferocity. The stale bread and cup of water that came to his cell were welcome. The sergeant who first arrived on the scene delivered it. The man slipped a piece of jerky onto the tray.

"For all the extras you've slipped in my meals before," he said with a sad smile.

I knew I had seen him before. Sergeant…Dougliss?? "Thanks," Tallen whispered.

Even the extra jerky did not help for long. By noon, his stomach called for more. *I wonder if bread is all they ever serve here?*

A sudden commotion erupted from the outer room. He heard raised voices – voices that sounded used to being raised. Several had a ring of familiarity about them. A few dog barks were followed by a low growl. Tallen stood up from his pallet when the door opened with a bang.

"I told you there is no way this young man did the crime!" Tallen recognized the gruff voice from their encounter a few weeks ago. He would never forget the stare that had accompanied it. "The timeline is impossible. The people at the inn would have seen blood on him without a doubt. I have observed what little of the scene your men left untrampled. To be frank, it looks more like orc work than anything."

"Joz!" shouted a second familiar voice. "There is no certainty regarding that!"

The gruff voice paused before it replied. "Fair enough Boris, but it is obvious the Westar lad did not commit the murder."

"We have no disagreement on that issue."

When they entered the room, the Bluecloaks brought a wave of sudden hope to Tallen's heart. *I never thought I'd be glad to see that mage again.* The soldiers brightened the room, pristine compared to the filth in which he had spent the night. The two faces above the cloaks were even more welcome.

"Open the door, Captain Haesby," the mustachioed Bluecloak ordered. "The young man did not kill your son. Since different weapons were used, there had to be multiple assailants."

"And the killers were trained warriors." The gray-eyed mage returned his stare to Tallen. "Which he obviously is not."

"But he had to be one of them! He had accomplices!" Ardric's father cried without much heart in his words. His crestfallen look reminded Tallen of the pain in his own chest. He handed the key to the mage, who stepped toward the door.

Leaping to his feet, Tallen's dry voice croaked. "Thank you, sir."

"We'll see if you thank me in the end." The mage laughed an odd chuckle. He waved his hand once the door was open. "Come on lad."

Ardric's father looked at Tallen with sour scorn. He walked to the man. "I am sorry about Ardric, sir. I would never have meant him any harm. I—"

"Begone, boy," he spat. "I'll hear none of your words."

Tallen nodded his head and stepped out the door.

Glynn and Dawne both waited in the outer room. Dawne tackled him with a hug. His brother slapped him on the back, a bright smile upon his face.

"Told you I'd get you out! Lucky these gentlemen showed up on their way back east to have some of your stew."

Tallen gulped behind his smile. "I'll make some fresh for you right away, sirs."

The mage lifted an eyebrow. "Enjoy your kitchen. It will be your last night there for a long while."

Sobering his tone, Tallen cocked his head. "What do you mean? I just got free"

Glynn's smile faded, and Dawne squeezed him harder.

The mage's grin widened. "You'll be coming with us. And you're mine to train until you leave for the Isle of Wizards."

Tallen's heart thumped in his throat. He wondered if it pounded out of fear or excitement. "Why?"

The mage inclined his head. "You are definitely a Dreamer. That often brings a great deal more with it. Strength in the Aspect of Psoul usually means strength in one or more of the others."

"Oh, Tallen!" Dawne cried into his chest.

The general turned that predator gaze on him again, sinking Tallen's heart even further. He replaced it with a smile, almost hidden behind his untrimmed mustache – a smile that gave Tallen hope. "My name is Earl Boris Mourne." The general nodded his head and stretched out his hand. "My men will tell you that I don't stand on formality, so you may call me Boris."

The mage slapped leather gloves against his hip. "My name is Magus Joslyn Britt. You will address me as Magus Britt." He gestured toward the door. "By the way, if you intend on serving us a stew tonight, you had better get to it. We leave at dawn tomorrow."

CHAPTER 7

And the Paladin Farina laid her hands upon Danewid. Her power closed his grievous wounds, drawing him back from death. They kissed one last time, before he drew his flaming sword and returned to the battle.
— "A Legend of Forbidden Love" by Mardon Transton

The mist spraying from one of the dozen falls forming Crystal Lake exhilarated Tomas Harte. He climbed along the slick, mossy rock at its edge. Spring brought warmth earlier than usual this year. Once he reached the top of the little lip of stone, Tomas looked out over the plain of Harlong. Harte Castle rose on a hill not half a mile away. He turned to his left and gazed upon the vast stretch of the Northwood. It folded in green waves all the way into the Dragonscale Mountains looming beyond.

Tomas watched the spray plummet to the wide, clear water below. The Crystal Lake earned its name, filled by a dozen streams that tumbled down from the tallest peaks of the Dragonscales. The snowmelt, remaining cold when it reached the lower plain, flowed onward to Crystalport and the Green Bay.

I find real peace only in my family home. Too bad I am the last of us. He reached his hands into the shower of water, cupped them, and pulled the sweet coolness to his lips. The minerals from the crisp mountain water danced on his tongue. Tomas pulled in a deep draught, the tattooed sigil on the back of his right hand glittering in the sunlight, when he shook off the remaining drops of water. The pearlescent half of his paladin's mark shimmered against the coal black half. It reminded him of why he hid in this beautiful desolation.

He sighed in futility. "The High Elder is not the only power in the Temple."

Tomas remembered the brisk autumn day last year when he had entered the High Elder's private study at the Cathedral. He had watched the entire Isle prepare for winter's arrival while awaiting the last ship home to Harlong. Varon Hastrian bundled himself in his heavy robes and stoked the fire with fresh pine. The fat man looked no more than a pile of laundry sitting in a wide, comfortable chair near the flames.

The elder pushed pursed lips out from his jowls. "Will you spend winter upon the Isle, Brother Tomas?"

Removing his gloves, Tomas draped them through his swordbelt. "I had considered returning to the capital. I am the only paladin in Gannon right now."

The elder steepled chubby fingers in front of his squat nose. "Do you intend to take your family seat upon the Common Council? It has been years since you sat there."

Tomas warmed his fingers at the fire. "I made the decision long ago that my vows as a Paladin of Balance superseded my role on the council. I have offered to name a proxy to speak for the people of Harlong."

Shaking his head, the elder waved a single finger at Tomas. "The Common Council is not for common people, despite its name. You know the law states that a proxy must be a member of the ruling house." Hastrian reached to the tray on his side table. It held a dozen pickled baby eels. Their green skin glittered in the firelight. The black and white robed man slurped one down with a slight giggle.

"You really should try one." He gestured toward the tray. "They are quite spectacular."

"Thank you, elder, no." Tomas straightened his leather cuirass with a sharp, downward tug. "Speaking of the council—I know that the rules of the priestly order are less…stringent…than those of the paladins, but do you think it appropriate for any ordained member of the Temple of Balance to sit upon the High Council? Especially one so exalted as…" Tomas swallowed. "…the High Elder. When you took the Lord Magister's seat, did you not see how you threaten to shift the Balance yourself?"

Hastrian swallowed another eel. He did not seem to notice that the liquor spilled out the corner of his mouth and ran down his flabby chin. "I did not *take* the Lord Magister's seat. King Arathan *offered* it to me. The Lord Magister willingly stepped down to the Common Council. The vacancy he took had sat there for years, much like your own position."

Tomas' beard itched in frustration, despite the fact he kept it neatly trimmed. "The Druidess left the council because she felt the imbalance even before I did. She chose to hide. I choose to meet it."

"Hah!" The elder slurped another eel, this one juiced with a lemon. He gulped it down with a ravenous smile, before wiping his face on a sleeve. "The Druidess is a fool. Let her rot in the Deepwood. You should not be a fool. *You* should take your seat on the Commons in support of the Temple. Work with me to build our future along with that of Gannon." His smile widened, spreading wrinkles of fat across his jowls and neck. "This imbalance you say you feel…" The elder did not fool Tomas with his false sincerity. "…would it not behoove you to fight it with me from the next tier of the royal dais? You could bring a great deal of wisdom to the entire council."

Shaking his head, Tomas turned his back on the High Elder. "You do not understand. It is the Temple's very involvement in Gannon's rule that threatens the Balance. Too much Order can be as harmful to the Balance as too much Chaos. It is not the place of the Temple to rule the people." He shook his head. "We offer them wisdom, perhaps give them justice, but we do not command. I will have no part in it." Tomas stalked out of the High Elder's study.

He had given the ship captain a hefty purse to take him directly to Crystalport. His ride up the Crystal River had brought back more memories. The winter that followed was cold, but the hearths of Harte Castle kindled bright and cheery fires. Now, however, the inevitable arrival of spring brought sequestered thoughts back to Tomas' mind.

"I cannot hide here forever," he said to the waterfalls. They answered with nothing but babble.

If only father had known his youngest son would be forced to inherit. He would never have made me take my vows. Then I could fairly sit on the council seat for the people of Harlong. I could fight the elder and his cronies. "But I will not compromise my vows," he called out to the oblivious torrents surrounding him. "I swore to maintain the Balance, not skew it to any particular advantage—not even my own." Tomas sighed, allowing his emotions to boil off into the cascade. "Not even my own people…" He focused on the rainbow formed under the noonday sun by the mists, using the techniques of his order to calm his mind and spirit. "One cannot fight Fire with Fire…"

Winds that whipped down from the Dragonscales remained his only answer from the world. With one last draught of the fresh, mountain water, he descended from the pinnacle. His hands grasped the slippery rock with the certainty of having climbed here many times before, seeking solace and center to his being.

A loud snort greeted him when he returned to the lake's edge. Fireheart trotted over, his gray coat still somewhat thick from winter's chill. The stallion nudged Tomas with a wide muzzle.

"I wish I had oats for you, old boy." Tomas scratched the horse's head. "We'll get you fed back at the castle." He pulled his swordbelt from the saddle horn and slipped it around his waist. Steelsheen's weight felt reassuring on his hip.

With a quick hop into the saddle, he guided Fireheart toward Harte Castle. The stallion made good time, eager for spring exercise.

Tomas caught the scent of blossoms still clinging to the cherry and apple trees in the old orchard where he had played as a child. *Summer is the most beautiful season in Harlong. Perhaps I will stay here with my people. They need me as much as anyone does.* Fireheart tromped across the drawbridge before he knew it, so distracted were his thoughts. He looked down and smiled at the large swirls moving over the surface of the moat. *It would not hurt my own inner Balance to spend a little time with a fishing pole.*

Inside the central courtyard, Tomas dismounted, and with a good pat of Fireheart's withers, he passed the reins to his groom. The young man bowed and led the stallion off toward the stable. Before Tomas climbed the steps to the inner keep, a woman with a pinched face and her hair pulled into a tight, white bun greeted him with a sniff.

"Did Milord enjoy his morning ride?"

Tomas tugged off his gauntlets. "It served its purpose, Manifred."

"These are the preliminary lists of planted fields and what the farmers have sown in them," she said, handing him a sheaf of papers and pulling a stylus from her hair bun. "There is also a list of fallow plots. The remaining documents list the likely lumbering areas for this summer, as well as estimates of animal reproduction."

Tomas groaned. He missed his older brothers often, but seldom so much as when the details of running Harlong required his eye. "Must I?" He smiled at the crease in the woman's forehead and reached for the papers. "I will take them with me to my study and go over them in detail, Mani. Please send up a lunch."

Her frown lessened. "Of course, Milord. Just be certain to initial each page as you finish it."

Tucking the sheaf under his arm, Tomas chuckled. He trotted up the last few steps to the front doors. Inside stretched the great hall of his fathers, though it was not so large by modern Gannonite standards. *Only because it is older than all of their buildings. My ancestors remained during the Exile. My ancestor knelt to the Navigator upon his return…all in the name of peace.*

Twisting the steel band on his finger, he trotted up the staircase to his private floor. The Harte signet ring carried more centuries upon it than the castle. One of Tomas' ancestors had etched words upon it in a language that predated Common Tongue, a human derivation of ancient Elvish. *Copus Eptu* — Face Facts.

"Grandfather," he had asked as a child after a visit by one of the Snowbourne Barons, "why does our family not have a motto like that of House Darax? *Strong as Stone.* Ours seems weak by comparison."

His grandfather had laughed. The old Lord Harte had been a jovial man, unlike Tomas' aloof father. "I'd like to see Baron Maydon punch the walls of Harte Castle. Then we would see just how 'Strong as Stone' his fist really is." The old man's face sharpened. He cupped his grandson's shoulders. "Facing facts means accepting reality, even when you don't want to believe it. It means knowing when you can fight, or – like Roman Harte did four centuries ago – knowing when you cannot. He was outnumbered a thousand to one when Aravath the Navigator turned his eyes northward."

The memory tasted bittersweet, as did most thoughts of Tomas' long lost family.

Slipping off the leather cuirass, he walked down a long, windowed hall overlooking the courtyard. A line of doors on his left led to several rooms reserved for the members of House Harte. Most sat empty, with sheet-covered furnishings. Tomas had not entered some of those rooms since his eldest brother died with his entire family during the Bloody Flux.

If only I had been here at the time… Ten years I have ruled this house. Ten years it has ruled me. I love it, but I am chained to it.

One of the last doors opened into his study. He basked in the wave of nostalgia that washed over him as he entered. When he was a child, this room had been his father's private refuge. Tomas draped his cuirass over the leather sofa, and then hung his steel on the back of a chair. The warm smell of books and centuries of good pipe smoke calmed his nerves.

"Perhaps I will remain in my homeland for the summer." Tomas gazed out the wavy glass windows onto the slate roof of the great hall. "The Balance knows I have paperwork to keep me busy." He tossed the sheaf of parchment onto his grandfather's desk and sat down. "I trust that Mani knows what she is doing. She's been doing it since *I* was a child."

However, his sense of duty would not allow him to simply sign each page. Tomas took the time to skim the first few. Before long, their content trapped his inquisitive mind in a twisting maze of numbers and facts. He was engrossed in a report concerning the new piglet population when a knock came at his door. His stomach growled a reply before his mouth could.

"Please, come in."

The girl who brought the platter in had been born on the castle grounds. She gave a quick curtsey before entering the room.

"Thank you, Denna." Tomas gave her a generous smile. "You may place it on the desk and go get your own lunch."

The girl set the tray of roast beef, brown bread, and spring radishes on the table. Curtsying again before turning to leave, she flashed a smile and closed the study door behind her.

Tomas smeared a daub of mustard onto the bread and followed it with a large slice of the peppered beef. He turned the pages with one hand and held his sandwich with the other. Soon the entire meal disappeared, though he had not yet read half the papers. Steeling himself with a deep, refreshing swig from the mug of ale, he dived into the rest of the sheaf.

By the time he initialed the last page, the sun had set a deep orange through the windows behind him. He placed the goose quill pen into its stand and gazed at the fiery heavens through glass so aged that the panes thinned at their tops.

"At least that is done." He rose from the leather chair, soft with age. He caressed its back, remembering the many generations who had sat there.

My vows are not of chastity, but I may take no wife, and I will not leave a bastard that must fight to inherit from me. He shook his head. "Perhaps that is my only choice," he admitted aloud.

Perhaps a meal and a good night's rest will help me lose this melancholy.

Buckling his sword belt around his waist, Tomas descended the stairs to the great hall. The banner of House Harte, a pale green stag on a violet field, hung above the front table. Next to it draped the black and white circle of his order, split by a sinuous line. A dot of each color nested in the other half. *Reminders that there are no absolutes.*

He wandered into the kitchens, where the household servants and soldiers ate. The smell of roasted pork and herbed potatoes put his mouth to watering. He served himself at the counter just like any other soldier. Translucent onions smothering his plate, Tomas headed for a table where a laughing squad of young guards sat. They scrambled to their feet when he approached, each straightening his purple tunic and saluting.

"At ease, lads. It's a small castle. I'm just here for supper too."

The soldiers seated themselves, with nods and sheepish grins aimed at their lord. Tomas placed himself at the end of the table and dug in.

He looked at one of the now silent men. "You mind passing the bread?" The soldier scooped it to him with military precision. "Thank you, corporal." Tomas tore a roll in half and dipped it into the onion gravy. "You know," he mumbled around the bread. "You are allowed to tell jokes when I'm here." Tomas grinned. "Just not bad ones."

The corporal who passed the breadbasket snorted a stifled laugh. His sergeant, not much older than him, scowled.

Tomas pointed his roll at the man who laughed. "Do you know a good joke, Corporal Dibbs?"

The sergeant spoke up before the corporal could. "If he does know a joke, Milord, it is no doubt a bad one."

Dibbs smile faded as he ducked his head. "Indeed, Milord. The only jokes I know are bad ones."

Tomas curled his lip into a rueful smile. "That is a shame. You should learn some good ones before next we break bread."

Dibbs saluted. "I will endeavor, sir."

The men spoke through the rest of the meal, but in hushed tones. Tomas exchanged a few more words with them, before he rose and returned his empty plate.

"Good night, sir," the corporal called with a nod of respect.

Tomas winked. "Have a good night, lads."

Picking up a lit candle, Tomas climbed the stairs back to his study. The shadows of a nearly moonless night hung within. Lighting the oil lamp on the desk, he adjusted the brass valve so it brightened the room enough to read. The book on his desk had called to him all day. *The Beginnings of Balance* concerned the earliest history of his order. Midnight closed in when he finally place the aged green ribbon back into the spine of the tome.

Rising from his chair, Tomas passed through the side door to his bedchamber. He removed his boots first and sat on a mat in the center of the room. With a deep breath to settle his mind, he entered the trance of his order.

Tomas reached out with his life force and sensed the energies surrounding him. Inside the castle walls, he discerned the servants and soldiers, bright flames of life, each separate and identifiable. The horses in the stable blazed as well, Fireheart in particular. Outside the walls, Tomas sensed the vast ocean of life within the forest. Wolves and bears, complex and intelligent, hunted through the background noise of their prey. Even a few of the eldest trees stood out in Tomas' mind. Villages dotted the Northwood, each a small island of human sparks in the sea of wilderness.

Brother Mardon laughed at me when I told him that one day I would reach twenty miles with my senses. If only he were still alive today.

Tomas, about to abandon his trance, stirred. A disturbance leaped into his perception – a sudden spike in fear tore along the edge of his range. Behind it burned a deep, frothing anger, one he recognized from expeditions many years before.

"Orcs!"

Jumping to his feet, Tomas gathered his boots and pulled them on, hopping on one leg into the study. He grabbed Steelsheen from the back of his chair and belted it tight, snatching his cuirass as he left. He ran down the hall, taking the stairs two steps at a time.

"Awake! Awaken Harte Castle! Orcs raid the Northwood!"

By the time he reached the bottom step, the keep bustled with activity. The officer of the watch greeted him at the front door.

"Shall I wake the captain, sir?" A single star gleamed from the man's collar.

"Do so, Lieutenant! Then gather a platoon of cavalry to ride out immediately. Garrettown is under attack as we speak."

The officer saluted before dashing away. Every resident of Harte Castle knew their lord's paladin powers.

Wondering if he needed his chainmail, Tomas stuffed his head through the cuirass. "This will have to do," he whispered to himself.

"Milord?" asked a guard standing at the ready.

"Never mind..." Tomas noticed the two bronze discs. "... Corporal Dibbs..." Tomas laughed. "The Balance sometimes tells us its own jokes, does it not, Corporal?"

"At least we got a good dinner first, sir," the man said with a salute, "if you'll allow me the honor of joining you."

"Get a horse, Dibbs." A stableboy brought Fireheart out from his stall, and Tomas leaped into the saddle. He waited while the platoon gathered around him, reaching out with his senses. At last the patrol was mounted, some armed with crossbows and most carrying torches. "We ride for Garrettown," he shouted above the stamp of horses. "Orcs already attack there. We must make haste!"

They dashed out into the night, thundering across the drawbridge. Tomas heard it clank shut as they made their way down along the edge of the woods. Ahead lay the logging road that led toward the hamlets dotting the Northwood. He led the charge along the sparse gravel, Fireheart's sure hooves making good time in the faint torchlight. Garrettown nestled deep in the forest, and dawn hid only a couple of hours away.

Fires dotted the village when they reined in at the edge of the hamlet's clearing. Thatch and log huts burned. Dark shapes ran through the orange light glinting off their steel.

Tomas twisted to look back at his soldiers. They wore worried frowns. "Stay together. We may be outnumbered, but we have them by surprise." Pulling Steelsheen from its scabbard, he embraced the power of the paladins, and blue-white flame surged along the blade. Lifting it high into the night, the sword burst forth with the brightness of his strength. The soldiers about him cheered. All knew rumor of their lord's power, but very few had ever seen it in full glory.

"With me!"

Fireheart reared up and launched his body toward the burning homes, the other horses following close behind. The ardent light of Steelsheen clashed eerily against the russet glow of the fires. The black shapes clarified into armored orcs, their red eyes dancing in the mixed light. Some carried loot from the houses. Others fed on slaughtered livestock.

Tomas yelled with fury as his men rode them down. Crossbow bolts skewered by surprise those that stepped out of burning buildings. His teeth gritted, Tomas swung Steelsheen in wide burning arcs, cutting down his enemies. He focused his emotions into a stream of power, focused on his sword. The flames brightened, and the steel within glowed white-hot. He urged Fireheart forward.

One orc stood his ground, his face curled in a vicious snarl. Thick yellow fangs protruded from his jaw, and a wide scimitar reflected the light of Steelsheen and the burning village. Tomas answered his challenge, and his first blow was met with a resounding clang. Blue fire scattered along with sparks of ordinary orc steel. Tomas swung again as Fireheart danced to one side, maneuvering on his own to create an opening in the attacker's guard.

Tomas caught the orc's eyes darting toward the movement of his men. He took the opening, lashing out with Steelsheen in an arc of blue-white flame. The steel collar protecting the orc's neck split like butter under the blade's razor edge. The head bounced twice along the ground before the body knew it was dead.

Other orcs felt the steel of his soldiers' swords as they ran from the burning fires of a Tomas' weapon. Once his eyes caught the scattered bodies of the inhabitants of Garrettown, his valiant rage took over, clearing his mind of all but battle. Dozens fell before Steelsheen. Fireheart took down his share as well with steel shod hooves.

They dashed back and forth along the small central street of the hamlet, cutting down the enemy where they stood and fought, or running them down from behind when they ran. Tomas kept his rage under a tight leash. The heat of it flowed into his weapon, fanning its fires and draining his emotions, allowing him to concentrate on the battle surrounding him. With his anger drained by feeding his fires, Tomas thoughts danced with clarity, noticing every movement of the battle. Blood sprayed across his face with another swing, but he took no heed. The flames of Steelsheen danced in the night.

Quiet descended on the village with a sudden finality. Tomas heard only the shouts of a few of his men above the crackle of flame. He bounded from Fireheart's saddle. One of the orcs struggled to crawl into the forest. From the trail of blood left behind, Tomas doubted he would make it much farther. He reached down to roll the weakened warrior over. The guts squeezing between the orc's claws caused even Tomas to grimace. *It would take a great deal of will to move at all with that wound, much less hold it in. It is far beyond my power to heal.*

"Why do you roam my lands, orc?" Tomas held Steelsheen aloft, casting its light down upon the dying warrior. "I will give you the gift of death by the Fires if you answer me."

The orc attempted a laugh, spitting up blood. "We don't want *your* land, human fool." In the white light of his sword, Tomas caught the deep crimson running down the orc's chin. "You will taste the power that comes. Then we will take *all* lands from you." He cried out in agony, and Tomas gave him peace.

He searched the body of the orc, but found nothing of interest in his pockets. Tomas did notice the tattoo on the warrior's neck, however – a hammerhead shark.

"So." His voice hid beneath the crackle of fire. "The Shark Clan has turned to raiding beyond the Dragon's Teeth this year. That has not happened for decades."

"Sir," a voice called from behind him. Tomas turned to see Corporal Dibbs limping, his face smudged with soot and blood. "We found about two dozen villagers hidden within a grove of spreading pines. They appear to be the only survivors." A mix of pride and pain washed over his face. "We lost Barend and Cloyne – both good fellows."

Extinguishing Steelsheen with a release of his power, Tomas caught a glimpse of the sunrise over the trees. "Stand close, Corporal. Watch over me." He sat down to enter a trance and reach out with his life force, stretching his senses. He felt no more anger, only the daytime life of the forest awakening around him.

"Gather the men and the survivors." Tomas stood. "We will all ride for Harte Castle."

As his riders bustled about, Tomas wandered among the corpses of the orcs, seeking a sign of their purpose. He noticed their gear shone with sharp edges and good maintenance. None wore chainmail – each equipped more for stealth and a long journey than a simple raid. Tomas shifted a body.

"A Boar Clan tattoo?" He leaned in close, and the bristling pig with curling tusks popped out in bright red against the fallen warrior's greenish skin. "Boris would not believe this. Shark and Boar working together." Tomas jogged back to Fireheart, his mind working through the potential dangers. *I must take this to the King, myself.*

The return trip took quite a bit longer than the ride out. Everyone stumbled along in exhaustion by the time Harte Castle peaked out of the trees ahead. Tomas sighed in relief once the portcullis had dropped and the gatekeepers raised the drawbridge behind them. More soldiers drilled in the courtyard and marched along the walls and ramparts. Local townsfolk already gathered within the safety of the castle, many bringing their livestock and supplies with them.

Manifred Adella jogged over with her usual dignity. Captain Jondon Maycrest ran without heed to his pride.

"What are your orders, Milord?" Captain Maycrest saluted. "Were you successful in Garrettown?"

"For some." Tomas tossed his leg over the saddle horn and slid to the ground. "Many were killed, including two of our soldiers. I want you to start extensive patrols of the Northwood. If you see any sign of incursions, bring in the inhabitants of the forest hamlets." He took a swig from a cup of water offered him. "Thank you, Denna. Some bread and meat would be nice, too." She curtsied and stepped away before he added, "And prepare a pack of travel provisions for me, one that will last a journey of several weeks."

"You will leave us, Milord?" Manifred deepened her eternal frown. "In an hour of such need?"

"I must, Mani." Tomas steeled himself against his sinking heart. He lifted his gaze in resolve. "I have hidden here for too long. There is far more at stake than just Harlong. I must return to the capital with this news of orc incursions. Any other messenger would go unheeded."

He turned to Captain Maycrest. "Send messages to the Duke of Wellsfield and warn the Barons of Snowbourne Fork. In the meantime, begin recruitment. Start with the survivors of Garrettown. Scout the Northwood in force. Use the safety of the castle if you encounter numbers." He shifted his gaze to Manifred. Her steady face settled him in his decision. "Use the closed rooms if you need them. I must go to Daynon. You will rule in my stead – you do it anyway. Maycrest has command of the soldiers, but you run Harlong." Tomas placed his hands upon her shoulders. "Protect it for me. I leave to protect the entire kingdom, maybe even the Balance itself."

Manifred stared at him, an unrecognizable look on her face. With a sudden burst of tears, she grabbed and hugged him. "I have known you thirty years, since you were a little boy," she whispered. "I have always known your strength. I am certain it is enough for the many who will lean on you in dark times."

Tomas returned her embrace, the weight of years lifting from his shoulders, though a darker shadow still hovered in the back of his mind.

The Balance has shifted indeed.

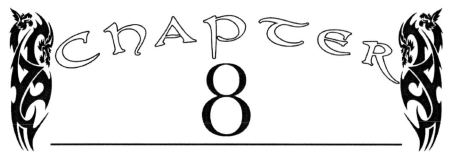

CHAPTER 8

"The Cataclysm has not destroyed our people! It has saved us while we remained in refuge. Look at these new mountains upon our very doorstep. The Iron Mountains were empty. These will be fresh with once deeply hidden veins of gold, silver, iron, and copper. Who better than we dwarves to pull out those resources? We will rebuild our great civilization with them, as we discover what change has wrought."
— King Varathar of the Dwarves at the hour of Exodus

Darve Northtower stepped out onto a wide platform at the top of the stone edifice that gave his family its name. He gazed over the city as evening sweeping into the sky. Only the royal palace at the peak of the Rock maintained a greater view of the lumbering Dragonscales. The wind caught his light robe and whipped it about him. His gray streaked beard and the few long wisps that clung to his scalp fluttered in the breeze.

"Not bad for a dwarf of over two hundred," he chuckled to the setting sun while brushing his hand through the bristles on his chin.

"You're that old!"

Darve turned to see that Bran and his twin Brax had joined him for evening air, their youthful laughter breaking the silence.

"You will hope to look as good as your uncle," he mock-scolded the dwarf of only sixty.

"Bran will hope to look as good as me," Brax added with a harsh laugh.

The two young dwarves appeared identical in Darve's eyes, save for a small scar over Brax's left brow. However, Darve had watched their personalities diverge, even during childhood.

"What?" Bran looked at his brother with a face full of shock. "And have your constant frown pasted upon my lips?" He laughed a bright chuckle. "I would rather leap from this tower right now to avoid that."

"I would toss you now..." Brax charged at his brother,

stopping short. "…to avoid the next couple centuries living with you."

"Silence!" Darve sliced the air with his hand. "My patience for your gibberish is limited today. I wish to witness this sunset in peace." He waved toward the door back into the tower. "If you wish to babble like the children I thought you no longer were then go back inside."

The twins quieted, though not without first each giving the other a good elbowing.

With a sigh of exasperation, Darve stepped onto the small platform at the center of the terrace. Upon it hung a bronze bell cast almost a thousand years ago, replated and refurbished over the generations.

Darve lifted an eyebrow at his nephews. "Do you young men know why Northtower was built? Do you know where your family comes from?"

Brax folded his arms with a scowl. "Of course we do, Uncle. We are not fools."

Darve shook his head. "I did not say you were. I only asked a question."

"It was built by Carnac Northtower," Bran said, flashing a smirk at his brother, "when what remained of our people exited the Rock after the Cataclysm."

"Yes…" Darve raised a finger. "…but what was his name before the Cataclysm?"

"Carnac Bywater." Brax folded his arms and raised an eyebrow at Bran. "And he was not born among the people of the Rock or the Iron Hills."

Darve nodded. "Yes. Our ancestors sought refuge with King Varathar when he sealed his people inside the Rock during the Cataclysm, but they were not born his subjects. Carnac hailed from the far south, from a group of dwarves we do not believe survived the Dragon Wars. He had come to trade with the dwarves of what once were called the Iron Mountains." He furrowed his brow at the twins. "What does this teach us?"

Brax rolled a snide grin across his lips. "Not to cause another Cataclysm?"

"Dwarves did not cause the Cataclysm!" Darve knit his brow and thrust his finger at his nephew. "You will stop with that 'Galdrian Cult' nonsense. It is a thing for young fools and jackanapes. I thought you well beyond that, Brax."

The young dwarf nodded with a bashful face. "I am sorry,

Uncle. I really am. It just popped out of me – a joke in poor taste." He folded his hands together in a pleading gesture. "My involvement with them was the mistake of a young man. I abandoned that two decades ago. I would never allow their heresy in my presence again."

"Good." Darve gripped Brax's fingers with his own. "I knew it." He reached one hand over to his other nephew. Bran offered a bright smile. "Come," Darve said. "Let us look upon the city our ancestors founded together, from the tower Carnac built." Releasing their hands, he pointed at the dwarf runes carved around the edge of the ancient bell. "*To guard His Majesty's northern flank. To watch the mountains from whence came our destruction.*" He ran his finger along the etched runes as he read them, feeling their age. "It is our family's grave responsibility."

The dwarves stood there in thought, their eyes fixed on the soaring Dragonscales. Darve filled his lungs with the fresh air that blew down from them. Something odd tickled his nostrils. He did not recognize the scent, yet it set the hairs on his back to dancing.

"Do you sme—" Darve stopped when his eyesight caught something moving against the horizon, darker than the sky, but lighter in shade than the mountain slopes. The hazy shape reminded him of a flock of birds – an extremely large flock of birds. "From Earth's heart…" he whispered. A moment later, his brain snapped into action. Darve dashed over to the small chest next to a set of divans. Flipping open the lid, he dug down through the contents to pull out a brass and crystal spyglass. Running back over to the top of the platform, he leaned against the bell. The glass went to his eye, and he swung it toward the mountains.

A green-scaled face leaped into the circle of his vision. Sharp fangs dripped slather into the wind, while muscular forearms pumped leathery wings against it. Darve adjusted the focus, and his heart leapt about inside his chest. Dozens more reptilian shapes flew out of the mountains, each one a different mesh of colors. His glass caught glimpse of a massive black beast with scarlet tipped wings. Darve's bouncing heart sank like a stone.

"Dragons!" His hand grabbed the old stone hammer and pounded it against the bell. Even after centuries unused, its tone still rang true. It tolled out over the entire city, echoing against the mountain home of the dwarven king. Soon other bells took up the call, as more folk noticed the wavering shapes on the horizon.

"Gather the house defenses!" Darve ran toward the far side of the tower's crown where a heavy ballista sat. A crew of dwarves on guard had already begun to load and crank it. "Sergeant Marrax! Prepare to target the beasts as they come at us. Aim for the face or underbelly." Darve turned back to his nephews. "Bran! Get that mage you brought with you. Bring him up here!" Both young dwarves ran for the door. "Brax! You check that every weapon platform is in action. I will command up here."

"Yes, Uncle," they shouted back in unison.

Darve turned to the ballista crew. Their faces paled, but they stood with the weapon loaded, ready to launch. Sergeant Marrax Redarm manned the aiming winches.

I would almost believe he might have faced the beasts before from his cool. But there has been no dragon raid on the Rock for at least six centuries. Marrax may be older than I am, but he's not that much older.

"Wait for them, Sergeant." Darve patted the air with both hands, gesturing for calm. "I have never seen one myself. However, I have read family records on how to fight them." The sergeant leaned in close, his eyes squinting at Darve. "You want to wait until they get right up on you. But you have to be quick, or you get burned. The open mouth is listed as the best place to put a shaft." Darve knitted his brow. "But they usually open right before they blast you with fire so timing is critical."

"Aye, Maester Northtower." Marrax turned to his crew. "You dogs heard the maester! Get yer eggs in place." He leaned toward Darve and whispered, "What is this, sir? Dragons? In a flight?"

Shaking his head with his own disbelief, Darve searched for an answer to give the warrior who had so long served his family. "I do not know, Marrax." He lifted a hand in futility. "We can only react as warriors must."

The sergeant nodded, firmness setting his features once again. "Aye, sir. That we will." He turned back to the crew. "Ready you dogs! I want the sluices and sand barrels opened." The soldiers scattered at his orders. Marrax turned back. "Maester, you have no armor or weapon. You must take refuge inside the tower."

Darve opened his mouth to protest, but dozens of archers and crossbowmen bursting out onto the terrace interrupted him. They took up places near the parapet, their faces nervous. A shaven-headed dwarf trotted behind them, his beard oiled to a fine point. Yrik wore simple robes not that different from Darve's. Bran stalked behind him. He had already donned his finest chainmail and carried a heavy crossbow.

Screams climbed to Darve's ears from the city far below. The reptilian shapes swooped upon the lower buildings, toppling stone and ripping prey from where they ran. Some of the dragons reached the size of houses, while others looked to be no larger than a pony.

"One bearing on the tower, Maester!" came a shout from Darve's left. Several of the more stalwart archers bunched together along the western parapet.

"Spread out!" Darve waved his arms about in the air. "Concentrate your fire, but don't let the damn thing wipe out an entire squad with one breath."

Brax trotted out onto the roof. He carried a heavy leather tunic treated with a fireproofing salve for Darve. The younger dwarf also handed Darve the Northtower family helm. "Can they really spit fire, Uncle?"

"I think you are about to find out," Darve said with surety, slipping the tunic over his robe. He took his great grandfather's helm, wrought of stainless steel in the form of a squat tower.

Sergeant Marrax pointed into the sky. "It's the big black one!"

Darve clamped the helm down upon his head. "Then swing that ballista this way, sergeant."

Marrax cranked the heavy handle. Darve's engineers maintained the weapons designed during the Dragon Wars. *They've been tested, yes, but never fired in actual battle.*

Above the noise of the weapon's gears and the shouts of his men, Darve heard a whooshing of air. Time slowed when the beast, both magnificent and terrifying, swept over the rim of the tower. In that bare moment, Darve saw its ruby eyes scanning the rooftop. He noticed the scarlet edging on its ebony appendages. The veins that webbed their way through its leathery wings throbbed in time with the beat of its massive heart. The beast latched its strong rear legs onto the parapet and stretched its wingspan, casting a shadow on Darve's entire company.

"Aim and loose!"

Greenish curls of flame erupted over the front rows of Darve's men. A few managed to leap away, but three were burned to ash where they stood. A half dozen more rolled about screaming, their comrades dousing the flames as best they could.

Many archers loosed their arrows, but only a few missiles found purchase in the dragon's scaly armor. One crossbow bolt ripped a hole through its wing. Darve looked at Marrax as the ebony monster sucked in for another blast. The older warrior held one eye closed, his other trained on the beast. Sergeant Marrax heaved against the vertical adjustment, tilting the ballista slightly higher.

"Launch!" Marrax sliced the air with one hand. A soldier slapped a lever, and the three-yard shaft of oak and steel flashed out at the dragon. It scraped the beast's face, dazing the monster and ripping away a layer of scales. The dragon heaved away from the tower's edge, flapping for altitude and roaring in rage. It curved away toward the stadium where hundreds of other dwarves gathered for refuge.

Darve waved his arms at the crew. "Reload!"

Brax looked back and cupped a hand to his mouth. "Another is headed toward us, Uncle!"

Darve grabbed the mage friend of his nephew by the sleeve. "If you have the powers you claim, sir mage, I would think now a perfect time to use them."

"I assure you, Maester Northtower, the next dragon to attack this tower will feel my power." Yrik stretched out his fingers. "You may then see how invaluable my service would be to a house such as yours."

Darve narrowed his eyes. "If you kill one of these beasts, Magus, I'll give you twice the stipend you ask."

Yrik returned a narrow, pasty smile, one that looked unfamiliar on that face. He bowed with a great deal of grace and flourish.

"Here one comes!" An archer waved from the parapet. The dwarves near that edge of the tower spread apart, pulling their bows.

This time the dragon did not loom so large, but still it overshadowed the platoon of archers. Purple ridges crawled along its emerald wings. A forked, red tongue lashed about behind needle-like fangs. Flame with a slight purple tint poured from its maw. The blast did not carry as much heat as the ebony dragon's fire had, yet still Darve lost another two of his company before they launched a shot.

In his gut Darve felt a sudden concussion. Stone, broken from the parapet by their first attacker, leaped up from the rooftop and smashed into the face of the beast.

"Launch!" Marrax shouted when the dragon toppled backward. The ballista bolt darted toward it and lodged under its chin. The steel tip ripped out the back of its green head, pinning the jaws shut. The body tumbled backward and crashed to the street and gardens below.

A cheer sprang up from the men. Bran slapped Yrik on the back with a laugh. Brax granted them a rare smile.

"Reload!" Darve hollered out to everyone. "There are fifty more where that one came from!"

The entire group wore chastised faces, including the mage. They scrambled to positions, pulling arrows and bolts from quivers. The ballista cranked into readiness, and its crew hefted another shaft into place.

Three beasts came at once, each not much bigger than a human's horse, but still able to breathe fire. They were a dull gray with mottled brown, not nearly as striking as the first two. Arrows caught these with more ease. Soon they scampered away into the air, one falling at last, overwhelmed by a dozen shafts.

Darve noticed the black one not far away, swooping into the open marketplace and pulling a fat dwarf from the ground. The dragon tossed its victim into the air and snapped down on the body, swallowing it with a single gulp.

Another beast caught his eye, a crimson one with bright blue rides on his spine and head. *Spirits of Earth, it's almost as big as the black one.*

The dragon's gaze passed over Northtower, and it curved its wings to swoop toward the dwarf emplacement. It swelled, pulling in the air it needed to feed its fires.

"Marrax," Darve shouted, his eyes transfixed on the dragon, "do you have another shaft ready?"

"Aye, sir!"

Darve took a step back, as the dragon swept forward. He felt the red and bronze eyes focusing on him, their catlike slits tightening on his presence. The dragon cracked its maw, and a black soot drifted out in the wind of its flight. "Any time, Sergeant."

The missile launched, shooting out as if it was pulled on a line toward the dragon's mouth. It darted forward, a pin of steel and oak. The beast opened its jaw to lay fire upon the tower just as the shaft struck, burying itself deep in the dragon's throat. The creature spasmed violently, scrambling as if to stop its flight and cut off its breath.

The dragon's head exploded in a flash of green flame, leaving a sinewy neck to flop with a caustic, burning ooze flinging about as the body crashed to the streets below.

Another cheer rose from the soldiers.

From the top of Northtower, Darve watched night swallow the valley of the Stonebourne Fork. Fires raged through the city.

Forest hamlets in the surrounding mountain vales dotted the distance with kindled flames. The flight of dragons gathered above the fiery wreckage of their attack and soared off northward. Fewer returned over the mountains than had come. However, the glow that still hung on the mountain's shoulders after the sun disappeared, left evidence of the destruction abandoned in their wake.

"Second platoon! Spread through the tower and city." Darve ripped the helm from his head, sweat making the leather padding sticky. "See if anyone needs aid – and I do mean anyone." He pointed to Sergeant Marrax. "Keep your crew ready in case one returns."

Half the archers dashed toward the door leading down to the street level.

"I will go with them, Uncle." Bran gave a quick salute. He pointed at Brax and Yrik. "You two stay here and protect him."

Brax nodded, his eyebrows knit in conviction. "Aye, brother."

Darve walked to the mage. "You are hired, Magus Yrik." He extended his hand. "Welcome to the Northtower family." The mage's grip, weak at first, strengthened as Darve shook it.

Natural gypsum chandeliers sparkled along the ceiling of the Cavern of Beginnings where it vaulted far over Darve's head. Dozens of long chains hung from that expanse of rock, suspending oil lamps at odd intervals. The effect dizzied Darve, even though he had been deep under the mountain dozens of times before.

Unlike the palace, the gardens, or the Magnum Room, the Cavern of Beginnings is not meant to be beautiful. It means to humble those who walk through it. Yet it still achieves beauty, even in its austerity.

Darve's gaze settled on the stone chair that stood alone within the vast chamber. Carvings depicting the history of the dwarves wrapped around the throne. Wide patches remained untouched by chisel and hammer, the bare stone awaiting heroes yet to be born. *They say when the last space is carved, the throne will crack, and our people will disappear from the world.*

A laugh escaped his lips at the idea, drawing looks from some of the other dwarves gathered round the seat of their king. Heat rose in Darve's cheeks and ears. He bowed his head in apology.

"Twenty-one carcasses have been gathered of the lesser

beasts," General Weldrin continued over the slight interruption. "Five of the large ones fell, including two downed by the guards of Northtower." He inclined his head in Darve's direction.

"Thank you, General." Darve offered a bow. "If only we could have killed more."

Weldrin nodded in return. His rare, trimmed beard had faded to white where a scar ran down his cheek. "Another beast fell over the forest village of Bearburough." He waved toward a fair-haired maid that tried her best to hide behind a group of dwarves dressed in foresting leathers. "Tilli Broadoak, a young huntress of the woods, placed a single shaft in its eye when it passed over the village in the dark. A shot blessed by the Earth itself."

King Berik II rested on the carved throne, his chin upon his fist. He gazed out over the assembled lords with an unfocused stare, despite the rare gravity of the situation. "Then I shall name her Tilli Dragonslayer. Let all men know her deeds."

Weldrin paused long enough to allow the applause to die down. The flush of color on the huntress' face made Darve reappraise what he had at first thought a rather plain girl. *If she were in the right dress instead of those leathers…and those golden curls done up by a good maidservant…*

The general cleared his throat before continuing. "Many of our forces did not do so well. We lost near seven hundred soldiers." A soft gasp rustled through the crowd. "However, reports from Stone Town are that civilian casualties remained light. Quick reaction to the warning bells *and* Earth's blessings be praised."

"That is not the case, however, in Wood Town!" Tribune Adaron Shipborne swept from the far corner to the front of the assembly, his white robe of office rippling. "Thousands are believed dead – thousands more homeless and injured. Some of the fires still burn!"

Another noble stepped forward. Darve sniffed in derision at Lord Rockcastle. *His family is old and rich, but he is a fool.*

"Tell me then, Tribune," Rockcastle said, his hands tucked in his belt, "where are these ruffians of Wood Town to go? Are we to take them into our own homes?" He looked about at his peers as if it were an absurd suggestion.

"That would be a good start, Lord Rockcastle." The Tribune's sharp blue eyes fixed him. "Your considerable mansions would house a great many."

"Yes, but it would take a decade to get the stench out." Rockcastle laughed, slapping his thighs.

A large percentage of the nobles chuckled as well. Others stared at Rockcastle, their expressions incensed. Darve counted himself among the latter. The Tribune looked ready to explode.

"Your disrespect for the people of this nation is disgusting, My Lord." The Tribune's lips curled into a sneer of derision for the noble. He pointed toward the exit of the hall. "They still die out there while you joke at their expense. Likely the only stench you could smell in Wood Town today is burning timber and flesh."

Rockcastle stepped back, his fist raised as if to strike the Tribune.

"Enough!" Berik waved a languid hand in the air. The young king still maintained his disinterested gaze.

Apparently, the shouting bothers his ruminations. He inherited too early. It was a bad omen for any prince, when King Karedon died in that rockslide.

Tribune Adaron dropped the suppressed rage from his features and focused on his monarch. "I do have a far more constructive solution, Your Majesty. Perhaps we could open the Magnum Room along the eastern face. It has more than enough space to temporarily shelter thousands, along with easy access to emergency food stores." Adaron raised his hand toward the mountain piled on top of them. "They would also be in a place of safety, should the enemy return."

Scattered applause erupted from some of the dwarven nobility. General Weldrin also clapped his thick hands. Darve knew that Weldrin had joined the army from the dock fronts of Wood Town. His own heart stirred, and Darve slapped his hands together too.

"Fairly suggested, Tribune Adaron." The king yawned. "I tire of these reports. We must see to action." Berik cast his eyes over the crowd. "Refugees shall be allowed within the Magnum Room. Your office, dear Tribune, shall pay for their needs in care and blankets. I will grant them food from my private store. I am a king with a heart for his people."

Berik rose and turned to the general. "See that there are sufficient troops to ensure security. I don't want a riot breaking out where I plan on holding this year's Midwinter Ball." The king stretched and looked over his shoulder at the throne. "Damned thing is even harder than it looks."

An aghast murmur rippled through the crowd. The king seemed not to notice. However, Darve lifted an eyebrow when he caught the hint of a smile crossing the lips both the king and Adaron.

Am I the only one who saw? Darve cast his gaze about the room. He bowed with the rest of the crowd when the king strode to the edge of the throne's platform. *If stories be true, then 'twas Berik who found Adaron near the docks of Wood Town as children. Berik was a daring child who often snuck out of his father's palace. But current gossip says that the twain have fallen out since Berik took the throne. Perhaps the gossip is not so true.*

"Maester Northtower." The king stepped down from his dais. "Would you join me on my ride to the palace? I wish to thank you personally for your family's vigilance. If only all of our defenses had been so prepared."

Another murmur passed the nobles, curdling Darve's stomach. *Few have ever been invited to ride with the king in his private lift!*

Darve bowed, his nose nearly touching the rough stone floor. "I am honored beyond words, Majesty." He straightened and lifted one hand. "Let me also add that House Northtower will donate ten thousand gold marks to the Tribune, so that we might aid his cause for the people."

Adaron bowed to Darve, his sandy beard tucked behind one forearm.

"Well and good, lords." The king gestured toward the rear of the hall. "I believe we have a lift to catch. Maester, if you would come?"

"Of course, Your Majesty." Darve trotted to join the king as he marched to the edge of the cavern. A gold inlaid brass carriage awaited there, suspended on long iron chains that disappeared far above. A guard swung the intricate mesh door open, and the king stepped through, motioning for Darve to follow.

He climbed on board. When the soldier moved to join them, Berik held up his hand. "Follow with the others. I wish to speak with Maester Northtower alone."

Shock crossed the guard's face. "Your Majesty..." he stammered, "...I am to stay at your side."

Berik frowned. "The shaft is sealed in solid rock from here until it arrives at the palace. I should be safe from attack."

The guard's bright eyes searched Darve, a skeptical wrinkle forming on his brow. "But..."

With an insulted huff the king placed his fists on his hips. "Maester Northtower is a hero of my kingdom. I will have no such attitude from a soldier on my guard. His family has stood with the dwarves of the Rock for a millennium. Even if they were not first born among us, generations of Northtowers have been since." The king slammed the door of the carriage. "Report to garrison duty. Some time in the forest will remind you how good palace service is."

The crestfallen guard ducked his head. "Yes, Your Majesty. Forgive my improper and impertinent words." He turned to Darve. "And please forgive my reticence as well, Maester Northtower. I did not mean to impugn you personally."

Darve shook his head. "I do not take offense, soldier. You only wish to protect your king." He nodded toward the pedestrian exit. "Seek out the Northtower garrison. Tell Master Sergeant Marrax Redarm that I sent you."

The soldier saluted and bowed his head. "Thank you, Maester."

Smooth and graceful, the carriage lifted into the colossal openness of the cavern. The chains did not jingle or jerk hauling their burden upward. Darve pulled in deep breaths seeing the gypsum ceiling rush out of the darkness.

That hole is way too small for this carriage! He could not help clamping his eyes shut when the rock engulfed them. A moment later, he opened his lids to see a smiling king, his face lit only by the twin oil lamps built into the brass construction.

"The first time rattles everyone." Berik's eyes reflected the lamplight and his kind smile. "I wanted an excuse for privacy." The king pursed his lips. "As your family cannot seek the throne, I fear you are one of the few in my court I can trust."

He cleared his throat. The smile shifted from uncertainty, back to kindness. "I have a mission for you that might well save our people from destruction far greater than that wrought upon us last eve." The king's eyes sharpened. The vapid child sitting on the throne disappeared. Instead, a ruler had taken that child's place in the confident stare. "You must go to the humans of Gannon and inform them of this attack. You have some of our most extensive connections with the nobility of their kingdom. Your trade deals have made many of them almost as rich as they have made us."

Darve swallowed. The passing stone discomfited him, but his senses had begun to adjust. "I thank you for the compliment, Majesty."

King Berik smiled again. Darve weakly returned the expression, his stomach still doing short flips.

"You earned it, Northtower, in more ways than one." The king stepped closer to Darve, lowering his tone. "You must warn the humans to look to the north. Too long have we ignored the orcs and the dark powers they are capable of stirring. I have many plans for our people, Maester Northtower – plans I think you might approve of – but chaos in the Northlands can only hinder our success."

Darve bowed his head. "I will carry your message to the humans at once, Your Majesty. I have extensive relations within Gavanor. I will go to Duke Aginor first."

The king raised a finger. "I also want you to take someone with you. Someone I believe fate has blessed. This Tilli Dragonslayer, the girl from Bearburough." Berik shook his head. "A shot in the dark that slew a big one…"

Darve ducked his head. "Of course, Your Majesty. If she can slay a dragon, she can join my travelling party any day." He wobbled when the pressure in the shaft adjusted. A duct, built into the wall to allow fresh air to enter, passed with dizzying speed.

"We are half way up the mountain now." Berik gazed upward at the taut chains still disappearing into darkness. "After you have spoken with Duke Aginor, I want you to travel on to visit the 'Old King' in his capital at Daynon." Berik chuckled. The idea of an old king being less than a century in age amused Darve as well. "Arathan is the military power in this part of Tarmor. Only Gannon has the strength to stand against an enemy that can gather a flight of dragons."

"Do you think the humans have the mettle?" Darve cocked a dubious eyebrow. "I know the men of Gannon as well as any dwarf, I suppose. They are fair traders. And they have a stout heart in battle, I'll grant." He shook his head. "But humans have a hard time standing up until they have no other choice. By then, it is often too late."

Berik sighed, and his smile slipped. "We shall see, I suppose. Perhaps there are a few among them with the courage to do what needs to be done."

CHAPTER 9

"Placed with the Grace of the Balance in the year 96 A.R. by the Royal Hand of Prince Gelron, Grandson of the Navigator."
— *Cornerstone carving, Citadel of Gavanor*

The pepper is right, but something is missing…

Tallen stopped stirring and reached into the bag he had brought with him from the Gryphon. Tucked in the back, behind a wooden saltcellar, hid a pouch of thyme. He crushed a sprig of the dried herb into the stewpot, and its fragrant bouquet wafted out when it hit the steaming soup. The spoon glistened as he mixed it in, careful to watch that the campfire did not get too hot.

The big sergeant sniffed the air. "Damn, I'm gonna like travelling with a good innkeeper. I'm also glad I found those turtles today." The wolfhound sat immediately beside him, a strand of drool running from the corner of his mouth.

Tallen took a sip from the spoon and looked up. "You certainly appear to have the lead in our little competition now, Sergeant Hall. I think this might just beat the doe Corporal Magrudy shot two days ago."

Magrudy huffed from where he sat on a large root. "Only because you're here to cook it. That doe was succulent. Turtle takes a very fine hand to even make it edible."

Tallen tilted his head, thinking of the way the fresh venison had melted on his tongue. "You have a point there. It was delicious."

"I believe Boris and I are the final judges." Magus Joslyn Britt folded his arms across his barrel chest. "Whoever hunts down the best animal for Tallen to cook on the road to Gavanor stays with the officers at Lilly's Pad in Bridgedale – that *was* the proposed wager."

Settling himself near the fire, Boris lifted one of his black eyebrows. "A fair prize in any contest."

Tallen avoided direct stares from the Bluecloak officers. *He hasn't watched me like the Magus, but I still see his gaze from time to time. At least the soldiers adopted me as a little brother – once I told them about Jaerd.*

"It's ready." He scooped out generous portions of the turtle stew to each soldier, saving the choice bits of meat from the back of the shell and upper leg to give to the judges. Brawny cocked his head and stared at Tallen with huge, brown eyes, until he scooped out an extra bowl for the hound. Boris tore into the stew with a piece of day old bread purchased in one of the small towns along the River Road. Magus Britt took more time with his dinner, sampling first the soup alone, then a spoonful with meat. Even his stony face softened with delight, if only for a split second. Then he was all Battlemage again.

"Delicious," Boris proclaimed, wiping the bowl clean and popping the bread into his mouth. "Winner."

"I have not made my decision yet," Magus Britt mumbled around another bite.

"He's right though." Corporal Magrudy had nearly finished with his bowl. "It is better than the venison."

The mage nodded in grudging agreement. Brawny scoured his wooden dish with a fat tongue.

Sergeant Hall drained his bowl as if it were a teacup. He motioned for Tallen to refill it. "I knew we would make a hell of a team, lad." The corners of the man's eyes crinkled when he laughed. "You'll stay with us at the Pad too, if I have to pay for it from my own purse."

The man's huge hand smacked Tallen on the shoulder. The pat did not send him reeling as expected. It only rattled his jaw. *If the calluses on those hands came from that battle-axe, he has seen a lot of action.*

"His captain will pay the tab." Boris waved his bowl for more. "Only he must cook for us every night in camp until we get there."

Tallen's face sank, and the Bluecloaks guffawed with laughter.

Snorting around a stifled chuckle Boris held up his hand. "Fear not, lad. The inns get much closer together east of Gavanor."

Setting an empty bowl aside, Magus Britt rose to his feet. "Come on Tallen," he said with a huff of breath. "Time for you to meditate with me."

Tallen stood up, leaving his unemptied bowl upon the ground. The soldiers swarmed toward it, scrapping at what remained within the pot. Hiding his smile, Tallen followed the Battlemage off to the edge of the firelight where the camp met prairie grass.

"I've not done much teaching." Magus Britt laid his dog's head staff to one side. "However I was taught once myself. I still remember some of those days." The two of them sat down facing each other with legs folded. Magus Britt spread his red-trimmed cloak neatly underneath him. "Draw in deep breaths. Breathing is a key part of this exercise."

Tallen closed his eyes and concentrated on inhaling and exhaling, deep and steady.

"In through the nose," the mage droned, "out through the mouth." Tallen heard the mage's breath in time with his. "Do you see the colors again?"

"Yes. They flutter about in my mind, circling each other."

"How many colors do you see?"

Tallen heard an odd, tentative tone in the mage's question. "Several. Blue and red, definitely. Yellow and green too, I think." He paused, finding concentration difficult. He stiffened his resolve and focused his mind. "It is all overshadowed by a...a dusky grayish light." Tallen frowned behind his closed eyes. "It makes them hard to distinguish."

The Battlemage remained silent while Tallen centered his thoughts. He focused on those colors, their lights dancing in his head. They became almost physical, as if he could touch them. His senses reached.

"Not yet!" the mage snapped. "You must first learn control. You may well have access to all four elemental Aspects, although I have never heard of such a thing in modern times. Open your eyes."

Tallen obeyed and saw that Magus Britt stood over him. He hopped to his feet.

"You should not reach for the Aspects, not until I have taught you more." The mage's voice held more than a hint of warning. "Your strength may be very great, Tallen. I cannot tell for certain. Varana may be the only one who can. She is the only wizard I know of who has access to all the elemental Aspects of magic." His brow knitted further. "However, she is no Dreamer. I only know of one still alive, and he is not likely to be anywhere close to the Isle of Wizards."

The mage's words deepened Tallen's concern. He already felt a great deal of pressure weighing upon him. Jennette's death, his night in jail, and the intensity of their travel, all put a great strain on his emotions. He felt stretched tight, covering a hidden wave of despair that might overwhelm him if he faced it. The promise of direct tutelage under the Elf sorceress of legend did not settle his nerves any further. *The books I've read say that she has helped to shape history since the Cataclysm. Many of the stories do not end well for those who encounter her.*

The mage interrupted his thoughts. "So, ask your one question."

Tallen abandoned the labyrinth his mind wandered and tried to focus. *I have to make my nightly question count.* "Have you ever been to the Dreamrealm yourself?" he blurted without knowing quite why.

The mage snorted. "Once, a long time before you were born. An erstwhile friend led me there. It takes a Dreamer to escort a normal mage into the Dreamrealm."

"Who was your friend?"

"Your question is already asked." Magus Britt turned his head away with fierceness. "You need your rest. We will arrive at Gavanor before noon tomorrow."

Tallen's blankets did not offer him enough comfort that night for sleep.

The land sloped gently downward across a long, open stretch. There the road split into a trident that stabbed toward three gates in the towering western wall of Gavanor. The wall stretched all the way from the Stonebourne Fork to the banks of the Andon, cutting off the triangle of land between the rivers in which the city lay. Tremendous towers sprang up on both rivers' edges, over two miles apart. The wall connected them, and a dozen smaller towers stood guard between the gates.

Tallen stared in awe. *To think Jaerd has served here for ten years!*

Shading the sun with his hand, Tallen cast his eyes beyond the wall. He could not see much of the city, only a few scattered towers and a slight haze of smoke. In the distance, the duke's citadel rose on a pinnacle of rock overlooking the confluence of the two rivers. Tallen had heard stories in the great room of the Gryphon, stories that told of how the violent energies of the Cataclysm cast Malador's Stone out from the Dragonscales when the mountains rose. *I doubt the tales are true, but it does seem odd sticking up from the middle of the prairie.*

Boris leaned forward in the saddle of his black stallion. Tallen had learned the hard way that the beast snapped at any human other than the earl who tried to touch it. "We take the northernmost fork. I told Aginor to watch for our return through the Wolfsgate."

Magus Britt put a heel to his sorrel mare. "Then let's get there. I look forward to the duke's hospitality tonight."

Tallen spurred his old palfrey to follow. His father had purchased the horse just before he died, and Tallen had named him Stew after the animal threw him on his first ride. *Because I threatened to make one of him if he ever did it again. Ever since, he's been a fine horse.* He patted Stew's neck. "Might I have time to look for my brother?"

"Possibly." Magus Britt kept his gaze upon the gate ahead. "We will remain in Gavanor only one night."

Boris frowned at the Battlemage. "We will make time for you to find your brother. How long has it been since you've seen him?"

"Near five years, sir."

The Bluecloak general nodded. "I will see that he is invited to what will almost certainly be a delightful banquet in our honor."

"Now you're talking, Milord," Sergeant Hall added with a pat of his stomach and a spur of his thick-legged horse.

The road became more crowded with more travelers as they neared the Wolfsgate. Hundreds gathered at each entrance. Boris led his squad around the throng. Brawny stayed close to Sergeant Hall's stirrup. Only a few annoyed stares followed the Bluecloaks. Most people nodded with respect. One or two old teamsters saluted.

When they reached the gate, the doors leaning back against the stone were fashioned of iron as thick as Tallen's waist. Artisans had cast each door of the Wolfsgate in half the semblance of a snarling, lupine head. When closed, the complete face stared out at any approaching enemy with baleful eyes.

"They don't even shut them at night any more," Corporal Magrudy whispered to Tallen, who stared open-mouthed, "so continuous is the traffic."

Earl Boris trotted his stallion over to meet the young lieutenant in emerald green questioning the entrants. "I need to see your captain. My men and I are here on urgent kingdom business."

The lieutenant studied the stars on Boris' collar before snapping a sharp salute. "If you will wait but a moment, my lord General." He tapped a corporal. "Get the captain, on the double!"

The man dashed off. Only a few seconds passed before he returned with another green-cloaked man, this one wearing two silver stars. Tallen stared at him for only a moment, before he leaped from Stew's back.

"Jaerd! It's you!" He ran forward and embraced the man.

"By the Waters…Tallen?" An astonished look blanketed the soldier's face, as he tried to salute through his brother's hug. "What are you doing with…with a Bluecloak elite team?" Jaerd returned the hug with melting reticence. "By the Waters. It *is* you."

Boris spoke before Tallen could answer his brother. "He travels with us because we required it. Anything further should not be discussed here."

Tallen could not read his brother's face, save for the shock. The expression lingered only a moment, and he stood before Tallen with the expressionless mask of an officer of Gavanor. He snapped another, tighter salute to Boris. "Yes, Milord. Allow me to fetch a horse, and I will escort the lot of you directly to the citadel."

The group followed Jaerd under the shadow of the gates. It took time for Tallen's eyesight to adjust to the darkness, but he could not hide the smile on his face at greeting his brother. A cool breeze chilled him within the shade under the wall. They passed beneath dozens of murder holes carved into the archway over his head. Tallen sensed the age and weight of the stone. Though he wanted to inspect every passing feature, the presence of his brother distracted much of his attention. A thousand questions bubbled up in his mind. *Boris' business is serious, much more serious than just retrieving me. Jaerd and I will have time to talk later.*

Tallen blinked as they emerged from the darkness into the city. It spread out before him, covering the spearhead of land between the rivers and behind the wall. Hundreds of thousands had to live in that twisted warren of streets, houses, and shops. Gavanor was a city to remind him just how small a town he had come from. He snapped his jaw shut, but could not pull his eyes from the sight.

Jaerd waved at the throng directly in front of them. "This, of course, is Gatesmarket."

Tallen had smelled it before they rode out into the light, hundreds upon hundreds of booths scattered in a winding maze. Some were spacious enough to sell horses, even camels, while others stood no wider than the man who hawked his goods. One section sported a variety of produce, some of which Tallen could not even recognize. The scents from the spice merchant stalls tickled Tallen's nose with pungent and enticing sensations. Farther along, he saw stands run by dwarves, mostly for metal goods and stoneware. A fair-haired elf in a stand with thick curtains sold books. Near the center gate of the western wall, a street of weapon vendors hustled their wares.

"Which gate is that?"

"Lionsgate," Jaerd answered to Tallen's query. "And Bearsgate is on to the south."

With a nod of reply, Tallen returned to studying the myriad goods available in the Gatesmarket. A vendor rushed out into the street, aiming directly for him. He carried a tray of steaming pies for a copper penny. Tallen handed the man a coin, before taking the pie and biting into it. It burst with chicken, leeks, and cheese. In his rush to taste it, he scalded the top of his mouth, leaving a painful strand of burned flesh to hang from his palate.

Magus Britt waved his hand. "Come on, Tallen. We cannot dawdle."

Tallen urged Stew after the others. Eventually the party waded its way through the swarm of people and their goods, emerging from the bustle of Gatesmarket into a sudden silence. Beyond a triple hedge of tall poplar trees spread an open meadow, with dozens of tended gardens, large statues, and sparkling fountains. Wide oaks and elms stood scattered about with groves of pine and spruce between.

Tallen's eyes spread wide with wonder. "What is this place?"

"Statuary Park," Jaerd replied with obvious pride. "The duke's family put aside this area many years ago for the use of all the people of Gavanor. House Varlan pays to maintain it still."

The ride through the park calmed Tallen's spirit. The bucolic landscape brought peaceful thoughts to mind. Couples and families wandered the gravel pathways. Ducks glided on a small pond where a boy skipped stones.

They left the peace of the tended meadow and entered an area of tall townhouses, gated mansions, and upscale mercantile. Tallen noticed the signs of jewelers, counting houses, importers, and premium grocers. Trees lined some of the streets, and well-tended cobblestones lined them all.

"This is Bailey Square." Jaerd waved his hand in an encompassing gesture. "The nice part of town." His voice carried a hint of sarcasm. "Most nobles have town homes here, as do the richest merchants."

Tallen's sharp eyes caught the mansion guards glaring at Boris' Bluecloaks as they rode past. A few of the compounds resembled small fortresses patrolled with many men.

Soon the road sloped up toward the outer wall of the citadel. On Tallen's left, the Western Priory of the Temple of Balance climbed into the sky. The dual steeples curved toward one another, one of white marble, the other of black basalt. The imposing structure loomed above them, brooding over the brighter homes of the well-to-do Gavanorans.

"The prior is a foul man," Jaerd whispered to Tallen from behind his leather gauntlet. "And he allows only one Water temple in this whole city."

Tallen cocked a single eyebrow. "Why does the duke allow the Temple of Balance to set a limit on other temples?"

Jaerd moved to reply but stopped with a frowning glance at the others. He gave Tallen a significant expression.

I definitely remember that look. He might tell me more in private.

They climbed the lower slopes of Malador's Stone, the paved road continuing right up to the outer gate. There, Jaerd acknowledged the officer on duty.

"Wolfsgate Captain" The lieutenant saluted. "Please escort your party through."

Within, a wide plaza of cobblestone spread out. Tallen caught glimpse of armories, stables, and other buildings lining the walls. Jaerd led Tallen and the others up a flagged road that climbed the last shoulder of Malador's Stone. A far more ornate gate towered overhead, with silver tipped cornices on several of the battlements. Above it, the emerald green banner of the duke with its gray stone wall snapped in the breeze. Adjacent fluttered the rampant silver dragon on blue of Gannon.

Another officer with two stars greeted Jaerd and immediately waved them inward. The captain saluted Boris when he passed. He gave Tallen only an inquisitive stare.

The citadel of Gavanor swept into the sky with grace. Built of grey granite and white marble, its central tower climbed upward over a hundred yards, while the attached spire rose another fifty. Tallen swayed in the saddle, staring at the pinnacle, its height spinning his perception.

A dozen men strode from the silver bound oak doors and trotted down the wide steps. The majority wore green cloaks like Jaerd's, while a few others wore midnight blue or maroon. A sour faced man wore a black and scarlet check pattern. The noble in front of them held an air of command. Even though the dark gray hair on his scalp thinned, a great deal of life still danced in his eyes.

"Earl Boris." The man turned to the Battlemage. "And Magus Britt. I am overjoyed to see you returned from your mission. We must speak in my private chambers immediately. My sons and liegemen will join us."

Boris nodded to the others huddled behind the duke. Most of the men returned the earl's gesture. "Thank you for greeting us, Duke Aginor. Our road has been a long one." He gave a small nod toward Tallen. "And certain surprises delayed us."

Tallen hung his head and dismounted without a sound. He held his horse's reins until a groomsman from the duke's stables took them with a bow. Tallen cringed without Stew to hide behind.

Jaerd waited back while the others entered the citadel. "Tallen, go with this gentleman." He pointed to a servant wearing a green tabard embroidered with a gray wall. "He will take you to a room where you can clean up and wait for us." Jaerd pointed at the man. "My brother will be staying with the Earl, so find him someplace nice."

The servant nodded and gestured toward a side entry. "Right this way, sir."

After passing through the edge of the main hall and up the spiral stairwell within the central tower, the servant opened a door carved with wheat sheaves. Tallen stepped inside to see an outer salon with four doors, painted in a deep forest green. Lavish divans and a table and chairs rested in comfortable positions. A wide window looked out onto the Stonebourne Fork and the River Road where it continued eastward on the far side of the water.

The servant waved his hand toward the nearest door. "You may use this bedchamber." He pointed to another. "The bath is through there. Hot water is on its way. Towels are in your bedchamber." The man bowed a final time and exited.

By the time Tallen entered the blue and white tiled bathroom wearing only a towel, steam rose from one of three large copper tubs. He unwound the towel, placing it and another folded one on a small table.

He cursed at the heat, first slipping one foot and then the other into the water. He dropped down to his neck with a yelp before the water sloshed over the sides. The soothing heat sank into his bones. Tallen held his head underwater for a moment, enjoying the womb-like embrace. He raised it when his lungs threatened to burst, and rested against a folded washcloth. His eyes closed.

The familiar darkness swirled about him. It coalesced into the galaxy of the Dreamrealm. He oriented himself with ease, but his heart beat in apprehension that the silvery spirit might return. Tallen found no other presence. *But I cannot be certain of anything here.*

The starpoints glittered around him, dancing sparkles in the night. One drew his spirit, the one he noticed before. It flickered a dusky white. Tallen reached out and touched it.

A ghostly city spread around him, filled with empty streets. A large temple with fiery sconces loomed, and a townhouse sprang up before of him. A girl with dark hair and an obscured face slipped into the building through the roof. Tallen followed.

Shadowy shapes moved about. The moon cast an eerie glow through high windows. The girl entered a room with a single desk and crawled beneath it. A huge lock closed a door in the floor. The girl struggled to open it. Tallen stretched to help her…

Awareness splashed into Tallen's face with a dose of frigidity. He spluttered awake, snorting water from his sinus – his bath now lukewarm. Magus Britt held an empty cup and wore a smile.

"Sorry for the rude awakening, lad, but you aren't allowed to Dream until we reach the Isle. I can barely sense the Psoul Aspect myself, yet I could tell you were there." The mage waved his hands over Tallen's face. A weird numbness sank into his brain. "That will keep you inside your own head. You will be able to perceive your power and tap into it; however, you will not be able to enter the Dreamrealm."

Boris stepped up behind the mage, a towel wrapped around his waist. Tallen barely noticed the muscles ripple under his black hair. Long scars scattered about the earl's torso drew his eyes instead. "Looks like the boy's water has gone cold. Show him how Joz."

Magus Britt waved his hand. "I am tired. I'd rather just do it the old fashioned way."

Tallen lifted a pruned hand. "Please. I really wouldn't want to put the magus out if he can't—" Warmth sank into him again when

Magus Britt lifted his hand. Tallen could almost see the trickle of Fire heating his bath. He nodded when the power stopped, just before it became uncomfortable. "Thank you, Magus."

Magus Britt waved him off, but Boris winked. The earl and the mage then took to their own steaming tubs. This time, however, Tallen picked up the fresh razor laid out.

"Don't dull that thing on your peach fuzz." Boris laughed. "We both have to use it too."

Most of the road at last washed away, Tallen wrapped himself in the soft towel. Boris worked the razor, and Magus Britt rested with a washcloth over his eyes

"The banquet begins at sunset." Boris spoke in a pinched voice, holding in his lower lip for the blade. "Main hall. You'll be at the head table with us…and your brother."

Tallen's heart leaped.

"I took the liberty of finding something for you wear," Magus Britt mumbled, eyes still covered. "Something befitting an apprentice wizard."

When Tallen entered the chamber, his good mood sank a fraction. A plain robe of rough woven cotton lay on the bed next to trousers and tunic of the same material. A wide leather belt lay next to it. *It's rather plain. At least everyone will know what it means.*

The apprentice garb reassured him as he pulled it on – the cut felt right on his shoulders. Freshly polished boots stood by the door. *Servants must do everything for these people! It's like living in a fine inn all the time!* He laid upon the satin-covered bed and spread his arms wide, the smile on his face stretching to match.

Some minutes later, he woke with a startled snort. The sky had darkened to deep blue outside his window. After leaping into his boots, he trotted down the spiral stairwell of the citadel's main tower. Tallen felt as new as his clothes. He beamed when he heard music drifting up from the party below.

The great hall of the citadel stretched out before him, its arched roof spreading overhead. He entered through the side door from the tower. Many people had gathered in the wide hall, milling about between the tables, while others perched on seats. Dozens of colors splashed across their finery. Tallen recognized many of the house markings – the maroon and cougars of Whitehall and the midnight blue with crescent and stars of House Magdon, each with matching jewelry. The Darilla family, attired in red and black, huddled in a far corner wearing chains with onyx and ruby pendants. Tallen also saw a few scattered nobles in black and gold, the colors of House Farseer, a small family whose holdings bordered the Iron Hills and Dwarf territory.

Most of the emerald green cloaks gathered around Duke Aginor at the front table on a small dais. A silver tower set with sparkling emeralds hung on a thick chain about the duke's neck. Tallen spied Jaerd among the royal blue cloaks of Boris, Magus Britt, and Sergeant Hall, who must have taken far shorter baths than he. Straightening his new robe, Tallen hurried to join them.

"Brother!" Jaerd nodded in approval when he approached. "The look suits you. We will be seated here at the end." He leaned in closer when Tallen stepped up onto the dais. "A piece of advice – stay as far away from nobles as you can, *when* you can, especially at dinner."

With his stomach grumbling, Tallen caught scent of the fresh baked bread. Slathering it in fresh butter, he and Jaerd devoured the first loaf set before them. From there, the meal sped by, timed to the musicians' rhythm. The brothers caught up on recent events, both with the family and in the town of Dadric.

When the tale caught up to Jennette's death, Tallen told it in as few words as possible. "It was awful, Jaerd. She was…mutilated." He fought tears as he looked into his brother's eyes. Jaerd stared back with sympathy. "I don't really want to talk about it."

"I understand," Jaerd whispered with a simple pat on Tallen's shoulder.

The rack of lamb arriving at their table, served with potatoes, onions, and herbs, livened their mood. Tallen even laughed when he and Jaerd almost came to blows over the last rib.

Jaerd won and took a huge bite, but gave the bone to Tallen to gnaw on, which he did with abandon. The fresh berries and cream showed up last, and his stomach, thought to be full, found spare room. More wine followed and soon the brothers sat satiated enough to talk again.

Jaerd patted his stomach. "Would you be able to see part of the town with me tonight? My lieutenant has the night watch. There are several places where we could find some trouble – er, I mean fun." He winked.

Tallen laughed. "I remember waking up to Dad yelling at you for your 'fun'. That was a long time ago." He raised his wine cup. "To Dad."

"To Dad." Jaerd spilled a little wine from his cup when he clacked it against Tallen's. The brothers drained their drinks. "What do you think he would say about you becoming a wizard?"

Tallen shrugged. "He would have told me he expected as much. He always thought each of us had more potential than we imagined."

A commotion began at the back of the hall, near the main entrance. Soldiers made a path through the crowd. Someone followed who Tallen could not see over the soldiers' heads. Seated at the middle of the table, Duke Aginor and Earl Boris rose to their feet.

The soldiers in green parted, and Tallen realized why he could not tell whom they escorted. A party of dwarves, still dusty from the road, pooled in front of the duke's dais.

"Your Grace, Duke Aginor of House Varlan." The lead dwarf bowed so deep his gray and black beard brushed the stone flags. "You may remember that I am Darve Northtower, emissary and trade negotiator for his Majesty Berik II, King of the Rock and the Iron Hills."

"Of course, Maester Northtower." Aginor dipped his chin with respect. "We have received you many times as our friend. What brings you to Gavanor in such obvious haste?"

Gravity hung about the dwarf's tone and visage. "Dragons, my lord."

A hush covered the crowd. Only nervous, scattered laughs broke the sudden silence.

"Dragons?" Duke Aginor's brow knitted itself together into a frown. Tallen saw Boris and Magus Britt both leaning forward, intense looks plastered on their faces.

Maester Northtower reached under his travelling cloak and pulled out a long object on a leather thong around his neck. At first, Tallen believed it a deer's antler, almost as long as the dwarf's arm and curved to a deadly point. His heart skipped a beat when he realized it could only be a tooth. A murmur rippled the crowd and covered his intake of breath. Two women near the front fainted into startled arms.

"This is the tooth of one brought down by my men and I." Darve waved at his companions. He pointed at a dwarf girl with blond hair hiding near the rear of the group. "Tilli Broadoak, now known among our people as Dragonslayer, brought another down when it passed over her forest home. Tilli, please."

The girl held up another tooth, nearly as long as the first. She had attached a handle to it, creating a rather vicious looking dagger.

The crowd grumbled.

Aginor's voice contained a nervous undertone. "Maester Northtower, how many dragons assaulted your people?"

"Dragons are extinct!" shouted a voice from the red and black corner.

"Silence!" The duke held up an annoyed hand. "Have respect for our visitors." He turned back to the dwarf. "How many?"

"Perhaps a hundred – dozens the size of this one." Darve lifted the tooth again. "Many of our people have died. Parts of Wood Town and the forest still burned when we left our city." The dwarf let the tooth fall against his chest. It hung down to his groin. "Please, Duke Aginor, send healers and grain to help our people. Since Aravath set foot upon these shores five centuries ago, our peoples have been fast allies. Now are the times that test those friendships."

Duke Aginor nodded, his arms folded in thought. "I will send a battalion with healers and engineers at once. And forty wagons of grain. More once we can gather it."

"Thank you, My Lord Duke," the dwarf intoned, bowing again. "Your generosity and the compassion of your people..." He waved toward the crowd. "...shall be carved into the throne of the dwarven kings, as a part of the panel commissioned to remember this attack. It shall forever become part of our recorded history."

"Please," Duke Aginor said with a gracious voice and a gesture toward the table. "Take part in our banquet, if you wish. Or rooms may be provided if you prefer rest. We will talk further once you have taken repast."

Darve looked about with a smile. "We would be honored to take place in this wonderful feast." At his signal, the other dwarves joined a table not far from Tallen and Jaerd. They dug in to the food served once they sat. Even the young woman ate heartily.

Jaerd whispered into Tallen's ear. "You're full, right?"

Tallen belched in reply.

"Then let's get out of here." Jaerd nudged him with an elbow. "I have already asked your Magus' permission. We have only a few hours, and I have many places to take you."

Tallen left his seat with reluctance. "But Jaerd...dragons." He pointed at the leader of the dwarves whose leaned close in conversation with Earl Boris and the duke. Magus Britt hung beside them, a black look on his face. Tallen paused. "Perhaps I can find out later. Let's go."

CHAPTER 10

Upon a third conviction, a thief shall be hanged by the neck until they are dead. Their bodies shall be fed to swine.
— Gannonite legal code

Sipping wine as sour as her mood, Maddi tried to shake the eerie chill left by the dream. She had been back in Dern, climbing through the empty townhouse again. This time, however, someone else had been there. She could not describe the person, nor could she be certain it even was a person. Upon awakening, the dream weighed upon her mind. It followed her to the Spendthrift Sailor, a quiet inn along the edge of the Gavanor docks, often frequented by middle class merchants and artisans. Few of the patrons carried many more years than she did.

I would bet that most of them inherited that gold they throw around. She snorted in disgust. *Any one of them would make an easy mark. I just don't know that I feel it tonight, or at all any more. Memories of that last job in Dern still haunt my dreams.*

She thumbed the tiny golden chalice she kept in her pocket for luck. Rubbing the likeness of the Fifth Talisman offered her strength and calmed her roiling emotions. She hoped it might drive way the ghosts of her dream.

The barmaid wandered by the corner table from which Maddi watched the sparse crowd. "You want another cup, miss? Or something to fill your pipe?"

Shaking her head, Maddi downed the last of her wine as two men walked into the inn. One wore the gray embroidered green tunic of a Gavanoran officer, pressed as if he had just come from parade – the younger one attired in a simple robe and tunic of cotton. Their stride and smiles were so similar, Maddi guessed the two for brothers. The younger had more hazel than gray in his green eyes, and he stood a little bit taller, but otherwise they looked much the same.

What is it about him? Why does he draw my attention so? He is far younger than the men I usually find interesting.

Maddi stopped the barmaid before she left the table. "On second thought, I'll have another spot of the Avarosan red." She held up her cup for the refill, but her gaze never left the two men. Shifting so she might better hear the two, she sipped at her wine and listened.

"Hoy, fellows," the elder greeted, "this is my brother Tallen, the finest chef in all the Western Realm."

"Jaerd, old boy, grand to see you." One of the young men that had flashed the most coin sauntered over to the officer. "Or should I call you Captain now, since you wore your Temple Day best."

"Jaerd is just fine Nikko," the soldier replied, raising two fingers to the barkeep. "I *am* off duty. My brother and I were so busy with the banquet in the citadel that I had no time to change out of my uniform." He smiled at Nikko. "It was in his honor. He is on his way to the Isle so that he might be trained to become a powerful wizard."

Maddi noticed the robed brother's cheeks redden. *A wizard? Looks a little fresh to be a wizard. I imagine the other will claim to be a paladin next.*

The brothers joined Nikko's table once they had their drinks. Soon, good-natured ribbing and general boasting rang throughout the inn. The brothers drank their wine and slapped one another on the back. Maddi heard them laugh at comments that made no sense. *Must be inside jokes. They sound like they had a few before showing up here.*

She sipped at her second cup of wine, watching the two men over its rim. After a few more rounds, the green-clad brother rose.

"Come on, Tallen." His voice slurred a tad. "I have another couple of places I want to show you."

"I assume you'll be ending the night at Madame Gename's," Nikko suggested, raising his mug in farewell. "Make sure he gets a taste of the special there."

The older brother laughed. The other smiled a sheepish grin. "Maybe. I'm not sure he would survive the special. Ginny might kill the lad."

With another round of farewells, the two headed for the door.

Uncertain exactly why, Maddi followed, leaving a silver coin worth far more than her wine lying on the table. She slipped outside, lifting her hood and wrapping a dark cloak about her body.

She took a deep breath of the fresh night air. The wind blew from the north, carrying the smells of Gavanor and its rougher sections southward over the river. She watched the brothers saunter down the cobblestones, not far ahead. Both carried a flagon from the Spendthrift Sailor. They took long pulls from them while they wandered through the narrow, unlit streets.

Why am I out here? These two don't have any real coin. Nor are they likely to lead me to any. And why does the one draw me so? She shook off the uncomfortable feeling that she did not remain in control of herself, yet she continued to follow. The men stumbled some and shared a great deal of laughter. At one point, the older brother stepped to the side of the street. Maddi feared she had been made, and ducked farther into the shadows, but the man simply struck a dwarven match to light his pipe and continued onward with a slap to his brother's back.

"Why am I stalking these men?" she whispered to herself resuming her hunt.

They passed through a small plaza. She hugged the shadows while her quarry marched across its center.

Something is not right. It's too quiet here. Her ears perked up. A sound drifted from the recesses of a narrow alley connected to the plaza. She leaned in against a building. The noise crept out of the next alley over, a muffled scrape of leather on leather – the shuffling of feet not as silent as they wished to be. She heard a grunt.

Pulling her dirk from where it hung at the back of her belt, Maddi took a deep, steadying breath. Another throwing knife jumped to her left hand from a sleeve.

I refuse to take chances since Dern. She held her position deep in the shadows of a closed cooper's shop, while the brothers wandered across the middle of the plaza. From their rambling stance, they appeared oblivious to the hidden rustle.

Half a dozen cloaked shapes darted from the alley Maddi watched. They had the men surrounded before the brothers became aware.

A rough voice snarled from a shadowed hood. "You two are coming with us."

"Hold there, now." The older brother flipped the flagon over in his hand to make a serviceable weapon. He took the stance of a seasoned fighter. The younger stood frozen. "We've little coin on us. You are welcome to it. But any thief in this city should know the tunic I wear. Are you certain you want the attention that comes with kidnapping the Wolfsgate Captain of Gavanor?" He backed closer to his brother, who at last shifted into the posture of someone who had been in a brawl or two. He also appeared experienced in using a wine flagon for more than drinking.

The shape nearest the younger man dashed in and swung a club. The robed brother dodged. The sound of his flagon breaking over the attacker's neck echoed across the cobblestones. The figure shook its head but continued on its feet. Two more closed in, while the other three made feints at the elder. A frown of deep concern crossed his face, while the younger brother's eyes widened in fear.

I can't just let them be taken. He's too cute to let some ruffians beat his face in. Maddi charged forward in silence, throwing her smaller dagger hard. It struck one black cloaked figure in the neck, dropping it to the ground. The others looked about, trying to find the source of the sudden attack. She caught one in the face with a second hidden dagger. The hood slipped somewhat as he fell.

"Fiery Hells, you guys are ugly!"

And short. Are they women? Or skinny dwarves? Grunting, Maddi cut back toward the edge of the plaza. Holding her dirk in a defensive stance, she pulled yet a third dagger from her bootleg. The brother in the officer's tunic made his move. He crushed the flagon over one's head and slammed a couple of punches to his face. The soldier shouldered his opponent, taking the smaller figure to the ground. Maddi saw the man's knee go into his attacker's groin before he rolled away toward one of her victims and pulled the throwing dagger from his face. He then rolled back, and planted the knife in the neck of his enemy. Hopping back to his feet with the knife still in his hands, the soldier looked for his next opponent, while his last writhed in agony at his feet.

The other three hooded figures rushed the younger brother, one smacking him over the head with a club. The man dropped to his knees, hands cupping his scalp.

That club is a blackjack, or his brains would be splattered across the street. They want these fellows alive.

One of the attackers grabbed the dazed brother and slapped a hood over his head. The other two rushed the soldier, steel gleaming in the dark as they drew daggers of their own.

"No you don't," Maddi muttered, hurling her last throwing knife. At this distance, it only found a spot in his thigh. A guttural scream of pain followed.

Definitely not women, then. Maddi moved toward one of the

bodies that sheathed her previous daggers. Pulling her weapon from the gore, she kept her eyes on the live targets.

The soldier again took advantage of the distraction. He plunged his knife up under the wounded attacker's chin and ripped it back out. Blood splattered across the plaza, black in the moonlight.

Baring his teeth, the soldier snarled in sudden pain. His last opponent slipped under his guard and planted a knife in his shoulder. He twisted hard, and then returned the favor, his own strike finding the attacker's eye socket. The enemy crumpled to the ground, lifeless.

"Tallen!" Blood darkened the shoulder of the man's tunic. Maddi saw it spreading. He charged the last attacker, the one dragging his brother away.

The figure dropped his victim, who slumped, listless. He drew his knife and faced the wounded soldier. Casting her retrieved dagger, Maddi charged. It glanced off the figure's arm and clattered across the cobblestones.

Maddi slowed, moving with more caution now that she held only her dirk. She noticed the older brother eye her as she closed. His focus returned to the remaining enemy. Maddi noticed the wince of pain when he moved.

"You can live if you put that down," the soldier said with a wave of the borrowed knife. "Your friends can't say that much."

"For Galdreth!" the figure screamed. With a snarl, it charged.

The soldier dodged one wild swing and then another, waiting for advantage. The man moved with fluidity despite his injury. When he found an opening, he thrust clean and quick to the kidney from behind. He stabbed again when the figure went to its knees, this time to the neck. The spurt of blood arced outward.

Maddi spun to search for any other opponents. She only saw a pair of lanterns coming in the hands of the Gavanor watch.

"By the Waters!" The older brother breathed heavily. "It is about time one of you bastards showed up!"

The two men in plain green tunics gawked at the scene their lanterns revealed. They appeared even more startled to see one of their officers.

One blinked at the stars on the older brother's tunic. "Captain?"

Ignoring his wound, the captain pointed to a guardsman. "Gather your entire squad and return here immediately." The guard ran away, the thud of his boots echoing off the cobblestones. The captain turned to the other. "You begin pulling these bodies into a line right here." He faced Maddi. "And you Miss – I don't know how to thank you. We would be dead or worse had you not shown up. If you would remain here for a few minutes…"

Maddi gulped, looking for a way out.

The younger brother moaned as the captain pulled the bag from his head. He knelt down, a concerned furrow in his brow.

"I know some healing," Maddi admitted and squatted beside them. She reached into her bag and pulled out a clean cloth, first making certain the bleeding on the young man's scalp stopped, before taking out another to staunch the captain's wounds. "This will need stitches or Talent." She stuck a second bandage upon his shoulder. "I was walking home for the night and saw them jump you. I don't like an unfair fight."

The captain smiled. "I noticed you following us. I had thought you perchance a thief from the way you used the darkness."

Maddi gave an offended huff. "Your eyes would have been better used on the rest of your surroundings, it seems."

The captain nodded, Maddi catching a hint of color on the tips of his ears in the lamplight. "Fair enough. You are our savior, and here I am with poorly-veiled accusations." He held the bandage on his shoulder while she tied it. "I am Captain Jaerd Westar of the Gavanor guard. And this…" He grunted, helping the other to his feet. "…is my brother Tallen."

The young man's eyes met hers. Even dazed as they were by the blow, they focused on her face with an intelligent gaze. "Thank you, Miss. You saved my life. That bugger had a hold on me, and I was too addled to think straight." He brushed gingerly at his wound. "I don't know what he hit me with, but it knocked me right out."

"It was risky, but I could not let them have you." Maddi pulled him down to get a better look at his head. It did not need a stitch, but he would have a goose egg for a few days. "My name is Maddi. As I told your brother, I do not like an uneven fight."

The guard returned and the last body went onto the pile. Shouts broke the nighttime silence. An entire squad dashed into the plaza. Maddi's heart skipped a beat at the sight of so many green-cloaked soldiers.

"Sir?" The guardsman's voice quivered as he stared at their bodies. "I think there is something wrong with these dead men." The man's voice broke again. "The light, sir – it showed me their faces."

"They are not men, corporal." The captain waved over the

guards who entered the plaza. "And you will keep that to yourself, or I'll have you guarding the latrine outflows."

Maddi gasped when she looked closer at the pile of bodies. The lantern showed their greenish skin. Their heavy jaws hung slack, exposing large, upward-protruding canines. The foreheads sloped more than a human, while the few open eyes gleamed blood red in the light.

"Are those…orcs?" she whispered in shock.

With guards swarming around them, the brothers looked at one another. Several of the soldiers murmured in surprise at the sight of the corpses.

Captain Westar pointed at the senior sergeant. "Take these bodies directly to the citadel. Keep them under guard until I or someone of higher rank comes to inspect them." He pointed his finger at each of the men in turn. "All of you are under strict orders to remain silent as to what you see here."

Maddi took a couple of steps backward, searching for an escape route.

The captain turned to her with a concerned frown. "I'm sorry, miss. But I must insist that you remain with us."

"Am I under arrest?" Maddi glanced around for a way out, but saw none. More guards arrived, setting up a perimeter to ensure the few midnight passersby avoided the scene.

The officer smiled. "Consider yourself a guest, if you prefer. Either way, there are questions that will need answering."

Maddi shifted her feet. *Fighting won't help me now. At least I may have made a friend in high places. This will teach me to follow a man because he is cute!* She sighed in resignation. "Very well, Captain. I will wait here – for now. Since I saved you."

The younger brother, Tallen, smiled at her with the kind of smile that infected others. "Don't worry." His grin widened. "You aren't the first to be taken into custody lately. It's not so bad."

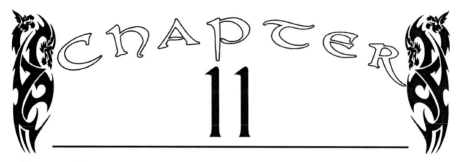

CHAPTER 11

The Orcs have seldom risen in force since the Dragon Wars. The Dragonscales block most of their entry into the southern nations of Tarmor. Highspur plugs the only gap. Those that might miss the patrols of the Unified Guard stationed there must still cross the wastes of lost Lond. Reports claim that Orcs have also been known to sail through the treacherous Dragons' Teeth. This Historian could not confirm these reports.

— Elyn Bravano's "History of Gannon, Appendix D"

Shuddering, Tallen watched the horse-drawn cart stacked with corpses. A tarp had been spread across the wagon trundling away from the scene, concealing every hint of green skin.

The citadel towers loomed over his head, set against the half full moon. Nearly a dozen guards gathered around, each wearing strict determination or masked fear on their faces. They had followed the cart through the streets of Gavanor, keeping any citizens from peeking too closely. Now they appeared to wonder what to do with themselves.

"Hold still." The yellow-fringed Bluecloak took his hands from Jaerd. He turned his pinched face to Tallen and reached for his head. In an instant, he felt a cool tingle where the orc had struck him. He sensed the skin knit itself together. A prickle ran across his scalp, as if his hair grew faster. He had known the touch of a Talented healer only once before. *But then I was just a kid who had fallen out of a tree. This is entirely different.*

From the corner of his eye, Tallen watched his brother bark a command at the sergeant in charge. "Set four men to watch the morgue once the bodies are taken inside." He turned to the others and pointed. "The rest of you are dismissed for the night. Remember your silence."

The men nodded before running off to their duties. The sergeant led his four chosen soldiers to follow the cart carrying the bodies.

Jaerd faced the young woman. "You must come with me for now. The duke will decide whether to trust your silence. I will recommend that he does."

Tallen thought it cute the way her nose crinkled when she scowled at Jaerd.

"It's not right that I become a prisoner for saving your lives." Maddi balled her fists. "Who knows where the two of you might be right now had I not been there?"

Tallen looked at Jaerd. "She's got a point, you know."

"If it were up to me, I would trust her word, but it is not." Jaerd held out his hand toward the door that entered the great hall of the citadel. "Please."

Tallen waited for Maddi to walk before joining in beside her. His nose caught a hint of jasmine. Her pale blue eyes drew him in, and the slim curve of her hip awakened other senses. *She also has spirit and wit. I like that as much as anything.*

Inside, servants still cleaned the remains of the evening banquet. One or two nobles chatted in quiet corners over a final goblet of wine, but most had left for the night. Jaerd led them along the side and through the door into the central tower. Before they took ten steps, two blue cloaks swirled around the corner.

"Tallen...and Captain Westar." Boris smiled, his face unsurprised. "And another friend I have not met."

An acid tone laced her reply. "Maddi."

Magus Britt laughed. "She doesn't seem that happy to be returning from a night out with the two of you."

Tallen felt the young woman bristle. He jumped in before she could say anything harsh to his teacher. "She saved our lives. Jaerd and I were in the city. We were attacked by orcs!"

"What!?" Magus Britt spat. Earl Boris took a half step forward, a sudden wariness on his features.

Raising a finger to his lips, Jaerd shushed his younger brother. "Not so loud, and not in the hall." Tallen felt heat rising in his ears, when Jaerd turned back to the Bluecloaks and snapped a quick salute. "The bodies are in the morgue, sirs. Only a dozen men know something is up, and only a few of those know for certain what happened." Jaerd folded his arms across the two rows of steel buttons on his chest. "I gave them strict commands to silence. I believe they can be trusted – for the time being."

Boris gave Magus Britt a hard look. "Get down to that morgue. Go over those bodies with a Jade Isles comb." He lifted an eyebrow. "Don't miss anything."

The Battlemage nodded and hurried out the front door faster than Tallen had ever seen him move.

"The rest of you come with me." Boris' voice was firm. "We just left the duke in his private study. He should still be there. We must make him aware of what has happened."

Jaerd nodded. "Informing the duke in private was my original plan, until the beans got spilled." A sidelong glance at his brother made Tallen blush again. "No offense to you, My Lord Earl."

Boris held up his hand. "You are loyal to your liege. I cannot find fault with that."

Tallen followed the two soldiers at a short distance, noting how Boris and Jaerd stalked the hall with a similar carriage. Maddi walked beside Tallen, her eyes scanning the surroundings like a trapped animal.

"You can breathe easy," Tallen whispered to her. Her scent filled his nostrils when he leaned closer. "These are fair nobles to deal with. Some are far worse, believe me."

"Lessons on nobles from a farm boy." Maddi gave him a disdainful look, tossing a hand through the air. "Or perhaps you are a minor noble yourself? Is that how your brother reached his rank?" She looked him up and down, cocking an eyebrow. "What's with your clothing, by the way? You look like your mother turned the old curtains into a wizard robe for you to play in."

This time the heat rushed to his cheekbones. He feared pink might become his natural color around her. "I am not playing." He kept his voice stern. "Nor am I a farmer. And I am certainly no noble." Tallen straightened his shoulders. "I am chef at the finest inn west of Gavanor. And these Bluecloaks you so distrust are escorting me to the Isle of Wizards so that I might become a mage myself."

The young woman paused in her steps. Tallen sped up so that he might leave her farther behind. He heard the shift of a guard's mail, followed by her quick steps back to his side.

"Then why did you not use your magic to save yourself from the…the attackers?" she asked, catching up.

Tallen shrugged. Magus Britt's slow teaching style frustrated him. "I am not yet allowed to use my power. Not until I have received training." He grumbled. "I'm not even allowed to Dream any more."

Scrunching up her nose again, Maddi shook her head. "That seems foolish. Someone is obviously out to get you. Someone should teach you to protect yourself."

"I intend to do just that," Jaerd announced from ahead. He and Boris mounted the stairwell that spiraled up the tower. "It was foolish enough for me to go out without arming myself. I will see to it that he is not without protection again." The captain in green looked at the earl in blue. "I will ask leave of my duties to join you in escorting my brother, Lord Earl, if that is acceptable to you."

Boris appraised Jaerd with a discerning gaze. "I would not object to your company as we continue eastward. A group of dwarves has asked to join us as well. I did not expect to need numbers to guard us." With a nod of approval, the earl returned his focus to the stairs. "We will take a boat upon the Andon at first light. It will be safer and faster than the road."

Half a dozen flights up, they reached the duke's study. Tallen breathed a sigh of relief when they approached it, and Boris knocked at the door. Jaerd snapped to attention when it opened.

"My Lord Duke," he began before Boris could say a word. "I have urgent news from the city. I must deliver it to you behind closed doors."

Duke Aginor stood with a half-empty glass of brandy. The smell of pipe and hickory smoke wafted out from behind him. "Then please come in, Captain. And your companions?"

Jaerd nodded. "They are witnesses, Your Grace."

The duke swung the door wide and waved them all inside.

Stone-flagged walls greeted Tallen, as did the brisk night air blowing in through the open windows. Almost five hundred yards above the surface of the river, the early summer nights were still cool. A fire crackled away around split logs in the hearth along the outer wall. Tallen perched on the wide settee to which the duke pointed. He could not stop the smile that cracked his lips when Maddi positioned herself beside him, her eyes searching the room like a trapped cat. Jaerd stood at attention near the door, and Boris rubbed his hands by the fire.

Duke Aginor pulled out a tray with crystal glasses and a decanter filled with a caramel liquid. "I believe you enjoyed this when you last came to Gavanor, My Lord Earl." He looked at the others, lifting his own glass. "Anyone care for a snort with their bad news? I often do."

Boris nodded, and the duke filled one for him.

"Sure, why not?" Maddi held out her hand. "If it's the duke's personal stock, who am I to turn it down?"

Aginor smiled and handed her a couple of fingers of the

golden liquor. Its bouquet warmed Tallen's nose, even at this distance.

It smells wonderful, but since Jaerd isn't having any…

The duke joined Boris near the fire. "Go ahead, Captain."

Jaerd nodded and explained, his voice crisp with formality. "Tallen and I had just entered Cooper's Plaza when six cloaked figures jumped us. They demanded we accompany them. I refused. Lucky for us, this young woman came along. She was very handy with her knives."

Boris raised an eyebrow, as did the duke.

"What did these men want with you?" Aginor sipped from his brandy, staring intently at his officer.

"I believe it was Tallen they were after, my lord." Jaerd nodded with certainty. "They hit him with a blackjack and threw a bag over his head. Then they had no compunction drawing daggers on me." He nodded again. "It is obvious that my brother was their intended prize."

Boris raised a fist to his lips and nodded his head as if something clicked inside it.

"There is something more though, isn't there?" The duke's eyes focused on Jaerd while he took another sip.

Jaerd's voice remained as flat as if he said that rain was wet. "They were orcs, sir."

The duke set his brandy down on the windowsill and stared out into the night.

"Joslyn is examining the bodies," Boris said while the duke focused silently on his city. "Captain Westar brought them here in strict secrecy. They are in the morgue."

Duke Aginor gulped down the rest of his brandy and moved to pour another. "Orcs within the city. Are you certain?"

"As certain as I can be, Your Grace," Jaerd replied, still at attention. "I have not fought them before, but I know them by description. Greenish skin – almost as short as dwarves but not quite as stocky. Blood red eyes."

"That's an orc," Boris said, slamming a fist into his hand. "I knew something stirred. The mood at Highspur was unmistakable."

The duke set down his drink. "You told me things were peaceful there."

Boris nodded his fist back on his chin. "They are. Too peaceful. The Northlands remained silent this spring. It worries me."

A knock rang at the door, insistent and impertinent. Without waiting, Magus Britt stomped in, huffing for breath. Tallen shifted upon seeing his teacher enter, and his knee brushed Maddi's. The touch lasted only a moment, but it made his heart quicken far more than the mention of Highspur.

"They are orcs, or I've never seen one." From the growl in his tone, Tallen was certain Magus Britt had seen them. "A crack squad, I would say. Boar Clan from the tattoos." The Battlemage stepped forward, reaching into his red-fringed cloak. "I found these. I intend on doing a full autopsy yet tonight, but I thought my discoveries important enough to report them first."

He pulled out a smooth, dark stone. It appeared made of a small piece of smoky glass, worn smooth from centuries of water. He held it in the palm of his hand.

"It is magical." The mage's voice hovered in a reverent tone. "Deep, strong magic. I have been unable to probe it very far as yet." He scratched his forehead.

I've never seen Magus Britt so concerned.

"What is it Joz?" Boris whispered. "You have a suspicion…"

"I'm not certain, and I hesitate to speculate." The mage looked at Tallen. "But its power became clearer to me when I entered this room. It's almost as if it seeks something, or someone, nearby."

"What do you mean?" Tallen's voice squeaked. He cleared his throat when he noticed Maddi's mocking smile.

"There is something else." Magus Britt's eyes pierced into Tallen. They held more compassion than normal. The mage reached into his cloak again, pulling out a tangled web of gold. A pink and green ribbon twisted about it. "Do you recognize this, Tallen?"

He tried to rise from the settee and step forward, but his knees refused to work properly. His breath came quick and harsh. Forcing strength to his limbs, Tallen stood and took the twist of hair and ribbon.

"Jennette's braid," he muttered. "How did these orcs…"

"I believe you were their true target in Dadric, Tallen." Boris softened his expression. "They killed your friend and the young man by mistake – as I originally suspected." He looked at Magus Britt. "The braid confirms it."

"Why take her hair?" Tallen's mind went numb with grief. Tears crept out from under his eyelids. His head hurt with the pain of suppressing them.

"A trophy." Magus Britt's tone remained soft. "Blond hair is very rare in the Northlands."

Jaerd raised his hand in the air like a student in class. "If I may, sirs? They did not seek to kill him tonight. In fact, they went out of their way to keep him alive."

Boris nodded, scrubbing his mustache with his hand. "Yes, Captain. I think they followed your brother that night at the Sowing Festival. His confrontation with the victims probably saved his life. The orcs tracked him and Jennette into the warehouses, but found Jennette and Ardric when they made their move." The Bluecloak sipped his brandy. "They wanted Tallen alive. When they discovered that Ardric was not Tallen, they killed both young people to cover their tracks."

Duke Aginor paced from the door to the fire. "How did they get into my city? What do they want with this boy?"

Magus Britt pointed to the glasses and decanter. The duke nodded with a tip of his glass. The mage poured a drink and took a long gulp. "I don't know the answer to either of those questions," he said at last with a deep breath. "I will find the answer. I will begin by returning to the morgue." He topped off the glass before he nodded to the duke and Boris, and then headed toward the door. At the last moment he stopped, squinting at Maddi. "You have the healer's Talent, don't you girl? Do not deny it. I can see it almost as clearly as I see the power in untrained mages." Magus Britt looked to Boris. "We must take her to Daynon as well. We need her kind as much as we need mages."

Boris raised an eyebrow. "You knew this, young lady?"

Scooting back in her seat, Maddi folded her arms. "I have been told of the possibility. However, I have not yet had a true Doctor open my Talent. I was told I would have the best success at the Doctor's College in Daynon."

Nodding, Magus Britt kept his gaze fixed on Maddi. It reminded Tallen of the night he had met the Battlemage in the Sleeping Gryphon.

I almost feel sorry for her.

Magus Britt grasped the door handle. "Then Daynon is where we will take you." He stepped out, mumbling. "I have ravens to send tonight."

Offering a hand to Maddi, Boris took a step closer to the divan. "Then you will accompany us to Daynon."

Maddi exploded from her seat. "This is not right! I should have some say in what happens with my life! I have cannot abandon my herbalist shop here." Her eyes glittered in the firelight, squinting in anger. "I also own a home in Bailey Square. What am I to do with that?"

110

Boris held firm but shifted his offered hand to a placating gesture. "I am sorry, miss, but you have been involved in a very violent affair, one that must be kept secret for now." He cocked an eye at her. "I can tell your accent is from the Free Cities – Dern if I'm not mistaken." He picked at a stray ash upon the fireplace mantle. "Strange that so young a woman, a foreigner from such a small town, would own property in one of the nicest districts within the capital of the Western Realm."

A portion of the anger slipped from Maddi's face. She nibbled at a lip, and the squint of her eyes refocused. "That is not fair. My father died and left me an inheritance. I brought it here because I *thought* this was a free country." She pulled at a long strand of her glossy, near-black hair. It glittered like onyx in the firelight when she twisted it. "Perhaps I was wrong."

Boris pursed his lips. "No one is truly free from all duty. Especially when calamity comes calling."

The duke stepped away from the fireplace. "My dear, I will see that your possessions are secured. I assure you my clerks will make full inventory of everything."

Maddi frowned. "Much of my inventory will spoil if left uncared for. Who is going to pay for that?"

Boris raised a finger. "I will. We will also take care of any expenses you have at the College."

Raising an eyebrow, Maddi's face slipped from scowl to grin. "And a stipend?"

The earl could not help a small grin of his own. "Perhaps. Do not push your luck too far with me, my dear."

Excited that Maddi would join them, Tallen sank back into his seat. His eyes returned to Jennette's braid, nestled in the palm of his hand. His chest heated, and a great pressure pulsed at his temples. Two crystal drops fell from his eyes onto the golden locks. *I had thought my feelings for her dealt with, but I…* Another droplet fell, and he sniffed.

Retaking her seat next to him, Maddi leaned toward Tallen. "Were the two of you close?" Her voice hummed in his ear, soft and sweet. She reached out her hand and placed it upon his wrist. "I'm sorry. I know the pain of loss."

Tallen dabbed his eyes with a sleeve. *I doubt I look much the wizard to her, wiping tears with my robe.*

"We were close, at one point." The words weighed heavy on his spirit. "Though we grew apart in the last year, I suppose."

Maddi nodded and patted his wrist. Her sympathy helped

111

him maintain control, but he could not entirely hide his emotions.

"You must use this, Tallen." Boris formed his hands into fists that shook with intensity. "Use it to drive your training. Think of the pain you feel right now when you hear of the deaths of your countrymen. Each of them leaves others behind who also feel the pain you harbor now." The Bluecloak put a hand on Tallen's shoulder. "This is why we do what we do – because we know the suffering and because we know it is right to fight it. The greatest test for those who are strong is in what they do with that strength – and in how they treat those who are weak."

Nodding his head, Tallen tossed Jennette's hair into the fire. "May she rest in the Waters." It curled and blackened, before disappearing in gray smoke.

CHAPTER 12

Arguments abound as to what exactly caused the Cataclysm. Most mages blame the wild use of magic at the end of the Dragon Wars for setting off a chain reaction. The Temple claims that it was due to a terrible skewing of the Balance. No written records remain from the time, save among the Elves. Those few texts are rarely shown to human eyes. When asked about the cause, the Elven ambassador to the Royal Court simply said, "Foolishness."
– Baelor Magdon's "What We Know of the Elder Days"

Slar spat a gobbet of dust and phlegm onto the ground. His arm scraped at the sweat and grime upon his brow until Radgred handed him a goatskin of water. The cool sweetness ran down his dry throat, cooling his insides.

"Blackstone was much nicer." The old sergeant closed the last flap over the pole Slar had just hoisted. "These huts won't last us through the winter."

"We won't need them then." Slar took another slurp from the goatskin and wiped his chin with the back of his fist. "Those left behind here will have begun construction of a far greater fortress than Blackstone. You and I will be long gone."

Radgred grunted agreement. "Let us hope so."

Slar picked up a folded doeskin, wiping the remainder of the sweat from his brow and neck with its soft surface. He sighed. "Midsummer arrives soon. It will be Sharrog's naming day."

The old orc's brow creased beyond his age and battle wrinkles. "I am glad you two have begun speaking again after your disagreement at Blackstone." He took his own sip from the waterskin. "But I can tell that things are still not right between you."

Slinging the doeskin around his neck, Slar shook his head. "My son and I do not see eye to eye on Galdreth, nor on our battle plan." He started back through the trees toward the cavern entrance into the depths of Dragonsclaw. "However, he will come around when our forces gather. The power of Galdreth is undeniable."

Following at a short distance, Radgred scratched at an ear. "I hope so." He raised an eyebrow. "What of Grindar? How go his training maneuvers?"

Slar smiled. "Grindar will be chieftain of the Boar Clan someday, like is grandfather before. He knows how to command warriors, and how to earn their respect." He watched a hawk alight upon the dead branch of an old pine tree. "My eldest will lead the Boar warriors when we make our move."

The hole in the side of the mountain gaped at them, and they climbed toward it, leaving the Boar Clan tents down on the lower slopes of Dragonsclaw. Inside the cavern's mouth, Slar made out the lodges of shamans from four clans. *The fools claim they desire to be closer to Galdreth, yet I know each one of them shakes in their cowl when the spirit appears.*

Radgred growled at the sight of the lodges. "You should have a Warchief's lodge here among them. It is not right that you stay in your small tent among the Boar. You command all the clans in Galdreth's name." Radgred turned and headed for the tents of their clan. "I will see to it immediately."

Slar reached out to stop his friend until he saw the expression on Radgred's face. "Very well. If I must play the part."

Radgred stopped, pointing his finger at Slar. "You play no part!" He barked, the yellow-clawed finger stabbing at Slar again. "You *are* the Warchief!"

I've never seen such wrath from Radgred. At least not aimed at me. Slar nodded to his longtime friend and advisor. "Your words ring true, as always. However, you will join me there as my second. I will not suffer alone."

Nodding in acquiescence, Radgred lowered the finger. "As you wish, Warchief. It will be a grand lodge indeed." He resumed his jog back down the hill.

Shaking his head, Slar turned to enter the cavern. The shamans within it weighed upon his mind. *Boar and Ram. Now Shark and Wolf. Soon the Bear and the Snake. How will I manage them all?*

Slowing his pace to think, Slar allowed the surrounding forest to distract him. The trees rose to great heights, spread wide with summer-green branches. Squirrels scampered from limb to limb, chattering throughout the chase of their courtship. The politics of the clans wandered far from his mind.

"Ho, there, old comrade." A voice broke into his thoughts.

Fargon of the Wolf Clan trotted up from the slopes on which the Wolves had gathered their tents.

"I welcome you, my friend." Slar slapped a fist to his chest. "How did you fare in your travels?"

"They were calm." Fargon bowed his head, before reaching out a hand of greeting.

Slar grabbed it with a hearty clasp. "Has your father come?" Trepidation laced his voice, for Slar knew he would need the other chieftains to balance the power of the shamans in council.

"Valgrar gathers more of our people." Fargon held his pink eyes steady. "I lead the twenty thousand Wolf warriors who now gather on the lower shoulders of Dragonsclaw." He released Slar's wrist with the friendly growl of comrades. "Over five thousand Sharks have come too, a big number for their small tribe." Fargon cast his eyes back down the slope he had climbed. "The Sharks delivered the teams as you commanded, and now ply the waters of the Teeth."

Slar nodded his head. "Their longboats have been invaluable to our cause." He gestured for Fargon to join him. "I have a favor to ask of you, my old friend."

Fargon laughed from his belly. "Twenty thousand warriors is not a favor already?"

Slar smiled. "It is indeed. But this is something more subtle."

Laughing even louder, Slar's childhood friend slapped his knee. "Subtlety is not a trait for a Wolf. Perhaps you should ask a Snake when they arrive."

A bitter smile crossed Slar's lips. "I will likely ask the same of Sarinn or his sons when they arrive, but I need your help most of all."

Slowing his steps, Fargon placed his hand upon Slar's shoulder. "What is it you need, Warchief?"

His eyes are so like Nalan's, so like Naleera's were. Those pink eyes run deep in the blood of the Wolves. They were part of what drew me to her. "It is a simple thing," Slar stated.

Fargon paused a moment. "Then ask."

Slar folded his hands behind his back as he walked. "I need you to place your chieftain's lodge within the mouth of the cavern. Radgred has insisted I place mine there." He paused, the cavern just within view beyond the trees. He watched a few orcs in wolfskin capes enter its shadow. "We must make certain that the chieftains speak for the people. The shamans are only interested in speaking for Galdreth."

Fargon frowned. "I thought you spoke for Galdreth."

Thoughts of his argument with Sharrog floated through Slar's mind. "I do. But I also speak for our people."

Slar remained silent while they marched the rest of the way up the slope. The hulking black mass of the mountain hanging over them reminded Slar of his future. Something dark and shadowy hung over it as well, and he could not shake a deep foreboding.

Within the outer mouth of the cave, nearly two dozen lodges of varying size perched on rocky outcroppings. A labyrinth of passages twisted into the mountain's bowels behind them. Slar knew what lay in those depths. *That's why I had hoped to stay out in the open with my people for as long as we could. But these shamans are fools. They seek to be closer to Galdreth. My heart tries to push me away.* "At least our people will find glory on the path," he whispered, distracted by his thoughts.

"It will not be so difficult living among them." Fargon raised his eyes to the group of orcs hoisting lodges for the Wolf shamans. "A dozen of them came with me. More may come with father." He smiled at Slar. "Perhaps the Wolf shamans listen to their chieftains more than in your clans."

"You just wait until they get together with the others." Slar snorted. "Shamans stick together, even across clan lines."

Fargon raised an eyebrow in thought. "Perhaps then, we chieftains must stick together as well." Cupping his mouth with his hands, he shouted to the orcs setting up lodges. "Hoy! When you finish those, bring my lodge up here. The chieftains shall join Warchief Slar within the halls of Dragonsclaw!"

In response, Brother Ortax sidled over from a cluster of shamans. "Warchief, it is an honor to have you among the camp of shamans. But what is this about you setting a tent here?" He shrugged his shoulders. "I had thought you planned to stay among our people. Will they not need your guidance?"

Oh, now I am definitely setting my lodge here. "Our people have many sources of guidance," Slar said, squinting his eyes to examine Ortax. "Our shamans will need guidance from their Warchief as well." Murmurs floated through the knot of Ortax's allies. "Let us not forget whom Galdreth has chosen."

The murmurs stopped.

Brother Ortax raised an eyebrow. "Speaking of those our master has chosen – how goes the search for Galdreth's vessel? Is that not one of your most important charges from our master?"

Balling clawed hands into fists, Slar craved the feel of his scimitar, but it lay in his lodge down with the Boar Clan. "Elite squads are now operating within Gannon." He held his voice even. "All you need know is that the vessel is being tracked." He folded his arms to squelch the longing to caress his absent sword. "A major asset has been moved into place. Galdreth has also explained to me that there are other powers beyond the Clans that search for the vessel."

Ortax scoffed. "Like the dragons?" Other shamans grumbled. "Their raid upon the dwarves did nothing save expose our hand. It wasted several of their strongest. Other dragons have since abandoned us."

"Most of their numbers remain at Galdreth's command," Slar said, raising his wide, dimpled chin. "Dozens of them rest within the deeper mountains, not far from here. They will be ready when needed." He pointed his finger at Ortax. "You need not worry about dragons or the other powers at Galdreth's call. You need only worry about what our master demands of you."

The rustle of dozens of feet born down with heavy loads shuffled behind him. Slar turned to see Radgred leading a group of orcs carrying the components of his lodge. Behind him strutted Balthor of the Ram and his own lodge bearers. Farther down the slope came a group of Wolves and Sharks with poles and skins for at least two more dwellings.

"Warchief," Radgred called. "Your honor guard brings your lodge so that you, the chosen of Galdreth, may rest within our master's holy mountain." He spread his scarred arms. "Your chieftains join you at your command."

"Hoy! Hoy!" Fargon saluted fist to heart and bowed his head.

All those who came with Radgred followed suit, including Balthor, who walked forward to stand next to Fargon. Near a third of the shamans from all the clans bowed their heads as well.

Slar waved a hand toward the bearers. "Then about your business."

Radgred pointed them further within the mountain, behind the shaman lodges, but still within reach of daylight.

With a scowl, Ortax spun on his heel and stalked back to his dwelling.

Slar looked at Fargon and Balthor, giving them each a nod of respect. They bowed back and joined the workers in directing the placement of their residences. Shaking his head, Slar faced Radgred. "Thank you, my friend. You are as strong an ally within council chambers as you are on the battlefield."

Radgred offered a deep and formal bow. "I am always yours, Warchief."

"Come," Slar said with an outstretched arm. "Let us see where we will stay." He looked into the depths of the caverns under Dragonsclaw. "Let us also explore just how much space we have at our disposal here. This place will be very useful in hiding our plans."

Pebble scree clattered down the mountainside as Slar's feet scrambled along the steep ledge. A scream from some predatory bird gave warning of the danger.

"You need not tell me," he whispered back. His claws ached from clamping onto the rocky wall beside him. His boot slipped again, and another batch of stones tumbled downward. Slar scuttled around a boulder, and the ground opened up in front of him.

"You make enough noise to cause an avalanche, orc." The sonorous voice spoke with a slight slur, as if the jaw did not quite move well enough to speak Common Tongue. "Good thing that I have already eaten all the predators hereabouts." A deep chuckle rolled out.

A black and scarlet head almost Slar's size rose up from behind the lip of a small depression. The crimson eyes burned with an inner fire, and a serpentine tongue lashed about from behind a field of sharp teeth.

Slar steeled his nerves and returned the dragon's stare. "Lord Vordrex. It is good to see you returned from your raid against the dwarves." He stepped closer to the ponderous beast. The obsidian scales glittered in the slanted afternoon light. "You obtained more treasure for your nest, I hope."

Vordrex belched, and a greenish haze floated from his nostrils. "One dwarf gave me indigestion, though he did wear a great deal of gold upon his person. Some emeralds and diamonds did come up with his bones as well." The dragon's smile sent an unbidden shiver down Slar's spine. "However, I did gain this." He touched a winged foreclaw to his cheek. A long strip of scales had been ripped away. "It may take a century for it to fade."

"Scars remind us that the past was real," Slar muttered, more to himself than the beast.

The dragon's harsh laugh rang out across the mountainside. "Is that ancient orc wisdom?"

Ignoring the creature's words, Slar focused on his purpose for climbing so high this late in the day. "I have come to inform you of a need – a need within Galdreth's plan. Should my warriors fulfill a certain quest, we will need a…an extraction…from enemy territory. I was hoping…"

The dragon snorted again. This time a sooty film floated out from his nostrils and mouth. "I am not a steed for a meddling orc!" Vordrex shifted his black bulk around. "I am no slave to your Galdreth's call, like the many scurrying ants I watch below."

"I did not mean—"

"I will bring my kin when you begin your move against the Humans," Vordrex growled, his forked tongue lashing out. "There is enough treasure on that path to make it worthwhile." He turned toward the cavern hidden behind the depression. "But I will not cross the Dragonscales alone on some fool mission. The last one cost my kind enough. I will not do it again – not even at Galdreth's command."

Slar watched him stalk into his cave then turned back to the path homeward when Vordrex disappeared.

"Drown him in the Waters," he grumbled under his breath. He picked up his pace when he looked at the westering sun. *I'll have to move to get back before dark.*

He scrambled down through a ravine, and then back up the far side. Shadows cast by the tall pines marked his remaining time. Once he slid down the pebble-strewn slope into the second ravine, a deeper shade surrounded him. Willing his legs for more speed, Slar followed the small rivulet of water at the bottom where it led down toward the foothills encircling Dragonsclaw. *The hills will be easier to travel in the dark than these damned mountains.*

The trickle of water grew while he descended. His feet moved with certainty, even in the fading light. He was about to begin humming a tune his grandfather taught him, when heard the snap of a twig from the surrounding bush.

He had only a moment to turn his head toward the sound before a leathery shape hurtled from the darkness. A hard, bony head rammed into his sternum and rolled his body to the ground. Slar screamed out in pain when a set of sharp teeth sank into his shoulder.

He kicked out with all his strength and felt his boots make contact with something soft on the creature's body. A wail of pain erupted from the beast, loosening its deadly grip. Slar kicked again in the same spot. His free hand scrabbled at his belt, desperate to find the lone dagger he had worn into the mountains.

In his mind, he heard the words his father would have used had he been there to witness his son's demise. *Fool! I hope your sword is safe back in the lodge!*

The cold hardness of metal met his fingers. The beast twisted, hurling him over onto his side, and pinning his free hand away from the dagger handle. They slid together as one down a dozen yards of sharp-rocked mountainside and skidded to a halt. His hand remained far away from his knife, but in this new position, he could shift his feet underneath himself.

Slar heaved against the scaly creature flailing him with sharp claws. Its teeth clamped harder against his shoulder, certain of a death grip.

Slar screamed with pain and flung his muscle and mass against the attacker. The creature stumbled back, far enough for him to clasp his fingers around the handle of his knife. Drawing it free from its sheath, Slar shouted with rage and thrust it repeatedly into any part of the creature he could reach.

A roar of agony burst forth from the small, fireless dragon. It lashed about, releasing its grip on Slar's shoulder. He pushed it away, falling back onto his haunches. The fading light offered him a glimpse of the reptilian shape as it retreated.

"Damn you!" Slar thrust the bloody dagger out toward the dragon. "We are on the same side!"

The beast, not much larger than a big dog, hissed in response. Slar smelled the sulfur on its breath. He shifted his weight again, ready for another attack. *I forget that the smaller they are, the dumber they are.*

With a final spit of stinking gas, the dragon turned about and scampered back into the forest, limping the entire way. One folded wing hanging askew from its forearm, the creature disappeared into the shadows between the trees.

Slar touched his wounded shoulder and winced. Sticky blood came away on his fingers. His fist closed when he flexed it, which was good news. He could bend his elbow, but only with a great deal of pain.

Down in the valley below, in a wide band that encircled the blacker-than-night shoulders of Dragonsclaw, thousands of fires winked alight a few at a time. The sight gave him hope, despite the aching pain in his arm and shoulder. He clasped his hand over his wound and made his way toward the lights, his grandfather's tune at last finding its way to his lips.

13

Before the Exile, our ancestors lived along this very river. The waters of the Andon still flow in our blood. It is now an even greater river than before the Cataclysm. So shall it be with the People of Gan.
— Aravath the Navigator, 3 A.R.

Tallen struggled not to wince as Jaerd hoisted him back to his feet with a strong arm.

Magus Britt wiped his beard clean of the cheese crumbs from his lunch. "You understand that someday the lad will be able to destroy a battalion of swordsmen while standing still?"

"Well, Magus, you haven't taught him that just yet." Jaerd handed back the dagger he had easily taken from Tallen's grasp. Tallen noticed the tightening of the mage's eyes. "So I intend on teaching him everything I can in the meantime."

Magus Britt glared Jaerd a moment then turned to Tallen, who tucked the dagger in its sheath at his belt. "Perhaps you have a point. Come with me, lad. It is time you touched your power."

"Thank you, sir." Jaerd saluted the mage who was also his superior officer. "If he is able to better defend himself it will take some of the weight off my mind." He winked at Tallen. "I'm going below for a bite to eat."

Waving a quick good-bye to his brother, Tallen followed Magus Britt over to the rail of the *Shasta*. The Andon rolled by, slightly faster than the riverboat on which they rode. Lightly wooded farmlands, broken by occasional cottages and hamlets, lined the banks. Only a few crewmembers moved about on board, and Captain Daneric stood at the wheel. The river's flow provided velocity for the *Shasta*, her men only there to help guide her. When they returned against the current, Tallen supposed it would be another story.

"This time I want you to find the Aspects without closing your eyes." Magus Britt's brow drew down, but the rest of his face did not show the customary frown. "No wizard can fight with his eyes closed. You must be able to sense your power while still granting most of your attention to the physical world around you."

Tallen nodded, but inside his stomach turned.

I had to concentrate so hard just to sense those colors while meditating. How will I ever do it in a battle?

Magus Britt folded his arms. "Can you focus enough to do it? Or am I just wasting my time with you?"

Tallen thought of the fluttering hues of light in his mind, and they popped into his perception with ready ease. He discerned them more clearly than ever before. The different colors – the different Aspects – each had their own quality beyond just a chromatic splash in his mind's eye. The red felt warm, like the Fire Magus Britt claimed it to be. Blue soothed Tallen's spirit, cool as a summer dip in the pond behind the Gryphon. Yellow and green clashed about, one fluttering and playful, the other solid and reassuring. A cast of silvery white inundated everything – the Aspect of Psoul. It tickled his gut with excitement and curdled it with fear at the same time. Tallen sensed its overwhelming power. He heard its call for him to unleash it. He began to reach.

"Easy there." Magus Britt held up a hand. "Focus. Only touch your power, don't draw it in yet. I would suggest Water first." The mage wagged a finger. "Psoul is a tricky thing, even if you know what you are doing with it. Neither of us does."

Shifting his reach to the azure call of Water, Tallen brushed its surface. Like dipping his fingers into a lake, the touch cooled his senses. The Water began to climb up the reach of his consciousness, running in rivulets into his mind. At first he pushed it away, but its soothing call drew him forward.

"Only allow a trickle in." Magus Britt studied him with an intense stare. "Pool it in your mind. Hold it within your body. You will know your limits when you feel the strain across your forehead. Do not push yourself anywhere near them."

As if opening himself to the flow of a river, Tallen took in some of the swirling power. He felt it gathering within his consciousness, begging him to unleash it into the world. He clamped down on the stream, wary of its siren call.

"Now, release it into the river." The mage's voice echoed in the back of Tallen's mind. "Push against the water already there and speed our boat forward. Easy at first. Maintain control."

Tallen opened the flow, the Water pulling against his will like a puppy tugging the other end of a rope. *Only this puppy feels as if he could eat Brawny in a single bite.* He opened himself a little more and let the magic pour out into the water.

The breeze whipped about his ears, and the landscape drifted by with greater speed. A smile crept over Magus Britt's face, though Tallen knew his own pinched in concentration. A slight creak emanated from the boat's shallow keel.

"Hoy!" Captain Daneric cupped his lips. "She's not gonna like much more than that, my lord mages!"

"Ease back Tallen." Magus Britt nodded in approval. "Let go of the Water. Let's try something else."

The sweet taste of Water tempted Tallen, along with the more raw sensation of his assembled energy. It called upon him to cast it all out in a rush of glory and power. He smiled, and carefully let it dissipate. The Water settled back into the pool within his mind. The riverboat eased back to its regular pace.

"Good." Magus Britt graced Tallen with a rare smile. "A mage's power can be his greatest weakness as well as his strength. Those who are too weak in spirit can succumb to it, like an addiction." His eyes watched the river. "They burn themselves out, living broken lives sunken in madness. Or worse. Some destroy themselves, taking everything else that they can with them." He turned to face Tallen, fixing those gray eyes on his. "You must learn control. With the level of your power, it will be your greatest trial and temptation. Do not lose yourself."

Tallen nodded. "I understand, sir. Now, after finally touching it, I realize what you mean about it being a temptation." He paused, searching for the words. "It's as if it *wants* to be used."

Magus Britt stared into Tallen's eyes, an unreadable expression on his face. "You already surpass what most can do after weeks of training. For most mages, their power only grows with use, and the more powerful the mage, the longer they live. I can't imagine where your strength might lead you some day."

Tallen gulped. The weight of his future settled onto his shoulders. "I never thought I would do anything bigger than maybe opening up another Sleeping Gryphon in Gavanor, once I got tired of Glynn." His face shifted into a nervous smile. "Do you think I could be a member of the Circle of Wizards some day?"

A laugh sounded from behind him. "I can feel your power, young man." The dwarf mage Yrik stood leaning against the rail. He must have emerged from below decks while Tallen focused on his spell. "You could squash half the Circle before they sensed you draw on your power." He shook his bald head. "Why you would join with them, I do not understand."

Magus Britt frowned at the dwarf. "Because the Circle gives our mages safety in unity. Plus, it helps us to keep an eye on our brethren." His concentrated his gaze upon Yrik. "Keeps those interested in dark things from exploring them too far."

Yrik put a knuckle to his lip. "You may be right. With the number of you humans, I suppose you must have more structure. There are so few mages among my people – we all know each other quite well." He bowed, his oily, pointed beard bending against his chest. It popped right back into position when he straightened. "Best of luck in your studies, young apprentice." He strolled toward the bow.

Magus Britt cleared his throat. "Come. Back to your lesson." He waved at the passing shoreline. "Now, I want you to reach out with the Air Aspect and grab a branch from one of those trees."

He sighed, and followed the mage's lead.

Tallen stoked the brazier, sending sparks flying off into the night. Their reflections danced upon the Andon River, harmonious with their partners in reality. *Just like the reflection of Fire in my mind. Only mine can actually burn you.*

"So, have you learned enough to protect yourself without my help yet?" Maddi's voice startled him from his thoughts. The scent of jasmine reached his nose. He breathed it in deeply.

"Maybe. If they attack us in a boat, I could certainly flip it." He grinned. "Anything more exciting may have to wait for another couple of lessons."

The girl held her hands over the brazier. Tallen stretched his own out alongside them. The breeze off the water chilled, even in early summer.

"Do you think more of them will come?" Maddi spoke in a steady voice, but the fact that she asked at all gave hint to her fear.

"We are only getting farther into the heart of the kingdom." Tallen pursed his lips with doubt. "I can't image any..." He looked about for boat crew, only spying the man on watch at the wheel. He also saw the fair-haired dwarf maiden watching the moon dance on the river. "...any of *them* getting back east. The Eastern Realm is much more populated, with a half dozen cities the size of Gavanor and larger, each with thousands of soldiers and watchmen."

Folding her arms, Maddi shook her head doubtfully. "If they can slip inside Gavanor…"

Tallen shrugged and reached out to pat her on the shoulder. She did not flinch from his touch. He returned to warming his hands. "Everyone is on alert now. We are protected by some of the best fighters in the land, not to mention a pack of stalwart dwarves." He inclined his head toward the dwarf woman. "One of whom apparently slew a dragon."

"I heard." A slight smile crept onto her lips, a pretty one Tallen had seldom seen. "Their leader, the Maester Northtower, told the story twice at breakfast."

Tallen snorted. "Dwarves do love their tales. Many of those that stopped in the Gryphon told them regularly – to the great pleasure of the crowd." He looked at her sideways. Her eyes focused on the fire. "But you are from Dern, so I'm sure you know dwarves quite well."

Shaking her head, Maddi reached out toward the brazier again. She rubbed her supple hands not far from his. "No. There are no dwarves left to speak of in Dern. They really only live in Kirath and Kerrigeir. The Free Cities are not the same places they were in old tales."

Tallen nodded, hoping the firelight hid the flush in his cheeks. "No doubt. Nothing is."

Maddi turned from the fire and headed below deck.

Damn. I've made her think I'm stupid.

Her shadow stopped before it disappeared. "I enjoyed our talk."

Tallen stood there by the brazier, unaware of the grin plastered to his face until well after the next crewman took his turn at the tiller.

Tallen swayed while his eyes tracked the towering heights of the Crimson Spike. Tumbled shoulders of reddish stone pierced up from the center of the Andon, forcing it to flow to either side. The southward channel churned, white and frothy, through scattered boulders that pierced the water's surface. Beyond the southern bank, the Red Hills continued into the distance, folding over one another in russet mounds of scrub dotted gravel. The *Shasta* took the northern passage, filled with slower waters.

Beyond the stacked red stone of the island, the tall tower climbing up from its peak drew Tallen's eye. It reached almost a thousand yards above the river's surface. Built of the same, ruddy stone, the Crimson Spike towered over everything for leagues.

"Its foundations are from before the Cataclysm." Boris shaded his eyes, staring upward at the tower. "They are one of the few human made structures to survive it. King Arathan III rebuilt the tower almost three centuries ago."

Tallen watched a small pier pass by. No boats docked there, but it appeared to be in good repair. "Does anyone live up there?"

Boris nodded. "A garrison still mans it much of the time, though it is mostly out of tradition."

"Unlike Highspur," Tallen blurted out. He watched Boris' face for a reaction. He got little.

"Highspur is essential to the security of all the southern lands, not just Gannon." Boris folded his arms. "Though it is hard to make most of them see that." He looked toward several of the dwarves and Sergeant Hall gathered about a barrel. Brawny hung close to his master, the expression in his eyes similar to when Tallen cooked around the huge hound. "Come. Let's see what they've found."

Maester Northtower slapped his hand on the top of the barrel. "I paid the captain five gold marks for it, and I say we crack it open." His twin nephews and the grizzled sergeant named Marrax Redarm nodded in response. "That way when we reach Magdonton at dusk, we'll have a half snoot full before we visit her inns!" The other dwarves applauded.

"You can count me in…" Sergeant Hall began, clapping his huge hands together. Then he noticed Boris. "With My Lord Earl's permission, of course."

Boris laughed. "Why not? I'll have a mug myself, if Maester Northtower is sharing."

The dwarf held out the first full tankard, his dark eyes sparkling. "I insist, My Lord."

Boris took the oversized mug and gave it a sip. He hoisted it with a smile. "It's good!" He wiped the froth from his mustache with a hand, while Hall and the dwarves gave a cheer. Tallen joined in. Hall even set a bowl of the brew on the deck for Brawny to lap at with vigor.

Before long, most of the group had wandered over by the barrel of ale. Maddi and Tilli joined in with a cup. After a few, Darve invited even the off-duty crew to come over for a taste. Magus Britt joined them, clinking his mug against Boris'.

Darve turned to Sergeant Hall. "So, how is that axe holding up?"

Hall patted the steel behemoth that never rested far from his side. "Good. I care for it quite well. I know how rare a dwarf-made axe large enough to fit me is."

Darve nodded. "You saved my life during the Border Skirmishes. A Northtower does not forget a debt."

"You all knew each other in the Border Skirmishes?" Tallen seated himself as close to Maddi as he could without being obvious.

"Not all of us," Boris answered. "Darve and his dwarves were to remain as neutral observers when they arrived. Hall was in the guard detachment of King Arathan's emissary among them."

A wry grin wrinkled Magus Britt's lips. "The Earl and I were…helping a band of Yadushii Highlanders raid deep inside Hadonese territory."

"I was only a corporal then." Hall stared at his mug wistfully.

"Bah!" Corporal Magrudy waved his hand in dismissal. "You came out of your mother's womb a hard-assed sergeant!"

Hall lifted an eyebrow as he drank, but Tallen noticed the smile behind his mug.

Magus Britt downed his cup and placed it upon the barrel. "Thank you gentlemen, but my apprentice and I are both limited to one drink." He looked at Tallen, his head tilted back to examine him. "I have a special lesson planned for you tonight in Magdonton. There is a garden that I wish for you to visit. It is the perfect time of year to show you one of the most popular, and most tricky, applications of Water."

Tallen looked into his cup, nearing its bottom. He poured the remainder into Brawny's empty bowl.

The docks of Magdonton rambled along the north shore of the Andon River. Hundreds of boats, for transport, fishing, and pleasure, lined up in relative order. The *Shasta* glided into berth next to an empty grain barge that floated high in the water.

Tallen hopped onto the dock immediately behind Magus Britt. "Easy lad, you'll catch my boot heel."

"Sorry, Magus." Tallen ducked his head in apology. "I'm eager to be about our lesson."

"Good. Just remember to temper your eagerness with caution." Magus Britt looked over his shoulder, the dog-headed staff clacking time against the cobblestones. "You mess with very powerful forces, Tallen. Far too powerful for one of your age and skill. You must learn to control yourself, as well as controlling your power."

Jaerd hovered nearby, his eyes upon the darkening streets. Maddi and Boris looked at each other and the dwarves and Hall who walked away to find a tavern, laughing coarsely. The normally silent Brawny bounced around them barking.

Boris lifted one eyebrow. "Mind if we join you?"

Maddi shook her head up and down in vigorous agreement. "A walk in a garden is just what my legs need after days on a boat."

Magus Britt shrugged. "Why not?"

Several blocks into the city, a stone-walled orchard appeared around a street corner. A tired old guard stood near its entry, his tunic of midnight blue spangled with a crescent and stars. He straightened from leaning against the wall when he saw Magus Britt's blue cloak.

"General Magus." The man still had a sharp salute for his age. "Do you wish entry to Milord's garden?"

Magus Britt returned the salute. "Those apple trees still grow here, do they not?"

"Aye, sir. They do. Just setting new fruit now, sir."

The guard opened the rusty iron gate, which creaked with disuse. Tallen followed the mage inside and looked about.

Obviously, the gardener comes through a different gate, because he is here every day.

Narrow slate paths webbed their way between ankle high bluegrass. Rose hedges lined many of the routes, vibrant in white, yellow, and a dozen hues of red.

Magus Britt led them down toward the eastern end, where several rows of apple trees grew against the shortened wall. Jaerd remained close, his eyes upon the entrance. Boris and Maddi strolled along the paths while the sunlight disappeared behind the trees. A few stars pricked the eastern horizon.

Surely, an Earl isn't going to…

Tallen squinted to watch the two disappear on the far side of the garden.

He might not marry her, but that never stopped a noble from dipping below his station for a little fun!

Noticing his expression, Magus Britt chuckled under his breath. "Don't worry. She's far too young for Boris' tastes." He cleared his throat and raised his bushy eyebrows. "Now focus on me."

The Bluecloak mage reached up into the branches of the tree. An odd tingle rippled up Tallen's spine. A long branch with several pea-sized apples came loose in Magus Britt's hand, its edge cut with precision.

Tallen slapped his hands together, his thoughts regarding Maddi driven away for a moment. "I think I felt you touch your power!"

Magus Britt nodded. "It happens soon after you first embrace your own. That was Air – a very tiny bit like a thin knife to slice through the tree branch. You are not only powerful, but you learn quickly." He cleared his throat and forced the pending smile from his face. "That is a good thing, because you have a great deal to learn. Moreover, since you are so intelligent, I shall be expecting a great deal from you. Come."

He walked over to the edge of the apple orchard. A dead tree stood there, trimmed of its branches, with a small red ribbon tied about its trunk. The Battlemage embraced his power again, and Tallen felt the tingle in his spine once more. He could almost see a fine sliver of Air as it cut its way through the tree trunk, down into the ground, and around its dead stump. Another tingle and the tree's remains flew over toward a brush pile stacked along the wall.

Pointing toward the empty hole in the ground where a few roots still stuck up, severed perfectly across their grain, Magus Britt waved the apple branch in front of Tallen. "Take it and stick it into the soil. Pull enough dirt around so that it stands on its own."

Tallen did as the mage asked, the smell of sour apple brushing his nose with the branch.

"Now embrace your power, but do not draw upon it yet." Magus Britt watched Tallen with a keen eye. "Because of the nature if things, which I *hope* your father or one of your brothers has explained to you, each apple seed is a cross between its two parent trees. This means that you cannot be certain that an apple from a new tree is sweet until you bite into it, and that can take years of waiting and tending to get a tree to maturity."

The mage's voice slid along the back of Tallen's consciousness. He heard the words and listened to their meaning. However, most of his perception remained focused on his power and the five Aspects that each called to him with their own, individual voice.

"Therefore it is one of the most important jobs among those mages skilled strictly in the Aspect of Water to make new apple trees from the older, taste-tested ones. That way you know the fruit will be identical." Magus Britt pointed at the branch, leaning limp against Tallen's dirt work. "Use Water, Tallen. Send it into the branch. Feel the wood, and touch the leaves. Imagine the roots spreading into the ground, twisting about in search of the natural water. Grow the tree, but slowly, with control. Do not grow the apples, just the tree and its roots."

Tallen touched the Water, its cool embrace becoming more familiar with each dip. It traveled up his consciousness, flowing about his mind. He focused it into the tree limb, feeling the Water course along the veins in the wood. The miniscule buds scattered about the center branch stretched outward, creating new limbs and sprouting new leaves. The original twig swelled into a trunk. When he felt the new tree start to lean, Tallen focused his attention downward, extending new roots out into the deep, loamy soil. His own power drew upon the natural water, pulling it into the tree to replace the magical Aspect.

"Easy…" Magus Britt whispered, his mouth agape at Tallen's work.

A giggle sounded from behind. Tallen heard Boris' belly laugh, and the giggle grew into a joyous cackle.

His concentration slipped. The Water rushed through him unchecked for only a moment. The tree strained to take all the power, shooting out blossoms that popped with a dust of pollen. Many of the blooms grew into small fruits that inflated and turned red.

Magus Britt shook his shoulder. "Stop!"

Tallen let go of his power, forgetting the tree. His balance wavered, and he nearly lost his feet. Magus Britt grabbed his arm to steady him.

"What did I tell you about control?" He pointed to the tree. "Look!"

Dozens of ripe, out of season apples hung from the tree, weighing down its spindly new branches.

"That was too much." He shook his head. "It is done by rich fools to have apples when they shouldn't, but you might well have killed that tree. It certainly won't bear fruit again for several years." Magus Britt let go of Tallen when he nodded. "It has also been known to kill the mage, when the fool wasn't strong enough. You obviously are, but that does not mean you have no limit. You must learn that there are consequences to each of your actions."

Magus Britt took a step back. "Watch." His hands reached out, and this time Tallen felt the tingle deep in his gut. A small globe of fire appeared in between the mage's palms. It grew until it was the size of one of the overgrown apples on the nearby tree. "The fire is small, but it warms the air around it." He grew the globe again. Several of the branches above began to sway. "The fire warms the air, the air moves the trees, the trees shake their fruit – all is connected." He threw the fireball into the sky. It roiled and spiraled as it darted upward, growing in size. Magus Britt snapped his fingers. The ball exploded far above, spreading across the night in an umbrella of red and orange that twinkled and faded away.

"Now imagine if that fireball had exploded right here. This would be a far different place." Magus Britt brushed his hands together several times. "That is what magic can do, Tallen. If that had been Fire you were working with at that moment, you could have killed us all."

The mage's words sunk into Tallen's heart. He mulled them over, considering the bare moment he had lost control of the Water. *He's right. And that was only the tip of what I could have drawn.*

"I understand, Magus." Tallen nodded meekly. "It was my mistake. I will learn control."

Maddi and Boris walked up, both staring at the ripe apples with surprise.

"Tallen made these?" Boris walked over, picked one, and bit into it with relish. He took a few chews, and then closed his eyes, munching away. "Oh, this is delicious…" He tore into another bite, ripping away several chucks of white flesh. "I have rarely tasted as good. Crisp, clean, sweet." He grabbed another, then two more for his satchel.

Maddi pulled one from the tree for herself and bit into it. The juice trickled down her chin, catching a facet of the last light of day. Her face widened as she turned her eyes on him, rewarding his magic with a smile.

The giggle he heard before escaped her lips once again.

CHAPTER 14

"Bridgeway to the West"
– inscription on the Tearbridge

Stew nudged Tallen's shoulder, insisting on another apple to follow the one used to coax him across the gangplank.

"I don't have any more." Tallen pushed the palfrey's nose away. "Why I kept you of all father's horses, I'll never understand. You know you're a girl's horse."

Stew snorted.

"The stable at Lilly's Pad has a wonderful paddock." Sergeant Hall scratched Stew's neck. "You'll be able to stretch those legs there, old boy."

"Let's be on." Boris swung into the seat of his black stallion, his steel-shod hooves clattering against the concrete of the pier. Boris clucked his tongue, and the horse quick stepped toward the main avenue leading to where the River Road passed through West Bridgedale.

Tallen took stirrup and heaved himself into the saddle. Stew trotted forward to catch up with the Bluecloak horses. The dwarves rode on spotted ponies. Tallen pulled back on the reins, casting his eyes over his shoulder.

"Am I to jog behind you, Milord?"

Maddi stood upon the pier with her arms folded.

"You brought no horse on board." Tallen's face reddened, and he extended a hand. "You don't look like too much to add to old Stew." He kicked his foot out of the stirrup. "Come on, before we lose them."

Slapping her gloved hand into his, Maddi hoisted herself up. After settling in, she gave him back his stirrup and wrapped her arms around his torso. Tallen tapped Stew's reins. The horse skittered once upon the cobblestones, but soon adjusted to the girl's added weight.

They caught up to the others at the junction with the River

132

Road. Around the corner of a tall manor, Tallen glimpsed the bridge that gave the town its name.

Spanning the Snowbourne Fork on three concrete and stone pylons, Aelron's Bridge leaped into the sky in long arcs of bronze between the huge columns driven into riverbed. Several pieces sparkled reddish-brown, newly placed along the metal arches. However, most of them ran with long streaks of faded green.

His nose filled with Maddi's jasmine scent, Tallen pointed at the yard-wide bars of bronze. "The streaks are why most people call it Tearbridge. Not that I've seen it before, myself. I just read about it."

"It's beautiful."

Tallen gave Stew free rein, and the old horse slowed for a drink at the sparkling fountain in the center of the intersection. The lowering sun bounced off the water as it sprayed into the clear pool. The rays glittered off the Tearbridge too, although Tallen had difficulty focusing on anything other than Maddi's hands resting on his waist.

"Tallen!" Jaerd turned his horse back from the others, who continued down a side street curving off from the River Road. "Stay close!" He trotted back toward them.

Tallen frowned at his brother. "You stay close!" He spurred Stew forward. "We're the ones riding double."

Jaerd nodded his head. "Fair enough. I did not realize Maddi had no horse on board the *Shasta*. My mistake." He frowned. "I'm supposed to be keeping an eye on you."

"You were." Tallen smiled. "You just called for me, remember?"

Jaerd waved them forward, turning his own horse about. "Come on. Let's be on to Lilly's. I hear it's quite the place."

Tallen clucked his tongue to urge Stew forward, and he noticed that Sergeant Hall lingered at the edge of the square on his thick-legged horse. The soldier looked away quickly, but Tallen knew the man had been watching over him as well. Brawny sniffed in Tallen's direction, and then loped after the sergeant.

"There you are." Magus Britt met them where a side street left the River Road. "You do dawdle from time to time."

Lilly's Pad sat on an entire city block, not far from the northernmost pier along the Snowbourne. It rose three stories into the air, with several outbuildings including an elegant stable with a well-tended, ringed paddock. A large garden of both flowers and vegetables grew in a plot. Cheerful candles lit the windows, and the wide double doors stood open and inviting. The rest of their party waited for them.

Boris made a gesture toward Corporal Magrudy. "You and your squad are dismissed, Corporal. Report to the local garrison for barracks. We will pick you up when we return westward." Boris frowned. "I hope no later than Midsummer."

"Aye, Milord." Magrudy saluted, fist over heart. He repeated the gesture to Sergeant Hall, before urging his horse back the way they had come. His squad followed close behind.

Maddi hopped down from behind Tallen, his heart leaping with regret as her hands slipped away. "Your bony nag is breaking my backside."

"He's not bony," Tallen said in a mockingly sweet tone to Stew. He swung out of the saddle. "He's just...seasoned."

Maddi walked away, shaking her head. Tallen could not help but notice that her bruised backside looked no worse for wear.

The dwarves had disappeared inside at the first opportunity, but Boris and Magus Britt waited with Hall at the door. At Boris' insistence, the sergeant barked at Brawny and pointed at the stable. The big dog trotted inside, his head and tail hanging. Jaerd passed off his reins to a stableboy, and Tallen did the same, watching the others disappear through the doorway.

"Is it the food or the hospitality that gives this place its reputation?"

"Both, as I understand." Jaerd led him toward the door. "I've only passed through Bridgedale, so I've never been here before." He shrugged. "But I *have* heard of it, so that must say something."

Tallen stepped through the door, and the first thing to greet him was the scent of fresh rushes scattered about – light and sweet on the nose. Behind that hung the distant smell of roasting meat from the kitchen.

Lamb with rosemary and garlic.

Dozens of lamps and candles, resting on richly carved tables of dark, warm wood, kept the dining room comfortably lit. A few well-dressed patrons sat in hushed groups. A wide bar lined the back wall, and behind it hung the largest glass mirror Tallen had ever seen. Placed in neat rows in front of it were bottles from vintages and distillers of which Tallen had only heard lavish tales, some with labels in languages he did not recognize.

Tallen followed Maddi toward the bar, while a maid led the dwarves up the wide staircase along the back wall. He heard her mention something about hot baths.

"Why, the Earl of Mourne has returned to my humble Pad! And he has brought my favorite gentlemen with him." The brassy voice preceded the buxom woman who entered from the swinging door behind the bar. "And some new friends, as well. And here I am unprepared and looking of the dregs." She fussed with the mound of fire-red hair stacked upon her head.

"You are lovely as always, Mistress Lilly." Boris offered a short bow.

"Indeed." Sergeant Hall's eyes passed over the woman without restraint. Lilly smiled in return. "You are as beautiful as the new spring in bloom, just as you have always been."

Mistress Lilly giggled, an oddly girlish sound from a woman with such a strong frame. "Why, My Lord Earl. Bringing the enlisted men into a place too expensive for junior officers." She covered her mouth in mock startlement. "Whatever would the nobility think?"

Boris chuckled. "I am the nobility, my dear." He shrugged, still maintaining his grin. "Besides, Hall won the hunting contest. The prize was a night here. I am bound by the rules of the gamble."

"Really? Then I am ever so glad he won." Lilly cast her eyes up at the man who towered over her, one of the few men Tallen had met who might.

Hall grinned, his large, white teeth peeking out from behind stony lips. "It was all my luck, thanks to my good friend here." He swung his meaty hand toward Tallen. "The chef who will become a wizard."

"A chef?" Mistress Lilly raised one eyebrow in Tallen's direction. "Wherever at, my dear young man?"

"You've likely not heard of it. It's called the Sleeping Gryphon, way out in Dadric."

The other eyebrow leaped onto Mistress Lilly's forehead. "Why, the Gryphon is known from realm to realm as one of the finest establishments in the kingdom. It is certainly one of the oldest and most honored in our history." She snapped at the bartender who stood silently behind her. "Some of the *rangeli*, the real Urian label, not the fake stuff they make down in Avaros." She turned back to her guests. "The man may know oil and wine, but Vonstrass couldn't distill almond to save his considerable ass."

The bartender set out seven small glasses and poured a couple of fingers of the amber liquor into six. He gestured to Lilly. "For madame?"

"Since we have such honored guests tonight, I will join them. Go ahead, Julan." Lilly bowed to her guests. Tallen brought a glass to his nose. The aroma met him long before it came close. The almond hint melded with an oaky scent that made his mouth water almost as much as the lamb that wafted from the kitchen.

The proprietor hoisted her glass. "To King Arathan and his worthy men!"

"King Arathan!" Jaerd and the Bluecloaks said in unison before tipping their drinks. Tallen mumbled the same, while Maddi closed her eyes, her lips moving slightly.

The *rangeli* soothed his tongue with a honey coat and coursed down the back of his throat, warming him from within as it dripped into his stomach.

"Nice," he whispered, the bite of alcohol catching in his throat when he tried to breathe.

"Very," Maddi said firmly and tipped her empty glass to the bartender. He poured her a second from the cobalt bottle, which she sipped more slowly than the last.

"We have but five tubs in our men's bath," Lilly said over her drink. "Maester Northtower paid well for first chance at them." She nodded to Maddi. "There are open tubs in our ladies' room, however, if you would care to join the pretty dwarf girl."

"I think I will." Maddi flashed her blue eyes at Tallen before disappearing up the staircase. His imagination spun with images of her slipping into a bath, and he quickly shifted his focus back to his glass.

"In the meantime, perhaps you gents might like another?" Lilly gestured to the bartender, who filled another round.

They managed another couple before the dwarves at last emerged, clean and trimmed. Either Yrik had not washed his pointy beard, or he had taken the time to oil it again before coming down. Tallen watched him more closely of late, hoping to catch a glimpse of the dwarf mage's power. As yet, he had seen nothing.

The bath was warm and refreshing, and Tallen would have liked to linger. However, his stomach had other demands. He had craved the roasted lamb in the kitchens below the moment he caught his first whiff of it. Even after he had taken his comfortable chair in the dining room, he could not stop staring at the swinging door from whence the aroma drifted. Three waiters finally came through, each carrying an overloaded platter.

Tallen tore into the fresh, crusty bread, after dipping it in a peppered olive oil. Jaerd went straight to the roast lamb, as did Marrax Redarm. They both added a dollop of a creamy sauce that smelled of horseradish. Tallen chose the mint jelly instead, while

Maddi took mostly from the heaping pile of roasted potatoes and peas. This time Tallen had no need to wrestle with his brother for the last rib. As soon as their platter started to look empty, another with a fresh rack replaced it.

"Say, youngsters," Marrax said around a mouthful of peas. "Do you happen to know how many orcs it takes to wield an axe?"

Jaerd and Tallen looked at each other with a dubious expression. Maddi however, kept right on eating and answered, "I don't know, how many?"

The wrinkled dwarf sergeant washed down his mouthful with a gulp from his wine. "Just one." He began to snicker. "But he has a hard time getting his hand around the blade!" He broke into guffaws of laughter, slapping his thigh with his hand.

Maddi chuckled. "Good one."

Dwarf humor.

From the look on Jaerd's face, Tallen guessed it was not the first dwarven joke his brother had heard. He shook his head as he took another bite of the lamb to drown out the dwarf's cackling.

Fresh strawberries and cream followed dinner, before a group of musicians filed into the common room and onto a small stage in the corner. Two kitchen boys came out and moved empty tables around to provide space in front. Tallen raised a fresh mug of ale to them when they began to play *Open the Door and Come on In*, a quick, fun song popular for years in the Western Realm.

A small crowd began to trickle into Lilly's Pad, many in very fine dress and bedecked with jewels and jade encrusted gold bridges. One or two of the older patrons looked down their nose at the dwarves and soldiers. Some, however, seemed to recognize Boris. Tallen heard several whispers of "the Earl of Mourne". At one point, once the ale had been flowing for a while, he heard someone say "the Bastard of Mourne", followed by a conspiratorial chuckle.

What does that mean?

He did not have time to ponder it. Maddi suddenly leaned close and slipped her arm through his. One of the younger nobles had approached while Tallen listened to the crowd.

"No thanks," Maddi said to the silk-clad man. She inclined her head toward Tallen. "I only dance with him."

A rush of heat filled Tallen's ears. He took a gulp from his mug to hide it. The ale tasted as sweet as Maddi's scent. He set the mug down on the table and twined his fingers through hers.

"And I only dance with her."

The young nobleman nodded with grace and returned sheepishly to his groaning friends.

Maddi squeezed his hand once then let go and leaned back into her own space. "Thanks for the help. Sometimes a girl just wants a mug and a pipe in peace, you know."

He nodded, regretfully allowing her reclaim her arm. "I understand. I'm always here for you."

"We'll see." She laughed and took a long drink. The musicians began a fast tune that Tallen did not recognize. Maddi smiled behind her cup then set it down next to his. "Come on! This is one of my favorites." She stood up and reached out her hand to him, bouncing as she backed toward the dance floor. "Join me!" She eyed the cluster of noble boys. "Please," she mouthed in silence.

Tallen stood and took her hand, and they spun about the dance floor. He noticed Maester Northtower offer Tilli his hand, and she took it with a shy grin. They joined the much younger humans twirling about. Then Maddi's sky blue eyes drew Tallen's gaze, twinkling as she laughed, spinning about him. He lost track of everything else, drifting in that moment. The other dancers and the room about them blurred. The music and her brilliant eyes melded together in his mind, drawing him ever toward her.

It ended far too fast. Everyone laughed, breaking into applause for the band. Maddi squeezed Tallen's grip. She leaned forward for a moment, then hesitated, and lightly brushed his cheek with her lips.

Clearing her throat, she released his hands one at a time. "I need some rest tonight. Thanks for…for being nice." She darted away through the back of the room and slipped up the staircase. Tallen watched her go, confused and elated, but mostly just sad to see her leave.

"Women," Jaerd huffed, handing Tallen a small glass of bourbon.

"I'll drink to that." Boris hefted his mug and nudged the bleary-eyed Battlemage sitting next to him. "How about you, Joz?"

The mage grumbled and downed his ale.

The bourbon burned when Tallen sent it to the back of his throat, slamming the glass down next to his brother's.

I hope we get to sleep in late before we have to board that boat tomorrow.

Tallen was uncertain whether it was the pounding in his head or the straining of his bladder that woke him. Jaerd snored away on the other bed in the small room they shared. Knowing that the pressure would get no better, Tallen swung his legs over the edge and stood up. The chamber pot rested underneath the window. As he stepped over toward it his foot caught on his belt, rattling the dagger Jaerd had given him.

Jaerd mumbled something, shifting under his covers. He sat up. "Oh, it's just you." He shook his head. "Must have been a weird dream I was having."

After he finished, Tallen sat back down on his bed. Brawny barked out in the stable, his throaty voice carrying through the open window. Someone shouted at him from down the street. Tallen dug through his pack, searching for his pipe. He stuffed the bowl and reached into his power for the tiniest trickle of Fire. An orange ember began to glow. He smiled at the ease with which he could use his magic. *I'll never need to buy matches again.*

Jaerd shifted his covers. "Here, give me a puff of that, so I don't have to fill my own."

Tallen passed the pipe to his brother. As he leaned over the chamber pot, a harsh stench wafted up to his nose. "I'll get rid of that."

Standing up, Tallen grabbed the pot and carried it toward the open windows. He dumped the malodorous contents toward the street below.

"Flaming... piss!" a growling voice shouted from outside the window.

"What the..." Jaerd leapt to the window. "Thieves and enemies!" He grabbed his sword propped against the bed, pulled the scabbard away, and cast it aside. He shouted at the top of his lungs. "Enemies on the walls!"

Tallen stumbled away as Jaerd thrust his sword out the window and downward. A scream of pain responded. When he drew the sword back, darkness covered the first six inches of its lustrous steel. Jaerd pushed Tallen toward the door, handing him his dagger.

"Get out! There are three more on a ladder." He opened the door and shoved Tallen through. "It's you they want!" Jaerd turned back toward the window before slamming the door shut with his foot. Tallen heard the bar drop behind it.

He banged on the door to Boris' room. "Earl Boris! Magus Britt! Everyone wake up! They are climbing in the windows!"

Tallen sensed a tingle deep within his gut, and knew someone summoned the Fire Aspect. Boris came stomping out, his silvery longsword in hand. Magus Britt followed close behind. Tallen sensed more Fire, then a vague itching in his forehead – just the tiniest bit of Water.

A bolt of white-hot lightning shot out from Magus Britt's fingertips and crackled about the two figures within their room. They jerked stiff then collapsed as the lighting receded, snapping one last time over their prone, smoking bodies.

Magus Britt shook his hand as if it stung. "I've burned their ladder, and the others on this side of the inn. They are probably coming in the other windows too."

As if in answer, Sergeant Hall came crashing out the rearmost door. He held a broken bedpost in one hand and carried an unconscious Mistress Lilly over his other shoulder. Blood ran from his temple. He nodded to Boris. "They won't be coming through that room."

Tallen tugged Magus Britt's cloak. "Jaerd barred himself in!"

He felt an odd thump in his chest. It could only be the Earth Aspect. Another door burst open, and Darve and Yrik tumbled out. The clash of steel rang loudly behind them. A young nobleman stumbled out of his own room, his neck opened into a second, gaping red mouth. Blood spurted from between his fingers. He tumbled to his knees, as two dark figures in leather armor charged out from behind him.

"Orcs!" Darve ran one through from behind with his rune-carved longsword.

Boris grabbed Tallen's arm in a tight grip and shoved him towards Hall. "Get him to cover behind the bar. That's where we will fall back."

Hall nodded, his wrinkled brow obscured by seeping red. He pulled Tallen toward the stairs.

He did not struggle against the sergeant, if that were even possible. Instead, he shouted toward Boris, "Get Jaerd!"

Down in the main room he heard a thumping noise, each blow followed by a creaking sound.

"They're coming in the main door." Sergeant Hall set Lilly down behind the bar. "You stay here with her, and keep your head down." He disappeared.

Tallen leaned over the inn's proprietor, searching for a wound he might bind. Lilly moaned and struggled limply against his touch. Suddenly the scent of jasmine wafted to Tallen's nose. That alone prevented him from screaming when the cool hand covered his mouth.

"It's me," Maddi whispered in his ear. "This inn is a death trap. We have to find a way out." She paused. "To get some help."

At first, Tallen thought to protest. But when he looked into her eyes, when he saw the resolve hiding fear. He gave in. "If I know anything about kitchens, there is always a rear entry for deliveries."

"Then let's go." She grabbed his hand and pulled him toward back.

The rear door was secured with a bar. They paused for a second, listening, but no sounds of intruders passed through. Tallen crouched close behind Maddi, who held a knife in each hand. He gripped Jaerd's dagger more tightly in his own.

The bar slid back easily, and Tallen pulled the door open to find himself face to face with a surprised orc. An acrid stench stung his nose as it exhaled a startled breath. He lashed out with a controlled blast of Air, throwing the snarling warrior across the alley to crumple against a stone wall. A second orc hurdled its fallen comrade and lunged towards him. Tallen scrambled to grab Air again, but not before Maddi leaped around him to stick a dirk in the orc's neck with a swift, sudden strike.

"Thanks," he gasped, trying to regain his breath.

The banging against the front door intensified, and a massive crash resounded through the inn. Shouts of rage and pain followed, mingled with the ring of steel on steel.

"Go! Before they send anyone else here." Maddi pushed him into the alley, slipping along the inn's rear wall. Tallen followed, copying her movements as closely as he could.

The plaza on the north side of the inn stood empty. A few figures carrying torches gathered in the distance by the docks.

"Those must be the dockside night watch." Maddi ran toward them, dashing out into the open square.

"Maddi, wait!" Tallen raced after her, casting his eyes over his shoulder toward the inn's entrance. A half dozen armed figures pushed their way through the front door, though he saw no signs of more entering through the second story windows.

He turned his eyes back toward Maddi, who was already closing on the docks. He sucked air in short, painful bursts as he strained for his longest stride. His heart pounded in fear, but inside his head, he was strangely calm. The colors of the Aspects floated near his perception.

If only Magus Britt had taught me something more useful than growing apple trees and moving seeds of grain!

Maddi skidded to a halt in front of him, her eyes fixed on several small boats tied up along the Snowbourne. The dozen dark figures stopped their random movement, coalesced together, and began to trot toward her. Tallen heard the sound of steel sliding along leather. The light of a torch caught a pair of eyes.

Red! Orcs!

"Maddi!" She looked back at him. "This way!" He waved her toward another side road, leading to a closer turn of the river. Maddi ran toward him, and the orc squad charged.

Tallen caught her wrist at full speed, taking care to avoid the knife. He looked to their right upon reaching the pier. The docks ended with nowhere to go but the river. They turned left, pounding up the wharf toward the set of small boats they had seen before. The orcs followed them around the corner, shouting with anger and the thrill of the chase.

Maddi spun and cast a dagger into the face of the lead orc, dropping him like a sack of flour. The others surged forward, snarling in rage. Maddi grabbed Tallen's hand and pulled him toward the nearest boat, tied to a cleat at the edge of the pier.

"We can escape on the river!" She hauled him closer.

An inexplicable sense of dread sunk into Tallen's mind. The silvery white presence of the Psoul Aspect throbbed. He turned his head toward the inn, now far up the street. The orcs chasing them slowed and quieted. They shifted their direction toward the figure approaching Tallen and Maddi.

The beast loomed over the three orcs flanking it. Each clung onto a chain attached to a collar around the creature's neck. Its wide shoulders hunched over, and the long, thick arms ended in meaty fists that almost dragged on the ground. A hide covering, thick and colored much like its own, covered its chest and loins. The thick jaw and protruding lower fangs reminded Tallen of the orcs who leashed it, as did the faintly glowing pink eyes. But those eyes held nothing of the orcs' cruel intelligence, only ignorant malice.

The monster roared, sending ripples across the moonlit Snowbourne.

"By the Talismans…" Maddi's dirk hung loose in her fingers. "Troll!"

The main group of orcs joined with the beast and its handlers. Together they moved cautiously forward, certain their prey stood trapped with its back to the water.

Maddi backed towards the boat, her eyes locked on the lumbering troll. Her foot caught on the rope, and she tripped backward. Tallen heard the sick thump of her head smacking against the gunwale.

"Maddi!" Tallen scrambled down to her, cradling her body. She moaned, eyes fluttering, and her hand gripped the front of his shirt, while the other still clung desperately to her dirk. He stood up, lifting her surprisingly light body in his arms.

Opening his mind and spirit, Tallen embraced the colors fluttering around inside his head. He remembered watching Magus Britt inside the inn just a few minutes ago. The red-hot inferno of Fire roiled to the forefront. Tallen let it come to him, let the Fire flow into his body. He focused on the rushing troll and orcs, their approach slowed down to the moments between heartbeats by his accelerated awareness. He took a second part of his mind and dipped it into the cool familiarity of Water. He pulled it forth, bringing it into contact with the Fire.

The lightning did not erupt from his fingers, as he had witnessed with Magus Britt. Instead, it ripped up from the ground beneath the orcs, leaping from them to the troll, silent in the split second of time. Blinding light crackled around the creatures and a single burning column shot into the night sky, punching a hole through the darkness. Tallen released all of his gathered power into the electrical stream, cutting it off with a stroke of finality.

The concussion smashed him to the ground, Maddi's body landing on top of him. He scrambled, thoughts wheeling out of control, and a strong smell of cauterized meat in his nostrils. He struggled to haul her body into the boat then tumbled onboard himself. The dagger Jaerd had given him lay where he had dropped it on the wharf. With his last conscious thought, Tallen grabbed it and cut the rope tying the boat to the dock. The knife clattered to the stone pier from his limp hand, as the boat gently bumped its way into the current.

CHAPTER 15

Trolls do not appear in any recorded history before the Cataclysm. Considering that, and their obvious physical similarities with orcs, most scholars have theorized that the chaotic powers of the Cataclysm caused a mutation of the orc. The result was the troll, a largely mindless creature found strictly in the mountain passages of the Dragonscales.
— "The Tarmorian Bestiary" by Dorias Ravenhawke

Jaerd slammed the bar down behind his brother and spun on his heel. Two figures jumped through the window, each carrying a scimitar and leather wrapped cudgel.

They still want him alive, or they would have burned us out!

Jaerd blinked as an orange glow leaped up outside the window. It died down as fast as it began. He heard the screaming of orcs in pain.

Must be Magus Britt.

The two orcs advanced warily, holding their weapons out in front of them. Jaerd tightened his grip on his sword.

Come on Shar'leen, don't let me down, girl.

He let them make the first move, one daring a careless thrust of his scimitar. Shar'leen rang true as Jaerd parried the blow, and his riposte took the orc's hand from his arm.

It bellowed with pain and backed away, dropping the cudgel next to the sword and hand already lying on the floor. The wounded creature staggered back towards the window as the second orc moved across as if to protect it. He swung his scimitar at Jaerd, far more careful to preserve his guard.

The curved sword clattered against Shar'leen. Jaerd parried a second and third swing. The wounded orc slipped over the window's edge. Jaerd heard it tumble to the ground over the increasing ruckus of battle echoing through the rest of the inn.

"Are you certain that you don't want to follow your friend?"

The orc lunged forward with a roar, swinging his blade in a swift arc. Jaerd batted it away, turning his movement into a thrust that ran the orc through its upper chest. The red eyes blinked in surprise.

"You should have followed the other one."

Jaerd twisted the blade.

Wild barking from the locked stable wrenched him out of his battle lust. He drew Shar'leen free of her bloody sheath and turned from the empty window. Tossing the bar up, he swung the door open onto chaos. Jaerd tasted brimstone on the air, and he smelled cooked flesh. Boris stood close to his door, an eerily keen longsword in his hands. Magus Britt hovered behind him, still in his nightshirt.

"How many?" Jaerd stepped into the hall. Several of the dwarves stood there in varying states of dress and armament. Orc corpses littered the floor. Jaerd saw the bodies of at least two human patrons among them. "And where is Tallen?"

"Joslyn and Yrik have eliminated their ladders," Earl Boris told him as he checked each room of the second floor for any other attackers. "Hall has your brother under cover behind the bar." A sudden banging sounded from downstairs. "I think we should join them."

With Boris in the lead, they raced down to the common room. The heavy bar over the front door strained with each blow. Jaerd saw Sergeant Hall standing there, a large bedpost in one hand and a chair in the other. His massive axe was nowhere to be seen. Tilli clambered onto the bar with her bow, an arrow already nocked. Yrik and Magus Britt stood in front of her.

"Is Tallen…" The inward crashing of the front doors cut off Jaerd's words.

Tilli's arrow caught the lead orc in the neck, turning its scream into a gurgle. More followed, swarming towards the defenders.

"The Bluecloaks!" Hall bellowed, throwing the chair. It crashed into another orc, shattering upon impact and driving splinters into the creature's red eyes. The sergeant rushed forward, swinging the broken bedpost. Another arrow from Tilli flew over him, claiming a second victim.

Earl Boris gestured to the skirmish line. "We'd better get in there before Hall kills them all. I want a prisoner."

"I can help with that." Yrik reached out his hand and an eldritch light flashed from it. Jaerd expected it to blind him, but when the flash receded, his eyes worked as well as before. That did not appear to be the same case with the orcs, who suddenly fumbled about, some stabbing their compatriots in blindness.

Magus Britt gave the dwarf a quizzical look. "Fire and Earth?"

The dwarf mage nodded. "The Earth focuses the light of Fire on each target specifically."

"Never mind theory!" Boris gripped his sword. "Cover us!"

Jaerd followed the earl into the melee. He tried to grab one of the blinded orcs, but several more charged in, forcing him to take the defensive. He parried and gave ground, conscious of the fact that he wore no armor. All fear was driven from his mind as he slipped into rhythm of battle. He focused on one assailant, hoping to gain a quick advantage, when another slipped through his left guard. A burning slice of pain shot up his thigh. Jaerd winced, his free hand dropping to the wound, while the other knocked away the orc's second blow.

"Damn you!" Jaerd spat as he thrust through a hole in the orc's guard, skewering his liver. Thick, crimson blood clung to Shar'leen when he pulled it free. The warrior's death did not ease the sting in his leg.

Lightning shot out from Magus Britt and coruscated across an attacker's skin. It dropped to the floor, eyes and hair smoking. Darve Northtower ran another orc through. Jaerd fell back behind the dwarf, gripping his wound and cursing.

Another arrow flew above Jaerd's head. He turned to see Hall deal one last assailant a massive deathblow. A dozen orcs twitched in a pile, strewn from the door almost to the bar. Brawny still barked outside, occasionally pausing to crash against the stable door.

"Damn!" Earl Boris turned a corpse over to see lifeless maroon eyes. "I wanted one alive."

Jaerd limped to the bar. Mistress Lilly huddled in the corner, eyes wide in fear, a bottle of wine held in her hand like a cudgel.

"Where's Tallen?" He stumbled behind the bar, his foot slipping in the blood that ran down his leg. Lilly looked at him, a stupefied expression on her face. *She's useless.* He grimaced, and threw open the kitchen door. The room stood empty, the rear door resting ajar. He hobbled back to the common room. "Has anyone—"

A thunderous clap ripped through the inn. Several windows shattered. Magus Britt fell hard on his rump, while Yrik collapsed, unmoving.

The sky was clear tonight.

Jaerd looked to Magus Britt, who held his head in pain. "Tallen?"

The Battlemage nodded, his face bleak. He pointed toward the front door, in the direction of the docks, gesturing madly.

"Let's go." Earl Boris darted out the door, a limping Sergeant Hall on his heels.

Darve Northtower and Marrax Redarm followed close behind him. Bran nursed both Yrik and Brax, who stared numbly at the orc knife protruding from his upper arm. Tilli offered her shoulder to help Jaerd. The bleeding appeared to have slowed in his thigh. He let go of the wound, placing his hand on Tilli's sturdy, yet feminine shoulder.

"Ready?" she whispered.

"Yep."

Stooping, he let her take some of his weight, and they made their way out to the street. The others ran a few dozen yards ahead. The shatter of breaking wood was followed closely by Brawny darting across the yard at full stride to chase after the soldiers. A few of the bravest citizens of Bridgedale stepped outside their doors, eyes blinking in surprise and alarm. Three torch-bearing watchmen ran toward Lilly's Pad, a pale green bridge stitched upon their brown tabards.

Jaerd tried to move faster, Tilli helping as much as she could. No sounds of battle came to his ears. Boris and the dwarves gathered not far from the docks around a dark, smoking mass. The stench hit Jaerd's nose when he approached the first pile, and his stomach turned. Pieces of glowing, slagged metal protruded from piles of ash and charred bone.

Boris kicked the massive chunk of char in the center. A huge, blackened tooth clattered across the cobblestone. Brawny crept forward, his teeth bared and a low growl in his throat. He sniffed the tooth tentatively, then snorted and backed away, his hackles thick on his shoulders.

"This had to be a troll." Boris rubbed his dimpled chin. "Nothing else has teeth like that."

Hall leaned on the broken bedpost, still clasped in his hand and covered with gore. "A troll, sir? This deep within the kingdom?" He patted Brawny's forehead as he bent over and picked up the tooth, juggling it in his hand as if it were still hot. "Down the Snowbourne, do you think?"

Pointing with his silvery longsword, Boris frowned at the plank boats tied up along the wharf. "It looks so." He walked over to the nearest and reached down to pull a heavy, black tarp up from its bottom. "Hidden in the night." The earl's brow furrowed and he knelt down.

Jaerd limped closer. "What is it, My Lord?"

Boris stretched out his hand, a look of deep concern in his eyes. A familiar dagger rested in it. A few drops of blood lay splattered about where the weapon had fallen. Suffocating panic welled up in Jaerd's chest.

"The dagger I gave Tallen," he whispered, taking it in his free hand. With the aid of his training, as well as his own natural willpower, he forced the anxiety down. He twisted it within his heart and forged it into resolve. "Do you think he drowned? He was a very strong swimmer."

Leaning closer to the wharf's edge, the earl reached downward, coming up with a piece of wet rope. "It's the same as the line that ties up those three boats." He ran his finger along the frayed edge. "But it's been freshly cut." Boris pulled the other end where it tied to a cleat. "Another boat was docked here."

Jaerd moved toward one of the remaining orc boats and tried to swing his leg over the gunwale. A hiss of pain escaped his lips as his wounded muscle failed to cooperate. Tilli stumbled under his shifted weight, but they did not fall.

"Damn them to the Fires." Jaerd slammed his fist against the boat. "We must go after them. We can't let them have Tallen."

"Oh, they've been damned to the Fires, alright." Magus Britt's voice barked from behind Jaerd. "Tallen's Fire."

Jaerd turned his head to see the mage stumbling around the burned corpses, some more recognizable as such now that he knew what they were.

"I don't think one of them survived." Magus Britt scanned the destruction, fists on hips. "And if I read the resonance right, and I usually do, it was Tallen and Maddi alone in that boat."

About to protest, Jaerd noticed the crowd gathering near the scattered ash piles, frightened faces curled in revulsion. One of the watchmen leaned close, a curious expression on his face. He jumped back with a shout when several bones settled at his touch. More men in brown tabards ran into the square.

"We need to deal with this." Jaerd nodded his head, the panic gone. "Then we can follow them." He looked to Magus Britt, who still rubbed his temples. "You can track him, right?"

The graying mage nodded his head, producing another wince. "I can find him." He knelt down next to one of the ash piles closest to the big one. He reached into it with a knife, digging around for a few moments. Jaerd frowned in distaste.

"Aha!" Magus Britt knocked a small, rounded stone free from the smoking ash and picked it up with his cloak. "Another tracing stone. I've had a chance to study the other one since Gavanor. They are definitely tuned to your brother." Magus Britt lifted his eyes, a small grin creeping onto his face. "I think I could use this to walk right up to him in a crowd of thousands."

"You can use them?" Earl Boris lifted an eyebrow. "You never told me that."

Tucking the smooth stone into a pouch, Magus Britt shrugged. "I just discovered it for myself, and only the presence of this second stone confirmed it for me."

A murmur began to pass through the mustering crowd as a second watchman pulled a fanged jawbone from an ash pile. Enough veterans lived in Bridgedale for Jaerd to pick the word "orc" out from among the hushed voices.

Magus Britt looked at Boris and thumbed over his shoulder. "You should probably see to that mess, and quit berating me."

The earl frowned, but said nothing as he marched toward the citizens. For the first time Jaerd realized he wore his travelling leathers and blue tunic. There was a black falcon stitched out upon the upper breast, usually hidden by his cloak. The three stars on his collar and the silver stitching of a Bluecloak officer glittered in the assembled torchlight.

The man must sleep in his uniform. Jaerd looked down at the ugly wound on his thigh. *Perhaps that's not such a bad idea.*

Marrax Redarm stepped over and offered Jaerd his shoulder, relieving a thankful Tilli of her burden. "Lean on me, you big malook."

The earl placed his sword point down on the cobblestones. "People of Bridgedale, I will not lie to you. These were orcs infiltrated by foul means within the borders of our kingdom." The murmurs turned to shouts. Several people looked about wildly as if dark figures with blood-red eyes might leap out upon them from the shadows.

"But know this." Boris swung his sword upward, brandishing it out before him. "We have wiped out this company, and now we know they are here." He nodded with confidence at the people. "More Bluecloaks will gather." He slapped a brown-coated watchman on the back. "The men of your city will be ready and redoubled." The earl pointed out toward the crowd. "Some of you will perhaps choose this moment to stand up and join your Baron's guard. Take the responsibility upon yourselves to stand a watch." He nodded to them again. "Be ready, but be brave. A time of change comes upon our land."

Saluting the crowd again with his sword brought on a few cheers. The assembled throng began to disperse, hurrying away to their homes. Candles popped up in the windows all along Dock Street.

With Marrax Redarm's help, Jaerd limped over toward Earl Boris and Magus Britt. "Well, said, sir."

"Indeed," Magus Britt added with a nod.

"Now what about Tallen?" Jaerd adjusted his grip upon Shar'leen's hilt.

"We will follow him within the hour." Boris furrowed his brow as he looked at Jaerd's leg, and then at Hall, who leaned against a wall with one hand pressed against his still bleeding head. "After we find a healer."

CHAPTER 16

*The Great River Andon and its many Forks are the very veins in which
courses the lifeblood of Gannon. Only the far-flung Southern Realm
does not touch one of its banks. Aravath the Navigator claimed the river
and its entire basin for the People of Gan when he brought them back
after their four century Exile ended.*
— "Second History of Gannon, Vol. II" by Elyn Bravano

A dull, throbbing pain drug Tallen from oblivion. It sharpened as his
senses woke, searing into his brain with every thump of his heart. He
blinked, one eye crusted over and barely opening. The glare of sun
sparkling off water honed the pain lancing through his skull. Tallen
smacked his lips and moaned around his numb, cottony tongue.

"I found a waterskin, if you need it."

Maddi's voice worked like a balm to his pain. Tallen rolled
over on one side, shifting to find comfort on the bottom of the
boat bouncing along the Andon.

"Please," he croaked, reaching blindly toward her voice.

His fingers met cool leather. Tallen squinted his good eye
open a crack, just enough to see the wooden stopper. He shifted
onto his back and pulled the cork free. The cool water washed
over his dry tongue, softening his cracked lips. It eased down
into his stomach like the front edge of a returned river washing
down its old, parched bed.

"You'll want to go easy on that at first, or you'll just—"

Tallen heaved over the gunwale, losing most of what had
reached his stomach.

"Never mind." Maddi's suppressed giggle rang in Tallen's
numbed ears.

"Sor...sorry," he whispered, his voice rough and broken.
He stretched out his hand, cupping a bit of the river water and
splashing it onto his face. Opening his crusted eye, he shifted
back into the boat and leaned against its curved wall. Tallen tried
another small sip of the water. This time, it stayed down.

"I also found another bag with some jerky in it," Maddi said, her voice filled with doubt. She held out a cloth pouch at arm's length. "It was in the back of the boat."

"The stern." Tallen's voice regained some of its strength, but the pain in his head remained.

Maddi titled her head to one side. "What?"

"The back of the boat – it's called the stern." He sipped from the waterskin, his stomach happily accepting the liquid.

Maddi snorted. "Whatever, *Admiral*." She shook the bag again. "I haven't had the nerve to try it. Who knows what an orc might eat."

Tallen took the offered bag and stuck his nose in it. "Smells like goat." He pulled out a piece and sniffed it closely. "Thyme, garlic, and smoke – I don't recognize the wood offhand." Tallen pulled a tentative bite and chewed. "Yep. Goat. I've made similar."

He took a second piece before handing the bag back to Maddi. She sniffed and set it down. Tallen shrugged and tore off a much larger bite, washing it down with a gulp of water.

Maddi nibbled at her lip, staring first at the bag, then at Tallen devouring his second piece. He heard her stomach rumble and reached to grab yet another strip.

"Hold on." Maddi snatched the bag away, her blue eyes catching the morning sunlight even though her scowl shaded them. "I'll try it."

Tallen watched her pull out a deep maroon piece. A few salt crystals reflected the sun back at the river, along with a golden flake of dried garlic. Maddi's nose wrinkled as she sniffed the jerky. A sudden wave bumped the boat and the piece almost went up her nostril. Her frown deepened, but her stomach growled again. Tallen smiled seeing her bite down on it, trying not to touch the meat with her lips. The grimace disappeared, though, while she chewed.

Tallen handed her the waterskin. "This helps."

She took a sip, chewed a little more, and then swallowed, her grimace returning.

He lifted an eyebrow. "Do you find it edible?"

"Barely."

Maddi shifted her cloak about her. He realized for the first time that was all she wore over thin nightclothes, and all he had on were his under breeches. He shivered when the breeze came off the water, suddenly far colder.

"Um, did they happen to leave any spare cloaks back there too?"

Maddi's chewing grimace became a roguish grin. "Sorry. I know better than to storm out into a nighttime battle without grabbing my cloak first."

Frowning made Tallen's head throb again, though it had eased since he first opened his eyes. "I didn't have much choice."

They sat in silence for a time, eating while they bobbed along near the northern shore of the Andon. When a tall pleasure boat sped by, sails full under the spring westerlies, Tallen waved for help. The group of young people, obviously from well to do noble and merchant families, waved back at the two of them, giggling behind sparkling glasses of white wine, while a string quartet played from the rear deck. Tallen caught a whiff of bacon, sausage, and other tasty morning foods floating out from the galley.

Maddi wrapped her cloak tighter about her body. "Rich kids on a pleasure cruise. Just what I needed this morning."

The boat sailed on ahead, the music drifting behind it. Tallen let his thoughts float on the wind with the melody. The pain in his head eased while he sipped on the waterskin, occasionally passing it back to Maddi.

He frowned with concern when he noticed the little fleck of dried blood along her hairline. "How's your head, by the way?"

Maddi's hand fluttered up to the wound, gingerly pressing at it. She winced. "It'll be fine. It's healing."

Tallen offered her a smile, despite the aching inside his skull. "Soon you'll be able to heal with a touch."

Curling her lip in doubt, Maddi shook her head. "I have a feeling it's a bit more complicated than that."

The smile faded from his lips. "No doubt."

"Speaking of complicated – what exactly happened after I… after I fell last night?" Maddi knit her dark eyebrows together. "That thing…that troll, I thought it would rip us apart." She wrung her hands. "I woke here and found us floating in the open river. At first, I thought you were dead. I had to search for your pulse before I moved you."

Tallen shook his head, the ache reminding him to remain still. *I remember what happened, but I don't want to. Even orcs scream in fear when they die.*

Dread crept up his spine when he remembered the faces of those he had killed. He blinked his eyes and stared out over the water, watching the shore pass by. Forcing his emotions down, he cleared his throat.

"I killed them, Maddi. Killed them all."

She frowned and leaned forward, resting her hand on his bare knee before speaking. "I've seen enough of your magic in the last few days to know that anything might be possible from you."

She leaned back and folded her hands in her lap. "You saved my life. Thank you."

Maddi's touch and soft words woke more than just his heart, sitting here alone on the river, the scent of her hair in his nostrils. He shifted in his seat and cleared his throat. "You saved me first… and my brother."

Her smile warmed him more than the early summer sun, now well above the bow of the boat. Tallen smiled back, before quickly turning his face sternward to hide the flush of color he felt rising on his cheeks.

A low prow bore down upon them, splitting the water before it. Three masts full of sail bulged forward, pulling the ship faster than the current.

Maddi's voice lowered and she wrapped herself deep in her cloak. "That's not the *Shasta*."

Tallen's stomach dropped. The dark-stained prow took on a menacing cast, slicing toward them. He reached for his power, but found his numbed senses fumbling. Only a bare hint of the Aspects hovered out of his reach. His headache flared anew, until he noticed the blue pennant snapping at the prow of the boat, a rampant silver dragon dancing in the wind.

"It's a Bluecloak craft," he whispered, squinting against the breeze to scan her deck.

Maddi leaned in behind him. "That doesn't comfort me as much as it does you."

A man stretched out from the prow with a looking glass. His sandy blond hair whipping about above a green tunic caught Tallen's eye. Blue cloaks fluttered behind him, and a large wolfhound leaned into the wind, his paws upon the gunwale and his tongue lolling out. The men waved and pointed at their little watercraft.

"That's Jaerd!" Tallen waved back, the boat wobbling as he stood.

"Easy!" Maddi grabbed her seat. "Don't drown us just before we get rescued."

The chasing boat swept up beside them, the faces of Magus Britt and Boris coming into focus, their expressions nearly as concerned as Jaerd's. Brawny bounced around, barking with glee. The crew reefed the sails, and the pilot brought the ship alongside the orc boat. Sailors tossed a rope to Tallen's outstretched hands.

Just as his feet touched the deck, and before even Jaerd could close the distance between, Magus Britt took Tallen in his grip. The Battlemage grabbed his temples, and drew him downward, staring deep into his eyes. He felt a wisp of Magus Britt's power, but had no sense of which Aspect he used, so clouded still were his senses.

"Young fool!" The mage found a way to look down his nose at Tallen, even though he stood almost half a yard shorter. "You could burn yourself out by doing things like that before you've been any damn use to anyone. I saw the damage you dealt. You could have killed that troll and those orcs with a fraction of the power you drew upon." His frown softened and Tallen felt the Battlemage's power switch off. "You haven't ruined yourself though, luck be upon us. I would bet your headache is one for the ages, however." He released Tallen and shook his head. "It should teach you the lesson about control that I have failed to."

Tallen nodded. He sensed Maddi hiding behind him, but she remained silent.

"I'm just glad to find you alive!" Jaerd pushed his way past the Bluecloak mage and threw his arms around his brother. "Damn it, boy. I thought I'd lost you." Jaerd stepped backward, still clasping Tallen's shoulders at arm's length. "Mother would have killed me. Glynn would have had to tell her, because I might have fled the kingdom." Jaerd's smile of relief shifted to a frown. "When I pushed you out of the room, I did not intend for you to flee the entire inn. What fool notion made you run to the docks? You should have stayed where we could protect you."

Tallen bowed his head. "I...I don't know. I just grabbed Maddi and ran, pulling her along." He felt her hand brush his back.

Magus Britt grumbled. "Again with the impulse reactions. You must learn to think before you act, boy. That is the first lesson of a true wizard, and I don't know that you'll ever learn it."

"Oh, come now, Joz," Boris said, putting a hand on the mage's shoulder. "The lad took out a troll and an entire orc platoon the first time he used magic in battle. That deserves some credit."

Magus Britt's scowl deepened. "Perhaps. Likely he will get enough of that in his life, if he survives." The Battlemage juggled a smooth, glassy stone in his hand, identical to the one they had found on the orcs in Gavanor. "However, he almost burned himself out in the process. Controlling your power – controlling yourself – will be your greatest trial in life."

With one hand still reluctant to leave Tallen's shoulder, Jaerd placed the other fist on his hip. "That is any man's greatest trial. My brother will be up to it." He turned back to Tallen. "You've learned a lesson here, right? Several, if I'm not mistaken."

Bowing his head meekly, Tallen folded his hands in front of him. "I have. And my head feels as if Sergeant Hall's axe split it."

155

Boris reached out with a folded bundle of brown wool. "Good! Now put a shirt on."

Tallen hurried to comply.

Tilli Broadoak stepped up from behind the humans with another rucksack Tallen recognized. She handed it to Maddi, who whispered thanks.

"Rule one for a new recruit – don't ever leave your squad." Jaerd nodded at him with a furrowed brow. "That's one you might find applicable here."

"I promise." Tallen fought to keep the red from his cheeks. He pulled on the cotton shirt, fumbling with the ties to hide his blush.

"Excellent." With a last pat on Tallen's shoulder Jaerd stepped toward the rear cabin. "Come on. I'll show you to the rest of your stuff. The *River Spike* is a much more impressive craft than the *Shasta*."

Tallen pulled the apprentice's tunic over his head before following Jaerd. He turned back to look at Maddi. "Are you coming?"

Hugging her rucksack to her chest, Maddi nodded. "I will not change out here for the crew to enjoy, that's for sure."

Tilli scowled at the men hovering nearby. "There is a small room for us to share next to theirs. I have the rest of your things there."

With a smile of thanks, Maddi started after her. Only then did Tallen turn to follow Jaerd. His older brother gave him a knowing look and a shake of his head before they ducked into the shade of the cabin.

"Get some rest," Magus Britt called after him. "We will train together after the evening meal, even if you still cannot touch your power."

It strained his mind close to the breaking point that evening, but with the Battlemage's guidance, Tallen eventually touched the source of his magic. Afterward, he collapsed onto the bunk next to Jaerd, asleep before his head touched the pillow.

His heart lightened by the speed of the ship, Tallen spent the next several days enjoying the last leg of their voyage. With a steady breeze pulling them along, the well-manicured fields, manors, and towns of the Eastern Realm flew by. Murky swamps eventually passed along the southern banks when the *River Spike* neared the confluence with the fast, deep waters of the Graybourne Fork.

He stood on deck and watched a large flotilla of commercial

ships gathered where the rivers met, some switching channels, while others sought the harbors of Forksmeet. They moved about like little toys engaged in an intricate dance. Each knew the steps by heart, as did the captain of the *River Spike*.

The three green trees on gold of House Bahalan fluttered from the tall towers rambling along the southern bank of the Andon and the eastern bank of the Graybourne. When they neared the city, Boris ordered a boat let over the side. A Bluecloak sailor hopped on board, and the earl handed him a leather tube, one that Tallen knew carried a message for Baron Dandric.

"The attack in Bridgedale could not be kept quiet, like the one in Gavanor," Jaerd said, watching the sailor heave against the oars of his dinghy. "Earl Boris issued a similar message to Baron Wilis before we left Bridgedale. What I wouldn't give to hear what he had to say to them. I just hope he didn't mention you."

Tallen shifted, uneasy. "Why would he?"

Jaerd kept his eyes on the messenger, and his voice remained level. "You're the one the orcs are hunting."

Looking down to see his whitened knuckles gripping the rail, Tallen forced himself to take deep breaths. Gradually, his hands released their death grip.

The Andon River slowed to a lazy pace and spread over two miles wide once it took on the waters of Graybourne Fork. The sailors spread all their canvas before the wind, and the *River Spike* shot past slower, heavier ships. Tallen watched the northern shore roll away in the distance, sloping uphill toward centuries-old, manicured farms that checkered the land. In a few places, the clustered buildings of a town broke the checkerboard. The southern shore crowded less, with only a few villages to break up the stretches of wild, swampy forests. In some places, aspen, cypress, and cottonwood spread their branches over the water wherever they could find refuge from human expansion.

As with every morning on the boat, Magus Britt called upon him early and dragged him out to meditate near the prow before they ate their breakfast. Tallen could not touch his power, only sense it, let it roil in the back of his mind. It tempted him, but the pain and fear of his mistake at Bridgedale remained a sturdy bulwark against his power's temptation. *I must learn control.*

When the evening sun sank toward the river, Magus Britt summoned him again. This time the mage let him touch his power, teaching him different uses for each Aspect. Tallen froze and boiled parts of the river with Fire and Water, careful to keep the two Aspects separate in his mind. Magus Britt helped him refine his use of lightning, too. A bolt flashed across the water, skipping across its surface like a well-cast stone.

Magus Britt raised an eyebrow. "Few mages with enough strength in Fire can also call upon the Water needed to set off lightning. I can barely do it myself. You, my boy, do not have that problem."

Tallen rubbed his hand. It still tingled from the bolt. "What can I do with the Psoul Aspect?"

The Bluecloak mage grimaced. "I knew you would ask that in time. I have very few answers for you." Magus Britt left the railing and waved for Tallen to follow him. He took a seat on a water barrel. "While I did once visit the Dreamrealm, it was not through my power. However, dreaming is not the only power tied to the Psoul Aspect. It may also be used to create illusions, or to…enter the minds of others. Some say it is the most powerful Aspect." The mage sounded reticent, as if uncertain how much he should tell Tallen. "There are others on the Isle far better versed in this than I. Though the only Dreamer I know still alive would likely never set foot there of his own free will."

Something about the mage's tone made Tallen lean closer. "Who is that?"

Magus Britt's bushy eyebrows closed together. "He is commonly known as the Ravenhawke."

A tingle of excitement shot up Tallen's spine, not so unlike the bolt of lightning. "Dorias Ravenhawke? The man who wrote *The Tarmorian Bestiary*? That book is in the library at the Gryphon."

The Battlemage barked a harsh laugh. "That thing is still in print?" The laugh faded while Magus Britt stared at the passing river. "It's probably the only one of his writings to survive the breaking of the Wizard's Circle. Everything else was destroyed when he and his fellows were declared rogue."

"So he is the only one who could teach me about the Psoul Aspect – why is it so different from the others?"

The mage adjusted his cloak. "What do you mean by 'different'? Each Aspect is unique."

Tallen searched for the words to describe what he meant. "Well, it's like this – you always describe the five Aspects as if they were the points of a star. It is well known that the pentagram is a symbol for magic."

Magus Britt nodded. "Go on."

"But, it's not quite like that for me." Tallen stared at his hands, his mind working ahead of his mouth. "Psoul stands out. I almost have to reach around it – or maybe through it – to get to the other

Aspects. Rather than a point of a star, it's…it's almost like the center of a circle."

Magus Britt blinked, and for a moment the color drained from his face. Tallen shivered as the last of the sun dropped below the horizon, and he searched for another way to explain himself.

"That's enough," Magus Britt held up his hand, his face unreadable. "That's precisely the kind of talk the Ravenhawke started decades ago. It ended with thirteen wizards abandoning the Circle." The mage shook his head, his age showing more heavily on his features. "Do not say that again, especially not in the presence of Varana Calais, if she teaches you." He stood and walked away. "Damn fool rogues."

Tallen watched his teacher, shocked at his reaction. The mage said nothing more to him as he stalked to the boat's cabin.

I'd best keep my ideas to myself…for now.

The next morning the Andon began to branch. The *River Spike's* pilot kept her to the northernmost passage at each fork. The banks became crowded with townhomes and docks, manors and inns. A few houses and orchards scattered across sparsely populated islands, one or two with a single manse and dock. Most of the sandbars and islands looked rather temporary, shifting with the constant change of flowing water.

Tallen had not seen much of Maddi during the voyage, so it surprised him when she wordlessly joined him at the prow. They watched the traffic and the people on the shore slip by. Pink river dolphins cruised alongside. Few words passed between the two of them. Tallen simply enjoyed standing near her, breathing in the jasmine scent of her hair carried on the breeze. He placed his hand precariously close to hers on the rail.

She leaned in and nudged his shoulder with hers. "I bet you could mess with the wind in some of those old ship captains' sails." Maddi's lips curled in a mischievous grin. "It might be funny to see a few of them bump into each other."

"I don't think that would fit into Magus Britt's idea of self-control," Tallen told her.

Maddi laughed. "Don't give me such a sour look. I'm just kidding." She leaned closer to the rail. "But it would be funny."

He gave in to her grin with one of his own. "Maybe."

They watched a cluster of rocky hills rise in the northeast. They sparkled in the afternoon sun, covered in an unimaginable maze of buildings. As the boat came closer to the great capital of Daynon, Tallen picked out small palaces sprawling on the peaks of each hill, while a circular pattern of gradually smaller structures disappeared into the valleys. Brawny, his front paws set upon the railing, stuck his nose into the air. His chest pumped like a bellows, sniffing everything that wafted up from the river. Along the edge, hundreds of piers and docks stretched toward the Bay of Hope.

The famed Ivory Palace set upon the last hill, nestled in the corner between the northernmost finger of the river delta and the swooping curve of coastline. The palace sprawled over its entirety.

"It's known as Aravath's Lookout," Tallen whispered to Maddi, careful not to break the spell of awe cast upon her by sight of the royal capital. "It's where Aravath the Navigator landed with the first wave of the Return. It is the seed of Gannon. From here he claimed the entire Andon River basin."

Maddi's eyes remained locked on the palace. Tallen watched her studying the spiral towers, delicate skyways, and domed structures, and the way they captured the sunlight with silver roofs and colored glass windows. The buildings stood seamless, as if made from singular pieces of marble. Most curved with fluidity, giving a peaceful, almost surreal feeling to the architecture.

"How do they build such things?" Her eyes never left the skyline.

"Wizards." Tallen nodded his head, his own gaze captured by the palace. "Air mages lifted huge marble slabs, and Earth and Fire mages molded them together. It is almost five centuries of work." He laughed. "Though, I imagine Aravath spent that first night in a rather dingy tent."

A voice cleared from behind. "And you'll be spending your first night in the palace." Boris smiled when Tallen and Maddi jumped. Magus Britt stood behind the earl, homecoming in his grin. "Unless of course you would like King Aravath's tent... I'm certain it is somewhere within the museum dedicated to him."

The mage barked a harsh laugh. "Probably right next to his hallowed chamber pot."

"Undoubtedly." Tallen could not pick Boris' humor from the comment, but he did not think the earl found it as funny as Magus Britt. "However, we will be docking soon, so the two of you will want to gather your things." Boris scanned the city of the Gannonite kings, a wistful expression on his face. "Daynon will be our last stop together."

CHAPTER 17

When the Navigator set his foot upon the land,
Flowers sprang from his very hand.
The fields did grow and the river did flow.
And the ocean bowed upon the sand.
— Rhyme of the Navigator by Josun Vatris

Familiar as she was with the slow rock of the riverboat, Maddi's first few steps onto the stone pier wobbled. She stretched the backs of her legs, working the unsteady feeling from them.

"You'll get your legs back soon." The gruff Bluecloak mage squinted while his eyes focused on the crew unloading their horses and dwarf ponies. "The ride to the Ivory Palace is not far, but we will stable our horses there." He shifted his face to Tallen. "You will have no need of yours on the Isle."

The young man nodded and made his way toward the old palfrey he called Stew. Maddi followed.

"I suppose I could hitch a ride with you again." She noticed the grin that cracked his face at her words. "I doubt I'll need a horse at the Doctor's College." Maddi narrowed her eyes at the mage. "That is why I'm here, right? Will I need to buy a house to replace the one you forced me to abandon in Gavanor?"

Earl Boris held a hand up to his elder friend, and the mage bit his tongue. "There are dormitories at the Doctor's College for all students. Duke Aginor secured your home in Gavanor. It will await your return, once you have completed your time at the College." The earl tossed his cloak over one shoulder, exposing the black falcon. "For the next few days, however, you will all stay with us at the Palace as guests of the Royal Guard."

Tallen took Stew's reins from the crewman leading him across the cargo gangplank. "When do I leave for the Isle?"

Hoisting his leg over his own, shorter steed, the mage settled himself into the saddle. "Day after tomorrow. A ship will be waiting for you at first light. I sent a raven to the Isle from Bridgedale and received their reply when we docked in Barmor." He clattered away over the cobblestones. "You will not want to be late."

Boris mounted his black stallion, nodding toward Maddi before following his friend. Their big sergeant rode close behind.

Maddi watched Tallen's green-cloaked brother mount his cavalry horse. "Come on then, you two. I can stay tonight then I have to head back to Gavanor." He clicked his tongue at the mare. "Let's make the most of our time."

Once firmly seated behind Tallen on the palfrey, Maddi wrapped her arms around his waist. *He does have a slender build, for a soft innkeeper. And his eyes are so…spirited. I think he's a little younger than me, but I can't tell for certain.* She sniffed. *And he always smells clean…*

The horses gathered in a tight group around Maddi and Tallen as they joined the traffic on the main thoroughfare to the palace. The half dozen dwarves on ponies drew far more stares than a few Bluecloaks in the capital. Maddi smiled at the sight. Darve Northtower seemed to relish the attention, nodding and bowing to passersby as if he were a head of state on parade.

"Maybe he is," she murmured.

Tallen turned his head. "What was that?"

"Just admiring the beauty of the city."

The overwhelming size of the Ivory Palace became apparent once they rounded the corner. The sweeping, cream-colored towers captured Maddi's gaze. What had once appeared delicate and impossible at a distance, now looked magnificent and unyielding. More than a dozen towers leaped into the air, most taller than the pinnacle of the citadel in Gavanor. Domed buildings sprung between them, adding bulk to the sweeping towers. In the center of it all a wide, circular hall stood, its dome reaching half the height of the tallest tower. Maddi snapped her mouth shut.

Tallen's jaw still hung agape. "It's…bigger up close."

She snorted. "Most things are."

The traffic thinned upon reaching the outer wall of the palace, twenty yards in height and garrisoned by hundreds of Bluecloaks. Earl Boris led the entire party up to the captain in command.

"Welcome home, My Lord." The Bluecloak saluted and bowed his head. "I hope your journey was fruitful."

Boris frowned. "We'll find that out soon enough, Captain."

They rode into the palace grounds, Maddi admiring the dragons and knights wrought into the steel of the gates.

The beauty of this place is enchanting. Wide grass lawns spread between the marble buildings and towers. Stone pathways, most wide enough for a pair of wagons to pass each other unmolested, crisscrossed the grounds between groves of manicured trees and flower gardens. Lillies and roses blossomed all around in dozens of colors, while clematis and mandevilla vines climbed painted trellises and shaded gazebos. The soft breeze carried the scent to Maddi's nose, and she fluttered her eyes in pleasure.

Tallen shook his head, his voice distant in tone. "I've never seen anything like it."

Smiling at the look on Tallen's face, Maddi slid down from behind him. She let her hand linger on his hip a moment while she pretended to pick a stone from her boot. *He's certainly kind, and his eyes sparkle when he smiles.*

She had a difficult time focusing on her steps. Her eyes kept drifting toward the tops of the tall towers – blue and silver banners snapping from each. Save one. A long gray banner fluttered from the third tallest spire, blazoned with the half-black, half-white sigil of the Temple of Balance.

She looked at Tallen and his brother. "Do all the people of Gannon follow the Balance?"

The two men glanced at each other, their matching expressions ones of mixed humor and humility.

"No is the easy answer," Jaerd said with a frown. "Our family is as close to the Water as to the Balance, but the Westars settled near the source of the Andon long before the Temple sent its missionaries to the frontier." He gestured to Tallen. "Tell her about the shrine."

The younger brother smiled. "The Water priests say that the old spring behind the Gryphon was a holy site in the Elder Days, when Aspect worship was all that anyone practiced in our part of the world." Tallen nodded in her direction. "What tradition do you follow? Aren't all the Aspects hallowed in the Free Cities?"

"As is the Balance." She lifted her head, squinting at Tallen. "My father claimed that all the Aspects were worthy of respect, though they did little to help him when the Bloody Flux came." She shrugged. "I think the only thing we really have to believe in is ourselves."

Tallen nodded. "You can believe in me." The smile, dampened by her words, returned to his lips.

Groomsmen in blue livery trotted up, taking the horses and dwarf ponies at Boris' command. A Bluecloak officer closed with the earl and the Battlemage, the three whispering in a close huddle. Hefting his two-yard axe, Sergeant Hall saluted the earl, and dashed off toward the city. Brawny looked at Tallen and whined softly, then loped off after his master.

Boris bowed his head to the dwarf leader. "Maester Northtower, servants will show your men to accommodations. The king holds court at this hour, if you wish to show him your totem."

Darve nodded and turned to his followers. "Seek rest and food. I will carry the message of our people."

"We must hurry," Magus Britt barked at Tallen. He gestured to Maddi. "You should come as well."

The group followed Boris with haste. Jaerd slipped in close behind Tallen. "This place could be as dangerous as anything we've faced."

The wide steps of the High Hall led up to three steel wrought double-doors, each cast in shapes of knights and dragons battling, sometimes on the same side. The central door stood open, flanked by two Bluecloaks at attention. They gave Boris a sharp salute as he stomped past them.

They followed the earl into the High Hall, Maddi gaping at the dome spread wide above her. Its vastness was incomprehensible from outside. The dome had no seams, like the rest of the Ivory Palace. At its center, nearly a hundred yards over her head, a wide circle of light poured in through an opening, casting a beam that crawled slowly across the floor. At first, the hole appeared tiny, until a raven flew through it giving her some perspective.

Tallen leaned in close. "They say an Air mage is employed full time keeping the birds out so they…um…don't make a mess."

Maddi snickered. She stepped out onto the intricate inlay of the stone floor. Hundreds of different colors were set into the marble, marking out a huge map of the known world in precise, beautiful detail. Gannon, at the heart of the continent of Tarmor, stood at the very center of the room.

She nudged Tallen, pointing at an odd crisscross of wavy lines across the map. "Do you know what that is?"

Tallen cupped a hand around his mouth, directing his softened voice toward her. "I've read that it is a sort of calendar." He pointed toward the opening far above. "That beam of light follows it every day, shifting with the sun and seasons." His finger trailed down to where the pool stretched as it neared the edge of the map, marking the descent into night. "With each day the light moves southward, marking the shift from winter to summer, then back again. By its position, we are just shy of midsummer. It looks like it will head back the other way in just a week or so."

"You are a font of knowledge," she whispered. "I hope it's useful someday."

The Battlemage cleared his throat, and Boris raised an eyebrow.

"You'll want to keep quiet in the hall of the king." The earl straightened his tunic and adjusted his sword. "I wish that I could." He stepped out onto the inlaid stone, his black riding boots ringing against it.

At the far end of the hall, almost a hundred yards from them, a large cluster of finely dressed men and women gathered. Dozens of house sigils made from precious stones hung around noble necks on thick gold chains. Squinting as they walked closer, Maddi picked out every Gannonite crest that she knew, and many she did not recognize. Three elves stood close together near the edge of the nobility, their calm faces focused on the scene.

Beyond the bejeweled clutch of highborn, a four-tiered dais rose from the floor map just where the Dragonscale Mountains should be. The bottom step held nine chairs, each carved of hickory. Men concentrating on the proceedings occupied three of the chairs. One somewhat handsome young man wore the crest of House Belcester, a mother-of–pearl seahawk stretching its wings between amethysts and aquamarines. The second man, far older, wore a white robe with a rainbow sash. His white beard flowed over his chest, and he held a wooden staff. The third man lounged in his chair, his clothes and pointed beard well kempt. The pendant on his chest held only a single, large blue sapphire.

Tallen leaned in to whisper. "Those are the king's councils. The Common Council is on the lower step – peers of the kingdom. Mostly dukes of the different realms." He nodded toward one end. "Duke Aginor Varlan holds a seat there, though they usually all gather only in times of great peril."

"You seem to know a lot about the nobility for a cook," Maddi commented, a doubtful frown on her face.

The young man looked sheepish. "Politics is an obsessive hobby, I guess. I've read histories from all over the kingdom." He frowned slightly. "Plus, we do get news at the Gryphon."

Smiling at his offended tone, Maddi fell in step alongside him. Her gaze climbed to the second row of the dais, where five intricately carved mahogany chairs stood. Men sat in three of them, their cast rather diverse. One of the chairs overflowed with a grotesquely fat man dressed in black and white silk robes. Next to him sat a man the exact opposite in appearance: thin, attentive, dressed in a fastidious cloak of Gannon blue. Four silver stars glittered on the collar of his tunic.

When Maddi focused on the third man, her senses tingled. She noticed the sharp glint to his eyes and a thick mop of brown hair that tumbled across his forehead. *Well now, isn't he a handsome one. Looks like he knows it too. But there's something…familiar about him. Not his look, but something else.*

After clearing his throat, Tallen continued. "The second platform is for the High Council. They are they king's private advisors – the most powerful men in the kingdom." He pointed to the fastidious-looking Bluecloak. "That is the Lord Marshal himself." Tallen's voice sank even further. "He even outranks Earl Boris and Magus Britt."

Maddi squinted. "Alright, since you know so much, who is the one on the right, the fellow in brown robes?"

A smile spread across Tallen's lips. He looked proud to have an answer for her. "I believe that is the Lord Doctor. I forget his name." He tilted his head as if in thought. "You'll be meeting him soon, I suppose." Tallen frowned. "It's Lord Doctor…Marvin, Maerin? Something like that. I think he's only held office a few years."

Nodding, Maddi gestured for Tallen to continue as they crossed the open dome. The young man smiled even wider if possible.

"The third step of the dais has just the one seat. It's black because it is carved from a solid piece of ebony." Maddi turned her gaze to the empty chair. A single, plain piece of blue linen hung over its arms. Tallen leaned in close enough to place his hand at the small of her back. "No one has occupied the Seat of the Heir in decades."

The Battlemage stopped along the far edge of the crowd, close enough to see and hear the nobles. "The two of you wait here, since you cannot be silent." His frown lifted when his eyes fell on Jaerd. "I trust you can keep them out of trouble?"

Jaerd put a hand each on Maddi and Tallen's shoulders. "Yes, Magus-General."

The Battlemage turned to Darve Northtower. "If you would join us, Maester."

The dwarf nodded and followed the two Bluecloaks wending their way to the front of the crowd. More than a few nobles clapped Boris on the back, smiling at his sudden appearance. One or two stared daggers.

Looking up at the fourth and highest tier of the dais, Maddi studied the top chair, an imposing throne carved of a solid piece of what looked like ivory. *No elephant could be that big! Unless that isn't ivory…*

Upon the throne, his arms folded in an almost petulant fashion, an old man slouched. A few days growth of shimmering white beard shone against his pale, almost waxy cheek. A finely wrought crown rested on his head, twisting in multiple bands of gossamer silver. Dozens of opals, each deep blue passing to green with fuscia at their heart, bedecked the crown. A single one at its peak was the size of a chicken egg.

"…and what proof have you of these claims, Lord Harte?" A man dressed in charcoal robes of fine wool stalked about on the High Council's tier. His face was shaven smooth, and a small cap rested on his head. *It looks like he uses brownberry dye in his hair.*

"I have my word as the Lord of Harlong," returned a man with a finely trimmed, ruddy beard and fierce green eyes. He scowled at the speaker upon the dais. "And my honor as a paladin"

Cupping her mouth with one hand, Maddi whispered, "Who is the man up there?"

She watched Tallen count the chairs, mulling over his memory of the hundreds of books he claimed to have read.

"It must be the Lord Chancellor. I don't know his name, just the office."

Maddi's attention snapped back to the argument when the voice of the paladin rose above the crowd.

"I tell you, orcs are in the Northwood." Wrinkles covered the man's tunic, as if he had just removed his armor. A rather expensive looking sword hung from his hip. "I killed several of them myself. I found the markings of both Shark and Boar Clans." He held out a strip of worn leather. "I ripped this from the armor of one of their captains. It is clearly the mark of the hammerhead."

A collective shudder passed through the crowd. Two men with the almond skin and flowing robes of Hadoners whispered to one another.

"A painted piece of leather is no proof of invasion." The Lord Chancellor smoothed his robes. "Even if a few orcs raided your lands, it is no cause to rouse the entire kingdom. It is needless warmongering – perhaps even a pretext to stir dissention and chaos in a time of peace."

The Lord Harte stood as still as stone, fists planted firmly on his hips. Maddi watched his jaw work behind the beard. The paladin closed his eyes, and his chest rose and fell in a steady rhythm. When he lifted his lids, his jaw no longer clenched, and a veil of calm hung over his features.

"I do not understand why you are being purposefully obtuse." The lord folded his arms, releasing his balled fists as he did so. "This is far more than a simple raid. Boar and Shark do not raid together. If it were Wolf and Shark, I might accept your claims." Lord Harte raised a chestnut eyebrow. "I have never played your games, Chancellor Vyce. Your accusations that I might play politics would be a case of the sky calling the ocean blue."

Muffled chuckles rippled through the crowd.

The four-starred Bluecloak lifted a finger from the arm of his chair. "If I may, my fellow Lords." The Lord Chancellor nodded begrudgingly. "If there is one man who knows the ways of the Orc better than the Lord Harte, he has just entered this hallowed hall." The Lord Marshal nodded at Boris working his way to the front of the crowd. "As if by providence, the Earl of Mourne has just returned from a long journey to the very edge of the Northlands. He has been to Highspur."

Murmurs moved through the assembled nobles. Maddi even noticed a single raised eyebrow among the three elves.

"Your Majesty." Boris bowed to the king. Arathan did not respond. His stare remained fixed on nothing. "My Lords." Boris nodded to the dais first, and then the crowd. "I have a great deal to report, most in private council. But I must say that I find myself agreeing with the Lord Harte." The chancellor jerked his head in sarcastic surprise. "The north is on the move." The earl gestured to his side. "If I may introduce Maester Darve Northtower, emissary from the King of the Rock."

Darve stepped forward to the bottom of the dais and bowed deeply. "Your Majesty, King Arathan, honored friend and ally to the dwarven people and their king."

Arathan nodded, his first visible movement since Maddi entered the hall. "We have memory of receiving you before, Maester Northtower." The king's voice sounded aged, but it still held the iron of a man who fought a dozen wars. "Gannon is honored with a visit from our ever sturdy friends."

Darve straightened wearing a broad smile of friendship. "I am honored you would remember one such as me, Your Majesty." His face turned grave. "However, I have come with grave news, news which may add urgency to your lords' debate."

Maddi stared, transfixed as Darve reached into his cloak and pulled out the dragon tooth he had shown her during their journey upon the Andon. Tilli had also displayed the dagger she made from her own dragon kill. *It was not as large, but just as fearsome.*

More murmurs shook the crowd.

"It is the tooth of a dragon, Your Majesty." Darve raised the tooth above his head so all might see. "A beast unlike any seen since the Elder Days. They raided our city and homes, burning much of Wood Town. Thousands are feared dead." The dwarf went to one knee before the dais. "I humbly request your aid, Your Majesty, in the spirit of the long alliance between our peoples."

Arathan nodded, his distant stare fixing on Darve. "We are already aware of this, Maester Northtower. We are also aware that Aginor has dispatched aid." The king shifted slightly, his white satin tunic and pants glimmering in the faded daylight from the dome overhead. "However, we will dispatch a chest full of gold marks to Aginor to aid him in aiding you." A whisper of a smile flickered across the kings lips, gone before Maddi was certain she had seen it. "Thank you for the gift, Maester."

Frowning herself, Maddi watched Darve's brow wrinkle. The dwarf smoothed his face in an instant and laid the tooth upon the lowest step. He rose, bowed his head, and turned, disappearing into the crowd.

Earl Boris' eyes switched from Darve to the king. "There is more, Sire. Orcs have been found in far closer places than Highspur or Harlong." He took two steps forward, his shoulder close to the paladin's, who had listened to Darve with interest. "Gavanor and Bridgedale have both been scenes of attack."

Alarmed shouts rang out from the crowd. Maddi took a step back from the shudder of movement among the suddenly pale assembly. Near half a dozen men dashed from the room, each wearing a different crest upon his tunic and an urgency about his features. The men on the Common Council perked up.

However, while those on the High Council sat alert in their chairs, they did not appear shocked. Maddi caught the Lord Marshal nodding to Boris, almost imperceptibly. The fat man in Temple robes stared at the fingernails of one hand. He slipped what looked like a piece of candy into his mouth with the other. The handsome Lord Doctor moved nothing save for his sharp eyes. *They knew already, but no one else did.*

The Lord Chancellor waved his hands to calm the assemblage. "Peace! Peace… Your king is well aware of this." He turned to Boris, his plain features frowning as if disappointed with an unruly child. "Your ravens were well received from both locations, My Lord Earl. As I said to the Lord Harte, there is no need to unnecessarily alert the entire kingdom over a few raids."

"What we faced at Bridgedale was more than just a raid, Your Majesty," Magus Britt answered, nodding his head in deference to the king. "Their raid was targeted, coordinated, and extremely well equipped. I believe they could be the same orcs that entered the Northwood, come down via the Snowbourne."

The Lord Chancellor spread his hands in disbelief. "What was their target?"

Tallen shifted next to Maddi, his face pale. When she patted his arm in reassurance, he gripped her hand.

Boris placed his palm on the Battlemage's shoulder. "We are not certain."

Maddi heard Tallen exhale. She felt his hand relax, but it did not leave hers.

The earl folded his arms, his blue eyes focused on the king. "But, along with the Lord Harte's evidence and this unprecedented dragon raid upon the Rock, I believe we must increase our vigilance – begin a muster."

Shouts of "Aye!" echoed from the crowd. Three out of five heads nodded in clear agreement. The rest remained frozen. Maddi could almost smell their fear. "I do not like the mood change in here," she whispered into Tallen's ear. "Maybe we should leave."

Tallen turned his head to her, a doubtful squint in his eye. "Oh no, not again. We're staying where we were told."

Jaerd, vigilant behind them, patted her on the shoulder firmly. "He's a smart one, my brother – learns more quickly than others."

The Lord Chancellor again waved the crowd to silence. "We have already begun preparations." He looked at the paladin. "A dozen ships of the line were sent north to patrol the Dragon's Teeth. The primitive skiffs of the orcs will be no match for Admiral Lindon's fleet." The chancellor shifted his stare back to Boris, and narrowed his gaze. "And you, My Lord Earl, are to command of a battalion of reinforcements, which will leave for Highspur at once. You will then remain at the fortress long enough to discover the nature of this 'threat' you proclaim but cannot name."

The earl slammed a fist into his hand. "It should be a division, not a single battalion. We should muster the kingdom, and send two dozen more ships north of the Teeth." He folded his arms again. "Tomas is right. Boar and Shark working together means this is more than just raiding."

The Lord Chancellor shook his head. "These are the resources to be committed. The kingdom has many responsibilities, the protection of trade and commerce primary among them."

The paladin scoffed. "What matters commerce when the world is dead?"

Maddi watched Boris ignore the chancellor, his gaze never leaving the king. "Is this your command, Your Majesty?"

Arathan nodded, his watery blue eyes never leaving the blue-cloaked earl. "It is."

Boris bowed deeply to the king. "Then I shall depart upon the morrow."

The Lord Harte folded his hands behind his back. "And I shall join you."

Grinning, the chancellor raised a single finger. "There is one more thing, Lord Harte." He lifted an eyebrow toward the king. Arathan nodded back, ever so slightly, his chin now resting on a thumb. "As you have at last made your presence known among us at court, after such a long absence, perhaps you would take your seat upon the Common Council? The king is preparing a summons for all the council members. Would not representing the people of Harlong here be far more important than some wanderlust borne journey into the wild?"

Maddi backed into Jaerd when she saw the contempt in Lord Harte's stare. But his sharp eyes were not aimed at the Lord Chancellor. Instead, they flew toward the fat man in Temple of Balance robes. He paid no attention, but Maddi caught the barest hint of a grin creep upon his flabby lips.

The paladin's tone dripped with barely contained rage. "I have made it clear to His Majesty many times why I feel that the vows of my order preclude my involvement in the councils of the kingdom." He blinked again and drew in a deep breath. Some of the anger slipped from his voice. "Others would do well to remember as much. The Temple already involves itself too greatly in the political matters of this kingdom, rather than simply its spiritual matters."

The fat man upon the dais raised a chubby finger. "But the two are intertwined, Paladin Harte." His syrupy sweet voice took on a patronizing tone. "The spiritual matters of the kingdom are best addressed from the council, as are the political. I believe this is the point my friend the Lord Chancellor makes."

After a short nod toward the priest, a falsely beseeching tone slipped into the chancellor's voice. "Just so. In this time of great strife, your king requires that you advise him in council." His eyes narrowed and a thin smile formed on his smooth face, turning Maddi's stomach. "If you cannot take the seat of House Harte, then it will be granted to another house, as will rule of Harlong."

From the mumbling of the crowd, Maddi picked out some of the words, a mix of confusion and support. Grins grew on the face of a few greedy lords. *They see this as a chance to improve their own standing in this farce. Fools!*

The Lord Harte folded his hands behind his back. He stared at the floor before lifting his gaze toward the king. "I could send for a proxy, Your Majesty."

The chancellor shrugged, mock sympathy oozing through his voice. "I am afraid, My Lord, that the law requires that any proxy be a blood member of your house." He shook his head sadly, though Maddi still saw a hint of the smile. "As I understand it, you are the last Harte. You have no other family to appoint as proxy."

I do not like that chancellor. Not one bit. Maddi sneered at the surrounding nobles, who likely already schemed to get themselves seated on the dais. *That Lord Chancellor will use you just as easily.*

Lord Harte's face clouded into a stony mask. His green eyes stared at the floor, seeming to study the intricate stonework. When he finally lifted his gaze, it was with sadness in his eyes far more real than anything in the chancellor's expression. He fixed it upon the fat man, who squirmed under its ferocity.

"I see that the Balance has skewed much further than I had feared." The paladin's tone remained even, his face calm. However, his eyes burned with passion when he turned them toward the king, ignoring the chancellor's very existence. "Your Majesty rules in Gannon, and Harlong has been a part of it since my ancestor knelt to yours. It is yours to do with as you will." Lord Harte lifted his chin with pride. "I trust to Your Majesty's grace, and that he will remember my people are among his most loyal and loving subjects. Had my father, one of my brothers, or even a nephew lived to take this seat, I am certain they would be glad to do so. However, I took my vows with the Paladins of Balance well before they all passed into the beyond. Those vows are more binding than even the command of a king, may it please Your Majesty." The man bowed his head slightly. "I cannot serve two masters, and the Balance can be my only choice."

The vast room stood silent. No one moved or breathed. Even the elves remained rooted, their eyes fixed upon Arathan. The king did not shift on his throne. His eyes bounced between Lord Harte and the fat priest. They settled at last upon the Lord Chancellor, who waited for his king with a suppliant tilt of his head. King Arathan nodded, blinking his eyes.

"Then you are banished forthwith, *Paladin* Tomas Harte." The chancellor's tone verged on gleeful. "This is an order of his Majesty, King Arathan VII, Lord of the Andon, Arbiter of the Return. The seat of House Harte is dissolved, and a new Lord of Harlong shall be appointed." He gestured toward the westernmost chair on the lower tier. "By law, the king and High Council will decide who takes up the empty Common Council seat."

"Wow..." Tallen whispered, barely audible above the sudden rustle among the nobles. Maddi felt him squeeze her hand again, wondering if he even knew he did it.

She lifted her free hand to her lips. *Even Tallen was quiet while they talked. This must be a big deal in Gannon.*

The paladin bowed. A finger brushed the hilt of his massive sword before he brought his hands together and pressed them against his forehead. He held the bow for only a moment, before he stood and faced King Arathan.

"This kingdom has wrought its own destiny." The paladin's voice rang through the High Hall. "I fear the backlash when the Balance returns. Perhaps it has already begun to snap." When he spun on his heel, his gaze passed over Earl Boris. Maddi noticed the paladin's eyebrow lift. Boris shook his head in the negative, but that did not convince the former Lord Harte. He turned back toward the king. "So long as the Seat of the Heir sits empty – so long as the one man who deserves it is relegated to exile from his proper place – then I will gladly take exile upon myself as well."

The paladin marched from the High Hall, leaving through a side exit. A dark cloaked man with a raptor gaze and wings of gray at his temples trotted behind him. The raven Maddi had seen fly through the roof earlier followed the men, sticking close to the span of the dome. It fluttered into the exit. *Where is that bird going?*

King Arathan rose, unsteady on his feet. A page dashed to aid him. The king's thin frame became more obvious once upright, although he only leaned slightly upon the boy. A sour look gathered on his face. "I am done with this farce. I must find something to eat." He gestured for the page to lead him away.

Maddi noticed a concerned look cross the Lord Chancellor's face. *That is not concern for the king.*

The pretentious chancellor raised his hand. "Your Majesty… we had discussed a banquet in honor of the return of Earl Boris."

Maddi scoffed. *And his leaving again, no doubt.*

The king sighed. "I have no desire for a banquet. We have nothing to celebrate." He gestured to the page. "To my rooms, boy."

The entire crowd knelt. Maddi followed their example, letting Tallen's hand slip reluctantly from hers. Even the men upon the dais rose from their chairs, and then went onto one knee. The fat priest of Balance, never quite made it down completely. The king waved them off, muttering to himself while the wide-eyed page led the monarch through a door at the rear of the hall.

Maddi scratched her head when the crowd began to break up, most clustering in hushed conversation with their allies. Boris moved his way among a few, offering confident nods and words of encouragement.

Leaning closer to Tallen, she furrowed her brow. "Boris appears to be more important than he lets on. Where is his earldom?"

Tallen shook his head, his face overwhelmed by the swirl of political power around him. "There are no earldoms in Gannon. It is a title without land among our people – a title of honor, but not of wealth."

Maddi watched the Bluecloak general move among his people. Most treated him with deference far above that of a landless soldier. "There's something else to it." She took Tallen's arm in hand. His thoughtful frown switched to a smile when he turned his head to look at her. "What about that time we heard—"

"Captain Westar!" The voice of the rotund Battlemage broke over her question.

He has a knack for timing, Maddi thought with a frown.

Jaerd snapped to at his call, and the mage continued with his orders. "Escort your charges to Garrison Tower. Find Captain

Braverman. He is to put the three of you up for the next few nights under my orders." Jaerd saluted, fist over heart, while the mage nodded at Tallen. "Get something to eat there, and I will try to find you yet tonight. Boris and I leave in the morning, as will you upon the next."

A ripple of anxiety crossed Tallen's features. "I had hoped you might escort me to the Isle yourself…"

The mage shook his head. "I will not leave without speaking to you again, but our time together is at an end." He looked over his shoulder at Boris, who nodded. The earl made a hasty farewell to the green and gold-coated noble clasping his hand. "I must hurry off to see if I can find you an escort, and the perfect one just walked out. I must believe in your luck, because I do not believe in fate."

Maddi watched the Battlemage head toward the exit she had seen the paladin and his dark-eyed friend use. She turned to follow Jaerd and Tallen out the way they had entered. She could not help but stare at the back of the younger brother's neck.

It may be harder to say good-bye to him than it was to Renna.

She thumbed the golden chalice in her pocket, her thoughts clouding the last beams of sunlight.

CHAPTER 18

When Arathan VII rose to the throne but recently claimed by his grandfather, his uncle, his cousin, and his older brother, many assumed that the Year of the Five Kings (423 A.R.) would soon become the Year of the Six Kings. Instead, he shocked the world. Through his steely gaze and hearty words, a thirteen year old boy convinced the Bluecloaks to back him. He convinced the people to love him. The nobles, after a good drubbing at the Battle of the Andon Delta, learned to respect him. Historians, including this one, have named his reign a Golden Age while he still sits upon the throne.

— "History of Gannon, Epilogue" by Elyn Bravano

Dorias Ravenhawke trotted after his old friend, sensing Merl flapping along behind him. The paladin stomped ahead, hands behind his back, his face hung in sad reflection.

"I know that you doubtless have advice for me." He did not change his stance or pace, but Tomas Harte's voice hung weary in the air. "I do not think I wish to hear it. I will join Boris at Highspur, and I will go from there into the Northlands, alone if needs be, to find the darkness that weighs upon the Balance. It is there." He at last lifted his head, staring off into the northwest. "I sense it."

Merl landed upon the outstretched hand of a statue. He flapped his wings and clacked his obsidian beak. Nodding at the bird, Dorias rested his hand upon the paladin's shoulder. "Help me figure out what this darkness is first, then we will go together to face it."

"What do you mean?" Tomas turned to face him. "How can we discover what it is without seeking it out?"

Dorias folded his arms, raising a charcoal eyebrow in return. "There are other potential sources of information. Sources but a boat ride away." He cleared his throat. "But that is where I may need your aid."

"Do you think she would let you return, even if I claimed

the Temple's prerogative there?" Tomas hooked a thumb on his sword hilt. "Doubtful. You are barely tolerated in this city."

Dorias shrugged. He knew he treaded on shaky ground. "Varana has many things to hold against me. However, I have aided her thrice since the breaking of the Circle. She owes me."

Merl cawed in agreement.

Tomas shook his head, a doubtful expression on his features. "While the idea of joining you like old times is quite tempting, I have a feeling that Earl Boris will have need of me at Highspur."

The sound of fast moving boots echoed down the hall behind them. Dorias smiled at his luck when he saw the blue cloak and black mustache. "Perhaps we should ask him."

Tomas straightened at the earl's wave of greeting.

"My Lord Harte." The earl gave a nod to Dorias upon his approach. "Wizard Ravenhawke. While some might curse you in this city, you know I am not one of them. The fact that the two of you stand in the High Hall on the one day I am in Daynon must be proof of someone's faith, though I cannot know which."

Smiling sadly, Tomas returned Earl Boris' greeting. "I don't know that either of us still carries the titles you grant us, My Lord Earl. Perhaps you should only remember that we've stood side by side in battle." He reached out his hand, which Boris clasped with a hearty shake. "Friends address each other by name."

"Indeed, Tomas my friend, it is good to see you."

Dorias reached out to grab the earl's proffered hand and felt the presence of another powerful mage nearby. From the heat of Fire, he knew who it had to be. "And Magus Joslyn Britt." Dorias cast a nod toward the goateed man in a red-fringed cloak. "I still consider the Bluecloak Battlemages to be my brothers, as I did when I stood in the Circle."

"Ravenhawke." Joslyn's pale blue eyes searched Dorias, who returned the stare without blinking. "This is quite fortuitous, as Boris said. I have found someone you must meet – someone perhaps only you can teach properly." The mage's last few words came out from clenched teeth.

Dorias' interest piqued. "You sound as if you don't want to hand over this apprentice you've discovered." He tapped his lip then lifted one finger when the answer came. "You've found a Dreamer."

Joslyn gave a slow nod of his head. "I have taught him all I can. He…he appears to touch all the Aspects in strength – a strength I haven't seen…well…ever. I sent a raven to Varana, but

I had no idea you were already in the capital. Ravenhawke, you must escort him to the Isle. Watch over him. Train him in the use of Psoul."

"This young man has already been attacked twice by forces from the north," Earl Boris added. He looked at Tomas. "This is what I did not say in open council. The attacks in Gavanor and Bridgedale were targeted at him, and they wanted him alive."

Dorias tried to ignore the sudden prickling on the back of his neck. "Why would orcs want a Dreamer?"

Boris opened his mouth to speak but the mage beat him to it. "I am not certain, but I know that it is him they seek."

Tomas cocked his head. "How so?"

The Battlemage reached into a small pouch at his belt, pulling out a smooth, roundish stone. It glittered like smoky glass.

Dorias sensed the power radiating from the stone and reached out to touch it. "May I?"

Joslyn hesitated, then nodded and handed him the stone.

Calling his power with the ease that came from decades of use, Dorias slipped his senses into the familiar, misty embrace of the Psoul Aspect. He pulled upon it and delved into the stone that rested in his hand. Muddiness clouded the object, a dark shadow that reminded him of the force still holding him at bay when he tried to enter the Dreamrealm.

"The force within the stone is just a resonance." Dorias redirected the flow of his power. "It is trained to find someone specific, just as you determined." He flipped the stone in his hand. "However, what I find extremely interesting is the material. It is made of dragonrock."

Magus Britt frowned, scratching his grayed goatee with one hand. "I have not heard of that substance. Is it as powerful as it sounds?"

Dorias handed it to Tomas, and he sensed the paladin embracing his own power to test the stone. "It is certainly rare. It can only be formed when granite is burned by the fire of an Ancient One, the eldest – the first – of dragons. Few pieces that size have ever been found. That piece alone might be worth a hundred thousand marks to the right wizard." His eyes met Joslyn's. "There are half a dozen substances far less expensive that can be used to craft a tracing stone. Why dragonrock?"

The Bluecloak mage reached into his pouch again, pulling out another of the stones. "Both teams had one." He gestured to the one in Tomas' hands. "Keep it. You and the wizard should be able to use it to find Tallen." Joslyn tucked the second one away. "Also, the team in Bridgedale had a troll."

Sucking in his breath, Dorias looked to Boris. "How did they get a troll within a city at the heart of the kingdom?"

The earl ran his fingers along the nameplate of one of the royal statues. "I cannot be certain, but we know that they used boats on the Snowbourne. How they crossed the Dragonscales, I have not yet determined, though Tomas' information gives us a strong lead."

Merl chortled from his perch on the long dead general's outstretched hand, and Dorias looked up at his feathered friend. "Trolls live within the heights of the mountains. Crossing them is no problem for such a beast. It's just that they normally have no desire to do so. Someone drove it across."

Earl Boris raised a hand to his black mustache, scrubbing it in thought. "There were at least thirty orcs with it, possibly more. No party of orcs that size could cross the mountains."

"They could well have passed through my lands," Tomas said, staring at the stone-flagged floor. "Their attacks on the villages of the Northwood may have been a distraction so that crack teams could slip through undetected. What clan markings did you find?"

Boris jerked his tunic straight. "Boar and Ram, which are not uncommon together. But I also found Shark, same as you."

Tomas' gaze remained distant. "Indeed…"

"You know how many years it has been since I travelled in the Northlands," Dorias said to the paladin. "I do not understand the significance of this alliance."

Tomas folded his hands behind his back. "The Ram and Boar Clans have been in alliance for nearly a century, the oldest known alliance among the orc nations. This was forged during a long, open war with first the Mammoth then the Wolf Clan, who have themselves controlled the Shark Clan as a sort of sub-tribe for fifty years."

Dorias narrowed his eyes. "So seeing Sharks working with Boars means something significant has changed." A sudden dread sunk into his chest. "This does not bode well for my own suspicions."

Boris leaned forward. "What exactly are those suspicions?"

Dorias shifted his gaze from one man to the next. *If there are men in Gannon that can be trusted to do what is right, it is these men here. Perhaps this is a moment to turn the tide.* "I will not yet utter

the name of that which I fear. Not until I can find further proof."
Dorias looked to Tomas and added a sincere tone to his voice.
"This is why I need you to take me to the Isle as a guest of the
Temple. Their claim upon it is far older than the Circle or Varana's
academy. I need to do some research among their libraries. The
wizards on the Isle have the most extensive collection of writings
from the Elder Days collected there."

Tomas ran a finger over the dragonrock tracing stone. "You
think this power rises from that far back in time?"

Dorias shrugged. "That is what I must research."

The Bluecloak mage coughed. "You mean you wish to go to
the Isle of Wizards? I had thought I would have to coax you with
the boy's power."

Dorias eyed Joslyn. "This Dreamer who touches all Aspects –
this target of three orc clans?"

"The lad will need someone to watch over him," Boris said.
"To protect and train him. I can think of none better."

Dorias tapped a finger on his smoothly shaven upper lip. "I
have not seen another Dreamer in decades. Joslyn, you know
as well as any mage the danger faced by Dreamers who hide
from their power." The mage nodded, his face stony and his lips
locked in place. Dorias looked sidelong at Tomas. "And one of
your order might find interest in a young Dreamer's training."

The earl lifted his eyebrows in hope. "Then you will go with
him?"

Dorias nodded, hooking his fingers behind the belt of his vest.
"I, for one, must go to the Isle. And, as Joslyn suspected, I cannot
pass up the chance to train a new Dreamer." His smile faded
when he looked back at Tomas, the conflict on the paladin's face
plain to see. "You still will not go?"

Tomas looked to Boris. "I had intended to ride out with you
and join the garrison at Highspur. My talents might be greatly
needed in the Northlands."

"I too wish that I could have your aid there," Boris said. "Not
only would your paladin talents be of great aid, but so would
your cunning and your unmatched knowledge of the orc clans."
The earl's face revealed his own conflicted emotion. "However,
I agree with Joz. This young man might be more important to
our cause than any one of us here. The enemy has made it clear
that they want him alive, and almost certainly for some nefarious
purpose."

The paladin looked down at the smooth, glassy stone in his

hand. The dragonrock caught the sconce light and reflected it back onto the creamy marble of the hallway.

"I will escort the boy to the Isle." Tomas turned to Dorias. "And I will vouch for you as a guest of the Temple if Varana tries to forbid you."

Unaware that he had held his breath, Dorias let it out. "Good." He turned to Boris. "One thing, though…why did you not tell King Arathan of the lad? You said you did not know the orcs' target."

A torn look crossed the earl's face. He shifted his boots upon the stone floor. "I will just say that the fewer people who know about the lad right now, the safer he will be." Boris lifted a hand toward Tomas. "You know better than anyone how poisonous this court has become."

The paladin nodded his head sadly, his green eyes finding the floor.

"Then it is up to us to watch over him," Dorias said, Tomas nodding in agreement. "And I will do all I can to train him while we are there."

"Good." The expression of relief on Boris' face stood out. "That will be at least one concern off my mind while I'm on the frontier."

"Mine too," Joslyn added, his features softening.

Boris lifted his face to Dorias. "Can you give me any idea what it is you sense? What it is that we must face?" He turned to look at Tomas. "Anything?"

Tomas frowned. "The darkness I detect is very vague. I cannot put a finger on it. I wish I could help you more."

Dorias met the earl's gaze when it returned to him. "I cannot tell you much beyond that. I can only give you a warning." His eyes bored into the Bluecloak's. "Do not underestimate the powers you go to face. Orcs are only the edge of the sword."

19

If the truth be told, most modern scholars are completely uncertain as to whether the Dragonscales rose as a result of the Cataclysm, or whether they were the cause of it. As stated many times in this work, writings from the time are scarce. The widening of the Broken Bay was almost certainly a part of the Cataclysm. Few maps survived from the Elder Days, and this Historian has only seen one of those. It shows a much smaller bay (labeled as The Bay of Figs), and the Iron Mountains, set in the center of a vast plain. The Dragonscales do not appear, and the Andon is a much less significant river with only a few tributaries.
— "Second History of Gannon, Vol. I" by Elyn Bravano

The clank of heavy hammers on red hot metal bounced off the stone walls of the cavern. Ruddy light danced in the shadows, reflected from a hundred hot forges and twice as many sooty torches. Slar far preferred the open air of a Northlands meadow in summer, but the needs of an army were many – weapons and armor far from the least.

"We've got 'round twenty-two thousand scimitars laid away already, Warchief," the forge master growled. "Chainmail takes longer, but we will move more smiths over to its production when we get to quota on the swords."

Radgred nodded, his red eyes scanning the hundreds of smiths and apprentices scurrying about. Slar noticed a look close to approval on the old sergeant's face, something rarely seen, if ever.

"What about pike heads?" Slar folded his clawed hands behind his back. A twinge of tightness remained in his shoulder from the feral dragon's attack, even though a shaman had healed it not long afterward. "I will need half as many pikes as scimitars, but they are twice as important, especially when we face Human cavalry."

Radgred spit, and the forge master stared at the stone floor. *Our people are fools to fear horses so. Every other race uses them to great advantage. Even the dwarves ride ponies.*

"I have the pikes complete, Warchief." The forge master bowed his head, a smile of pride visible in the glow of the cavern. "We tempered the last one this morning."

"Good." Slar nodded. "Woodsmaster Farrol informed me that the poles have been properly cut. See to it that your work gets delivered to him."

"Aye, Warchief."

Raising an eyebrow, now marked with a fresh scar from his fight in the mountains, Slar leaned in closer to the forge master. "And the catapults – you received the designs?"

The burly smith nodded. "Indeed I did, Warchief. Most intricate, and most fascinating. I see no problem with production, as long as the vein within this mountain keeps producing."

Slar smiled. "It will." He tapped his chest with a fist. "Well done, Baylax. Keep at it. More smiths will come when the Snake and Bear Clans join us."

Master Baylax bowed again. "We will have forges and tools ready for them, Warchief."

Once they mounted the dirt ramp leading out of the pit, Radgred tilted his lips closer to Slar's ear. "That is the first you have mentioned of Snake and Bear joining us to anyone outside the war council. Was it purposeful, or are your wits aging faster than mine?"

Unconsciously rubbing the hilt of his father's sword, Slar smiled at his old friend. "It was purposeful. There is a smith here from every tribe, town, clan, and village – and they usually know everyone in that village." He nodded toward the swirl of fire and activity below. "When they go back to the camps tonight, the rumor will spread faster than molten iron."

"You wish a rumor rather than announcing to the people yourself?" Radgred ran a curved, yellow claw along his jawline. "You should take some of the credit yourself – fortify your position among the Clans."

Tilting his head to gain one last glimpse of the glowing forge pit, Slar led Radgred into the recently carved out tunnel. It twisted its way back up toward the main exit from Dragonsclaw. "That would be too presumptuous. A Warchief needs not claim credit, as credit is his due." His lips twisted into a cunning smile. "Believe me, old friend. We will be ready to greet Dradlo and Sarinn when they arrive with their people."

Radgred wrinkled his brow. "Those chieftains come with their warriors?"

"Yes. Apparently so moved were they by Galdreth's visit."

The old sergeant frowned. "I understand that, but why are you smiling like a white fox with a clutch of goose eggs? Valgrar did not come with Wolf, and he might even be seen as an ally." Radgred shook his head. "Maybe." The whites of his crimson-pupiled eyes glittered in the torchlight. "But none of the other clans sent their chieftain, and you have only recently worked out a rough truce in council with the shamans. The Bear and Snake will be far less amenable to you than the Wolf, Shark, and Ram."

Slar shrugged. "It is not me who needs inspire them. It is Galdreth who is our lord and master now."

Radgred frowned. "Then you haven't heard a word I've said."

Patting his old friend on the shoulder Slar watched a young orc in leather running toward them. "Just wait until they arrive, my friend. There are advantages to being Galdreth's *Chosen One*."

Radgred held his tongue as the courier stamped to a halt, breathing heavily from his run.

"Warchief," the messenger slipped between breaths. "A carrier pigeon arrived moments ago." He handed over a small piece of curled paper. "The message was relayed via Blackstone and Sourbay."

With a sideways glance at Radgred, Slar took the paper and dismissed the messenger with a wave. The young man saluted and dashed back the way he came.

"Well…read it," Radgred growled.

Leaning in underneath one of the torches hung upon the wall, Slar squinted to scan the message. Upon finishing it, the knot of fire and pain within his gut that had been silent for the last several weeks burned again. It throbbed, eating away at his insides. He suppressed a sudden urge to vomit. A bit of sour bile rose in his throat, and Slar tasted a hint of blood. He swallowed hard to prevent Radgred from noticing.

"What does it say?" From the expression on Radgred's face, Slar knew his friend could sense his anxiety.

"The second team has failed. None have reported back to base." Slar lifted the paper to a torch, watching it burn down to his claw. "I knew more strength was not the proper approach, and now we have exposed ourselves within the borders of the Human kingdom. One of our best-trained trolls, wasted." He spat on the floor, sending the gobbet into a corner to hide its pinkish color. "I will be forced to apologize to Galdreth for the failure of a plan our master forced upon me."

Frowning, Radgred folded his arms across his wide chest. "How will you deliver the news to the dark one?"

Slar led his friend onward. The fire in his belly subsided with movement. "It is certain that Galdreth will already know. Our master created the tracing stones that are trained on the vessel." Slar fought to hide the pain and dread from his former sergeant. "It is only a matter of time before Galdreth appears to me. Our master should soon be rested from its journey to the Bear and Snake." He clapped Radgred on the shoulder. "Come, old friend. Let us find some lunch, and then we will retire to await our rebuke for failing the impossible."

The swirling black form gathered over Slar, its bright eyes shining down upon his head. The piercing agony in his mind masked the pain in his gut. He winced, a scream gurgling its way to the top of his throat. As quick as it had begun, the pain stopped. The shattering thump within his mind disappeared, leaving only the familiar companion in his bowels. Slar turned his head to see Radgred panting heavily. The veil of pain hung plain in his eyes.

You have failed again, my Warchief. Or perhaps it is just the weakness of your entire race. The screech of rusty iron rang out from the formless face of Galdreth, its shining eyes glimmering in cadence with its words. Malevolence glared down on Slar. *Nevertheless, you are the only tools at my disposal. I only hope that when our victory is complete, your people will realize the honor I have granted them.*

The pain returned, and Slar fought to control his rage, knowing it to be futile. He drew heaving breaths into his lungs, and his claws clenched until they drew blood from his palms. Remaining in his prone position, he bowed his head even farther. *I must draw Galdreth's attention from Radgred. The old man cannot take this.*

"This was my mistake, my Master." Slar scrambled closer to the swirling mass of black smoke, placing himself between Galdreth and his friend. "I could not get enough soldiers inside the great cities of the humans. The vessel is now in their capital, protected by thousands." He stretched his hands out, noticing a slight quiver in them. "Perhaps we could find another…"

NO!

The concussion threw both orcs hard against the wall of the cave.

I have chosen my vessel because he is the only one strong enough and young enough for my purposes. I will have no other!

Climbing back to his unsteady feet, Slar dipped his hands in obeisance. "Forgive me, my Master, I beg of you. I did not know. I wish only to offer every idea my feeble mind might spawn." He knelt down again, casting his eyes in Radgred's direction. The tough old orc shook his head, fighting to come back to his senses. "We will spend every last warrior to capture your vessel, no matter where he flees. I have worked out a plan to slip into the city from the Great River delta. If we can—"

No, my Warchief.

The voice no longer pained Slar's ears. He noticed Radgred sit up from the periphery of his vision.

My vessel will move yet once again. They will send him to their Isle of Wizards. A sizzling chuckle rang through the cavern, lit only by a brazier and the lights of Galdreth's eyes. *It is more isolated than any of the human cities. But it will require true skill and stealth from your people to capture him there. Will they be ready?*

"I will lead a team myself, Master Galdreth."

No! Fierceness returned to the steely voice. The dark spirit roiled in a tempest, then calmed. The shining eyes focused upon him. *You must be the one to lead my army once the Bear and Snake arrive. However, this display will take a great deal of my energy, and I will be required to rest for some time before I can go unto the Mammoth Clan. Their lands are a great distance from my prison. It is unlikely I will return before you must move forward with our plans.*

"Yes, my Master." Despite the dark spirit hanging over Slar, a weight lifted from his heart and the tightness in his gut untwisted. *At least I have peace when Galdreth rests.*

Radgred tried to crawl up beside him. Slar gave the old orc a dark look and signaled him to freeze.

Now, as to the capture of my vessel. This time I want you to send shamans. The boy gains power even more quickly than I foresaw.

Slar tilted his head. "Will the wizards not detect our team with their magics?"

There is a certain place upon the Isle...

Smoke rose from a thousand campfires, clouding Slar's keen sense of smell. But no amount of charcoal could cover the scent of nearly one hundred thousand orcs gathered on the plain that spread below Dragonsclaw. Nearly as many orcs stood behind Slar, but their far more familiar scent blew upwind.

Fargon of the Wolf Clan folded his arms and drew air into his nostrils. "I think an actual, live bear would smell better…or a dead one, for that matter."

Folding his own arms, Radgred nodded. "And real snakes have almost no scent at all."

Coarse laughter passed among the shamans and war leaders gathered to greet the arrival of Bear and Snake Clans.

Brother Ortax frowned at their numbers. "Only two clans, yet they almost outnumber our four. It is a good thing they come as friends." He turned his scarlet stare upon Slar. "I hear the clan chieftains have come with their people. Can you control both Dradlo and Sarinn?"

Running his hand along the worn leather-wrapped handle of his sword, Slar stared at Ortax until the shaman lowered his gaze and covered his retreat with a cough. Slar turned his eyes back upon the newly arrived clans. "Our Master Galdreth has given me dominion as Warchief of the united clans. That will be sufficient."

Pulling the shining steel from its sheath, Slar lifted his ancient weapon into the sky in salute as two parties of orcs broke away from the mass. One group gathered beneath a brown banner sewn with a rampant black bear. Above the second fluttered a coiled green snake, poised to strike.

Slar's voice remained level. Not even Ortax could crawl under his skin at the moment. "Our Master will make his choice clear."

He strode forward to greet the arrivals, Radgred, Fargon, Balthor of the Ram, and Visron, son of the Shark chieftain marching behind him. Ortax and the other shamans hovered at the rear. *They have learned better their place, but shamans unite easily, no matter their clan. Sadly, it is different with us warriors.*

The rock-strewn distance between the parties closed. When only a hundred yards remained, a shadow passed over the sun, darkening the sky above the assembled orcs. The darkness continued to grow. Slar's companions mumbled and slowed in apprehension. Radgred kept pace, even though Slar had only given him a hint of today's events. The approaching Bear and Snake delegations wavered, but shouts from their leaders drove them on.

Their chieftains will not be cowed by a shadow. At least not yet. Slar stopped, his coterie gathered about him. The darkness swelled until it hid the noonday sun, and a false dusk covered the land. Dradlo of the Bear approached first, his chest puffed out and a great waraxe slung over his shoulder. Sarinn of the Snake hurried to keep pace with his companion, working the fingers of his clasped hands.

Dradlo offered Slar the nod of an equal. "Chieftain Slar, I gree—"

"*Warchief* Slar!" Radgred bellowed, his fingers rubbing his own axe.

Fargon growled in support of Slar. Dradlo shifted his stance, glaring directly at the Wolf chieftain's son.

His shamans closing about him, Sarinn spread his lips in an ophidian smile. "But tradition states that a Warchief may only be appointed with a vote of all seven clans. No more than one chieftain may dissent."

Dradlo slammed the butt of his waraxe into the hard ground. "And two dissenters stand before you!"

Slar sensed the hackles rising on his companions, including the representatives of Ram and Shark clans. He rested the blade of his sword over one shoulder and waved his allies to calm. Slar gazed at Dradlo and Sarinn. "You make a mistake challenging the chosen Warchief of Galdreth," he said in a calm voice. "Was it not our Master's command that you join my army at Dragonsclaw?"

The Snake chieftain folded his restless fingers. "Master Galdreth did summon us, yes." He paused while Dradlo glared at him. "But a Warchief of all clans may only be appointed through tradition. We cannot—"

What can you not do, Sarinn of the Snake? Obey my command? The metallic voice screeched from the sky, and the darkness surrounding them sank into night. A hushed cry of fear rose up from the thousands of orcs gathered at the feet of Dragonsclaw. Even those within the camp of clans already joined to Slar murmured in unease.

Upon hearing the voice, Radgred immediately fell into a prostrate position, as did Fargon, Balthor, and Visron. The shamans, including Ortax, followed suit without hesitation. Only Slar remained standing, one eyebrow cocked, and his family sword casually resting on his shoulder.

I must show casual courage, as if I held not an ounce of fear. The stirring in his gut told him otherwise. *What boils down there must not show on my face.*

Kneel before your chosen Warchief! The screech sounded across the vast plain of the Northlands. Slar remained steady on his feet, while a wave in the grass rippled out in a circle from where they stood. Dradlo of the Bear and Sarinn of the Snake collapsed to their knees, as did their entire guard, most with their faces pressed against the dirt. The thousands standing behind them fell onto their bellies, while most of the camp followed suit.

"I assume this means you no longer dissent." Slar walked forward, tapping first Dradlo, then Sarinn, upon the shoulder with the flat of his sword. "Then rise as chieftains, and members of my war council. Your shamans should join the others after they have seen to the needs of your people."

Sarinn stood swiftly, bowing again from the waist. Dradlo blinked first before clambering to his feet. He gave a quick, short nod, but one deeper than his first.

Slar gestured for his own supporters to rise.

The darkness that hid the day disappeared as if it had never been. The bright sun of deep summer, a sun that would not sleep long tonight, returned to the Northlands. It spread its warmth once again upon the flower-strewn meadows and glinted off the green and obsidian shoulders of Dragonsclaw.

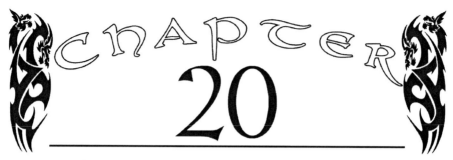

CHAPTER 20

Any man who comes to this land, willing to swear the Oath of Fealty to his new king, and swear the appropriate oaths to his liege lords, shall become a free subject of Gannon. The kingdom shall then grant unto him forty acres of unclaimed land to work, or grant equivalent kingdom marks to begin a trade should he display proof of knowledge or training in a recognized craft.
– Seventh Decree of the Navigator

The bare orange sphere of the sun peeked over the eastern wall of the Ivory Palace, setting alight the silver plated dome of the High Hall. Tallen watched the tall towers flare like torches, glowing with the first rays of morning. The blue and silver banners snapped with a steady westerly breeze, and the longest pennants reached out to brush light fingers upon the sun.

His heart hung heavy in his chest, and a slight pressure formed behind his eyes.

"Battalion! Mount!" Sergeant Hall's voice boomed out into the misty morning, its gray wisps just now melted by the sun's first warmth. A thousand Bluecloaks clambered into their saddles in unison, the ranks of horses standing steady as they took their riders. Lances settled into saddle boots, and the troops straightened their conical steel helmets. Hall's wolfhound sat still near his master's oversized horse, his eyes drifting along the line of Bluecloaks as if he were a general on inspection.

Tallen looked up at Jaerd, whose emerald green cloak stood out against the sea of blue. "Be careful," he whispered. "I wish we had more time together."

Nodding his head, Jaerd reached out his gauntleted hand. "Me too. You be careful also."

Tears threatening to well up, Tallen clasped his brother's hand with both of his own. They had already hugged good-bye earlier to avoid all these unwanted witnesses.

The wizard in dark green lifted his hand, and the raven on his shoulder flapped his wings. "We will keep a close eye on him."

The man fascinated Tallen. Magus Britt had arrived with him and the disinherited Paladin Lord from court before the break of dawn. *I'm to be watched over now by heroes even more famous than Boris Mourne and Joslyn Britt! Everyone has heard of the Paladin Tomas Harte, and I own a copy of Dorias Ravenhawke's book.*

"Good." Jaerd nodded to the wizard and paladin. "This young man means more to me than just his power."

Magus Britt edged his horse closer, while Boris conferred with one of his lieutenants. The mage reached out, a small, leather-bound tome in his hands. "Something I read a long time ago. You would be lucky to find ten copies in the kingdom." He looked at Dorias when Tallen took it from his hand. The cover, softened by use, held worn but well cared for pages. "It was written by the Ravenhawke, though I imagine it sold far fewer copies than his *Tarmorian Bestiary.*"

The dark-eyed wizard lifted an eyebrow. "Is that *The Five Pointed Star*?" He chuckled. "I doubt I even have a copy of that anymore." He turned his eyes to Tallen. "Read it cover to cover, lad. It's written specifically with Dreamers in mind." Narrowing his gaze, he turned to face Magus Britt, his expression both knowing and compassionate. "Why am I not surprised that you have this?"

The red-fringed Bluecloak frowned, reining his horse back. "Regardless, it has been a pleasure training an apt student, Tallen. I look forward to seeing what Varana and this rogue can draw out of you."

"So do I." Boris led his stallion closer, the black beast chomping at the bit. "Take care, lad. I wish I could stay with you longer, but duty calls me to the king's service – as it always does."

Tallen opened his mouth to speak, but the clatter of a single rider galloping up from the command barracks interrupted. He recognized the thin man who sat upon the High Council.

"Lord Marshal Magdon." Boris saluted his superior, who trotted his horse up to the head of the long line of Bluecloaks. "Have you come to give us a personal send off?"

"Nay, My Lord Earl, I come to join you."

A scowl of confusion swept over Boris' face, and the other officers muttered amongst each other. Magus Britt shook his head, as if he had already predicted this occurrence.

"Why, Lord Marshal?" Boris slow walked his stallion forward. "Just yesterday I received this command by King Arathan's order. Has he ordered me to stay?"

191

"No, he has not." The Lord Marshal shook his gray, thin face. "The king has ordered that I take command of Highspur – to ensure the security of the kingdom." The Lord Marshal held up a scroll of fresh paper. "He signed the orders this morning."

"The chancellor strikes again," Magus Britt muttered in an angry tone.

Boris shook his head. "There is nothing to be done but follow the king's decree." He looked at his superior officer. "Then I cede my command, My Lord. The detachment is yours."

Marshal Magdon ducked his head, sad eyes looking out under bushy eyebrows. "This is not what I wanted."

"We must all do things that we do not want." Boris gestured to the head of the line. "The battalion awaits your orders to march, My Lord."

The Lord Marshal spurred his horse forward. He gave a clipped nod of farewell to Paladin Tomas, who returned it. Dorias stared at the battalion, his eyes unfocused. Tallen noticed that the huge black bird upon the wizard's shoulder watched the troops with far more attention.

The marshal, his four silver stars catching dawn's light, nodded to the giant Bluecloak with four bronze discs. "Give the order, Master Sergeant."

After his salute, Sergeant Hall gave Tallen a short, confident nod. "Battalion! *Ho!*"

The several hundred-yards of flesh and steel lurched forward as one. The wagons at the rear, stuffed with barrels and sacks and covered mounds of goods, rolled over the cobblestone with an echo that rattled in Tallen's ears. Brawny jogged over to him, nudging his hand with a huge snout. He gave the wolfhound a good ear scratching. Brawny licked his fingers before loping back to the front of the line.

Tallen caught a glimpse of Boris leaning toward the Lord Marshal, whispering from behind a gauntleted hand. Magus Britt hung close. Jaerd looked back over his shoulder and nodded once at Tallen, before turning his face back to the front.

The pain behind Tallen's eyes swelled and threatened to burst forth in a flood of tears. He held his breath. When Maddi slipped her arm through his, patting his wrist, Tallen did not see her. He stared at the single green cloak in the mass of blue. He did not blink for fear of the trickle of salty sorrow that would flow down his cheek. When the head of the column disappeared underneath the front gate of the palace, Jaerd flung his hand up in a final wave.

"Let us go get some breakfast together," Tomas Harte whispered, placing his hand upon Tallen's shoulder.

"Yes, let's." Dorias rubbed his hands together. The raven on his shoulder cawed and hopped from one foot to the other. "Merl agrees."

Tallen let a small smile slip out at the raven's dance.

Maddi squeezed his elbow once before releasing it. "Food always helps a sad mood."

Paladin Tomas nodded in agreement. "You will make a very powerful healer, miss, and not just because of your Talent. You have so much potential. If I had the time, you could possibly even become a paladin."

"Doubtful," Maddi said, her nose wrinkling. "I don't put any stake in your Balance."

Tomas' tone did not change. "That is why you should become a Doctor."

A slow day passed. After a breakfast of bacon, eggs, and summer berries, Dorias excused himself to the city, claiming a need to find supplies. Maddi seemed in no hurry to leave the palace, and a silent agreement occurred to spend the day together before Tallen's ship left with the morning tide. Tomas, his watchful eye never roaming too far, remained close. His presence intruded on Tallen's desire to spend time alone with Maddi, though he knew the paladin only sought to protect him. *But I doubt orcs will come after me inside the palace.*

They sat under an ancient, spread black oak, the paladin lost in meditation, while Tallen and Maddi watched the blossoms of the palace gardens bounce in the summer breeze. At Tomas' request, a servant brought them lunch. The food soon disappeared, and mugs of ale sat half-empty. Tomas made the excuse of nature's call and left Tallen alone with Maddi as the sun tracked its way toward the western wall.

Tallen twisted a blade of grass between his fingers. "Tell me about your family, Maddi."

She leaned back against the trunk of the tree and eyed him over the rim of her mug. "Why do you ask?"

Surprised at her sudden suspicion, Tallen dipped his head. "I don't mean to pry. I'm just interested in you."

He saw a smile creep around the corners of her mouth. She took a sip to hide it.

When the mug came down, her eyes sank in sadness. "My father raised me until I was almost ten. He only told me that my mother died bearing me." Her gaze roamed toward the tower tops. "He died in the Bloody Flux."

Tallen sucked in a quick breath. "It took my father, too."

Maddi tilted her head at him, and then nodded, her eyes cast downward. "We have loss in common, I suppose." She pulled her legs up, wrapping her arms about her knees. "I was a lucky orphan, I guess, especially for Dern. My father's cousin, Renna, took me in. She is a Talented healer. She taught me almost everything I know. It was Renna who told me I had the Talent to become a Doctor." Her gaze drifted back to the tower tops. "She told me to come here, but I never really believed it would happen."

Tallen patted her hand and she clasped it for a brief moment. "I know what you mean," he said.

A flutter of strong wings on the air rustled over Tallen's head. Merl the raven alighted on the oak tree, flapping to settle his balance. He cawed a greeting.

A smile formed on Maddi's lips. "And the same to you, Merl."

"We thought perhaps you two might like to join us for dinner." Dorias' feet crunched on the crushed gravel path that led from the cobblestone to the oak tree. "I know of a wonderful place on Tarathine Hill, not far from the Avenue of Flowers. Tomas will meet us there before sunset." The wizard ducked under the tree to cast his raptor gaze back and forth between the two young people. "It's very quiet, very tasty, and I'm buying…"

Tallen stared at Dorias, hoping he might get his silent message. *I know they want to protect me, but I do not need a mother hen watching everything Maddi and I do and say.*

The wizard did not grasp it, but from her wry smile, Tallen thought maybe Maddi did. She said nothing, however, and followed Dorias toward the west gate. Tallen huffed before he joined them.

The Baron's House stood not far from the Palace, across a bridge between the two hills. "It was once the townhouse of a southern baron who long ago sold it for newer digs." The wizard rubbed the quilted leather vest covering his flat stomach. "An entrepreneurial friend of mine purchased it, and ever since, Baron's House has served the best beef steaks in Daynon."

Maddi laughed at Tallen's contented moan as he took the first, luxurious bite of his sirloin. However, when she put a bite in her mouth she made much the same noise. He laughed back.

"I told you." Dorias waved a fork with a piece of dripping pink beef skewered upon it. "Best in the kingdom." He stuck the bite in his mouth and chewed, eyes closed. He opened them and smiled, pointing with his empty fork toward the jug in the center of the table. "Try the wine. It's an Avarosan Red, House of the Red Tower vintage 484 -- just fabulous."

Tallen sniffed the bouquet before he sipped, fruity and oaky. The hearty wine warmed his insides as it went down. He smiled at Dorias with a nod of thanks as his nervous anticipation of tomorrow slipped away.

Cool night breezes, full of salty sea air, swept up from the Bay of Hope during their walk back to the Palace. Tallen could not help but jump at every shadow that moved along the thoroughfare, despite the satisfaction of his full stomach.

"Fear not, lad." Tomas nodded to him with confidence. "I assure you, no danger hovers nearby. I would sense any threat."

The towers of the Ivory Palace danced like ghosts in the moonlight under the shadow of thin clouds scudding through the night sky. Tallen saw only the brightest stars shining through the penumbra glow of the city lights. The scent of lilac bushes hung in the air as he walked onto the grounds.

The bulk of Garrison Tower cast a shadow over Tallen and his companions as they approached the gated yard. Within the tower, two hallways ran off to wings full of officer's quarters. As guests of Earl Boris Mourne, Tallen and Maddi stayed in rooms several flights up along the stone-carved staircase.

Tomas Harte turned the key to his room. "I will keep watch for the night with my paladin senses, so rest with ease." He nodded goodnight before closing the door behind him.

Merl burbled on Dorias' shoulder. The wizard turned to look at Tallen. "You can trust that. Many's the night on the road I awoke at dawn to find him still in his trance, the campfire still glowing." He stood there for an annoying moment, a strange smile on his face, until a caw from his raven echoed up the spiral tower. Dorias started as if woken from a nap. "Ah, yes. Fair enough, Merl. Goodnight to you both." He left them alone in the hall.

Tallen turned. "Well…I guess this is—"

Maddi's soft, sweet lips found his. He fumbled to put his arms around her and returned her kiss with passion. She held him for only a moment before pushing back, faced flushed and her breath quick.

"I…" she stammered, putting a hand to her mouth and a smile forming behind her fingers. "I should go to bed. I don't mean to tease, but I wanted you to know how I felt before you leave. Fires, I don't even know how I feel." Her nose wrinkled in that cute way, and a cloud of emotions crossed her face. She squeezed his hand. "Goodnight, Tallen."

Maddi scratched at the door with her key, having difficulty finding the lock. Even in the dim light, Tallen could see the crimson blossoming on the tips of her ears.

When the door at last opened, she looked at him. "Breakfast before your ship leaves?"

"Of course."

With a soft wave, Maddi closed the door behind her, leaving Tallen alone in the corridor, frustrated and elated in equal measure. Huffing a confused sigh, he turned toward the comfort of his lonely bed.

Few words passed among the four while they broke their fast. Tallen found no flavor in the eggs and the sausage too rich for his stomach. He drank his tea and ate a handful of rolled oats, hoping to settle the nervous movement in his gut. Dorias and Tomas ate their meal with haste, before excusing themselves to wait out in the sunshine. Merl cocked his head at Maddi and clacked his beak. She waved a soft farewell.

"My ship leaves in just over an hour." Tallen moved his eggs back and forth across the plate with a fork. "I will write you if I can."

Maddi nodded, her eyes fixed on her own untouched breakfast. "Please do. I promise I will write back."

Tallen tossed the fork down and rose to his feet. "I suppose I should go. It might take a while to find this ship."

Setting down her fork, Maddi shrugged and said in a spooky tone, "The paladin can probably *sense* it nearby." She fluttered her fingers around her face while she spoke.

Tallen laughed and held out his arms for a hug. Maddi hopped up into them, wrapping her own around his chest.

"Don't forget me when you are a wizard," she whispered into his ear. Her lips brushed his cheek before she stepped back.

"How could I?" He held her at arm's length. "You're amazing."

Maddi's eyes popped open. "I almost forgot..." She reached into her pocket and pulled out a little piece of gold, handing it to him. It was wrought in the shape of a noble's cup, but no bigger than a thimble. It sparkled when he spun it between his fingers. "It is Greal, the Fifth Talisman. The Talismans are important to the folk of the Free Cities, especially Greal. It is a symbol of peace between the races, as it was in the Elder Days...before the Dragon Wars came and the Cataclysm destroyed it all." She bit her lip. "I have had it for a very long time."

"It's beautiful." Tallen examined the intricate scrollwork surrounding the cup, stem, and base. "Thank you, Maddi."

She cleared her throat. "They also say that the Talismans and the Aspects are connected, and that Greal is tied to Psoul. Since you are a Dreamer I thought it appropriate."

Tallen gazed upon the tiny cup with more reverence. *There is so much I must learn.*

When she looked at Tallen, tears floated between her eyelids. She put her arms around his neck and kissed him on the lips, reminding him of their moment alone last night. This time she ducked away even faster.

"Goodbye, Tallen," she croaked, turning and dashing from the mess hall.

Watching her go left his throat dry and a heavy pressure behind his eyes. He swallowed and hoisted his rucksack. Dabbing his cheeks upon a sleeve, he left the hall in the opposite direction, following the wizard and his paladin friend.

"I see things were not easy," Dorias said when Tallen joined them in the courtyard of Garrison Tower. "They seldom are with women."

He forced a smile. "Exceptionally so with me."

Dorias patted him on the back. "Well, on the Isle, you will have little time to think about it. I remember my first few months...a long time ago. I hardly slept, ate everything I could get my hands on, and learned almost as much as I've learned since." Merl fluttered his wings, and the wizard reached up to scratch under the raven's beak. "Almost."

They passed beneath the main gate of the Ivory Palace and

entered the twist of city streets. Tallen watched the bird closely. "Merl is a special raven, isn't he?"

Dorias laughed, while the raven flapped over to settle on Tallen's shoulder. Merl rested far lighter than he had guessed from the bird's size. Noticing the soft grip of his talons, Tallen copied the wizard's regular gesture and reached up to scratch the raven's beak. Merl's eyelids fluttered with pleasure, and he chortled with joy.

"He likes you, but you can probably tell." A smile broadened the wizard's sharp features. "Merl is my familiar, a bond only we Dreamers can create. What's more, he is a friend. Wise beyond most humans–and fast…so fast." He smacked his hands together, one shooting off toward the sky. "I saw him outrun a pair of wyverns once. Left one with a broken wing when he drew it too close to a baobob tree."

Tomas nodded. "I remember that. Jahad is a vast land of beauty." He sighed. "Perhaps I might retire there."

The wizard smoothed a momentary frown, his steps quickening to join the paladin. "You will retire to Harte Castle, and I may join you there."

Pursing his lips, Tomas watched the constant crowd of people travelling along the avenue toward the docks. Tallen's eye followed the paladin's as they descended from the palace to the sea. He watched a dozen children playing hayball with the help of a few excited dogs.

"I may never see the stones of Harte Castle again," the paladin said with a sad tone, "or the beauty of Crystal Lake in summer. Arathan has taken from me what has been in my family since before his ancestors set foot upon these shores." His thumb rubbed the hilt of his sword. "However, it would pass to some other house upon my death, regardless. I suppose it is for the best that it happen now."

Dorias reached out and tapped the ruddy-bearded man's shoulder. "You could get married and have children."

Tomas shook his head again. "You know that the vows to my order forbid that."

"Who cares?" Dorias barked. "Did you notice how that *order* treated you in the High Hall? The High Elder schemed with Chancellor Vyce to turn the king against you. Arathan has understood your position for years. He accepted that you would manage the lands of Harlong, but you would not sit in council. Why has that changed now?"

"Because it was convenient," the paladin murmured. "Because the elder knows I oppose him. Because Arathan is losing his grip."

Dorias hushed his friend, casting his hawkish eyes about. "You should not let anyone in this city hear you say that. You are not on good terms with the king as it is."

His lips tight, Tomas nodded. "Fair enough. But I can sense it Dorias, as certainly as I could sense a broken arm. He is full of rage, sorrow, and regret – they all eat away at his sanity." He looked at the wizard. "And the chancellor is full of hate. It is directed, though I could not tell at whom."

Dorias hooked his thumbs behind the belt of his leather vest. "We have larger problems than the scheming of a royal court. That happens all the time. The darkness we have sensed, the shadow obscuring the Dreamrealm, these are things that have not happened before – at least, not since I began watching things."

Tomas snorted. "And that was indeed a very long time ago."

Dorias laughed heartily, and Tallen chanced a snicker. They turned a corner onto the main street lining the docks, crowded with carts and carters, horses and cargo.

The scent of horse crawled up Tallen's nostrils, and a spark of memory popped in his brain. "Magus…Paladin…sirs…"

The wizard waggled a finger. "Now, Tallen, we told you, Dorias and Tomas. We are to be friends, and someday you are likely to be more powerful than either of us, I think."

Tallen ducked his head. "I wonder, what of the horse I rode here? He's been mine for some time, and I left him at the royal stable in the palace."

"You show concern for lesser creatures," Tomas noted. "That is a good sign."

Dorias waved toward the top of the hill, where the towers of the palace peaked over the city buildings. "Earl Boris made me aware of this. My horse, Shade, stays in the same stable. I even made the point of introducing the two of them this morning. Shade will see that he is cared for."

"My own steed is there as well," Tomas added. "Fireheart and Shade are well acquainted."

"Here we are," the wizard said when they reached the pier. "It should be…oh, my." He turned to look at Tomas. "She sent her own ship."

Unfazed, Tomas strode forward. "Then we will arrive at the Isle all the faster."

They led Tallen to a ship unlike any he had ever seen or read about in the Gryphon's library. Its hull swooped in smooth lines like many of the other sea-going vessels in the harbor, but that was where the similarities ended. No masts rose from its deck, and no racks of oars lined its rails. A rainbow of color splashed along its hull, red, yellow, blue, green and silver – the colors of the five Aspects.

A short man with olive skin and dark eyes stood at the far end of the gangplank, his stare fixed on Dorias. Tallen sensed the power of a mage about the man, though he was not as strong as Dorias or Magus Britt. Tallen saw no other crew.

"I've come for the boy, Ravenhawke, not for you." The man frowned, his heavy, black eyebrows knitting together. "The Lady did not say anything about returning a rogue to the Isle."

Dorias spread his hands. "She could not have known, Yarro, and I will gladly pay for my passage. Otherwise, I could simply book a spot on the next cargo ship headed there. Either way, I intend to speak to Varana." He gave the mage a knowing look. "You were there when we found Malcolm, hidden in the Jade Isles. You also know that I never desired power beyond my own, and that I never wished to harm the Circle."

"I was there. I will not forget." The ship's captain shrugged. "And you might be surprised to know that I would like to have children myself some day."

Dorias peaked an eyebrow, but Tallen frowned at the comment. *What is that about?*

The ship captain smiled. "Don't tell the Lady I said that, if you wouldn't mind." Yarro stood aside and gestured for them to cross. "Welcome onboard the Fair Aspect, lad. New students rarely arrive at the Isle on Lady Varana's personal ship. You'll want to thank her for the privilege." Yarro turned to Tomas. "And you must be the Paladin Harte. Passage for paladins to the Isle is always offered freely and with respect. Your order resided there long before mine."

Tallen had no more than tossed his rucksack into the forward cabin than the boat thrummed below him. He felt the flow of magical power, the light tingle of the Air Aspect. Soon, the ship moved, pulling itself away from the stone and concrete pier. In only a few minutes, the boat's bow pointed out into the Bay of

Hope. The flow of Air increased, and it leaped forward, plowing through the waves. Tallen hopped up the gangway, where Tomas and Dorias both watched the passing water from the foredeck. Merl perched upon the prow of the ship, carved like a hawk spreading its wings over the whitecaps. He posed in a similar fashion.

"How does Air drive this ship with no sails?" Tallen blurted out, his curiosity overwhelming him.

Tomas raised a hand. "Perhaps I could explain this for you, eh, Dorias?"

The wizard gestured toward Tallen. "By all means."

The paladin nodded. "It is a combination of magic and something Dorias would call engineering, like the design of siege engines. The dwarves know a great deal of this art—"

"Science!" Dorias interrupted with an upthrust finger.

Tomas shrugged. "As you say." He looked back at Tallen. "I believe Dorias would also say that it is the future of all the races to learn this…science." The Ravenhawke nodded. "As for this vessel – a long shaft descents from the rear cabin, down through the hull and into the water. At the end of it is a star shaped device called a…" He looked to Dorias. "What do you call it?"

"A propeller. It propels the boat through the water."

"Ah, yes, a propeller." The paladin pointed toward the stern. "Yarro is in there right now, spinning this shaft with his power in Air. Usually two or three mages might handle a ship this size, but Yarro is very strong."

"And, at this speed, the ride does not take long." Dorias patted his stomach, a thoughtful expression crossing his features. "Perhaps it might be long enough to see what's down in the ship's galley."

Tomas scrunched his face in distaste. "Not if you are the one cooking."

Tallen laughed. "Let me see what I can do."

An hour later, their bellies full of salt pork, braised with potatoes in beer, and a mug in their hands, the three watched a blue mound rise up out of the horizon. Tallen's heart leaped and froze at the same time.

My life will never, ever be simple again.

CHAPTER 21

The allied powers signed the Great Concord in 122 A.R., just weeks after crushing the invasion of the Free Cities by Wild Tiger. That was the last time an orc host came south of the Dragonscales in force. Much of that security can be credited to the vigilance of the garrison at Highspur, founded as the core act of the Great Concord. All six signatory powers have sent troops to that isolated fortress. Even when those powers war amongst themselves, the soldiers of Highspur maintain their vigilance, no matter the nation or race of their birth.
— "History of Gannon" by Elyn Bravano

Captain Jaerd Westar stretched his back, one gauntleted hand still holding the reins of his horse. He watched Earl Boris, Magus Britt, and Sergeant Hall all move through various stages of the same act, and allowed himself a small smile.

Behind Jaerd, the Stonebourne Fork spread to join the Andon where dozens of ferries still unloaded blue-cloaked cavalry. To the south, Gavanor bustled beyond the western wall. Jaerd squinted at Wolfsgate. It stood open and peaceful as ever. *Those boys are in for a surprise when I arrive to inspect them.*

Magus Britt drew down his bushy brows and pointed toward a tight knot of blue and green-cloaked men on horseback. "It looks like we drew Aginor's attention, bringing a thousand men across the Stonebourne like that."

"I'm sure they are just coming to greet us, Joz," Earl Boris replied, giving his black stallion rein to scrabble at the grass. He scanned down the line of Bluecloaks falling out to make camp for the night. "Lord Marshal Magdon should be here for this."

Magus Britt leaned close to the earl. "He is not well. One of our healers attends him. He is too frail and should not have come."

Earl Boris puffed out his black, bushy mustache. "It is His Majesty's command, and Darron Magdon is far too noble to claim illness when his king orders a march."

Magus Britt snorted. "Sammin Vyce just wanted to get another

High Council vote out of the capital. It was also his idea to send the Lord Justice to Threeforts to handle an insignificant dispute with the Yadushi."

Frowning at the mage, the earl turned toward Sergeant Hall. "See to it that a camp is erected for the night. City privileges for any man who wants them, but only until midnight. I want this column ready to move an hour after dawn."

Hall knuckled his brow. "Yes, Milord."

Earl Boris leaped astride his charger. Magus Britt groaned, but also mounted.

The earl looked down at Jaerd. "If you would join us, Captain, you might want to greet your liege lord."

Ignoring the protests in his thighs and hips, Jaerd sighed and swung back into his saddle. He picked out Duke Aginor among the riders, along with his two elder sons Doran and Kent – Kent in Gannon blue – and several other officers within Jaerd's chain of command. He gave them a sharp salute when they met. Doran offered a friendly nod.

"My Lord Earl, it is an honor to host you again so soon within the Western Realm." Duke Aginor cast his gaze at the Bluecloak battalion setting up camp. "It appears the king listened to you."

The earl and the duke both dismounted. The rest of the parties followed suit. Boris and Aginor clasped hands, while Jaerd stood nearby at attention.

"Perhaps not as many men as I would have wanted." Earl Boris indicated the camp being assembled on the prairie behind him. "But they are the best in the kingdom."

"I can help you somewhat with your numbers." Duke Aginor nodded toward Lieutenant Kent Varlan. "Five hundred Bluecloaks supplement my own guard in the city. Kent will bring half of them with you. I can also send another two hundred of my own men." He nodded at Jaerd. "It appears you have already claimed one of my captains."

Magus Britt laughed, and Earl Boris reached into one of his saddlebags. He pulled out a folded blue tunic, trimmed in silver. Steel buttons ran in double rows down the front. "I suppose you have preempted my surprise, Duke Aginor." Boris turned to Jaerd. "I want you to join the Royal Guard, as a captain under my command."

Jaerd opened his mouth then snapped it shut. He looked at Duke Aginor, who nodded. Doran Varlan winked.

"Earl Boris gets who he wants in his Bluecloaks." The duke

sighed. "As I obviously have no choice, I relieve you, Wolfsgate Captain Westar." He cast a significant look at the earl. "Consider him on loan."

Jaerd took the blue-dyed wool from Earl Boris with a nod of thanks.

"Your cloak and other uniform requirements can be handled by the quartermaster."

Magus Britt cocked an examining eye. "You'll look good in blue."

Almost a week later, an unseasonably cool breeze swept down from the Dragonscales, chilling Jaerd through his mail and new wool. The wind drove the wheat fields around the Free City of Novon in green waves. Jaerd gazed up at the walls encircling the sizeable town, much closer to his childhood home than Gavanor. Many of the metal tools needed at the inn had come from Novon. A sooty smoke rose from the city to be drawn away by chill winds.

Jaerd wrapped himself in his blue cloak. *Dad would be proud. Fires, the whole bloody Westar clan would be proud!* He shifted in his saddle. *Half of me wishes I had stopped at the Gryphon, the other half is glad we had no time.*

A company of gray-clad soldiers wearing circular helmets and burnished mail rode out to greet Jaerd and the others.

"My Lord Earl of Mourne," their leader called with a bow from his saddle. "I am General Bryce Vahn. I bring a hundred men of the Free City guard to join you and reinforce our garrison at Highspur."

Earl Boris nodded his head.

When Lord Marshal Magdon's cough erupted into a silk kerchief, Jaerd noticed a spot of crimson. *He does not look well, but he insisted on joining us to greet the Free City men. And that officer – he does not command many men for the title* General.

"You are most welcome, General Vahn." Boris saluted the man whose long legs hung low in his stirrups. "Our thanks to the Mayors for sending you." He looked over the general's shoulder, passing his gaze over every soldier. "And to your men who sacrifice time at home with their families to join us in protecting all the free peoples of Tarmor. You will be honored as heroes when you return home."

A smile curled at the corner of Jaerd's lips. *And with that, those men belong to Boris.*

Jaerd scanned the new company. About a hundred mounted cavalry with sabers and lances stood before him. A dozen wagons bulging with supplies followed, each with a pair of teamsters. Among the officers at the front, Jaerd noticed a woman wrapped in a dark blue cotton robe. When his eyes paused on her, she hoisted the hood over her hair. He caught only a glimpse of her golden-brown curls before she tucked them away. A carved harp stuck out from under a leather flap on her saddle. Reaching back, she flipped the bag closed.

"We should be off." Earl Boris waved to Sergeant Hall. "We still have a hard ride if we are to reach the fortress before winter sets in."

Groaning, Jaerd collapsed onto his bedroll and stared up at the stars. At last he had found time to fill his belly with a bowl of camp stew and a hard crust of bread. It tasted plain, but it warmed him against the cool night. Up here in the foothills of the Dragonscales, skirting the edge of the Wastes of Lost Lond, Jaerd needed to pull his blanket more tightly about him. The sky, however, twinkled with the light of a thousand pinpoints. He gazed at the River of Souls where it spread its milky haze across the heart of the firmament. *Already I can tell the nights are getting longer since we left the kingdom.*

He rested his head upon his pack, shifting it so that the pipe inside no longer poked him in the neck. He flung his cloak over the top of his blanket and closed his eyes.

The soft trickle of music danced across the camp. A melody formed from random notes, and a soft, beautiful voice carried along on the wind. *The woman who came with the Free City men.*

Crossing his boots, Jaerd settled in with a smile. The words of *Catching the Dream* carried him away from the cold wastes and into the warm bed of a private barracks.

But sleep did not come, so long as her song floated over the camp. *There's something about her voice… Have I heard this siren before?*

His eyes opened to see the heavens remained just as spectacular as when he had closed them. Snores resounded about the camp,

Magus Britt rattling the ground with each breath. Captain Silios Vonstrass, a younger nephew of the Duke of Avaros, slept in silence two bedrolls away. He commanded the Bluecloak rangers, who had long since traded their formal green-fringed garb for Fadecloaks, which shifted in the daylight and darkened at night, making their wearer more difficult to find.

Earl Boris, however, sat straight up, his eyes focused on the low-banked fire.

Jaerd tossed off his blanket and swung his mundane, unfringed blue cloak about his shoulders. The bard's song continued above the rumble of sleeping soldiers. Looking around and noticing no one other than Boris awake, Jaerd hopped to his feet. *Perhaps a short walk to burn off whatever keeps me from rest.*

He wandered among the sleeping forms, most wrapped in wool blankets, still wearing their boots. Jaerd paused. The music had stopped short of the song's end as he knew it. Realizing that he unconsciously made his way toward the bard, Jaerd took a few more quick steps. He rounded a knob of stone to see the young woman tucking her harp into its leather bag. She hid it hurriedly under her blankets and adjusted her hood.

"Your music is quite lovely." Jaerd folded his hands behind his back to show her his officer's tunic in the firelight. "I can't imagine why you would want to come with us to Highspur, but I'm thankful that you do. Men's spirits can fade in lonely places." He took a step closer. "If any of them seek more from you than your voice, you let me or one of the command staff know immediately."

The girl nodded, clearing her throat and tucking a dark lock of hair up under her hood.

Jaerd tilted his head. She would not meet his gaze. "Have I seen you play in Gavanor? What is your name?"

She tucked her hands up into the sleeves of her robe. "My name is Shaela, and no, I've never played in Gavanor."

Jaerd shrugged. "You sound familiar. Perhaps it is just the emptiness of the Wastes that makes my ear seek familiarity."

Shaela wrapped herself in her blankets. "I get that a lot."

He took a step back with a half-bow. "Then I will leave you to your rest. Goodnight."

Once he reached his bedroll, his eyes fluttered only once before he drifted off to sleep.

Jaerd cast his eyes down the long train of soldiers keeping tight to the foothills of the Dragonscales. They had skirted the Firewood then crossed the river Lond before reaching the shallow and swift Gallond. Jaerd turned his head to stare at the unchanging landscape of gray-brown grass sweeping away to the south. A few scraggly pioneer pines grew, twisted and deformed along the edge of the grass. Even though he knew autumn still reigned, winter hid in the wind whipping the drab grass. He shifted in his saddle to lean toward Magus Britt. "What happened here?"

Magus Britt turned to look at the sea of switchgrass. "The Cataclysm."

Frowning, Jaerd watched the Battlemage as he shifted back and forth with the gait of his horse. "I understand that, but what caused it? What could release enough power to destroy the elf kingdom which once existed here?"

Shifting his red-fringed cloak about him, the mage kept his gaze on the landscape ahead. "No one really knows, save maybe the elves who fled to Valen. As most people are aware, few records, in fact few things at all, survived the end of the Dragon Wars."

General Vahn tapped his steel gauntlet upon his shield. "The Free Cities survived."

Jaerd turned in his saddle to examine the man. His gray cloak spread across the hindquarters of his steed, as if he marched on parade. His mustache curled upward, sticking out from his helmet.

"How so, General?"

Vahn cleared his throat and folded his gauntlets on his saddle horn. "The Free Cities used to be called the Last Cities, before your people returned to this continent. Before that, they were a part of Lond." He sniffed with pride. "Kerrigier was a major seaport of the elves."

Jaerd wrinkled his brow. "I did not know that."

"Few do." Vahn clucked his tongue. "How quickly the past is forgotten by the men of your kingdom."

Magus Britt turned his shaggy brows upon the Free City General. "Aren't most humans in the Free Cities descended from the same settlers who returned with the Navigator?"

Vahn spluttered. "Well, I suppose…"

The Battlemage nodded, turning his gaze forward.

Silence consumed the van of the detachment. Jaerd watched

the Dragonscales drifting by, their tops capped in eternal white.

On the third morning after crossing the babbling Gallond, the last pinnacle in the continent-spanning range rose before them. Highspur stood out, taller than the last few peaks, and connected to them by a long ridge of sheer rock. A cone of white capped its gray cliffs, and its southern shoulder rose in a flawless, flat wall of stone.

Jaerd shifted in his saddle, following the sharp ridge with his gaze. "It looks like tools have worked that face."

Magus Britt gestured toward the cliff. "It is even steeper on its northern side."

Earl Boris glanced over his shoulder. "Three centuries of lonely garrison assignments create a need to keep busy. They have changed the shape of the entire mountain. Just wait until you see how they've carved the inside."

Lord Marshal Magdon lifted his thin finger toward the peak. His gray eyes fixed upon the snowy bluff. "You will see it any moment."

A flutter of motion appeared over a snowy hump – a long strand bouncing in the wind. After a few more strides of Jaerd's horse, it resolved into a long, sable banner, lifting from the conical point of a remote tower.

"Farseer's Spire," the marshal said.

Jaerd leaned in his saddle, his heart quickening at the sight. "I've seen the tapestry in the citadel at Gavanor. The tower is totally separate from the fortress, correct?"

"Accessible only by a narrow chimney of rock." Snorting in amusement, Magus Britt lifted a canteen to his lips. "They have a lift for Earl Brandon."

Shifting the reins in his hand, Jaerd stared at the twisting banner. The black pennant drew in the light of day. Where it hung from the top of the tower, a golden comet flared across its canton.

Lieutenant Kent Varlan piped in from behind Jaerd. "My father's bannerman, Baron Maylon Farseer of the Ironfort, is Earl Brandon Farseer's nephew. The Earl of Highspur has been a Farseer since Earl Brandon's grandfather took the name." The man's voice broke off, and Jaerd heard him shift his armor. "And I'm certain you all know this quite well. My apologies."

A pair of riders approached over a crest of rocky earth. One wore the green-trimmed blue cloak of a ranger; the other wore a Fadecloak that shifted in pattern as it flew out behind him. *Captain Silios wanted to be known, or he'd have his Fadecloak on too.*

Both Earl Boris and Magus Britt perked up in their saddles. Brawny the hound charged out to greet them.

"Silios returns." The earl leaned forward, shading his face with a gauntleted hand. "And I believe that would be Lord Gael."

The two arrivals cantered their horses up to walk alongside the command officers. Upon closer inspection, Jaerd saw that white hair topped a youngish face, but the pointed ears peeking out over his cowl told him for an elf. However, only one of his eyes glittered with the bright violet common among his race. A black eyepatch covered the other.

Earl Boris and the mage both nudged their steeds over to greet him.

"Gael!" Boris clasped the elf's outstretched wrist. Magus Britt nodded a friendly greeting.

"Boris. Joslyn." The elf bowed his head toward them both. "It is good to see you again so soon. Your last stay with us was far too brief." He cast his good eye over the line of cavalry behind them. "It looks as if you will remain a bit longer this time."

Nodding his head, Earl Boris released the elf's arm. "We will indeed. Possibly indefinitely."

Gael's white eyebrows dipped, bringing the band of the eye patch down with it. "You are not needed in your capital?"

Earl Boris waved a hand in dismissal. "I am not wanted in the capital – for now. However, I *am* needed here." He gazed toward the top of the mountain. "The north stirs more than we feared."

The frown remained upon the elf's brow. "Indeed. Your captain of rangers has informed us of the basics. Attacks within Gannon – a dragon raid upon the Rock…" He shook his head in disbelief.

The look of concern on Boris' face softened. "We have also brought a number of very Talented healers, if you would care to have one visit you."

His hand lifting half way toward the patch, Gael instead ran it through his close-cropped white hair. "I have almost gotten used to it. Likely, the wound is too old for them be able to accomplish anything."

Boris pushed his stallion into a trot. "Nevertheless, they will try. I know you see better than any human even with only one eye, but I have a feeling we will need both of them."

The elf spread his hands and shrugged. "Spirits of Air willing. Otherwise, I have two hundred more elf rangers whose sight is almost as sharp as mine ever was."

Their path dipped behind a heavy root of stone stretching out from Highspur Mountain. Around a tool-shorn corner of rock, a narrow gorge ran between two tall shoulders of granite, like the leftover cleft of a huge axe. Where the defile narrowed, the fortress of legend crawled up the side of Highspur. Jaerd held his breath at the sight.

Two thick towers stood upon the shoulders of the mountain. A stout wall of stone ran between them, meeting in the middle at a bulky gatehouse. Behind the wall, the slope of the mountainside steepened, and the carved out gorge narrowed even further. At its end a second wall rose, higher and of older stonework. Four lofty towers stabbed up from the wall, two at the center around the gate and two where the wall met the sheer cliffs of the mountainside. Beyond the inner wall the edge of the mountain climbed swiftly, bored with several entrances. Upon the last shoulder of the mountain he saw a square bastion keep, and from it six banners flew. Beyond there, the mountain peaked in white, with only Farseer's Spire near its pinnacle.

Magus Britt looked at Jaerd and chuckled.

Noticing that his chin almost touched his chest, Jaerd clicked his jaw shut.

"The fortress of Highspur looks quite impressive upon first sight." Earl Boris smiled behind his mustache. "I would imagine at least a thousand of the men behind us are reacting in the same manner right now."

Gathered upon the walls of the mighty fortress, several thousand soldiers in cloaks of blue, gray, green, and a dozen other colors raised swords, spears, and a mighty cheer to greet the new arrivals. The clangor rolled down the defile, bouncing between the mountain and its spurs. Two heavy thumps sounded above it all, and Jaerd cast his eyes skyward. Two arcs of flame passed far over their heads and into the northern foothills.

"Quickfire!" Magus Britt grumbled. "They need not waste it."

Earl Boris leaned on his saddle horn and turned to face the mage. "You do remember how much of it they have stored here? That's why we brought all that naphthous sulfite you wanted."

The mage picked at the double row of silver buttons on his tunic. "Exactly. We may need it, when this spot is swarming with orcs and trolls and the Fires know what else. I'll be kind enough then to not to say I told you so."

Boris laughed. "That'll be the day."

The fore gate stood open. Dozens of dwarves scrambled over the towers, hoisting the portcullis and swinging the doors with hidden mechanics.

Earl Boris turned to Jaerd. "You commanded men upon the

walls of Gavanor for years. Did you learn the inner workings of their defensive engines?"

Jaerd nodded to his commanding officer. "Yes, sir. I actually found a way to twist our ropes to add more tension without snapping them."

"Good. Just the thinking we need." Boris turned to his giant master sergeant. "Hall, have the men dismount in the outer courtyard and fold into the garrison. Bring the wagons inside after us."

Sergeant Hall snapped his salute and pulled a thick cigar from his pocket. "Magus Britt – would you be so kind?"

The Battlemage snapped his fingers, and a small flash sparked at the edge of the cigar. Sergeant Hall puffed away, and a bright red cherry began to glow.

"Thank you, sir. Much obliged." He turned to look down the parade of cavalry entering the outer courtyard. His wolfhound barked in unison, as if to emphasize his master's orders. "All right you maggots! Get those horses lined against the wall! Move it or I'll toss you and your beast over there with my own hands!"

The Earl of Mourne watched his sergeant march away, shouting orders even at the officers, who followed without question. "I've never seen him so happy."

Gael spurred his sorrel mare forward. "The captains of Highspur wait within." He gestured for them to follow. "What hospitality we have to offer is yours."

The inner gate hung over them, twice as tall and imposing as the outer. It also looked twice as old to Jaerd's journeyman eye.

They passed between the pair of hulking, steel inner doors and into a pristinely manicured courtyard of cut grass and white stone paths. Jaerd dismounted, handing his reins off to an almond-skinned Hadoner carrying a scimitar. A sharp-featured elf took the reins of Boris' stallion, and the two led the steeds into the lowest entry of the mountain. Carved horses reared in battle along its mouth.

"The stable is on the lowest level." Boris pointed up the mountainside at the series of carved entryways. A switchback stone staircase climbed upward along the mountainside to connect each level. "The second entrance is enlisted barracks and their mess hall, while the third leads to the infirmary, the armory and general quartermaster, along with a full forge." He lifted his finger to a door carved with watchful lions. "Fourth level is officers' barracks and mess."

Jaerd nodded. "I'll be bunking there."

"No, Captain." Boris pointed to the stone keep built upon the upper shoulder. "You will be joining us within the bastion. You are a command officer now."

They reached the top of the first flight of steps, a platform carved with figures of hunting wolves. Three men stood there, one dressed in blue with red fringe, one in black, and one in the loose, flowing clothes and lacquered armor of the Empire of Hadon.

Lord Marshal Magdon bowed his head to the elder man in a sable cape. "My Lord Earl, thank you for your welcome to Highspur. My men and I are greatly honored."

Earl Brandon Farseer returned the bow with a sour frown, his wispy white hair hanging down about his shoulders, and scraggly silver eyebrows covering parts of his face. "Why have you come here yourself, Lord Marshal? Is Earl Boris insufficient to supplant me?"

The marshal blinked. He folded his arms and scowled back at Farseer. "I am here at King Arathan's command. He is still your liege, Earl Brandon, regardless of your remote location."

Earl Boris stepped forward, patting the air in placation. "Please, my lords. We are here to supplant no one. Rather, we are here to support you."

Earl Brandon pursed his pale lips. "Very well. I will take my place within my tower. My eyes will gaze unceasingly into the north. This…" He waved at the fortress about him. "…is yours to command. I am old enough to read the subtle messages of court." The earl turned away and hobbled into the mountain entrance, his two black clad men-at-arms joining him.

Stepping into the awkward silence, the Hadoner bowed, his crimson and white lacquered armor glinting in the sunlight. "My lords. I am Khalem Shadar, quartermaster of Highspur and captain of the Emperor's expedition of Sunguard here. If there is anything you need, for yourselves or for your men, please do not hesitate to ask."

The man spoke with the fairness of court, but Jaerd recognized the lithe movement of a warrior. The handle of the decorated scimitar at his hip showed the wear of regular practice, and his brown hands the calluses of its use.

"Yes, Captain Shadar." Pretending not to notice Earl Brandon stalking away, Boris returned the nod of greeting. "We met briefly when Joslyn and I were here in the spring." The Bluecloak earl turned to the third man. "And Magus Eldester – we brought a squad of your compatriots as well."

The Battlemage with two stars upon his collar nodded to Joslyn Britt. "I am glad you have come, Magus-General. We are far too few as it is."

Magus Britt returned the nod. "We have other surprises as well."

Turning back to the Hadonese quartermaster, Earl Boris gestured toward his men. "Most have never served at Highspur before. They will need instruction."

The Hadoner bowed his head. A fine beard circled his honest smile. "I have already detailed Gannonite men to get them situated. A hot meal is currently being served in the mess hall." He gestured for them to follow him up the stairs. "The forge is fired, should any of your equipment need repair, and farriers stand ready in the stables to care for your mounts."

Khalem Shadar led them to the staircase, and they began to climb upward. "We have many excellent eyes here at Highspur. We have known of your approach for some time."

"My scouts watched you wet your toes in the Gallond," Gael added. "We knew the hour you would arrive."

Boris looked back to the quartermaster. "How are the stores?"

"Very full. And growing."

Earl Boris rubbed his black mustache. "Keep at it, Khalem. I want the deep stores bursting if anything comes down on us."

Once he set foot upon the third level, its walls carved with campfires and the vine-entangled hand of healing, Jaerd smelled bacon and roasted peppers, mingled with the yeasty aroma of fresh bread. His stomach gurgled, reminding him that he had not eaten since breakfast.

Boris smiled at him over his shoulder. "Not long now, Captain."

A blocky, soot covered form waddled out from the entrance. Jaerd focused on a dwarf, almost as wide as he was tall. His black beard was streaked with gray, though Jaerd could not be certain if it came from age or ash. Grime smudged every visible patch of the dwarf's skin. Upon his head he wore a helmet – the kind the dwarves wore for mining, not for battle. A white crystal was strapped to it.

The thing probably glows in the darkness below.

Earl Boris clasped hands heartily with the dwarf, heedless of the black soot rubbing onto his glove. "Tarrak! Good to see you again, my friend."

The dwarf laughed a sonorous bellow from his thick chest. "Good to see you again, lad. I was in the mines when you visited us last – found one heck of a vein – and never got word of your visit until you were already gone."

Earl Boris patted the dwarf on the shoulder and raised a puff of dust in the process. "Understood, my old friend. I only wish I had been able to stay long enough to visit you down there myself.

This time, however, I will be here for a while longer." He waved his hand at Jaerd. "Captain Jaerd Westar, I want to introduce you to the chief dwarf here at Highspur, Maester Tarrak Goldmar."

Jaerd shook the dwarf's hand, ignoring the soot as politely as the earl had.

"Jaerd served on the walls of Gavanor for many years," Boris said. "He has a particular knowledge of siege weapons. The two of you will have a lot of ideas to share over the next several months." He waved at the walls. "I want this place bristling."

"Good to meet you, lad." The dwarf rubbed his blackened hands together. "I can't wait to pick your brain for any of your Human secrets." He cackled, eyes glittering.

Jaerd looked at his commanding officer, uncertainty on his face.

"It's alright. Don't mind him." Boris laughed. "Tell him everything you know, with my permission."

Jaerd saluted, noticing the odd grin on Tarrak's face. "Yes, my lord." *I think this old codger and I might just get along.*

Boris turned to the elf ranger. "Can you have two dozen of your best ready to leave tomorrow?"

Squinting his eye, Gael nodded. "Aye. You wish to head out that quickly?"

The earl nodded. "Captain Silios will go with us too. We need not leave early – the men can rest tonight. We will discuss in council who I will take and what provisions we will need, but I will leave with at least a thousand cavalry tomorrow. We will scout deep into the Northlands." He cast his gaze over Highuspur's shoulders. "I intend on drawing them out. They've had enough time in control of the game board."

Magus Britt sighed, stretching his back. "And my ass was just beginning to enjoy being out of the saddle."

Earl Boris drew down his brows. "Nay, Joz. We've discussed this. You must stay here. You are the only one who can enhance the Quickfire."

The Battlemage set his hands on his hips. He opened his mouth to argue, but Boris forestalled him with an upthrust finger.

"Very well," he said at last, his eyes narrowing at Earl Boris. "But you are taking Gaeric and two of his best lieutenants with you."

Jaerd gazed at the wide stretch of desolation. *I'm glad I'm staying here.*

CHAPTER 22

The Doctor's College in Daynon dates back to King Arathan I, son of the Navigator. The Talent for healing hid within certain folk of the People of Gan, even during the Exile. Arathan I set the cornerstone of King's Hall, a building still used to this day. He commissioned the college not only to find those with Talent and make Doctors out of them, but also to teach the basics of herbology and medicine to anyone with the aptitude to learn.
— "Second History of Gannon, Vol. III" by Elyn Bravano

Maddi leaned forward in the squeaky wooden chair, hunching over the desk with an inkwell and quill holder. The handsome man she had seen upon the dais in the High Hall just a week ago stood glaring down at her and the dozen students in the class. Lord Doctor Tymin Marten was the most Talented doctor in the city, and his place upon the High Council stemmed from his position as headmaster at the college.

"It is rare I see so many students in this class." The Lord Doctor turned his eyes to Maddi, softening them and offering her the hint of a smile. "With our surprise addition this semester, you are the largest class I have ever taught to embrace their Talent." He scanned the crowd with his gaze. "You all have the potential, or I would not waste my time with you. Some of you will choose to join the Bluecloaks – the army always has need of healers for some reason." A soft chuckle emanated from the students. "A few of you may choose to teach here." He narrowed his eyes. "Very few."

Another soft laugh circled the classroom. Maddi even offered a slight grin, until a faint sound tickled her ears. *Was that a child's cough?*

The Lord Doctor folded his hands behind his back to continue. "Most of you know the basics of our current subject. Otherwise you would not be here. You have either been told by another Doctor or sensed it for yourself." Marten turned his head toward a shy young woman slumped in her seat near the rear of the

215

room. "Some of you even found a way to tap into your Talent already – warped though you have made it." The woman sunk further into her seat.

"You know about the life force," the doctor continued, "what the elves call the *psahn*. Healing Talent is far more common among the elves than humans, though less so among the dwarves." He shrugged his shoulders. "I do not know nor care what the rate is among orcs."

One boy near the front guffawed, receiving glares from some of the students.

After a short smile at the young man, as if proud of making him laugh so, Marten resumed his pacing. "Regardless, the *psahn* is the power that drives all life. It is in all living things – even the microbes that cause the diseases we cure." He waved his finger at the class. "When you learn to use the mind's eye of a healer and enter into your Talent, you will see the *psahn* as a glowing light, radiating from the life forms around you. The more complex the life, the more brilliant the glow."

A hand shot up from the boy who had laughed.

The doctor sighed. "Yes, Mister Darby?"

The young man shifted forward on his seat. "How soon will we learn to use it?"

The Lord Doctor barked a sharp chuckle. "Well, Mister Darby, if you are so enthusiastic, lets get right to it." He walked to a small door leading to a back room and opened it. "Come on out, little girl."

A wiry ball of stringy hair and rags stepped into the classroom. Her eyes widened in fear at seeing the assembled students, then closed as she lifted her hand to cover a hacking cough. Coming from deep within her chest, it wracked her tiny frame. Maddi started from her seat, her hand reaching out. She stopped herself when the Lord Doctor led the girl forward.

"We will try disease first. Wounds next." He pushed the girl forward, his fingertips pressuring her shoulders. "Mister Darby, you begin."

The young man hopped up from his seat and strode forward to face the Lord Doctor. Darby looked down on the little urchin, who wiped her nose in response. He grimaced, his face wrinkling in disgust.

"Shut your eyes, and put your hands on her shoulders." The Lord Doctor closed his own eyelids. "You will think of the girl, see her in your mind – see the glow of her *psahn*. Enter it with your mind. See the blackness of her sickness."

Darby's face lit up. "I see it!"

The Lord Doctor sighed. "No you don't. You may sit down, Mister Darby. I see that you need more time and concentration." Marten nodded to the disappointed student. "Read Lord Doctor Brathlaw's book on meditation. Use the techniques there to hone your mind and concentration."

Flopping down in his seat, Darby glared at the little girl.

As if it were her fault!

The poor girl hacked again, this time almost falling to her knees. Maddi half-stood. "Aren't you going to help her? She obviously needs camphor and *menthum*, with a good bath and bed rest in clean sheets. She needs warm stew three or four times every day, and whatever citrus juice you can get your hands on in this city. Lemon-grass and honey could help as well."

A small smile crept on Marten's lips. "Then why don't you help her yourself, Miss Conaleon? But not with your midwife's remedies, useful as they may be on the frontier." He gestured toward the girl. "Use your Talent."

Maddi crossed the room, aware of the other student's eyes upon her. She knelt in front of the girl, her face smoothing to a smile. "What is your name, sweetie?"

The girl sniffed. "Tanya."

"My name is Maddi." *She looks about the same age I was when father died. I imagine I looked just like her until Renna took me in.*

Maddi placed her hands on the child's shoulders, and the doctor placed his hands on hers. His finely manicured nails held not a speck of dirt, and his skin felt warm and soft.

"Close your eyes," Marten whispered. "Find her *psahn*."

In the darkness behind shut eyelids, Maddi imagined Tanya standing in front of her. Her hands upon the girl's shoulders anchored Maddi, giving her mind a seed from which to grow.

"Breathe." The Lord Doctor's voice came to her – distant – as if he called through a fog. "Open your mind. Open your Talent."

Maddi perceived a glowing shimmer gathering in the black. It swelled, shaping itself into the outline of a little girl. When Tanya coughed, Maddi barely heard it. Instead, she felt a lurch within the radiance of the girl's life force. More silvery shapes bloomed into her perception – the students surrounding them. The doctor's life force burst in front of her, becoming a brilliant glare once it fully resolved.

"Focus on the girl." His words floated on the edge of her consciousness. "Find the shadow of the disease that dwells within her. Find it and draw it out." He paused. "Take care to keep your own *psahn* clean."

Shifting her mind back to the girl's life force, Maddi concentrated on the shining form. Black specks flowed along within eddies of silver energy. They impeded it, dimming its brilliance.

Maddi reached into the light with her mind. A warm sensation flooded her cheeks and chest. She swept the specks of shadow together, like gathering corks upon a pool's surface. Pulling them in, she continued searching Tanya's life force. Drawing the disease inward, she held it away from her own sense of self.

The last of the impurities disappeared from the girl's energy. Maddi withdrew from her Talent and opened her eyes.

Tanya's color had brightened, a pink glow in the cheeks where once gray had reigned. She cleared her throat, but did not cough.

"By the Waters!" Marten covered his mouth with one hand. "I have never seen someone cure disease upon their first try." His voice hung low and breathless. "You are…ahem…you did well, Miss Conaleon."

When Maddi moved to rise, exhaustion rippled her muscles. She remained on her feet, however, standing without a wobble.

"You will want to sit and rest." The Lord Doctor put his hand underneath her elbow and escorted her to her chair. He only let go her arm once she looked him in the eye and nodded.

After a few deep breaths, her senses cleared. She pulled a strand of loose hair back behind her ear.

"Careful." Marten grabbed her wrist with a soft and steady grip.

A black, tar-like substance smudged the palm of her hand. The doctor reached over to a side table and set a large glass beaker of clear liquid on her desk. It smelled of the strongest liquor Maddi had ever sipped.

"Place your hand within, please. It is just a distilled spirit."

Maddi dipped her fist into the beaker, the cold shock waking her mind even further. "It will kill the disease," she said. "My foster mother also taught me to use strong spirits when cleaning wounds."

Marten nodded, a half smile creeping onto his lips. "You are correct." He scanned the gathered students. "This does not mean that drinking the spirits will do the same thing." More chuckles rose from the students. The doctor handed Maddi a towel. "I will have my eyes on you."

He walked over to the little girl, who had begun toying with a small metal contraption on the doctor's desk. "Here you go, young miss." He handed her a silver penny, the sight of which cause Tanya to gasp in excitement. "Go on back home now." He ushered her to the hall door, scooting her out and closing it behind her.

Maddi frowned, eyes narrowing at the doctor. "Shouldn't someone see her to her home?"

Marten knitted his brow, as if surprised by her question. "She is an urchin of the street. She knows her way about the city, I assure you." He huffed. "Probably better than either of us do."

The Lord Doctor waved his hand in dismissal and opened another side door. A large guardsman in the white and gray livery of the city watch entered the room. The man winced when the doctor unwrapped a folded bandage soaked with the guard's blood and exposed a nasty slash on the man's arm.

"Private Digson kindly agreed to let his wound sit open so that I might test another one of you. Who wants to try to repair this?"

Thoughts racing through her mind, Maddi sat in the chair, distantly observing several students fail to heal the guard. After six unsuccessful tries, the color of the guard's face began to shift past gray into ash. A small pool of blood gathered among the river rushes scattered on the stone floor. The doctor laughed at his students, closed his eyes, and touched the arm of the man. In seconds, the wound knitted closed, leaving only a small pink scar underneath the blood that had already leaked from the gash.

Those events hopped along the surface of Maddi's awareness. Her mind focused on what she had done, the potential she felt when embracing her Talent. She longed to do it again.

What does this mean for my other *career?*

When the yard bell rang to mark the hour, she rose, still numb, and shuffled out the door along with the other students. Her mind still tried to wrap itself around her power.

"Miss Conaleon, if you would stay a moment..."

Maddi took two more steps before the Lord Doctor's words registered in her head. She turned and walked back to him. His pale honey eyes narrowed in an examining stare.

"I have something for you." He held up his hand, a small key dangling from his fingers on a leather thong. "All new students, no matter how high their references, are required to live in the dormitory. You are assigned to room twenty-seven."

219

Maddi took the key from his hands. She stared at it.

"You are welcome, Miss Conaleon." The doctor chuckled, turning his chair back to his desk and focusing on the papers there. "See you tomorrow."

She wandered into the hall. *Just how powerful is this Talent?*

Leaning against the door marked "27", Maddi heard the sound of soft crying. She stood, listening until the sobs faded away. When no more sniffles drifted through the thick oak, Maddi turned the key and pushed her way inside.

Two narrow beds hugged the walls with the space of another between. Through a single window, draped in plain cotton, Maddi glimpsed the grassy space between college buildings. Curled up with a knitted blanket, the pretty, kind-faced student from Maddi's class sat on the left hand bed. *The one Marten accused of warping her Talent.* The young woman wiped a tear from under her eye, and offered a friendly smile.

"Hi…"

Maddi knelt down beside the woman. "Are you alright?"

The student nodded, dabbing her eyes again with a kerchief. "Yes. I'm sorry to meet you this way. The Lord Doctor can be… harsh." She reached out her hand. "I'm Amilia Magrone…Ami to my friends." Her smile broadened. "I hope we can be friends."

After shaking Ami's hand, Maddi sat down upon the bed next to her. "I'm Maddi, and I'd love to have a good friend. They are hard to find in this place." She tilted her head. "What did Doctor Marten mean when he called your Talent *warped*?"

Ami wrapped her blanket more tightly. "He doesn't know what he is talking about."

Patting the woman's knee with her free hand, Maddi leaned in closer. "I want to be your friend. Tell me what's wrong, and I will help if I can." She grinned with mischief. "After all, if that arrogant bastard can't bring us together, who can?"

Ami chuckled. "Fair enough." A calm look crossed the woman's thin features. "My parents both work at Belcester Palace in Wellsfield. My mother is a housemaid, while my father works in the stables." A slow smile split her narrow lips, one that grew with each line of her tale. "As a child, my mother taught me to clean the rooms of the palace and to help her with the laundry.

I hated it. Every time I could, I slipped away to see my father in the stables. I loved the horses." She laughed. "And the goats, and the dogs, and the cats…"

The young woman's eyes glittered, and Maddi could not help but grin with excitement.

"So one day – oh, I don't know, about three years ago – my mother and I were arguing about the wash. I threw the duke's undies into the basin and ran off." Ami folded her hands in her lap and stared up at the oak raftered ceiling. "I found the stable, searching for my father. He always consoled me and let me stay with the animals for a while. Then he would convince me to return to my mother and the duties of a maid." She looked down at her hands. "This time, however, there was a mare in foal. She screamed in pain. It was the most terrible sound I had ever heard."

Ami rubbed her hands. Maddi could almost see the memories playing through the woman's mind.

"I knelt down beside my father," she continued. "I can still remember the grave look on his face. When I…when I touched the mare's neck, her wild eyes settled and…and she lay there calmer, breathing hard." Ami looked up from her hands, her gaze boring into Maddi. "I closed my eyes and I reached out to her life force…her *psahn* as Doctor Marten calls it. I felt the baby inside her, separate yet connected by the fragile umbilical cord. The foal's life force flickered. I…I reached inside her with my mind – just as you did with the girl today – and I eased the baby out. I steadied the flow of its life force, and then healed the wounds inside the mother."

Maddi gasped, reaching out again with her hands to cup Ami's. "You opened your Talent without the help of another doctor?"

Ami nodded, her lips wrinkled in both fear and joy. "I saved the horse and its foal, but I scared my father. When he realized what had happened, he took me to the closest doctor, who recommended I come to the college." She rolled her eyes back, counting in her head. "I've been here over two years now."

"But what is warped about that?"

Shrugging, Ami shook her head. "I can only heal animals, not humans. I've even tried elves and dwarves. No good." She grinned. "Really, I don't see a problem with it. Animals deserve healing as much as people."

"More than most," Maddi agreed. She looked at Ami with a bright smile. "I think we will definitely be friends."

Doctor Witesell droned on, his voice a slow monotone that coaxed Maddi into drowsiness.

"The Red Death came to the Hadonese Empire through an unknown conduit. The contagion swept the empire. Thousands upon thousands died. Most of the deaths occurred north of the Hadonese Range, in the cities and towns surrounding Avaros and Lake Iyar. By the time Aravath the Navigator led the People of Gan in the Return, those entire regions of Tarmor were virtually unpopulated, the Red Death having mostly stayed north of the mountains. In fact, the Hadonese Empire was so decimated by the plague that the People of Gan quickly settled Avaros and Iyar, claiming them for the kingdom of Gannon."

Epidemic History is boring. What does the history of a disease have to do with curing it? She stared out of the window, watching the sunlight filter through leaves already shifting to autumn brown. The grass on the open quad still held its deep green hue, beckoning her to lay down on it and nap until the warm sun left Daynon wrapped in a late summer evening.

The tolling of the yard bell awakened Maddi from her thoughts and tore the sleepiness from her mind.

"Very well, class. Read Aberson's History of Gout for next week." Doctor Witesell raised a finger, thin with age. "There will be a test."

The students shuffled out of the room, whispering quiet plans to one another. With no class tomorrow, many suggested going out into the city. *Maybe Ami will want to go too.*

The fresh air and late summer sun brought a smile to Maddi's face. She skipped down the brick steps and headed toward the dormitory.

A bundle of dirty clothes and spiky hair tackled her as she rounded the corner of Prince's Hall. A pair of sinewy white arms, streaked with mud, wrapped around Maddi's waist. She took a step back under the sudden onslaught.

"What the—"

A wail escaped the attacker. "Please...can you help my mommy the way you helped me?" A pair of pale green eyes looked up at Maddi from behind stringy hair that appeared red under all the dirt. "I've been looking for you so long." Tears left gray streaks down the little girl's cheeks.

"Tanya?" Maddi patted her hair. "Is that you?"

"Yes, Miss Maddi." The girl let go. Stepping back, she twisted her toe into the ground and stared at the grass. "My – my mother is sick, just like I was. You cured me." Her gaze strayed toward Maddi's face. "You could cure her too."

Maddi stood there, watching the little girl's lower lip tremble. She had no desire to follow her into the slums, and she let it show upon her face. Tanya stood her ground. Not a whimper escaped her throat.

The girl has a heart full of bravery, just like I did. If only someone had been there to save my father...

"How far away do you live?"

Tanya's face brightened. "Not far! Just down at the bottom of the hill." She grasped Maddi's unwilling fingers. "Please come!"

Her reluctance weighing down her steps, Maddi followed the girl. Behind Prince's Hall, the Avenue of Willows trailed down to the bottom of Jalanine Hill. With each intersection, the buildings grew more ramshackle, stone and brick becoming far scarcer materials. Mud splattered the streets and the clothing of the people living there. The few open shops hawked goods for survival, or more likely, the goods of debauchery. The further they descended, the more the scent of wine, vomit, and rare opiates rose to Maddi's nose.

"You live down here?"

Tanya pulled her along, her path direct and purposeful. "Yep. In a flop over here on Green Street."

Maddi cast her eyes about, rubbing the hilt of the dagger hanging just above the cuff of her sleeve. Most of the passersby remained focused on their own drudgery. A few drunks passed a bottle behind a dilapidated stoop. A single, wiry fellow watched her from across the street. A good hard stare from her, and the man disappeared into an alley.

"This way!" Tanya pulled her toward a three-story building tucked between a locked warehouse and a makeshift tavern. Dingy paint peeled in strips from the walls and doorframe. The hinges creaked when the girl pushed it open. A fog of human stench washed over Maddi, hot and musty as it belched forth from the darkness.

Wrinkling her nose, Tanya gave Maddi a telling nod. "You'll get used to it. Come on."

The stench within clung to the inside of Maddi's nose. It coated her mouth when she tried breathing through it. She swatted at fat, green flies that buzzed about her head. Movement from behind a worn desk caught her attention.

"You'll have to pay for your new friend, Tanya. No free visitors."

Maddi squinted against the darkness. Her eyes adjusted when the light pouring in through the door spread to the room's corners. A thin, greasy man brushed blackened fingers over the few long strands of hair still clinging to his scalp. Bucked teeth and a needle grin turned from Tanya to look at her.

"Well, now aren't you a fine lass to be wandering about down here?" His grin shifted to an angry scowl, and his simpering voice became a snarl. "What are you up to, Tanya?"

"I'm tryin' to save my mom!" Tanya crossed her arms and stuck out her lower lip. "You leave me alone, Briscoe. My friend is an important doctor, and she won't let you touch me."

Maddi shifted her stance into a more dangerous posture. "She's right about that." The dagger rested a hair's breadth from her fingers. "I'm here as a representative of the Doctor's College, and I will see to this girl's mother."

The man took a step back, his brows raised. "I would not harm the girl. I am the landlord's representative, and I must know who enters the building…for safety's sake." His fingers fidgeted and he sniffed. "There is a visitor fee…"

Maddi set her jaw and scowled at the man.

He held his hands up in surrender. "…but I will waive it for a doctor."

Staring at the man until he skittered back behind his desk, Maddi followed the girl up the rickety staircase to the second floor.

Tanya pointed to a weak spot in the floor. "Watch the hole!"

Six rooms lined the hall, two of which had no doors. Maddi cast quick glances into them as she passed, following Tanya. Stained mattresses and worn chairs lay scattered about in both rooms. Bare wall slats showed through the plaster. Distant memories of painted flowers clung to it behind layers of filth and grime.

Twisting the knob on the last door, Tanya waved for Maddi to follow. "You get your door when you pay the rent."

Inside, a small window with cracked, dirty glass let in enough light for Maddi to see a woman curled up on a narrow bed.

This room is cleaner than anything else in this building, but old and dilapidated can only be tidied so much.

A moan escaped from the woman.

"I brought the doctor, Momma!" Tanya drug Maddi toward her mother, whose ashen face gleamed with a sheen of sweat. "She's the one who cured me!" Her nervous eyes looked up at Maddi, on the verge of tears. "Please...will you help her?"

Kneeling down beside the bed, Maddi placed her hands upon the woman's shoulder and arm. Ice-cold flesh met her fingers, when she had expected the heat of fever.

Not good... She looked at Tanya. "I will try. Bring me clean water and towels."

The little girl nodded. She grabbed a few folded rags from a small trunk in the corner, and then dashed away with a cracked pitcher in her hand.

Closing her eyes, Maddi delved into her Talent. She conjured up a mind's-eye view of the life forces swirling about her. Dozens surrounded Maddi in the building, surprising her with their crowded numbers. Some flickered with sickness. Tanya, however, stood out bright and strong when she returned, free from any taint of disease.

Her mother appeared far different.

Oily blackness oozed over the surface of the woman's life force, sinking into it, dimming the light of its glow. Steadying herself with a deep breath, Maddi dived in, careful to use the techniques the Lord Doctor had taught to keep her own life force safe and separate.

She drew the oiliness toward her, wrapping it in pockets of *psahn*. She pulled it out with her Talent, wiping black tar onto the towels Tanya provided. A dozen times she went into the woman, drawing some of the poisonous disease out with each attempt. Her shoulders and back ached as though she had been fighting all day. Sweat beaded on her forehead, running down to nestle within her dark eyebrows. Her breaths became hurried.

Yet still the blackness held sway over the woman's life force. Every time Maddi thought one part was clear, the disease would spring back elsewhere. All the while, the brilliance of the woman's *psahn* faded, until at last Maddi broke away from her Talent, gasping for breath. She wiped the sweat from her brow with the back of a blackened hand.

"I must rest," she panted, thankfully gulping down a cup of water offered by Tanya. "Now give some to your mother while I collect my strength."

Tanya refilled the cup from the pitcher and held it to her mother's lips, cradling the woman's head with her other hand.

Her mother did not drink. When Maddi scooted closer to help, the woman popped open her eyes, pale green like her daughter's.

"Tanya! Is that you?" Her voice weakened swiftly. "I...I want you to be...to be a good girl." A weak cough brought a small spray of crimson that spattered across her threadbare coverlet. Those feverish green eyes stared at Maddi. "Care for her..."

The rattle of her last breath left those eyes gazing at Maddi, who fought down heat rising in her chest. Pulling herself together with a sniff, she reached over and closed the woman's eyelids. Tanya collapsed against the still form with silent tears. The little girl stroked her mother's hands while she folded them together.

She's seen death before. Maddi rubbed Tanya's back in sympathy. *She's a tough little thing. Who does that remind me of?* Maddi stood and put hands on her hips. "Come with me, Tanya. You cannot stay here."

The girl clasped onto her mother's gray arm even more tightly. "But what about Momma?"

Maddi knelt down, her eyes searching Tanya's. "I will make certain she is taken care of. I promise." She looked out into the hall. "And everyone else here." She turned back to the girl, who nibbled on her lower lip. "Do you have anything you need to bring with you?"

Tanya rubbed her pants pocket in search of something precious. Her eyes brightened before she shook her head in the negative.

"Fine, you can stay with me for now. Come on." Taking Tanya by the hand, Maddi led her down the stairs. The coughs and moans of other residents rang through the closed doors.

When she reached the ground floor, Maddi stormed up to the proprietor. "You run a cesspit, sir! Plague has taken hold in your establishment." She slammed her fist onto the desk, jostling the mess upon it. Briscoe jerked his head. "I will be back with more healers – and with the city watch." Maddi jammed a finger at the greasy man, wishing it were one of her knives. "You will treat the dead in this building – and I know there are more – with respect."

Briscoe squinted at her, folding his hands and clearing his throat. He leaned forward upon his desk, eyes bouncing back and forth between Tanya and Maddi's finger. "I can make use of the girl here. She can...clean things – uh – help me clean things up." His lips thinned. "You can leave her with me. She's a terrible burden."

Grabbing the edge of the desk, Maddi heaved it over, flipping it onto its side and scattering papers and a half-eaten sandwich across the room. Briscoe toppled back onto his chair, crashing to the ground and sprawling against the back wall.

"You will *not* keep her!" Anger overtook Maddi, and she pulled one of her knives. She charged forward, slamming his shoulder against the floor and bringing the dagger within an inch of his cheekbone. "I want you to understand clearly with whom you are dealing. I will take the girl, and I *will* return to clean out the plague."

Maddi leaped back, slipping the dagger away. She watched the apple in his throat bounce and noticed a dark patch spreading at his groin. She took Tanya by the hand. "Come now, Tanya. Let's leave this place. It suddenly reeks in here."

Evening slipped into the air while they walked back. Halfway to the college Tanya stumbled, her steps slow with exhaustion. Without a word, Maddi scooped her up in her arms and cradled Tanya's head upon her shoulder. The little girl clung tight, her face nuzzling into Maddi's neck. Ignoring the child's weight, Maddi carried her all the way back to her room.

Ami waited within, her nose buried deep within a book. "Is that the girl from class a few weeks ago?"

Maddi nodded, fighting back tears. "Her mother has died of the same disease that threatened her. Their whole tenement is in danger of the same." She reached out to Ami. "I need your help. We must get her clean – I have to get clean." Maddi cast her head about, searching for something she could not find. "I suppose I need a towel...I..."

Closing her book, Ami reached out to grab Maddi's hand. "Of course I will help you. We can hide her here for a long time – if she can stay quiet."

A few hours later, Maddi lay cuddled up under her blanket, a freshly scrubbed Tanya rolled up beside her. She reached her arm around the little girl, who hugged it tight.

What have I gotten myself into?

227

CHAPTER 23

Any smart sailor will tell you to avoid the Isle of Wizards when you can.
A wise one will tell you to never, ever go there.
— *Captain Sully's Maritime Guide*

Tallen Westar shifted his weight to maintain balance as the boat turned to dock along the stone pier. The thrum beneath his feet changed frequency, and water burbled out from under the hull. The rainbow ship nudged the pier resembling a single cut boulder drawn up from the water.

"Looks like a special welcome for you, lad." Dorias Ravenhawke squinted at a group of people gathered on the dock. "I hope some of it rubs off on me."

Tomas Harte stepped closer to the gangway. "I will take the initial brunt of the attack."

Dorias chuckled. "As usual."

Two stevedores tied the gangway in place, and the paladin led Tallen and the wizard onto the pier. Tallen stared at the group of robed figures moving forward, each as different in face and stature as the next. Three human females stood there, one with the caramel skin of a Handoner and two others who appeared very Gannonite to Tallen's eye. A dwarf, his beard trimmed short, scowled at the new arrivals and fingered a twisted oak staff. Two elves stood near the rear of the group, one male and short, with ash-colored hair and cobalt blue eyes, the other female with golden hair and violet eyes. In front of all of them stood a third elf, her hands lifted in greeting.

Tallen almost stumbled on the gangplank when he focused on the leader, her face calm and beautiful beyond any woman he had ever seen, framed by long, white hair, radiant in the sunlight. A samite robe matched her glowing tresses. Her smooth facial features complimented a gaze that carried a weight of centuries. When those violet eyes fixed on Tallen, they laid him bare to her, as if every sin, every skill, every thought in his mind were hers to claim.

Tomas bowed once his boots touched the pier. "Lady Varana. It is my honor to be in your presence. I have returned to the Isle to visit the great Cathedral of my order."

Varana dipped her head. "Welcome, Paladin Tomas. It is always our honor to host those of your order." Rich, melodious tones carried her words to Tallen's ear. She turned her gaze upon Tallen once again when he stepped onto the dock. "You must be Tallen Westar, the new find of Magus Joslyn Britt. Joslyn has sent me several interesting students. However, he has never sent one accompanied by such high praise."

Bowing his head, Tallen shifted his rucksack to the other shoulder. "Thank you, My Lady. I am honored to be here."

Varana's eyes narrowed when Dorias' boots tapped the stone. "And you, Ravenhawke. What brings you to the Isle? You may have chosen exile from the Circle, but that does not mean it is your choice to end it."

The wizard bowed his head. "I am here only because of a great need, Varana, I assure you." He looked up, his hawk-like gaze settling on her. "Something dark stirs in the Dreamrealm – something I cannot name. I hope to search the libraries upon the Isle for clues as to what it is or what its purpose may be." He dipped his head toward Tallen. "The fact that the first Dreamer in decades has been found at the same time cannot be mere chance."

Tomas nodded his head. "I agree. The Balance shifts as the Balance will."

Varana folded her hands behind her back. She looked first at the elf woman in her entourage, who shook her head. Varana then sought one of the Gannonite women. The blond mage shrugged, pulling her sky blue robes about her body.

"You understand my reluctance to allow you upon the Isle," Varana said, turning back to Dorias. "It was you who led twelve of your fellows to rebel against the Circle's guidance. Each of their stories ended badly – save for yours." A flash of fire leaped into her eyes. "You betrayed not only me, but the trust every one of *them* placed in you."

Dorias focused on the stone pier, his voice a controlled monotone. "You know that I did not intend that they choose the paths they did. You were there when I slew Malcolm with my own power." Merl warbled from his perch on the dock rail. Dorias' voice dropped even further. "As for my betrayal of you, that happened long before I left the Circle. And we both know it was not a true betrayal by that time." The wizard cleared his throat. "And Kaela paid enough for both our debts, even if my aid against Malcolm was not enough."

"The Ravenhawke speaks the truth." The caramel-skinned woman's dark eyes shifted between Dorias and Varana. "He has aided us – and several other lands – with honor since he left." She fixed her gaze on Varana. "He is the only Dreamer left."

Smoothing the front of her dress, Varana looked at her companion. She stared at the Hadoner while the woman's face remained set in stone. Varana turned back to Dorias. "I will allow you your search, Ravenhawke. However, you may not stay at the Academy. You will find lodgings in one of the abandoned towers on the Isle. Yours no longer stands." Raising a finger, Varana tightened her lips. "Take care with those who rest upon the Isle. Have respect for the Circle of Wizards which you so carelessly abandoned."

Dorias bowed to his waist. "I have nothing but respect for those retired to this island."

"See that it is so." Varana narrowed her gaze. "And see that you share any information you find with me. If this dark power is so daunting as to bring the great Ravehawke back to my island begging for help, then perhaps I should be aware of it as well."

Straightening from his bow, Dorias covered his heart with one hand. "I promise, Varana – on the friendship we once shared." Merl fluttered to his shoulder, rubbing his beak behind the wizard's ear.

Varana did not respond, though Tallen noticed a hint of pink rising at the tips of her ears. The sorceress turned to him. "And you, young man, shall begin the most intense training of your life. I sense the power of all Aspects within you." A strange grin curled on her lips. "Perhaps even enough to rival mine."

Her gaze shifted back to Dorias, who stroked Merl's wing. "He does have a distinct connection to Psoul, and Yasmine is correct, you are the only known Dreamer." Varana paused, her thoughts making no impression on her calm face. "You must take a hand in his training from time to time – so long as you remain upon the Isle."

Dipping his head again, Dorias spread his hands in submission. "As you wish."

The elegant elf woman laughed aloud – a crystalline sound that trickled over the docks. It drew Tallen toward her. "I have no doubt this is your wish as well, Ravenhawke. You could never pass up a chance with a promising student." She wagged a finger at him, still smiling. "But you must wait your turn." With that said, she spun away, the retinue joining her without hesitation. "Come, Tallen. We will take you to the dormitory. I will teach your first lesson myself. Then many other wizards will spend some time with you."

Dorias patted his shoulder, and Merl croaked a farewell. "I will visit soon enough."

The paladin saluted, fist over heart. "As will I." He tapped a gauntleted finger to the side of his head. "And fear not. This island is small enough I can sense an enemy anywhere upon it."

Tallen smiled and waved thanks before jogging after the knot of mages.

"Now fold the metal with your Earth Aspect. Your goal is to line up the particles of iron perfectly with the coke evenly distributed."

Varana's voice hung at the edge of Tallen's perception. His entire being focused on the strip of steel warping and writhing in his hand. Sunlight bounced off the metal while it smoothed out to a length of several inches, thinning as it stretched. Tallen poured Earth into it, giving him rein to shape the steel to his will. It was the most complex task he had undertaken in the week since his arrival.

"That is correct." Tallen heard a hint of surprise in Varana's voice. "Now remember, you must focus on strengthening the heart of the dagger. The edge need not be perfect; it can be sharpened. However, it must be as hard and compact as you can make it. The blacksmith will shape the hilt separately. The handle can be wood, ivory, or wrapped leather just like any other knife." She placed her hand lightly on his shoulder, where he knelt outside the Academy's smithy. The warmth of the sun was a distant murmur next to his power. "Now is the time to infuse it with magic. There are many useful ways to do so. Some of the most powerful artifacts in history began as simple devices like this."

Tallen's own voice echoed in his head from far away. "What do I do?"

"That is for you to decide. It is different for every mage, depending on their strength and what Aspects they can touch – especially the first time." Varana leaned in closer to his ear. "You have almost anything at your call. The possibilities are endless." Her voice became a whisper, but one that rang clearly within his mind. "We have taught you the basics of what each Aspect can do. Choose one of them – I will not allow you to call on multiple Aspects in artifact conjuring just yet – and infuse your choice into the knife just as you finish it. Remember to force it into as compact a form as you can. Condense the metal. That is what gives it strength."

Reaching the relative shape and length he remembered, Tallen compressed the steel with the Earth Aspect, careful that its weight balanced where the hilt belonged. He withdrew the Aspect, while reaching toward the Water that bubbled next to Earth. Drawing upon it, Tallen pushed the Water into the dagger in the instant he extracted Earth. The knife pulled in the Water, lapping it from him as he drew more.

"That's enough, Tallen," Varana called through the roar of his power. "Release the Aspects."

For half a second more, Tallen let the Water pour into the dagger. Then he let it loose.

A sudden exhaustion rushed over him, worse than his usual afternoon fatigue during the last week of training. He gasped for breath as if he had been running rather than kneeling under a shade tree. The dagger blade glittered. It held a slight curve to it that he had not planned.

"Damn." Tallen sighed. "That will probably make it harder to throw."

Varana knelt down beside him to examine the knife. "It is not balanced properly for a throwing knife, if that is what you intended. The weight of the added handle and hilt will throw off its balance." She held out her hand, and Tallen passed the dagger to her. "What magic did you intend to infuse? I know you used Water."

Tallen shifted back on his haunches. "I have learned to use Water to aid in healing. I hoped to make the dagger heal the person who used it."

A bright laughter trickled from Varana's lips and across the Academy yard. She covered her fine lips with even finer fingers. "Forgive me, Tallen. Your power is great, but your ambition may be greater. Even I have never been able to create such a powerful artifact." She shrugged. "Besides, such a weapon would also likely heal the person it stabbed." Varana turned the blade in her hand. "Let us see what you have made."

Tallen felt her embrace her power, but the mix of Aspects became too complex for him to follow. Varana's brow drew down and she focused. A slight smile of pride formed on her face. "Come. Walk with me and watch your dagger."

Rising from her position beside Tallen, Varana strode off toward the small fountain bubbling up in the center of the yard. He rushed to follow her, his eyes fixed on the blade he had created. As they approached the fountain, a faint blue glow emanated from the dagger. It distinctly lit up Varana's creamy skin, even in the bright afternoon sunlight. Brighter it blossomed, until Varana dipped it into the pool surrounding the fountain. Bright sparks of blue coursed up and down the metal. They danced harmlessly around Varana's fingers.

"It appears that you have created a blade that finds water." Fascination tinged her voice. "This is an amazing accomplishment for a first attempt. Few students even make a serviceable stabbing tool on their first try, and this…" She cast her smile upon him. "Do you know that there are nomad chieftains in Hadon who would pay you a thousand goats and one of their daughters for this blade?" Her laughter put the dancing sound of the fountain to shame. "Well done. I look forward to your next experiment."

Tapping the blade against her open palm, Varana looked toward the sun. "I believe you have an appointment with Magus Trevarie to work on your use of Fire."

And that old windbag lives on the far side of the Isle! Tallen nodded to Varana. "Yes, My Lady. I should get going. It is quite some way out to his tower." He raised an eyebrow. "My knife?"

Varana lifted the blade to point toward the smithy. "I will have Jerome put an edge on it and affix a hilt." She lifted a corner of her mouth. "And this weapon deserves a finer one than the average first attempt." Fixing her violet eyes on him, Varana granted a gracious smile. "I wish to study it a bit more as well. I will have it for you in a few days."

"Thank you, My Lady." He turned to begin his jog across the island.

"By the way, Tallen," Varana called after him. He stopped and looked back. "You will be certain to avoid the forest in the depression between Walnut Hill and Acorn Hill. I understand that some think it a shortcut to Magus Trevarie's tower. I have made it clear to students that no one is to pass through there." She knit her brow. "It is a cursed area that interferes with magic. It is forbidden to everyone."

Tallen knuckled his brow. He had heard rumors from other students. "Yes, My Lady." *Damn. They said that makes the journey twice as long, though none have dared to try the shortcut.* His eyes drifted toward the deep woods in the distance. *I don't think I will either.*

Peaceful calm covered Tallen. He focused his thoughts on breathing, ignoring the sounds of the Academy grounds surrounding him. The twitter of birds and the breeze in the tree limbs passed over his consciousness, as did the chatter of students walking nearby. Tallen also avoided the rhythmic pulse of his power, churning about in the back of his mind. Instead, he drew his mind into a tight point, allowing only his breath to draw his attention.

"I would not interrupt so accomplished a trance, but I have not seen you since we arrived."

Tallen opened his eyes with a wide smile. Tomas Harte stood over him.

"Dorias sends his regrets." The paladin offered a hand to help Tallen to his feet. "He is captivated by this search of his. He currently roams Acorn Hill, exploring the empty structures there. I believe he intends to examine every scrap of paper and parchment on this island." Tomas gestured toward the pathway. "However, I made some inquiries and found you have some free time this afternoon. I wanted to show you something."

Tallen fell in beside the paladin. "What is that?"

The expression on Tomas' face mixed pride with sadness. "The temple where I took the vows of my order."

The paladin led Tallen eastward on a quiet stroll leaving the Academy grounds. The path widened and dipped down the edge of what the students affectionately called Peanut Hill, the rocky knoll on which the Academy sat. Soon it curved back upward where Walnut Hill began to rise. Scattered with the trees that gave the hill its name, the slope gradually steepened. A few dozen towers surged above the forest, only about half of which looked inhabited.

The two men climbed in silence, Tallen's gaze constantly drawn to the distant sea encircling the island. *At least the prairie rolls, and groves of trees break its horizon. That blue expanse does not end, and the horizon melts into the sky.*

Near the crest, only a few ancient trees remained. The terrain became rockier. Tomas stepped over the crest of the ridge, a faint light appearing in his emerald eyes. He gestured down into the vale below.

Tallen heaved himself up beside the paladin, his breath heavy from the climb. Below him, a wide, circular building sat nestled between two northern spurs of Walnut Hill. Built in two halves, it matched the sigil of the paladins and the Temple of Balance – one half built of glistening white marble, the other of a glossy, black granite, dark as obsidian. From each curved, droplet-shaped half climbed a tower, built in the opposite color stone. A silver and steel bridge extended from the top of one tower to the other, with a small platform resting at its center.

Tomas pointed to it as he began to descend the path leading to the temple. "The Cathedral of Balance predates the Cataclysm, as does my order. Sadly, much of what it has become since is mostly a bastardization, used by black-hearted men to gain power." The paladin shook his head. "The priestly order now controls the Temple, and only a handful of paladins remain."

He stopped, turning his eyes back to Tallen. "They do not *feel* the Balance the way we do when we sense the life forces around us. I admit, many priests want no more than to heal the sick and minister to the poor." His frown sharpened to anger. "Some, however, have other motives."

Listening to the paladin brought a creeping disquiet to Tallen's heart. He gaped at the white and black columns of the Cathedral rising before him. However, Tomas' words shook him more than the breathtaking sight.

Why does he tell me this?

"Father Vernin in Dadric was pretty nice." Tallen shrugged in order to hide his deeper thoughts. "I guess we did have worse in the past. Father Edric was a sour old despot." He could not help a laugh. Upon noticing Tomas did not share his mirth, Tallen quieted. He searched for a question to change the subject. "How come there are so few paladins left?"

Tomas' frown only deepened from anger to sadness.

Wrong question.

"Well, for one thing, the kingdom snatches up anyone sensitive to *psahn*, and makes them into healers for either the Doctor's College or the military." Tomas watched his feet on the path. "Add the fact that tradition requires that a paladin come from a noble house – *and* that paladins, like wizards of the Circle, may not marry – and it becomes even more difficult to find true Talent."

Tallen knitted his brow. "You mean those with Talent, like Maddi, are like you – they could become paladins?"

"Perhaps," Tomas said, his expression lightening. "It does require a great deal of training. And the...rules...are far more strict. Maddi could probably learn. She has the athletic ability to handle the physical training, and from what I have seen she has a keen, strong mind."

They crossed a round space of trimmed grass and scattered trees. Tallen felt the unnervingly cold shadow of the stone temple pass over his face.

Tomas led him up the white marble steps, and under the wide, colonnaded roof. The Cathedral of Balance loomed before them, open on all sides. From where he stood, Tallen saw the gated entries to the towers. The soft breeze flowing between the pillars created a ghostly whistle.

Turning to face Tallen as he stepped backward, Tomas nodded his head. "You could probably be a paladin too."

"What?" Tallen's voice echoed through the deserted temple.

Tomas laughed, the first mirth Tallen had heard from the man all afternoon. "Again, perhaps. Dorias and I have been friends for a long time. We have spent many months together on ships, in lonely camps and in isolated inns. He has many theories – but I'm sure you have already noticed."

Tallen nodded. "Yeah. But I'd love to hear them all."

Clutching his stomach, Tomas laughed again. "Spoken like a true wizard." He turned about and strolled across the shining white marble. "Dorias' theory is that the Psoul Aspect of magic and the energy maintained by all life, what those with Talent can see and manipulate, are related. You will find the basics of it in that book Joslyn Britt gave you. Likely you could learn to use Psoul in much the same way I use *psahn*." Folding his hands behind his back, Tomas watched the columns. "Dorias is the only other Dreamer I have known. Even he has learned a few tricks from me. As young as you are and with your strength...who knows?"

Freezing in his steps, Tallen raised an eyebrow. "Could you teach me this?"

The paladin shrugged, an ironic grin curling his lips. "Again, perhaps. This is what I brought you here to discuss. As long as we are together, we can spend some time training as well. I know that you are quite busy already, but if we can find the time..." He spread his hands. "I will know quickly if it cannot work." Tomas laughed once more, and it echoed between the black and white pillars. "If it does, then you will just have to learn to become the first wizard paladin in over a thousand years."

A brisk breeze tumbled across the Isle, reminding Tallen that autumn hung just around the corner. Green still held prominence among the trees that swayed across his path. The short structure ahead sat not far from the Academy. Magus Yasmine's tower rose in the saddle between Peanut Hill and Walnut Hill, just where the slope began to climb again. *At least it is much closer than that windbag Trevarie's tower. And Magus Yasmine is far more pleasant to visit with!*

The door opened before Tallen could knock.

"Welcome," the lithe woman said, shading her dark, almond-shaped eyes from the morning sun. Her short black hair hung about her scalp in loose curls. "I suppose today is nice enough that we should work outside. Tahmat knows there are only so many left until your northern winter sets in." She gestured at an iron-wrought table and chairs that rested in the shade of a maple tree. Once seated, Yasmine leaned toward Tallen. "Are you excited about your first lesson in using multiple Aspects? I happen to be quite proficient in Fire and Earth, as well as the Air that I have been teaching you."

Tallen folded his hands upon the table. "I have used multiple Aspects before. In Bridgedale, when I killed the troll, I used lightning made from Fire and Water."

Magus Yasmine nodded, her chocolate colored smile warming him more than the sun. "Indeed. The casting of lightning is one of the most popular and most tricky of spells using multiple Aspects. Tricky because Fire and Water are opposing Aspects – popular because it is very powerful." She shrugged. "I do not have the strength in Water to create much more than a small shock. Terrible irony for me to be born in the deserts of Hadon, yet have no skill in Water. Nevertheless, we shall learn something simpler, if no less useful."

The mage closed her eyes, signaling Tallen to do the same. "Now I want you to take a small piece of Fire, no more than if you were lighting a torch."

The call of his power waited for him to find it. The five Aspects reached out to him, but the roiling warmth of Fire won over. He drew on the Aspect, holding it at the ready.

"Good." Yasmine's voice remained a pool of calmness beyond the torrent of his power. "Now wrap that Fire in Air, an equal amount. I want you to then invert both Aspects as you have been taught, so the spell self sustains."

Tallen stretched his will to grasp Air, whirling about next to Fire. He pulled a measure of it within himself, wrapped it around the strand of Fire, and then fastened the flow so it would remain once he let go.

"Now open your eyes."

A small ball of light floated in the air above his head, casting a faint glow that hid part of the tree's shadow.

Yasmine's smile widened, her teeth sparkling. "Imagine the usefulness of that little spell. Sadly, very few mages have the skill in Air and Fire to create it. It is such a simple thing…"

The globe dimmed almost imperceptibly while he watched. "How long will it last?"

"That is the trick. You must use finesse. Simply stuffing more power into it only makes it brighter. You must balance the Fire with Air and…squeeze the ball of light tighter." The smile leaped up to her coal eyes. "You will learn in time. Here, let us try something else…"

leaning against the tiny windowsill of his dormitory cell, Tallen drew in a deep breath of the night air. Cool winds drifted down from the north, bringing the fresh scent of the ocean to the Academy. In his weeks there, Tallen had learned to enjoy the salty aroma. It somehow soothed him, even though he had never seen the sea before he arrived in Daynon.

He stepped to his bed and collapsed. Exhaustion pervaded his mind and body. Not only did the wizards test every limit of his power, but they also tested his physical strength with the schedule he maintained. At the Academy, the students went to the teachers, no matter how far their towers sat from each other.

It's the running between them that has me so drained. My legs are ready to cry! Tallen forced himself to rise and move to the writing desk and stool. He reached into his pocket, pulled out a small, glittering object, and sat it on the desk. The golden cup Maddi had given him sparkled in the flickering lamplight. He smiled.

Underneath the lid of the desk, sheets of elegant white parchment hid. Tallen pulled one out, dipping the sharp goose quill into a well of squid ink.

Tallen wrote and rewrote the letter before settling on his words. After sealing it with plain gray wax, he wrote upon its outside.

Maddi Conaleon, Student – Doctor's College of Daynon

In the morning, a ship's captain leaving the Isle would take his coin to deliver it. *At least that's what the other students told me. The few that will talk to me, that is.*

Laying the letter aside, he picked up the worn book. Its soft leather cover had frayed slightly at the edges, but the pages remained crisp and clear. He traced Dorias Ravenhawke's name, scripted as the author in gold press upon the leather, and opened it to the first page.

CHAPTER 24

"May the holy Fires bless our sons, so they may be stronger than us. May the many battles we fight be so they need fight no more. Let the Fires grant they see better days."
— *Traditional prayer at Orcish birth ceremonies.*

Slar emerged from the dank lower tunnels and closed the heavy, iron gate behind him. He snapped shut the most intricate lock the forge master had been able to craft. His dark master's prison remained quiet, unmolested by the thousands of orcs that filled Dragonsclaw, save a few brave shamans and Slar himself. The fire in his gut had been quiet as of late, too. *No one will disturb Galdreth's rest, but perhaps I should set a guard?*

Above his master's tomb, the upper network of natural and orc-carved tunnels he passed through twisted with the speed of their excavation. The dozens of orc warriors, shamans, and stewards he passed within the mountain all offered deep nods of respect. Slar returned every one. *No need to waste the newfound respect Galdreth's display earned me.*

Where the main tunnel met a twisting, wooden staircase, he found Radgred standing next to a tall, wide-shouldered orc Slar had longed to see. An extra long scimitar slung over his shoulder, a gift from Slar long ago.

"Grindar!" Slar embraced his eldest son, who towered over him by several inches. "You have brought the reserve warriors from Blackstone?"

Grindar returned his father's gesture, his warmth less exuberant. "Father. It is well to see you." He pushed back a step to clasp Slar's arm in the greeting of a warrior. "I mustered twenty thousand more."

Releasing his son's wrist, Slar frowned. "But I ordered fifty. What is Lagdred hiding?"

Sighing, Grindar shook his head. "Lagdred is still chieftain of the Boar Clan, Father, even if he recognizes you as Warchief. You must remember, there has not been a true Warchief since Wild Tiger. Lagdred insists there are no more warriors with enough skill to wield a sword. He wants to keep a few strong backs at home for the harvest in just a few weeks." Grindar tilted his head. "And he is right. We have to feed this army somehow."

Slar wagged his finger, anger creeping into his voice. "We will feed off the fat of the humans once we move southward." He looked again at his son, who wrinkled his black brows in petulant grimace. "Did you at least bring more shamans? Bear and Snake each brought more than Boar, Ram, and Wolf combined." At the thought of the shamans, Slar's gut knot twisted after its long silence. "I believed fighting shamans from my own clan was difficult."

His grimace deepening, Grindar scratched the day old black scruff on his jawline. "Twelve joined us. I could find no more. Messages have been sent to the Ram Clan. Perhaps some more will come from them."

"Twelve!" Slar stopped in his tracks. Radgred hung behind him, watching the exchange with rare quiet. "There are that many alone still hiding up at Denwich Monastery. Did you not explain that Galdreth has ordered them here?"

Grindar's big shoulders heaved with a sigh. He looked down, his blood red eyes unable to meet his father's. "I did not have time to spend three weeks wandering in the Dragonscales to gather a handful of crazy old monks. I gathered what I could. You set the timetable. In the last several months I have gathered almost a hundred thousand Boars at your call. That is…what… half, maybe, of the men in our entire clan. Do you wish to teach women the sword, like my sister Shana learns to be a shaman? Shall our babies also die at Galdreth's command?"

Slar pulled his fist back as if to strike his son. Radgred moved to stop him, but Grindar held out his chin. Straining with all his will, Slar unclenched his fist. His stomach spun, a burning sensation like caustic ooze spread through his intestines. He forced a breath and lowered his arm.

"I will not argue this point with you, too." Slar stretched his fingers. "You are my left hand as Radgred is my right. Your younger brother may have room for such romanticized hyperbole, but you and I do not. We must lead our entire nation to war and victory."

Slar reached out a hand, and his son did not flinch. He grabbed the scruff of Grindar's coat and pulled him close. "Look at how many have gathered. Do you not understand that we cannot support these numbers trapped north of the Dragonscales? We must either grow or die off." Slar's tone sharpened. "Would you rather die on a Human spear, or have one of your sons die on a Mammoth Clan scimitar? They are beyond even the Bear and Snake in number. If they choose to turn on us, the Boar Clan will die." He clutched his son's strong shoulder. "Don't you see? Instead of the Mammoth looking at us, Galdreth and I have them looking to the south."

Watching the thoughtful look on his son's face, Slar paused.

"I see your point, father," Grindar said eventually. "The Boar, even allied with the Ram, are overshadowed by the Mammoth, and the Bear and Snake would certainly make alliance with them." He nodded with a grave frown. "We must use this moment to change the game board."

Slar clapped his son on the back. "I knew you would understand this where Sharrog does not." He gestured toward the staircase. "Come. We must attend the shaman's council. I need you to stand beside me."

"Thankfully, the Warchief has seen wisdom, and put a shaman from Boar Clan in command of our latest mission to obtain Galdreth's vessel." Brother Ortax smiled at Slar, who sat in his chair with Grindar and Radgred at his shoulders. "While dwelling in the past accomplishes little, I must wonder how much sooner the vessel might have been captured had this course of action been taken sooner."

Slar eyed the leader of the Boar shamans. *What does he think to do in weakening me? Does he not understand that the other clans are scheming against us?*

He signaled Radgred to lean in close. "We must have a private conversation with Brother Ortax."

Radgred nodded, fingering his axe hilt and watching Ortax from the corner of his eye. "Yes, Warchief."

Ortax strolled through the center of the semicircular chamber. Seven chairs sat in a curve facing what would eventually be a window cut into the mountainside. Six orcs rested in those chairs, Slar in the middle – the single empty one to his far left. Sargash of the Mammoth or his chosen leader would sit there. *If they come.*

Narrowing his gaze, Ortax retreated a step. "However, the Warchief is wise in his current plan." He bowed, deep and with respect, and then scanned the other chieftains and their proxies. "We shall have the Master's vessel soon."

The shamans gathered among the chairs tapped their staffs upon the stone floor. The clacking bounced off the walls in a cacophony of support. No Bear or Snake shamans applauded, however, and Slar understood from Ortax's frown that the Boar shaman noticed. *Perhaps Ortax begins to see what I mean. We must definitely speak in private.*

A shaman wrapped in a thick bearskin stalked out into the semicircle. He fluttered his cape about him, the head of the long dead grizzly fashioned into a hood. "Perhaps a closer involvement of the other clans in the planning process of these raids might yield a better result. For nearly a turn of seasons, the Warchief and the Boar Clan have been alone in their leadership." Fargon of the Wolf growled from the chair at Slar's right hand. The Bear Clan shaman ignored him. "And for a turn of seasons, they have failed to capture Galdreth's chosen." More growls rose from the Rams and Boars in the room. A few Bear and Snake shamans tapped their staffs. "If this mission does fail, then perhaps we might be consulted in the next plan."

Slar rose from his seat, making certain to shift the sword upon his hip. He kept his voice calm. "Perhaps it should be restated who commands the horde." His words were for the shaman, but his eyes did not leave Chieftain Dradlo. "I may be Warchief, but I am not the master of our people. It is Galdreth who commands – Galdreth who plans when and where we will strike, be it to find the vessel, or to strike with this horde. I would not have thought another display of our Master's power would be necessary so soon. Galdreth prepares to go unto the Mammoth Clan, but I am certain another demonstration can be arranged. I cannot, however, guarantee that it will be as painless as the last."

At mention of Galdreth's name, many of the boisterous shamans wilted back a step. Even Dradlo lowered his fire-orange eyes.

He has tasted Galdreth's wrath, just as the rest of us.

A sudden shuffle of feet and murmur of voices sounded from the side entrance of the chamber. A ripple of shamans opened a pathway. Two Boar warriors entered the room, one dirty and exhausted from the field. He stood with pride before his Warchief.

"Warchief Slar," the cleaner warrior began, "this messenger

has come in from the westward scouting parties." He looked about the room at the crowd. "Shall we adjourn to a private room, Warchief?"

Waving his hand at Dradlo and Sarinn, Slar shook his head. "We are all allies here, Sergeant, united under Galdreth. Any news from the scouts can be shared in this council room."

Radgred huffed from his position behind Slar's chair. Fargon and Grindar both frowned.

The scout bowed deeply. "Yes, my Warchief. It is an honor." He stood at attention. "The humans have placed a significant force out into the field. At least a thousand, mounted on horses." Slar heard a few spits of distaste from the assembly. "They are heavily armed and provisioned for an extensive march." A smile crept across his face when he bowed his head again. "They have seen nothing, Warchief. They have no idea that we are aware of them, or what numbers we have."

Slar slapped the leather wrapped handle of his scimitar. "We have them." He turned to Radgred and Grindar. "Prepare the last stages of our plans. We have had just enough time." Slar chuckled and grabbed Radgred's shoulders. The old orc offered a slight grin. "I knew they would come out of their hole if we pricked at them enough inside their own lands."

He turned his gaze back to the Bear and Snake chieftains. "You see, there is a greater plan at work here. They have turned their eyes toward us. Soon, the vessel will become complacent within the safety of his hiding place. Then we will strike." He looked at Fargon, Radgred, and his son in turn. "Before they understand what they truly face, we will have smashed their fortress and be eating their winter stores in the Free Cities."

CHAPTER 25

"The Northlands are barren. They would be our graveyard. How the Orcs survive at all, I do not understand. I think that was the plan when we signed the Great Concord, but somehow they still thrive. Perhaps they are tougher, or smarter, than we give them credit."
— *Lord Marshal Horatio Vonstrass, 284 A.R.*

Earl Boris Mourne, General of the Royal Guard, spat onto the long, green grass spreading about the knees of his horse. He wiped his untrimmed mustache with a leather-gauntleted hand, before lifting the brass and crystal spyglass to his eye and scanning the mountain ridge that loomed ahead. A long spur of the Dragonscales shot out to the north, capped by a bulk of piled, black stone known as Dragonsclaw.

"That's where we'll find them." He slapped the spyglass shut. "They are watching us – smiling at us."

Captain Silios Vonstrass trotted his gray charger forward. A mottled gray and green Fadecloak fluttered about him. "I will go out with the next squad. We will push all the way to the ridgeline."

Boris shook his head. "I don't want any scouts caught too far from the protection of the main detachment. We will move forward one more day, find a defensive position, and then send out parties to reconnoiter the ridge. I want an elf ranger with each unit. You will go with Gael himself once he returns." Boris held up his hand at the Bluecloak ranger captain, whose proud nose lifted toward the sky. "You are to follow him. His one eye is better than either of yours, and he has led rangers since before your greatest grandfather hopped the boat."

Silios saluted and spurred his mount forward, shouting orders to his team of men. Sergeant Hall rode a shaggy draft horse up beside Boris.

"He's a Vonstrass. He'll not like taking second position."

Boris wrinkled a lip at his oversized friend. "Since when did you become my court advisor?"

Hall chomped on the unlit cigar butt between his teeth. "Since you ordered Joslyn to stay behind at Highspur, sir." He pulled the butt out with sausage fingers and spit a piece of tobacco onto the ground. "I should have brought Brawny too."

Boris sniffed. "Just get the column ready to move, Sergeant."

Bowing from his saddle with a smirk wrapped around the cigar, Hall shouted back at the long line of men. "Mount up!"

His voice bellowed over the line, echoed by junior officers. The battalion heaved into their saddles, chainmail peeking out from under their blue cloaks. Steel-tipped lances glinted in the sunlight slipping over the dark ridge to the east.

In the distance, Boris heard the creaking wheels of the wagon train. *We will have to leave them behind before long.*

In little more than a minute, the detachment had mounted and sat in formation to advance. Boris nodded to Sergeant Hall.

"Battalion! Ho!"

A mid-toned, three-note sequence sounded out from the bugler. The long line of cavalry lurched forward, Boris at their head upon his black stallion.

"We'll find them soon, Balthar," he whispered to the chomping beast. He patted the stallion's withers. "Then you can run, boy."

Boris watched the sun sink far behind the train, dipping at last where Highspur Mountain hid in the haze of dusk. The swiftness with which it fell from the sky reminded him of how soon winter would sweep upon them. "This is a good spot." He looked at Hall, who still chewed on the same unlit cigar from that morning. "Break for camp, Master Sergeant."

The big man turned his heavy-footed steed back toward the column. "Detachment! Fall out!" He swung his leg over the saddle, hopping down with a grace that always surprised Boris. "I'll make certain our defense lines are tight." Hall looked up at Dragonsclaw, looming in the twilight. Boris thought he noticed a slight shudder. "Tighter."

Captain Vonstrass hopped onto a fresh horse brought up by one of his rangers. He had been silent all day. "I will double our screening scouts. I intend to lead a party myself, if that sits well with My Lord Earl."

Boris frowned at Silios. "Your actions do sit well with me,

Captain. Your command of the Bluecloak rangers is unquestioned. However, Lord Gael Calais commands all rangers attached to Highspur." Boris lowered his gaze. "When we scout the mountain, I want the two of you working together, not in competition."

Silios nodded his head. "Yes, My Lord, understood." He reined his horse around and rode out with two of his men close behind.

Magus Gaeric Taland trotted his brown steed up beside Boris' stallion. His red-trimmed blue cloak lay draped over the horse's haunches. "His Vonstrass pride could be trouble."

Boris shook his head. "Silios is a good soldier. He knows how to follow orders." He swung his leg over Balthar, hopping down to the ground with a groan he had not expected.

A yellow-trimmed Bluecloak with two silver stars trotted over from the command. "Do you need me to examine you, My Lord? I could ease the soreness in those joints."

Laughing, Boris shook his head and waved Doctor Forstra off. "No thank you, doctor. Save your Talent for our coming needs. I will work out the soreness myself."

For the next hour, Boris moved through the forms of the Lion's Stretch, flexing his muscles and strengthening them. When finished, he wiped the sweat dripping from his brow with a towel offered by his steward.

"Thank you, Private." Boris sighed. "What I wouldn't give for a good bath."

Private Delattre nodded, his face regretful. "We have extensive baths at Highspur, fed by the springs deep within the mountain." He sighed. "They wash away a hard day's ride quite well, Milord."

"I know." Boris opened the flap of his tent, no different from that of any other soldier, save he had no bunkmate. "It will be nice to get back there."

"I will find them." Gael Calais' one violet eye focused on Boris. "I sense them out there. We will do our best to draw them out and lead them back to you."

The marble-sized, magic-infused glowglobe on Boris' camp desk fought back the shadows within the tent. Outside the sun had not quite yet brightened the sky.

I got a solid four hours of sleep, Boris lied to himself.

"Good." He nodded to Gael. "You are the bait. This spot is as defensible as anything we have seen out here. Our base camp will remain nestled in this gully with mountains to our south and east." He looked at Hall, who took up most of the tent. "When I take the cavalry out to close the trap, you will stay here with a reserve company. You're better on foot than on horse and you know it." Boris turned to lay his hand on Gael's thin but sturdy shoulder. "We will be ready when you return."

Blowing out the little glowglobe, Boris held back the tent flap for Gael to exit. Hall followed close behind. Outside, Captain Vonstrass stood at attention with two dozen Fadecloaked rangers. He saluted Boris and Gael, fist over heart. His men followed suit.

"Good morning, My Lords," the captain said with a smile. "It is a fine day for a hunt."

His men whooped a single grunt in unison.

From the shadows, half a dozen elves in similar cloaks stalked into the light of the small fire. An amethyst eyed woman stepped to their fore.

"We are prepared as well, My Lords." Her voice did not hold the ferocity of the Bluecloaks, but the stares of the elves certainly did.

Boris nodded to both leaders. "Best of luck today. Keep your eyes and ears sharp."

Gael walked over and stood next to his second. "Ours are the sharpest."

"Indeed." Boris folded his hands behind his back, drawing his blue cloak with them to display the black falcon embroidered on his breast. "Just so, be as alert as you ever have been. Do not engage the enemy unless necessary. Draw them down here from the mountain where our cavalry will have advantage in the open." He rammed a fist into his vertical palm. "We are likely outnumbered, but we are not outclassed. Our steel will be ready."

With a second round of salutes, and a personal nod from Boris to both Silios and Gael, the scouts melded back into the dark. Boris turned his gaze to the eastern horizon. A small ribbon of silver hung high in the sky, tracing the line of Dragonsclaw. "The morning escapes the mountain," he muttered.

Boris stood next to Balthar, his other officers gathered nearby. Hall leaned against his battleaxe. The mountain loomed, its spurs reaching out toward Boris and his men. He shaded his eyes from the noonday sun, in danger of disappearing behind a storm that swarmed from the distant sea. Boris took a bite of the bacon sandwich in his other hand.

"Gael will find them, Milord." Hall held a similar sandwich, but with twice as much bacon. "And Captain Vonstrass' men are the best in Gannon."

Healer-Captain Ian Forstra folded his hands, a nervous look on his face. "We have a triage area set up to receive wounded scouts, and any of your men when you return from engagement."

Boris nodded and turned to Magus-Captain Taland. "Gaeric, you will remain at the base camp. I will take most of the soldiers with me. You and your mages will provide for their defense, along with Master Sergeant Hall and a platoon of lancers."

Gearic frowned, his hands twisting each other. "Magus Britt gave me strict orders not to leave your side, Milord."

Washing down the last of his sandwich with a gulp from a canteen, Boris scraped his thick, leather gauntlet across his mustache. "And since I am Magus Britt's superior officer, I have countermanded that order."

The mage bowed his head in acquiescence, but his frown remained when he backed away.

Boris slapped a cork down into the canteen and hung it from his saddle horn. He boosted himself into his seat, Balthar standing firm until Boris had his second stirrup. Shifting his sword, Greyiron, into position, Boris watched the mountain from the higher vantage. With a stamp of hoof, Balthar and two of the other horses snorted. The distant thunder of hooves found the edge of Boris' hearing.

A pair of horses darted around a curve of hill, churning the grassy earth with their strides. Fadecloaks flew out from their riders. Behind Boris, the wind ahead of the oncoming storm began to pick up.

Reaching into a saddlebag, Boris ripped out his spyglass and popped it open. He brought it to his eye and adjusted the crystals to find the riders. "It's Captain Vonstrass and one of his men. They do not spare their steeds." Slapping the spyglass shut, he turned to his captains. "Get companies one through four mounted." Boris looked at Captain Belecond of Fifth Company. "Five is to protect the basecamp. Magus-Captain Taland will be in command." Captain Belecond saluted, as did the others. All five rode back toward the camp in haste.

Sergeant Hall flexed his fingers around the shaft of his battle-axe. "Are you certain you want both Gaeric and I to stay behind?"

Boris focused on the approaching scouts. "You heard my orders, Sergeant."

The moments stretched out while Silios and his partner rode up. Their mounts stamped about, chewing at their bits and throwing foamy lather from their sides.

The ranger captain leaped down and gestured to the other scout. "Trade our mounts in for fresh ones. I will report to the Earl." His compatriot nodded and jogged away leading the two horses. Captain Vonstrass turned to his commander with a salute. "My Lord Earl, we found the enemy."

Noticing the sweat on Silios' brow and the rip in his cloak, Boris folded his arms. "Report."

Captain Vontrass lowered his salute with a snap. "My Lord, the enemy appears to have hidden within the mountain itself. Companies of orcs just appeared out of tunnels in the rock. Lord Gael ordered me to bring the message to you immediately, while he and the elves provided a distraction." He sniffed, wiping a wind-reddened nose with his glove. "Their numbers are quite large. I saw at least two or three thousand spread over the mountainside. They progress in our direction."

Nodding at the horizon, Boris gripped tighter on his reins. "Well done, Captain. Get that new mount and initiate a screening pattern ahead of the main force. If we are outnumbered, I don't want to be caught by surprise."

Silios saluted again and dashed after his fellow ranger, who returned with two fresh horses. He hopped into the saddle. Giving spur and a wordless shout, the two riders galloped back the way they had come, steel-shod hooves tossing up clods behind them.

Boris reined his stallion around and rode over the rise to the gully along which the detachment was camped. Eight hundred lancers already mounted and waited in ranks, while the remainder of his men scurried to make the camp more defensible. They circled the wagons of supplies around the huge waterwagon, made by dwarves from two huge wine aging casks placed on a bending frame. The half a dozen mules that formed its team grazed close by.

Thinking back on Silios' report, Boris cantered Balthar up to the commander of Fifth Company. "Captain Belecond! Take half your company and get those wagons moving back to Highspur." A startled expression crossed the faces of several Bluecloaks. "This is just the tip of the spear. I have a feeling Lord Gael and the others will find a great deal more orcs than they already discovered. We will engage the lead of the enemy, then feint and fade across the Northlands back to Highspur."

Captain Belecond saluted and began passing orders out to his men.

Boris twisted his neck to find Hall standing nearby, his battle-axe planted. "Sergeant Hall, be ready to pull up stakes fast if we come back in a hurry." His face set in stone, Hall snapped a ferocious salute and pulled out a fresh cigar.

Boris looked to Doctor Forstra. "We may not have time to heal wounded before following the wagon train. Be ready to help the worst so they can at least move."

"Yes, My Lord." The doctor spun about and trotted off toward his triage area.

Gaeric saluted to Boris from where he and the other two mages prepared defenses. Boris nodded back and rode to the head of the armored column.

Pulling his helmet loose from the saddlehorn, Boris slapped it on his head. He swung a steel encased arm. "Forward ho!"

The bugler tooted the three-note sequence, and the entire train of men and horseflesh lurched forward. Boris barely tapped his stirrups to Balthar's flanks, and the great stallion leaped ahead.

Boris led the column through the hills, winding his way around outcroppings of rock. Balthar arched his neck, throwing his head as he stepped between the stones. Boris scanned every ridge and vale through the perpendicular slits of his helm. Twice, scouts rode in to report to him that they had found no enemy upon either flank.

A nervous hour passed before Boris spied Silios Vonstrass charging up a small ravine. "They are coming!" He turned his sweating horse in beside Boris. "At least two hundred orcs, and they are not much more than a hundred yards behind me."

Boris swung back to his officers. "First company, ready to charge. Second company, draw bows. Third and fourth remain in reserve."

Orders passed along the column. The second company of men tied lances to saddles and readied their short horsebows.

Boris spun his neck forward, the blue-dyed horsehair tassel on his helmet bouncing away to reveal the first of his enemies trickling up the dry ravine. A hundred ebon-mailed forms marched forward, curved scimitars dancing over their heads. Boris picked out crimson eyes shadowed by leather and steel helms. The banners of Wolf and Ram Clans fluttered over them.

The metallic taste of adrenaline in the back of his mouth tingled across his tongue. Boris shouted over the rumble of nail-shod boots tromping up the ravine. "First company! Form wedge!"

Two hundred horsemen gathered in a staggered formation, just as wide as the ravine was narrow. Boris rode at its lead. Those soldiers with horsebows gathered behind the triangle of cavalry.

Drawing Greyiron, Boris lifted it on high. His heart pounded with excitement, yet his mind was singular and focused on their enemy. His sword caught the last rays of the westering sun just as scattered clouds along the approaching thunderhead overtook it.

"Formation! Charge!"

He flourished Greyiron, and the bugler sounded a series of bright, hopeful notes. Balthar leaped down the ravine, and the wedge of blue-tinged steel surged with him. The dragon spangled pennants snapped in the rush of air. A barrage of arrows passed overhead, dropping a few of their enemy, quickly replaced by their comrades. The thicket of steel and oak lances surrounding Boris tipped forward at the last moment. Boris growled a wordless shout of rage.

The heavy clatter of steel clashing on steel, of hooves crushing bone, and of leather and flesh ripping, echoed off the walls of the ravine. Screams of horses, orcs, and men resounded over all other clatter. The wedge of Bluecloaks rode over them, most shorter than Balthar's shoulders. Lances snapped, swords came out, and the killing continued.

Boris swung Greyiron with a heavy hand. A scar-faced veteran with a Wolf tattoo died swiftly, his throat slit by Greyiron's unnatural edge. A grunt, his beard little more than black fuzz, died watching his shoulder spurt arterial blood. Boris slashed through the steel clad skull of another orc, splitting the staff of the Ram banner he carried with the same stroke. Balthar's hooves dropped one like a loose sack of flesh.

Boris reached the rear of the orc force, riding into open ground. He reined Balthar around with the rest of his formation. His single-minded focus during the initial charge over, he looked back up the ravine.

An abattoir of churned flesh and bone scattered the rocky slope. Broken lances and swords formed a devastated forest of steel popping up from the gore. A few orcs stumbled about in a daze. One lacked an arm, bewilderedly searching for the lost limb among his fallen comrades. Boris' Second Company picked the stragglers off with bows, though most of the mopping up was complete. The metallic scent of blood, along with the more sour stench of spilled entrails, clung to the breeze. A single, riderless horse stood among the carnage. Boris noticed five or six more lying dead, their lumps of flesh protruding up like islands in a sea of death. Cloaks of blue draped several of them.

"Back to the main force." Boris waved Greyiron up the slope. "We cannot afford to be separated with no intelligence about the enemy's movements."

He spurred Balthar forward, casting his eyes back over his shoulder. The helmet obscured his vision, the slits only useful in close combat. He ripped it from his head, the sweat clinging to his long, black hair. He scanned the ridgeline, much closer than it had been at basecamp and more above him than ahead. He pulled out his spyglass.

"Whoa, boy – steady." Balthar stomped to a halt.

Putting the glass to his eye, Boris examined the tumbled shoulders of Dragonsclaw and the foothills leading toward him. Odd, barely perceptible movement rippled about the mountain, as if it were not entirely solid.

"What does that remind me of...dear Balance, it cannot be!"

Like ants roiling over a newly dug hill, orcs crawled over the slopes of Dragonsclaw. As the darkness of the oncoming storm deepened, the flicker of torches spread among the mass. Trees shook and fell, revealing gaping maws in the mountainside. Trolls poured out of the openings, hundreds, every one as large as the burned carcass Boris found in Bridgedale.

Boris lowered the glass, the warm sensation of panic slipping into his chest. He forced it down and gritted his teeth.

Balthar charged back through the butchery to the top of the ravine. There, Boris turned his glass once again to the mountainside. He noticed several large siege engines, trebuchets and catapults pulled by orcs and more trolls, rolling out of the holes. Organized formations of thousands of orcs crawled down the mountain, with more pouring out behind them. A flutter of movement from something extremely large caught the corner of his glass. He lowered it, squinting to catch what had passed between him and Dragonsclaw. A black, winged shape swooped around the corner of the mountain. It looked no bigger than a horsefly at this distance, but Boris knew it must be larger than a horse. *Balance and Spirits of Water protect us...*

"Captain!" Boris turned back to see his men in formation. "Double time back to the basecamp!"

The officer's face curled in a concerned expression. "What is it, sir?"

"We are no match for this enemy." He passed the glass to the captain. "I suspected the orcs gathered in force, but this…"

The Bluecloak captain's ashen face wilted behind the glass. "Is that a…a dragon?"

Boris feared his own face matched that of his subordinate. "This is why we must get back to basecamp quickly. We will then catch up with the wagon train, burn it, and retreat back across the Northlands to Highspur." He nodded to the captain. "If we keep together and move fast, we will all make it."

The ride back to camp seemed to take longer than the ride out. Along the way, Captain Silios Vonstrass and his rangers joined them.

"They outnumber us at least fifty to one. Probably more." The nobleman from the Southern Realm looked shaken, his eyes darting always behind them. His horse and his men appeared in no better state.

Boris kept the column at pace while he talked. "Have you seen sign of Lord Gael?"

A worried frown settled upon Silios' brow. "Not since this morning, when he ordered me to report to you."

Boris stared at Dragonsclaw. "Damn."

As they rounded the last outcrop before entering the gully, a sudden crackle of lightning forked into the sky. The storm still hung several miles to the west.

Boris looked to Silios. "That's Gaeric." He looked back at his men. "Battallion, full advance!"

The sweet notes of the bugle rang out over the rolling grass. The formation galloped up the slow trickle of water, churning it into a froth of mud. Boris pulled out Greyiron, and Silios drew his own saber alongside him.

When they arrived at the flat top where the camp set, Boris witnessed a churning morass of confusion. Hundreds of orcs swarmed about, engaging a knot of Bluecloaks. They stood defending the horse lines, while a dozen of their fellows scrambled into their saddles. A few yards away, Boris saw Sergeant Hall, swinging his axe in wide arcs. One blow cleaved an orc in half, while a stab of the weapon's butt crushed another's windpipe. Hall stood his ground in front of the triage area, while the healers scrambled for cover. Each mighty swing took out one or more of Hall's enemies, until only those wise enough to stay out of his range remained.

The sergeant staggered as a black feathered shaft seemed to sprout from his shoulder. Hall winced around the lit cigar between his teeth, but his onslaught continued.

"No!" Boris waved Greyiron, gritting his teeth. "Battalion! Charge!"

The arc of lancers swept forward, rolling over the orcs and crushing them from behind. Boris, however, did not get three strides closer to Sergeant Hall before a second arrow slammed into his chest. Hall backed up two steps, before bashing another orc warrior with the head of his axe.

"Hall!" Boris urged Balthar forward. The stallion jumped ahead under his heavy spur. He swung his sword about, cutting through bone, iron, leather, and sinew. Greyiron's enchanted edge sliced through where other weapons would glance and chip.

A third arrow struck Hall. He fell to one knee, lowering his guard a moment. An orc warrior rushed in, placing a quick thrust in the giant's side. Hall swung late, but still caught the fool in the side of the head, removing its top half. The momentum of the huge axe spun him around. He collapsed in a heap on top of his weapon.

Boris and his men swept past, charging over Hall's assailants.

Swinging his leg over Balthar's head, Boris leapt to the ground. He dropped Greyiron as he fell to his knees beside Hall, struggling to roll the man over. One of the arrows snapped in two as the body shifted.

Lifeless gray orbs stared up at a sky of the same color. Boris reached down to close them. Master Sergeant Jerome Hall still clenched the cigar stub between his teeth, his lips turned up in a ghostly smile. Boris held him tight, unaware of the two dozen mounted Bluecloaks gathered about him in a protective circle.

May you return to the Waters your family worshiped. And may the Balance return you to the cycle of life, my brother.

Boris lifted his head, at last taking in his surroundings. The rush of riders had passed, and most of the orcs lay dead. A few platoons chased those who fled, while the rest secured the site. Another field of scattered carnage spread before him. Boris watched it all in numb incoherence, while a healer knelt beside him.

"I'm sorry, My Lord Earl." Forstra's words skipped across his consciousness, like a pebble crossing a still pond. "Sergeant Hall has passed. His life force has left his body. I can do nothing for him."

"See to the others, then." Boris heard his words as if they came from another mouth. "See to the other wounded."

He rose to his feet and walked a dozen yards to the horselines, stepping around tumbled orc corpses. He took the halter of Hall's big draft horse and led him to where his master had fallen. Straining against the weight with a heavier heart, Boris heaved Sergeant Hall's bulk over the steed's back.

"One last ride back to the castle, my friend."

Boris turned to the nearest officer. "I want everyone gathered and mounted immediately. We must get to the wagon train before they are ambushed too." He climbed back into Balthar's saddle, a deep pain behind his heart. "Everyone stays together from now on."

A small pillar of black smoke billowed toward them, blown by the wind before the storm. The clouds hung thick overhead, but no snow had fallen yet. Several bat-like forms circled the column of smoke, swooping downward as if chasing scattered prey.

"Dragons!" Boris cast his eyes back toward Gaeric, whose red-fringed cloak fluttered out behind as they galloped. "You and your mages are our best defense against them. We will get the teams cut free and mount up their drivers." He shouted at the captain of Second Company. "Your men have already warmed up their bows. Use them on the beasts."

The train came into view on the open plain. One of the supply wagons burned, separate from where the others had circled. A green-scaled dragon with red trim along its wings passed over the cluster of Bluecloak teamsters. The beast belched a green gush of liquid fire. Where it landed on the wagons, it burned through metal and wood alike.

Boris watched Gaeric raise his hand. A flash of lightning darted out, skittering over the dragon's leathery wings, leaving them smoking. The beast roared in pain and pounded for the sky.

Urging his horse to more speed, Boris closed on the line of wagons. The ground beneath Balthar's hooves churned past. Through his knees Boris felt the stallion tense, gathering strength. Balthar bounded into the air, carrying them over the tumbled wagon in a single vault.

Gael knelt before him, a goose-feathered arrow nocked to his long elven bow. His single violet eye widened at the sight of Boris and his steed. "Spirits of Air, am I glad to see you."

Unable to stifle a sudden laugh of joy, Boris shook his head, whipping his horsehair tassel back and forth. "You are glad to see me? Ha!"

A second dragon swept downward, and a hundred arrows launched into the air to meet it. Few found lodging in the thickly scaled body, but more than a dozen stuck in the thin membrane of its wings. A fount of crimson sprayed from one of the veins that twisted through the leather. A bolt of lightning lashed out from Gaeric, wrapping the beast in blue-white sparks. One of the other mages gestured, and three Bluecloaks tossed their lances into the air. The mage sliced his hand forward, and the three projectiles launched toward the dragon at a fantastic speed, each planting in the beast's side. Its beating wings faltered, and the yellow and gray beast crashed into the ground, ripping a furrow in the earth. It came to a halt, its eyes rolled back and its tongue lolling out between still jaws. Its two companions winged for altitude, soaring their way back toward Dragonsclaw.

Boris returned Greyiron to its sheath and looked at Gael. "Where have you been? How did you find the wagon train?"

Gael lowered his bow and gazed off toward Dragonsclaw. "We were surprised when the enemy poured from the mountain in far greater numbers than we expected. I wouldn't doubt the entire mountain and ridge are tunneled out like a good piece of Gavanor cheese." His brows furrowed. "They killed Delena and Sharvis before we even knew we had been set upon. Their bones will lie upon the mountain forever." He shook his head. "Another two of our people passed on before having children."

Shifting in his saddle, Boris bowed his head to Gael. "I feel for your loss, my friend." He looked toward a large horse with a blue-cloaked body hung over it.

Placing one hand over his heart, Gael returned Boris' tilted nod. He took the reins of his gray horse from the man who brought it to him and mounted. "We were separated in the fighting. I saw smoke from the wagon train and led my scouts toward it."

Trotting Balthar closer, Boris licked his lips. "So you know what's coming?"

Gael nodded, his grim expression only accentuated by his eye patch.

Boris waved to the bugler. "Then we should get moving."

257

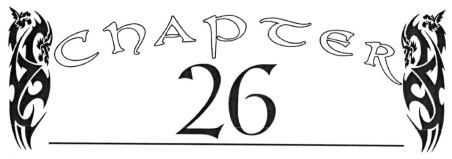

CHAPTER 26

Quickfire was invented in Uria centuries ago. Some believe they based it on the burning substance of dragon fire. Aravath brought the formula with him when he and the People of Gan returned to Tarmor. Over the centuries since, the kings of Gannon and their powerful mages have found it an even more useful substance than the Urian nobility ever did.
— "The Gannonite Arsenal" by Yahn Folore

Captain Jaerd Westar dragged his finger along the cold, rough stone as he climbed down the spiral staircase. With steps in the thousands, it wound its way down through Highspur Mountain, all the way from the roof of the bastion to the deepest storeroom. Jaerd sought the armory level.

He stepped off the stairs, through a carved arch, and a wide chamber opened before him. Scattered torches and magical glowglobes lit the room. To Jaerd's right, a crossed sword and shovel draped with a blue cloak hung above an entryway to the quartermaster corps. Thirty yards closer to the bright exit portal from the mountainside, another sigil hung – a hand wrapped in twisting grape vines. A dozen Talented healers, and twice as many trained in more mundane techniques, worked within the infirmary. Jaerd recognized three of the five healers that had travelled with his own forces.

Two ride with Earl Boris.

Off to his left, the clanking of the forge rang out. Jaerd took only a couple of steps toward it before the person he sought emerged from the red-lit interior.

"Ah, Captain Westar." Tarrak Goldmar waddled over closer to Jaerd, lifting up a curved bracket of metal. "This should work for those new catapults we're building along the inner wall."

Squinting in the faint light, Jaerd inspected the object that Tarrak turned with his tongs. The metal still radiated waves of heat, but it looked like it just might do the trick. "You have enough iron from the new vein you found to make this a dozen times over?"

Tarrak laughed, his thick shoulders bouncing. "That, and plenty more. I also thought we might get really ambitious and build two new trebuchets for the rim towers to match the older ones on the gate towers."

Jaerd nodded slowly. "Excellent."

Tarrak carried the new catapult part back to the forge. It radiated a comforting warmth. "We'll be ready, Captain."

"One more thing," Jaerd called at the dwarf's retreating back. "Do you still have all that extra pot metal lying around?"

Tarrak glanced over his shoulder. "Aye!" he shouted over the clanging from the smithy.

With a smile that left the dwarf wearing a puzzled expression, Jaerd turned back to the stairwell.

The clank of metal on metal followed him as he returned to the spiral steps, echoing up the long, carved-out tube. Sighing when he looked upward, Jaerd began his ascent back to the bastion. Dozens of soldiers – human, elf, and dwarf – dashed past. Every one of them seemed to salute in a different fashion, and he did his best to return the compliments correctly.

To think I was a gate lieutenant in Gavanor only four months ago. Now I get saluted by the elite soldiers of the greatest powers in Tarmor.

When he passed the officer's level, the scent of ham cooking filled his nose. His stomach growled, reminding him he had not eaten since breaking his fast at dawn. He stopped by the mess, picking up a tray of warm ham, brown bread, and a cup of rough-ground mustard.

"Put two mugs on the tray," Jaerd told the cook. "I have a meeting with another officer."

The pale ale, kept cool in deep storerooms of Highspur Mountain, bubbled to a frothy head. Jaerd grabbed a couple of wrinkly apples from a barrel in the corner. Grasping the tray, he returned to his ascent. With each step, the ale jostled a little closer to the rim of the mugs. *This is why I left the inn!*

Relieved that he wore no armor, Jaerd still breathed hard by the time he reached the second level of the bastion. He passed down a narrow hall, carpeted with thick rugs. Pushing his way through a double door, he entered the main library of Highspur.

A magnificent bay window opened along the northern wall, looking out over the Dragon's Feet and the Norvus River in the distance. The natural light spilled across a half dozen tables, each ringed with comfortable looking chairs. Rows and rows of shelves filled the rest of the room. In the center stood an ancient globe, scrawled with the continents of Tarmor, Uria, and Jahad. The lopsided circle of the Jade Isles drifted across the Eternal Ocean. Parts of the globe were clearly marked unknown.

"I brought you lunch, Magus." Jaerd walked to a table scattered with maps. Magus-General Joslyn Britt leaned over a sketch of the Northlands, frowning. Brawny lay curled up on a rug, his chin fixed to his feet, though his eyes followed Jaerd and the tray. "And a mug, if you like."

The Battlemage looked up. "Ah, Captain Westar…" He eyed the ale before returning to his figuring. "Boris estimated twenty days to Dragonsclaw, even at his slowest. The last dispatch rider put them exactly on schedule, five days from the mountain." The mage closed his eyes, counting on his fingers. "That courier reported in two days ago. Another one should arrive before evening."

Jaerd had done the same math himself while looking at that exact map. "So they should arrive there any day now." He sat the tray down on the next table, one empty of papers. "Is there a reason Boris is headed for that mountain?"

A low growl emanated from Magus Britt's stomach. Brawny's ears pricked at the sound. The mage pulled the tray closer and picked up a slice of ham. Slathering it in mustard, he stuffed it in his mouth. "We have seen proof of at least three orc clans working together. Boar and Ram may be allies, but Shark is allied with Wolf Clan. We know that Boar and Wolf fought a couple of wars against each other in the last century. So either Shark Clan has switched sides…" He mumbled around another mouthful. "…or Wolf and Boar are working together too."

Grabbing a piece of bread and a slice of ham for himself, Jaerd furrowed his brow. "I understand that part, but what does this new alliance have to do with Dragonsclaw Mountain?" Unable to resist the hound's eyes, Jaerd tossed the end piece from the ham toward Brawny. It disappeared in a snap.

"That black mountain is sacred to the orcs," Britt said. "The only time they have ever been known to gather there is when the clans unite, usually to strike at Highspur or raid the eastern coasts."

Jaerd shook his head, forcing himself to swallow a too-dry bite. "Ah." He picked up his mug to wash down the crumbs of bread. "It's like their Mootlawn."

Magus Britt cleaned his teeth with his tongue. "I suppose. Regardless, that is where Boris seeks to draw them out."

Setting down his mug, Jaerd folded his arms. He considered not asking the question, but he felt it his duty. "Do you believe his numbers are sufficient to such a task? If three or four orc clans are united, might they not have thousands of warriors to call upon?"

The mage turned away and carried his mug over to the wide bay window. Jaerd followed, close behind. The morning sunlight cascaded through the glass in dust-sparkled beams, bathing the older man's face in a yellow glow. It seemed to age him further, emphasizing the wrinkles behind his jaw and the lines on his forehead. Jaerd watched him stand there, casting his gray gaze over the long spread of the Northlands and the heavy shoulders of the Dragonscales that marched off to their right.

"They might well have those numbers." Magus Britt sipped from his mug, his other arm wrapped behind his back, holding onto his red-trimmed cloak. "From experience, though, I can tell you Boris' detachment could handle at least five times its number in orcs – maybe ten."

Jaerd stepped between the mage and the globe, his eyes tracing the northern parts of his home continent. "What if there is more than that?"

Sipping again from his mug, Magus Britt gazed out the window. For a long moment he said nothing, his lips pursed as if the ale tasted too bitter. "Boris will lead them back here, and we will smash them with the new toys you and Maester Goldmar are building." The Battlemage turned to stare at Jaerd. "How goes that project, by the way?"

Jaerd pointed at the tray. "That was part of the reason I sought you out bearing gifts. I heard you talking with Boris about a special, highly explosive form of Quickfire. Does it have something to do with that wagon full of naphthous sulfite we brought with us?"

"Yes." The mage's face perked up. "It can be made quite concussive when formulated by a powerful Fire mage." He lifted his head in pride. "I just happen to be one."

Jaerd smiled. "Well, I spoke to Tarrak about all the pot metal he has lying around…"

When the sun drifted from its height, a slight breeze picked up, cooling the perspiration on Jaerd's brow. He leaned against a battlement, watching the wind scoop up swirls of dust as it whipped down the approach to the gate. Working day and night for the last few weeks along the front wall, they had placed ten new turrets, each built of heavy oak beams and dwarf-cut stone. Scorpions that fired three, yard-long shafts at once sat mounted in each turret.

Casting his gaze up the slope at the secondary gate, he realized how much more formidable it was. *Tarrak said it is far older. I guess they really don't quite build them like they once did.*

A squad of men dug about underneath the foundations of the interior walls. They scurried in and out of man-sized holes that bored into the solid stone.

"What are they doing there?" Jaerd asked of Captain Dercester, a Bluecloak engineer who had served at Highspur for nearly a decade. "Are those boltholes if the forward wall falls?"

"Aye." The man in the brown-trimmed cloak nodded. He looked at the towering fortress above them. "When this outer wall was added, fifteen thousand men stood garrison here. Now, even with the men you brought, we are lucky to have seven." The grizzle faced engineer spat off the edge of the wall, watching the gobbet fall to the distant ground. "The Empire of Hadon has barely two hundred men here. The elves and dwarves little more. Saria hasn't sent a delegation for nearly a century, though I suppose that might be because their Union doesn't really exist any more." Dercester shrugged, clacking his tongue. "This front wall cannot be held if they send the kind of numbers against it you keep warning me about. It's why we keep the trebuchets and most of the catapults posted on the inner wall."

Jaerd lifted his eyebrow. "So it is customary to abandon the outer wall in the event of a siege?"

The captain spat again. "Nothing is customary. There hasn't been a siege of Highspur in over a century. I'm just telling you what can and cannot be done."

Folding his arms in thought, Jaerd looked at the gate towers above him. *Look at all that stone – the weight of it.* He stared at the newly finished turrets and noticed how small the men crawling about them looked. *And those scorpions would be turned around on us. The wall will give them cover – a raised platform to fire upon the inner wall.* The kernel of an idea sprouted in his mind. "I need to talk to Magus Britt again."

"Rider coming!" Lieutenant Kent Varlan waved down to Jaerd from his perch atop the gate tower. "It's one of our outriders!"

"Damn." Jaerd pounded his fist on the stone battlement. "I hoped it would be the dispatch courier from Boris."

The front portcullis lifted with a squeak of heavy iron, and a

rider in the mottled Fadecloak of a Bluecloak ranger trotted in..
Trotting down the steps along the inner side of the wall, Jaerd
returned the scout's salute.

"An armed force approaches along the southern road, sir.
You're not gonna believe who it is."

Jaerd heard a distant horn echo off the shoulders of Highspur.
"I don't recognize that call. Who comes, man?"

"Dwarves, sir. Hundreds of them."

Grabbing his cast-off tunic, Jaerd pushed the scout toward the
inner gate. "Take your message to the bastion. I will meet our
new friends."

The buttons on his tunic fought him as he marched toward
the main gate. Dust from his work clung to the blue wool. *They
arrive unannounced, they can expect a little informality.*

Another horn blasted up the defile, followed by a lower,
rhythmic beat. The tromping of hundreds of heavily armored
footsteps rang for quite some time before the horn blasted once
more. Jaerd noticed many of the garrison soldiers gathered on
the walls and towers. Nervous stares among them gave way to
cheers shouted down toward the marching dwarves.

"Sink me in the Waters," he whispered. "Looks like Northtower
kept his promise after all."

By the time the battalion of dwarf soldiers arrived outside the
gate, a delegation of officers had ridden down from the bastion,
including Lord Marshal Magdon. Even Earl Brandon Farseer had
left the seclusion of his tower, riding down with two of his sable-
cloaked armsmen.

Three dwarves marched out from the main force, stopping
at the very front of the gate. Maester Darve Northtower bowed
in greeting to the gathered commanders. "My Lords, in honor
of our ancient alliance, Berik II, King of the Rock and Iron Hills,
sends five hundred warriors to aid in the defense of Highspur."
He waved at the blond maiden next to him, now dressed in the
fine leathers of a ranger. "Tilli Dragonslayer has also brought a
hundred hunters with stout bows."

Lord Marshal Magdon swung down from his saddle, as did
Earl Brandon. When both men tottered, Jaerd rushed in to offer
an arm to the Lord Marshal. Farseer's retainers aided him.

"Greetings, Maester Northtower." The Lord Marshal released
Jaerd's arm to offer a short bow. "All men in Gannon know that
the promises of Dwarves are never broken. Your arrival is most
fortuitous."

Northtower nodded his head in response. "Marshal Magdon. We did not expect to find you here. Has the Earl Boris Mourne not come to Highspur?"

"He is in the field." Earl Brandon's gaze drifted to the north, a sour look on his features. "He insists on provoking our enemy."

Darve bowed to the earl. A ruby set into the pommel of the broadsword on his back sparkled in the dying sunlight. "You must be Earl Brandon Farseer. It is an honor to meet the commander of Highspur, My Lord. My men and I are at your service."

The earl nodded, some of the sourness slipping away from his expression. "Your valor is appreciated. However, it is the Lord Marshal Magdon in command here." He waved at the gray bearded Bluecloak. "He shall assign your positions." The earl swung his hand upward to point at his high tower. "I shall be watching for the Earl of Mourne's return."

Darve frowned. "Has the Earl Boris sent dispatches as to his location and the position of the enemy?"

Marshal Magdon nodded, combing his thin fingers through his beard. "His last dispatch came yesterday, reporting him within five leagues of Dragonsclaw Mountain. So far, he has encountered no enemies. However, he believes they wait for him at Dragonsclaw."

The dwarf commander nodded. "When do you expect the next dispatch?"

A low rumble of thunder tumbled down from a purple storm stretching from the Lone Ocean out over the Northlands. The breeze picked up, swirling little dust eddies down the defile through which the dwarves had just marched. A looming darkness hung over the fortress, and Jaerd felt it begin to creep into his heart.

Earl Brandon shook his head with a morose grimace. "There will be no more dispatches."

A long, mournful howl rang out from the fortress.

CHAPTER 27

"So that the art of Healing may be taught and spread to every corner of my father's kingdom."
— King Arathan I – carved into the cornerstone of King's Hall on the campus of the Doctor's College of Daynon

Maddi pushed against the heavy, iron-studded door of King's Hall. It swung open with far more ease than she expected of the monstrosity. Inside, the building smelled of old paper and pipe smoke. Classes had not been taught in King's Hall for years, as far as Maddi knew, but on the top floor, the Lord Doctor Tymin Marten kept his private office as headmaster of the college.

Maddi trotted up the wide steps of age-polished cherry wood, sliding her hand along wrought-iron railings that curved around each flight and stoop. After the third floor, she noticed her breath quickening. *I have to spend more time keeping fit and less time studying.* She jogged up the last two flights, forcing her breath to remain steady. On the fifth landing she paused.

I do not want to walk into his office panting. She drew in deep breaths to regain her wind, steadying herself quickly.

Brass trimmed the wide double doors of walnut with colored glass windows. Above the entrance hung a sign that read: *Lord Doctor Tymin Marten, Collegiate Headmaster, High Councilor of the Kingdom, Professor Medicinal.*

Maddi shook her head with a rueful smile. *Evidently the man likes his titles.*

She pushed the doors open into a waiting room with windows overlooking the quadrangle. A prim woman with pretty eyes and a slim figure sat behind a small desk, scratching away upon a parchment with a quill pen. She lifted her eyebrows at Maddi's entrance.

"Miss Conaleon, is it?" The woman placed the quill into its holder. "The Lord Doctor is not expecting you."

Maddi straightened her blouse and adjusted the red scarf

265

she had hastily tied around her neck. "It is important. If he is in, could you not at least ask?"

The woman glowered at Maddi, the tight bun in her hair pulling the skin of her face back. "Very well." She rose and walked into Doctor Marten's office. The woman was gone only a moment before returning and gesturing her in. "The Lord Doctor will see you now."

The inner office was twice the size of the outer. Paneled in rich walnut, the room held shelves full of exquisite art and artifacts. Maddi's eyes passed over objects worth enough money to supply a large Dernan family with a lifetime retirement. A wide mahogany desk rested in front of a semicircular fanlight overlooking the distant harbor. The Lord Doctor Marten sat behind the desk in a rich, brass-riveted leather chair. He watched Maddi over his steepled fingers.

"Miss Conaleon. How convenient that you have come here. I was just discussing you with Doctor Gramm."

My Herbology teacher? Shaking off her surprise, Maddi refocused on her reason for coming. "First, I must tell you what I have seen down in the slums along Jalanine Hill – down on Green Street, where the little girl you had me heal came from."

Marten folded his fingers together, and his gaze narrowed. "What were you doing down in that part of the city? Students, especially young women, should be careful where they travel in Daynon." He lowered his hands and leaned forward in his chair. "That area is particularly rough."

"It's no worse than some of the places where I grew up." Maddi planted her feet, a little offended at the doctor's attitude. "And that little girl *lives* down there. What's more, it is infested with plague. I'm not certain which one yet, but it is the same sickness that Tanya had. Her mother died of the disease, and I sensed it in several others within their tenement."

The doctor leaned back in his chair, brushing his strong chin with his finely manicured fingers. "Do you believe this disease will spread?"

Maddi cocked her head sideways, her voice filled with disdain. "What is it that disease does, Lord Doctor?"

Marten chuckled. "I suppose you have a point." He lifted his hands in a futile gesture. "Fine. Fine. As Lord Doctor the health of this city is somewhat within my purview, although my resources are extremely limited. I will mention it in council and pass this news to the Mayor."

The Lord Doctor pulled a paper from the side of his desk

to the center. "However, let me get to the reason I intended on summoning you myself – something far more important than a few sick people in the worst corner of town." He lifted the document toward Maddi. "This is your official commission as a teacher within the college. Doctor Gramm says that you exceed her in your knowledge of herbs and potions, and you should begin teaching an advanced class immediately. Apparently, she wants to take it."

Maddi's jaw dropped to her chest. Snapping it shut, she stood there, uncertain what to say.

The doctor smiled at her silence. "You are not yet a full doctor. You must complete your Anatomy and Viscera, as well as Diagnosis, and I still expect you to come to my class on Healing." His grin widened. "However, you are excused from Epidemic History, so that you may teach your class in that hour."

Her mind raced, thoughts of the slums long vanished from her thoughts. *I had thought Renna'a knowledge quaint, and that the doctors here would think the same. Perhaps that's not the case.*

The doctor gave her a doubtful expression. "You will accept, will you not?"

Maddi reached for the paper. "I've never taught before."

Marten laughed. "Most haven't when they get their first teaching job. You'll do fine." He gestured toward the door then picked up a pen to go back to work. "Your first class begins tomorrow. I suggest you prepare well. At least two doctors will be there, and several of our advanced students." He looked up at her. "You might want to be ready for them, as I have no doubt they will be very…inquisitive as to why a new student is teaching a class."

A few weeks later, her eyes drooping with exhaustion, Maddi entered her room. Tanya sat on her bed, munching away at an apple, while Ami looked up from a book on farm animal anatomy and smiled. Maddi laid her things on the narrow desk, before tousling Tanya's hair and crashing down beside her. "I am exhausted," she claimed, stretching out her arms. "Teaching a class is far more involved than taking one."

Tanya wiped the apple juice on her chin with a sleeve. "I wish I could take your class, Maddi."

Maddi smiled at the little girl. "Maybe someday." She turned to Ami and rolled her eyes. "Do you have any idea how many people have asked me in the last two weeks whether I can make a love potion?"

Ami's short laughed turned to a serious expression. "Can you?" She laughed again when the pillow hit her.

Lying back against the wall, Maddi watched Tanya finish the apple, leaving little more than the seeds and stem. The little girl smiled when she finished. She was quite cute, Maddi noticed, now that they had cleaned her up and she had a little more meat on her bones. *She is probably older than I first thought as well.*

The girl looked up at Maddi. "I visited Momma's ashes today."

Maddi lifted an eyebrow. "You know it is far too dangerous for you to go down there any more."

Tanya frowned, folding her arms. "I used to live there. It doesn't scare me. Besides, I wanted to talk to Momma." Leaning in closer to Maddi, Tanya whispered in a conspiratorial voice. "Did you know that Briscoe hasn't done anything? Even more people are sick in the old building." She mad an angry face. "I thought you were going to help everyone down there."

Maddi clenched her fists, memories of the dirty tenement building replaying in her mind.

No one cares for these people. I could have been like them if it weren't for Renna. Not everyone has someone to help them up when they fall. And it's not always their fault when they do. She took Tanya's hand in her own, squeezing it tight. The girl responded with a squeeze of her own.

"I will do something, Tanya. I promise."

A fly buzzed in through one open window and out through another. Maddi stared at Darby, hoping her face did not display the frustration and shock she felt inside herself. "Mr. Darby, it is the moral duty of healers to do what they can when they find illness. Do you have no compassion within you?"

Darby shook his head. "If they couldn't pay my price, then I would not heal them."

Maddi shook her head in surrender. "Then I suppose you should work on improving your skill level, since you believe it worth so much money." She passed her eyes over the class. Doctors Gramm and Darilla watched her with eagle eyes. They both respected her knowledge of herbology, but neither offered her the regard due a teacher at the college. "Did everyone study the ten herbs I introduced yesterday?" Nods passed around the room. "Good. Then let's start with wormroot. What are its primary uses?

Before any hands went up, Darby sighed. "What is the

practical use of all this? I am Talented. I'll never use herbs to cure anyone in my life."

"What about when there are so many sick around you that you spend your strength?" Maddi folded her arms and tapped her foot. "Sometimes a good potion or poultice will save a life just as easily as using your Talent – and it saves your strength, in case another challenge arises."

Darby laughed and waved his hand as if to shoo Maddi away. "Where would I ever come across that much sickness? I plan on being private healer to a duke somewhere."

Folding her arms, Maddi scowled at the young man. "What if plague broke out in his city? What if he ordered you to go among the people and cure them?"

The young man wrinkled his brow in confusion. "Why would he do that? I'd just stay in his castle and keep him and his family healthy while the plague burns itself out."

Maddi stared at him. She looked at each student, noticing expressions that varied from clear agreement with Darby to distracted indifference. Maddi noticed that Doctor Gramm eyed her with intense interest. Doctor Darilla sat there with a slight smile, obviously in agreement with Darby's sentiments. Anger rose in Maddi's throat, along with a good batch of confusion.

Why am I so worked up about this? What do I care about those people down there? I don't know if I'm more upset with these people not caring, or with myself for the fact that I care one whit about the people of this city.

Maddi furrowed her brow, her gaze stopping on Doctor Gramm. The older woman nodded barely, a look of encouragement in her eyes. Maddi turned to Darby, his smug, soft face fixed in a grin verging on a leer.

I'll bet there hasn't been a day in his life that he ever broke into a sweat. Those hands look like a ten year-old girl's. Fiery hells, Tanya has seen more hardship in a week of her short life than he has seen in his twenty odd years.

She looked at Doctor Darilla, who stared in anticipation of Maddi's next words. His fine, velvet robes splashed over the edge of his narrow chair. A chain of gold hung around his neck, and a garnet as big as a bean set in a healer's hand dangled at the bottom. Even the man's hat was sewn with thread of gold.

I am enraged because I would have been just like those living in the streets had Renna not taken me in. Those dying down there in filth could have been me. Tanya would have died down there if it weren't for me.

Maddi turned toward the door of the classroom. "Everyone, come with me." When no one moved, she spun around with a sharp glare. "The Lord Doctor ordered that I issue you doctors a grade for this class. If any of you want to pass, then you will come with me. Now!"

All the students snapped to their feet, grabbing their books and bags. Doctor Gramm rose with elegance, a soft smile on her face. Doctor Darilla frowned, remaining in his seat for a moment. At last he stood, brushing his fine robes with a cool stare.

Maddi stalked out the door, the class right behind her. She led them down the stairs and into the street.

Doctor Darilla eyed the passing crowd with distaste. "Where are we going?"

Ignoring his haughty tone, Maddi marched along the Avenue of Willows, down the Jalanine Hill. The students followed close to her, excited to be away from the campus and fascinated by where Maddi led them.

By the time they reached the dilapidated buildings of Green Street, all of the smiles had diminished. Cold stares from the inhabitants drove the students into a tighter knot around Maddi. They passed barely-dressed prostitutes leaning in doorways, one or two trying to get the attention of the male students. The boys recoiled in nervous fear. Maddi also noticed one or two darker figures watching from farther back in the alleyways.

She addressed the entire class, huddled in the shade of the cracked, gray buildings. "This is where the little girl Tanya lived. Some of you remember her from the first day of Healing class. Some of you have seen her since on campus." She looked up, gesturing toward the surrounding structures. "Many other children live down here, some treated far worse than Tanya. They are used as prostitutes, or sold into servitude." Looking at the doctors in particular, Maddi focused on each one of those in her group with opened Talent. "Many die of sickness. Feel the disease around you."

Embracing her Talent, Maddi sensed that the plague had worsened. It leaped from denizen to denizen, marking hundreds with its curse. Of the thousands of lives crammed into just a few blocks down in the vale between hills, the residue of disease blackened nearly half. A look of shock appeared on the faces of both doctors, Darilla's touched with a bit more disgust.

One of the younger girls in the class – one who had found her Talent – raised a trembling hand. Her eyes blinked away tears. "Is there nothing that can be done?"

Maddi breathed deeply, even though she inhaled the stench of sewer and rot into her lungs. With a calm expression covering her features, Maddi gazed at the students. Doctor Gramm's smile widened. Her eyes searched the buildings all around, and Maddi knew she still embraced her Talent.

"Only what we are willing to do, Denielle." Maddi lifted a hand toward Tanya's old tenement. "Let's begin here."

Maddi did not intend what began there. Every day afterward, she came down to the slums of Daynon, starting with those in the shadow of Jalanine Hill, gradually working her way through the city. At first, only Denielle, Ami, and a few of the more compassionate students came. Doctor Gramm often assisted, too.

As the days passed, others got wind of Maddi's mission, and she greeted both Talented and ordinary healers who wished to join her. Over two dozen faculty and students moved through the slums. A squad of city watchmen assigned to the college volunteered to provide security. Even Tanya helped, carrying water and supplies.

"Briscoe left because he heard you were coming back," she told Maddi on the third day, while wrapping a clean bandage over an old man's festering wound, caused by fall working at the docks. "I think you scared him off."

Maddi still taught her herbology class, though most of the students had joined her mission. Only Darby and Doctor Darilla abstained. Both men were consistently contrarian in class, but Maddi dealt with it all in stride. After her lecture, she headed directly down into the slums, and soon the immaterial concerns of two over-privileged men disappeared next to the pain of the suffering she witnessed.

Five days curing disease from the area surrounding Green Street, as well as healing the other wounds brought on by poverty and a harsh life, left Maddi wondering if she would ever be clean again. She knelt over a washbasin, scrubbing the blood that clung under her fingernails. Tossing the brush into the pinkish-gray water, Maddi lifted her hand to wipe the sweat beading on her brow. The water ran along her forearm and under the rolled up sleeves of her blood-streaked blouse. The trickle felt cool her against skin warmed by late summer sun.

A familiar voice called out from behind her. "What have you done to my college?"

Maddi turned to see the Lord Doctor Marten standing with his hands on his hips. A wry smile curved on his mouth instead of the dour frown Maddi expected. He reached out a hand to help her to her feet, heedless of the blood or any other soil on her hands.

"Students come down here, rather than go to class." The Lord Doctor wagged his finger at her. "Even my teachers have missed faculty meetings to follow this *mission* of yours. School resources – bandages and medicines and the like – have all been used." He squinted at her. "Tell me, Miss Conaleon, when were you going to invite me to join you?"

With a gasp of surprise, Maddi squeezed his hand. "You would join us down here?"

The Lord Doctor laughed, an out of place sound in the dreary backwaters of Daynon. "Not just me. I have committed the entire faculty and student body to this endeavor for the next four weeks." He smiled, his handsome face filled with wonder. "You have got me thinking, Miss Conaleon. Practical application is what we need more of at the College." He looked around. "This may not be exactly what I might have thought up, but it will do quite well."

Marten waved at a large group of gray-cloaked guards. "I also kept my promise about mentioning the sickness in council. The mayor has granted two companies of watchmen to aid us." He pointed at the semi-collapsed building behind her. "They are also commissioned to demolish any dangerous buildings – to burn out those infested with plague."

Not sure what to say, Maddi watched the city guards fan out. Their captain walked over to stand not far from the Lord Doctor, clearly awaiting his command. Behind the soldiers, dozens of teachers, doctors, and students milled about, uncertain what to do with themselves.

Maddi's stomach turned with nerves. She looked at Marten. "I think you've just made more work for me than I wanted."

The doctor laughed again. "Welcome to leadership."

Weeks passed, and autumn edged toward winter. Maddi and her mission spread throughout the city. Almost all the students, and a great number of the teachers, joined in with gusto. Maddi formed teams of doctors and students, each member with a different specialty. She matched up those with Talent with those who knew sewing and poultices. They spread throughout the five hills of the city, and as they spread, so did rumor of the woman who led them.

Doctor Marten wiped sweat from his smooth brow with a clean rag. He no longer wore the robes of a doctor and teacher, rather simple breeches and cotton shirt. The open laces at the top showed a smooth, muscular chest Maddi worked hard not to notice. Tanya stood just a few yards away, watching workers tear out the walls of her old tenement.

"Dozens of buildings have been marked for destruction." Marten tucked the rag into his belt. "The mayor has commissioned new tenements be built for those displaced." He grinned. "His Honor is always looking for a way to endear himself to the people. It looks as if you have given him the perfect opportunity."

Maddi's eyes fixed on Tanya as the girl watched them demolish her old home. "Good. I feared for what would happen to everyone who lost their homes to the disease. Without shelter, they would just get sick again."

Stepping closer behind Maddi, Marten spoke low. "You have made friends in many places, as well as a few enemies. Have you heard the name the people call you?"

Lifegiver. "I've heard. It's silly."

The doctor delivered a golden chuckle. "Ah, Maddi. Never underestimate the good will of the people. Kings spend lifetimes trying to gain what you have earned in just a couple of months."

Maddi waved her hand in dismissal. "I don't want it." She tapped Tanya, who turned as if awakened from a dream. "Come on, sweetie. The sun is almost down. We are done for today." Tanya reached up and took Maddi's outstretched hand.

Marten cleared his throat. "I do have some good news for the both of you."

Maddi turned her head to see the doctor's smile showing bright, straight teeth. "What is that?"

He sauntered closer, his hand behind his back. "It is inappropriate for a teacher, especially one whom the people are calling Lifegiver, to be housed in the dormitory." He held up a key. "The college owns houses for visiting teachers from far lands. I have commissioned one for you." Marten's eyes shifted to the little redhead. "Both of you."

Maddi took the key with a nod, uncertain what to say. "Thank you."

The Lord Doctor placed his hand on her shoulder. "If there is any other aid I can provide you, do not hesitate to ask."

Early the next morning, Maddi set down her rucksack, her gaze drifting over the wide central room of the house. "Why don't you stay here with us? It has three bedrooms."

Ami looked about, her eyes lingering on the kitchen and bath at the rear. "Do you mean it?"

Nodding her head with vigor, Maddi reached out her hand. "Absolutely. We can always use a friend here. The extra room is larger than our dorm, and it's even furnished."

Ami grabbed Maddi's fingers. "Then I will – if it won't get you in trouble."

Maddi laughed. "I'm not too worried about the Lord Doctor." She squeezed Ami's palm. "He's like putty in my hand."

Laughing together, they unpacked Maddi's few things. The sun peeked through the window.

"Fiery Hells," Maddi cursed as she realized the hour. "I have to get to Orange Street, and it's halfway across the city."

Ami stood with a book from the sack still in hand. "Why not have the people of the city come to you? You're the one being hospitable."

Stopping in her tracks, Maddi looked at her friend. "You may have an idea." She resumed her march out the door. "There is someone who promised to help me if I needed it..."

Before the sun climbed over the buildings of Daynon, Maddi stood in the Lord Doctor's office.

"I want to build a hospital – a free clinic for the poor and working people of the city." Maddi stared across the mahogany desk at Marten. "You could make it happen."

He frowned, leaning forward and resting his chin on a fist. "And just what would make you think that?"

Maddi threw up her hands. "You are the Lord Doctor of the Kingdom of Gannon! You sit upon the High Council. You speak to the mayor often, and even the king – or so I suppose." She paused and narrowed her gaze. "Perhaps you aren't as powerful as I thought."

Marten sat up straight, a ridge of anger flashing on his brow before he wiped it away. "I will bring it up in council. Money is tighter in this kingdom than you might imagine." He shifted back, reclining into the leather with a soft creak. "And what of your new home? Does it meet with your approval?" A soft smile crept onto his face. "I believe I chose the appropriate one."

Nodding, Maddi drug a finger along the desk. It felt warm and smooth. "It is quite lovely. Thank you. Tanya is beside herself with joy. She has never had her own room, much less a house for her family." She set one hip on the edge of the desk. "My roommate Ami has joined us, to help me care properly for Tanya – if that is alright with your Lordship?"

She noticed his eyes dart toward her hip, snug in the breeches she wore while leading her mission within the city. He immediately refocused on her face.

"That should be fine, if slightly irregular." Marten laughed his baritone chuckle. "Of course, everything at this college has been irregular since your arrival. You appear to be handling your class well, too. I have heard comments from teachers and students alike on your vast knowledge of herbs and potions."

Maddi snorted. "Do you have any idea how many have asked me if I can make a love potion? Men and women both. It's insane."

The Lord Doctor raised a dark eyebrow. "Can you?"

"You too!" Maddi threw up her hands and stalked from the room.

When the first morning chill appeared in the air, Maddi began taking a cloak during her walks into the slums. She did not need the protection of the watchmen who joined her, unless it was protection from a wave of loving admirers. They tossed flowers and tokens of affection to her, calling out "Livegiver!" whenever she strode past. By the time the first few flakes of snow fell, Maddi received letters of introduction from nobles within the city, offering generous donations to her cause if they could appear with her in public.

"It might be a good idea." Ami handed her back one of the brightly sealed letters. "It would help build support for the hospital."

Maddi shook her head. "They just want to use me for their own grandstanding. I hate nobles and politicians."

Ami shrugged. "It's all part of the game you have to play if you want to make things happen."

The next morning, Tanya rushed in through the door. "Maddi! You got *two* letters today!"

A glob of gray wax with no seal closed a folded parchment for one letter. The other was in a sealed linen envelope attached to a small box. Maddi read the outside of the parchment. It was addressed to her in a strong, confident script, while beneath the seal the sender had written a single word.

"Tallen," she whispered.

Tanya wrinkled her nose. "Who's Tallen?"

Maddi laid the letter aside, her emotions too strong and too mixed for her to read it now, especially in front of Tanya. "He is a very good friend. He is on the Isle of Wizards learning to be a mage."

"A wizard!" The girl clapped her hands. "Now open the box!"

Raising a single finger, Maddi admonished Tanya. "Always read the card first. It is respectful and proper manners."

She used her nail to pop open the envelope. The hint of a musky scent wafted to her nose. Maddi pulled out a fine, linen card. Exquisite calligraphy crawled across its creamy surface.

To the Lady Doctor Maddrix Conaleon,

By the grace of the Lord Doctor Tymin Marten, you are requested to attend the Midwinter Ball of his Royal Majesty Arathan VII, King of the People of Gan, Arbiter of the Return, Seeker of the Balance. Festivities begin at sundown within the High Hall of the Ivory Palace of Daynon.

At the bottom, a barely legible hand had scrawled a few extra words.

Please, I beg that you join me Maddi. I will have a coach arrive at your home just before sundown. I will have good news.

Tymin

PS – Wear something nice with the gift. Important people wish to meet you.

Maddi lifted the lid off the white cardboard box. Facets of sparkling blue met her eyes, and a grin brightened her face to meet them. A set of sapphire earrings surrounded by brilliant white diamonds dappled the room with the refracted sunlight flooding in through the eastern window.

Tanya hopped up and down. "Lemme see! Lemme see!"

Lowering the box for Tanya, Maddi shook her head.

That bastard. How can I tell him no now?

CHAPTER 28

Never let a mage catch you with spare time.
— Unofficial student motto on the Isle of Wizards

Tallen ignored the oil lamp, tying off a small piece of Fire and Air into a ball of light the way Magus Yasmine had taught him. A slight breeze floated in through the open window, not yet cool enough with autumn to make him uncomfortable. Midnight approached, yet he had so little time to spare. He grasped the old book Magus Britt had given him, refocusing his eyes on the tightly printed pages.

> *The Aspect of Earth is not the exact same substance as the actual element in our physical universe, just as the green light we see reflected from an object is not the same thing as the green object itself. Magical power is a potential for change. It is raw energy. We tap into the different Aspects of it to affect different parts of our physical world. The fact that we express the Aspects through the use of elemental terms is really just a semantic issue – they are analogs from two different realities.*
>
> *I believe that the four elemental Aspects, as they are often known, are just facets of one basic power, just as all elements are expressions of the same matter. I believe this power is closer to the Psoul "Aspect" than any of the others. I believe it is connected to the powers of Talented healers and the Paladins of Balance. All different forms of life reflect* psahn, *just as the different Aspects reflect this base magic.*
>
> *Now some of my colleagues complain that I am prejudiced as a Dreamer. But I ask this instead – why are there so few like myself who can touch the Psoul Aspect if it is just an equal point of the star?*
>
> *Writings from before the Cataclysm show...*

A flap of wings and rustle of feathers rattled his open window, drawing Tallen out of the book. The heavy black bird rested upon the sill, clacking his obsidian beak.

"Merl!" Tallen called. "I've been wondering what you and Dorias have been up to."

Merl croaked a burble that sounded suspiciously like the word "Hello." Pointing the black bead of one eye toward the door, he chortled again. This time, Tallen felt certain Merl said, "Wizard."

A knock sounded at the door.

Setting the book aside, Tallen reached for the latch. "Come in."

"Greetings, lad," Dorias Ravenhawke said, entering the room. "Sorry I haven't had the time to visit you over the last month or so. I've been all over this blasted island." He slumped into Tallen's single chair. "I have searched libraries passed from master to apprentice for hundreds of years. I have gone through every abandoned tower on both hills. Merl scouted from the sky to lead me to them. If I missed something, it is buried deeper than my powers can reach."

Shrugging his shoulders, Tallen shifted his legs over the side of the bed to lean against the wall. "What about the forbidden area Varana warned me about?"

A visible shudder rippled down Dorias' back. "I'm not desperate enough to search there yet. I have a few other ideas to try first." He rubbed his charcoal goatee and shifted his hawkish eyes onto Tallen. "Which brings me to one of the reasons I am here."

Dorias reached into a coat pocket and pulled out his pipe and pouch. He filled the bowl, offering the pouch to Tallen, who grabbed his own pipe – the gryphon carved gift from his brother. *He's probably on the walls of Gavanor right now. Living the big life in a big city, while I'm stuck on an island full of stuffy wizards.*

When both pipes had a good ember glowing, lit by their powers in the Aspect of Fire, Dorias leaned back. "I have found very little information, Tallen. The few Dreamer writings mention nothing like the black fog I feel over the Dreamrealm." He puffed his pipe and shifted forward to look Tallen in the eye. "Have you felt the same thing, lad? When last did you enter the Dreamrealm?"

Tallen rested the hand holding his pipe on his lap. "Several months ago, when I was in Gavanor. Magus Britt detected that I had gone there while sleeping. He wrapped my head in a spell that has kept me out since." He shrugged and furrowed his brow. "I guess I've been so consumed by learning the other parts of my power, I forgot about Dreaming."

Dorias leaned in close, setting his wolf's head pipe on Tallen's desk. "I see. I had not thought to look." He chuckled as Tallen felt him embrace a tiny filament of Psoul. "Very clumsy. So much Fire…but I suppose that is most of what he has to work with." The wizard passed his hand over Tallen's head. "There, I—"

A violent stab of pain ripped through Tallen's skull. He cried out in agony, tossing his pipe as his hands leaped to his head. The searing sensation built up a ball of pressure behind his nose, threatening to tear his brain apart. In his last vision, a startled Dorias leaned toward him with an expression of concerned panic.

Shadows spun around Tallen. He fought to steady himself, at first only aware that the pain no longer split his skull. Regardless of how long it had been since last he visited the Dreamrealm, it felt like slipping on a familiar sweater. The star-speckled night hung about him, and Tallen focused on it.

The barest of moments passed before he felt another presence. He froze, both unwilling and unable to move. A wisp of silvery light twisted about. The brilliant smoke curled and rolled, spinning itself out into a serpentine form that wrapped its luminous wings about him.

Tallen of the Humans that once called themselves my people, I only have a moment to warn you, then you must go from this place and not return.

"Who are you!" he shouted wordlessly at the shining light. "Why do you want me? Why do your orcs chase me?"

I am not the one who seeks you out, Human. It is my opposite and my twin. My counterpart is the one who desires you. Galdreth seeks your power. Only a Dreamer can fulfill Galdreth's purpose. The orcs simply serve Galdreth who is their ancient master.

The tendrils wrapped around him, possessive and protective. He attempted a struggle, but the force that held his mind tolerated no resistance.

You must understand that I am trapped, as is Galdreth. But the prison weakens for my counterpart far more quickly than for me. You must resist Galdreth. Chaos must not be unleashed alone upon the world.

The silver spirit shuddered, and a distance crept into its silken steel voice.

You must not come here again. You are vulnerable here. Otherwise, Galdreth requires you be brought to our prison.

Another shudder shook the smoky light, which wavered in the darkness. Tallen felt something pulling at him, tugging from a long distance away.

You must find a way to free me from this prison, so that I may balance Galdreth's Chaos. You must seek it out, in the mountain your people call Dragonsclaw. Now go!

Spinning about Tallen, the light disappeared, and a sucking sensation drew at his heart. His vision tunneled, and he opened his eyes.

Dorias knelt beside him, a worried peak to his eyebrows. Tallen coughed, though the agony no longer squeezed at his temples. A slight headache remained, as if he had drunk too much wine the night before. The wizard rubbed Tallen's back while he struggled with desperate breaths. When the room steadied around him, the rhythm of his lungs smoothed.

"Easy there, lad," Dorias whispered. "I thought I'd lost you. For a second, I thought I had killed you."

Tallen rubbed his throbbing head. His breathing eased a little. "I…I was pulled into the Dreamrealm."

Taking Tallen's head in his hands, Dorias knelt down beside him. A small trickle of Psoul magic flowed out from the wizard, and Tallen felt it caress his mind. "Does your head hurt?"

Tallen winced. "Somewhat, but not nearly as bad as before. How long was I out?"

"Only a few seconds." Dorias, apparently satisfied that Tallen remained intact, stopped the flow of his power. "I realized it in an instant and tried to pull you out." The wizard paused. "Only… something stopped me. It was similar to the cloud obscuring the Dreamrealm, yet still quite different – sharper perhaps."

A familiar scent drifted into Tallen's nostrils. "Something is burning…"

Where his pipe had flown and landed on the woolen blanket, a small ember had begun to smoke.

"Goodness me." The wizard snuffed it out with a tendril of Water. "Sorry lad, I should have noticed that before. I was focused on you."

Tallen nodded and his skull throbbed again. He placed the pipe back on his headboard. "Thanks for your concern. I appreciate it."

Reaching into his inner coat pocket, Dorias pulled out a delicate silver flask. He flicked open the lid with a small lever and took a sip. The wizard winced and sighed after the liquor went down. He reached out, offering it to Tallen. "Here lad, take a good slug of this. It will make you feel better."

Sniffing the mouth of the flask, Tallen caught a hint of blueberry and almond. He pulled hard on the liquor, which warmed his throat and stomach on its course through his body, the tingle flowing all the way to his fingers and toes. The throbbing in his head no longer made him wince.

Tallen passed the flask back to Dorias. "I think I've encountered this being before – back in Dadric before I left with Boris and Magus Britt." The warmth of embarrassment filled his ears. "I never mentioned it because my memory of that single dream is so hazy. Do you have any idea what this thing was?"

The wizard took another nip from the flask. He sat back in the narrow chair, his head shaking in doubt. "I'm not certain as yet. I think the presence that drew you into the Dreamrealm is the same or similar to the one that forbids me entrance. I could not pull you out. It released you. It is far too powerful." Dorias narrowed his gaze on Tallen and passed the flask back. "Can you describe it to me? I only sensed it from a distance."

Taking another gulp of the liquor sharpened Tallen's wits even further. He sat there, letting the cordial do its work. The tingling was not as strong this time, but his body warmed again and his mind focused.

"It was different from anything I've encountered in the Dreamrealm before. It gathered like...like silver smoke in the shape of a lizard..." His face snapped up to stare at Dorias. "...like a dragon."

"A dragon spirit?" Leaning back in his chair, Dorias drug his hand across his lips, and his complexion paled. "What did it say to you?"

"It's distant – like remembering a strange dream." Tallen shook his head. "Though, it is clearer than the last time I encountered it."

Dorias nodded, his acute gaze focused on Tallen. "Such can be the case with untrained Dreamers. I can teach you techniques that will help you focus in the Dreamrealm and carry what you learn there back with you. You can even help those mages you draw in with you to remember conversations. That is how long distance communication is done by Dreamers." He lifted a professorial finger. "There was a time when every monarch and many nobles had Dreamers employed to exchange messages between each other in an instant, but that was long ago."

Tallen sipped from the flask. The liquor invigorated him, wiping the last of his headache away. With its cleansing, the shattered parts of his memory began to knit back together. He snapped the lid on the flask closed, and handed it off to Dorias. "You'll have to teach me the recipe."

The wizard tapped the flask to his head before he slipped it into his pocket. "It is complex, but I am certain you could pick it up."

Drawing in a deep breath, Tallen closed his eyes and thought back to his experience in the Dreamrealm. "It was a warning. The...spirit said something about its...its..." Desperate for the word the visitor had used, he calmed his frustration with a long exhale. "...its *counterpart* being master of the orcs – the orcs who are after me."

Tallen heard the clatter of the wizard's pipe hitting the floor, followed by a short trickle of Water. Dorias' voice was strained. "Its counterpart is master of the orcs – you are certain the spirit used this term?"

Opening his eyes, Tallen nodded. "I'm certain. It also said that I was vulnerable to this counterpart when I'm in the Dreamrealm. The spirit warned me not to return there."

Popping to his feet, Dorias paced the few steps of Tallen's cell. Merl cooed, following Dorias with one eye. Tallen watched him in silence, an unnamed fear growing in his heart.

Dorias stopped and lifted an eyebrow. "What do you know about the Dragon Wars?"

Tallen gulped, and the unnamed fear expanded into his gut with a gurgle. He shook his head. "Not much. I read a book or two, mostly fiction about heroes." Tallen lifted his gaze to meet the wizard's. "All the races fought each other – dwarves and orcs against humans and elves. Dragons fought too. In the end, the dwarves switched sides, and the orcs were driven into the far north." He paused, wrinkling his brow. "Then the Cataclysm happened, and the humans, the People of Gan, fled..."

The fear dropped into his bowels, and Tallen fought a desire to run to the privy down the hall. Merl cocked his head, and Dorias tilted his in much the same way.

"What's wrong, Tallen?"

Blankly staring at his hands, Tallen's fear leaped into his throat. "In the dream before – at home – the creature named itself to me. It called itself Gan. It said I was one of its people." He shook his head in confusion. "I've heard us called the People of Gan, especially when our ancestors were in exile across the ocean. What is Gan?"

Dorias sighed, exhaling through tight lips. He tapped a toe while staring at Tallen, before sitting back down on the edge of his chair. "You already know more than most of the common folk of the kingdom, and I mean no offense, for you are nothing if not uncommon." He tilted his head. "Tell me something, Tallen. Have you ever heard of the Dragonsouls?"

The name hung over the room like a blanket of dread. Tallen watched the wizard's face, certain he had never seen such a serious expression on it. "No," he answered with trepidation. "Were they a part of the Dragon Wars?"

Dorias smiled. "You will make an excellent wizard some day." He returned to tamping his pipe. "The Dragonsouls were not just a part of the Dragon Wars – they were the cause of them. They should have been named the Dragon*soul* Wars."

A fruity scent lifted from the bowl as he packed it out of his soft leather pouch. "There were two spirits that appeared upon this world long ago – when only the dragons lived here, or so it was written in the Elder Days." He waved the stem of his refilled pipe at Tallen. "That is why they took on the rough shape of dragons, though no one ever described them as more than shadowy or shining spirits. 'Like wisps of smoke,' Talernicus wrote."

Tallen reached for the small pitcher of water by his bed, splashing a little when he poured it into his rough-hewn cup. He gulped it down with abandon, drops lapping over the corners of his mouth and onto his shirt. The water tasted brackish and warm, but it soothed his parched, nervous throat.

"That's it," he said with a gasp.

Dorias nodded gravely, his eyes narrowing in sympathy. Faint crow's feet formed in their corners. "I'm going to tell you the whole thing. It is better we know the truth and face it than hide behind a lie until it is too late." He pulled the flask back out, flicking it open and holding it out for Tallen. "Take another swig."

This time the liquor calmed his nerves and settled his stomach, allowing him to breathe easier. When he offered it back to Dorias, the wizard gestured for him to hold it for the moment.

"The lighter spirit – Gan as you have surmised – appealed to the humans and the elves of Tarmor. Its characteristics were of compassion and order. Some considered it the personification of Order, as in one half of the Balance." Dorias sniffed. "I consider it more likely the reverse – that the sect evolved from a Dragonsoul myth, but I doubt the Temple would like hearing me say that out loud. Regardless, that brings me to the other half of the circle – the Dragonsoul known as Galdreth."

Tallen sipped again from the flask, the name stirring fear that hid in the recesses of his being. "Gan mentioned that name. I could not remember it until you said it just now."

Dorias rubbed his face. "You'd better let me have a sip of that."

Tallen passed the flask reluctantly across. *I'm going to need more than a strong drink for this, I fear.*

"The dwarves and orcs at first followed Galdreth," Dorias continued, "because that spirit promised them the power and riches they craved. At times during the Elder Days, everything remained at peace, the two sides balanced and constructive. But at some point, Galdreth changed, as is the only constant with Chaos." Dorias puffed on his pipe. "Or perhaps, again, Galdreth was just a chaotic personality from whence developed a cult that still may exist among the dwarves. It obviously exists among the orcs."

He paused while the smoke rose about his face. "Regardless, these two sides could not remain at peace forever, and eventually the hostilities rose to the level of the Dragon Wars. Those wars ended with the Cataclysm, but they did not cause the Cataclysm." The orange glow of his pipe lit his face in shadows. "The Dragonsouls did."

Tallen sat with his half-filled pipe in hand. He stared at Dorias. "The power I felt in the Dreamrealm was great, but was it enough power to crack a continent?"

The wizard pulled his pipe from his mouth and pointed it at Tallen. "That is why I have searched this island like a madman – why I bowed and scraped to Varana to come here. When I sensed the darkness upon the Dreamrealm, something made me think of the chaos of the Dragon Wars." Dorias looked at Merl, who squawked in encouragement. "I am one of the few wizards who believes that the Dragonsouls were not destroyed in the Cataclysm, as most think. Rather, they were only trapped. However, I do not know what that trap is, how it works, or if it can be broken." He bit on his pipe and folded his arms, puffing away. "I'm looking for any record of it. There were thousands of mages during the Dragon Wars, and many fled to the Isle. Someone had to leave a copy of what happened. Those arrogant bastards wrote down every detail of their mundane lives." His voice lowered near a mumble. "As if future generations would care one whit about their preferences between shrimp and prawns."

Tallen lit his pipe with a tendril of Fire. Touching the power calmed his mind, as did drawing upon his brother's gryphon-carved gift. "You were saying about the trap?"

Dorias stared at Tallen with an open mouth. He laughed, a hearty chuckle that must have rung down the hall. "I do have a tendency to ramble off on a tangent, don't I, lad? Tomas used to have such polite ways of getting me back on point." Merl cawed in clear agreement, and Dorias shook his head. "Well, that's just the point. I can't find out anything about the trap. Now that I am certain Gan has visited you, and that Galdreth hides the Dreamrealm from me, it must be that they are imprisoned. It must also be that this prison grows weak."

"You are right," Tallen whispered. "I remember that now. Gan told me that their prison weakened, and that Galdreth would reach freedom much sooner."

The sinking in Tallen's belly must have shown on his face, because Dorias reached out and patted him on the knee. "Don't worry, lad, at least not yet. We still have many powerful friends on our side. I am going to teach you the ways of the Dreamer – some defenses that you can use within the Dreamrealm." He moved his hands over Tallen's head. "Pay attention. This will keep you from entering the Dreamrealm again, no matter what tries to drag you there."

A short wave of Psoul Aspect emanated from the wizard. Tallen watched the way the net of magic closed over his head. *I can do that – and undo it if I want.*

Dorias lowered his hands when finished. "There. Much more elegant than what Britt did."

Merl cawed and flapped his wide wings.

"Ah, yes, Merl. It is late. Perhaps we should let the young student rest. He has been through enough tonight as it is." Dorias offered a short bow before moving toward the door. "My search is more important now than ever, but I promise to visit more often in the evenings. I must teach you how to use your most powerful Aspect."

Merl squawked a soft farewell before he lighted from the window in a flutter of black feathers. Dorias slipped out.

For some time, Tallen lay there, waves of information sifting through his brain. Churning anxiety and excitement kept him awake, until at last, he drifted into a sleep full of fitful dreams and shadowy shapes.

CHAPTER 29

Each signatory power shall commit soldiers in proportion to their total military strength. Logistical support shall be provided in like proportion.
– The Great Concord, Article III Section 2

Music drifted down the stairs leading to the roof of the bastion. Jaerd tilted his head, straining to understand why the notes haunted him so. A sense of trepidation seeped into his bones. Shifting his sword belt, he trotted up the steps and out onto the roof.

The snap of fluttering banners gave background to the harp notes and poignant words. Six banners of the Great Concord signatories stood out against the brisk westerly wind. The five gold stars on gray of the Free Cities slapped against the long forest green banner of the elves, its rampant stag dancing in time to the music. The silver throne with gold crown on sable of the dwarves leaped about at one far corner of the bastion, while the white-rayed sun on red of Hadon rippled at the other. The first winds of winter already frolicked across the Northlands, and Jaerd pulled his cloak closer about his neck.

Following the soft trickle of music, he found Shaela, the bard from the Free Cities. She leaned against a granite parapet, strumming her harp and faintly singing the tune he recognized. When he lifted the blue banner of Gannon behind which she hid, she stopped her playing and pulled the hood tighter about her head.

"Hello again." Jaerd offered a gracious bow. "You play very well, and your voice is…enchanting." He noticed a strand of dark hair slip from her hood. "When you first joined us I thought you had hair the color of honey." Jaerd shrugged. "Must have been a trick of the light."

Shaela ducked her head, tucking in the strand of hair. She avoided his direct gaze, staring instead at the wide vista of the Northlands and the Dragonscales that spread below and about them. "Must have, My Lord."

Jaerd laughed, clapping his hands together. "I, my dear, am no lord – just a captain. You can call me Jaerd, if you wish."

She nodded, her focus drifting from pennant to pennant. Her eyes paused on one at the rear of the bastion. "I recognize most of the banners here. Ours of the Free Cities, yours of Gannon blue. The elves, the Hadonese Empire, and even the dwarves. But I do not know that one with a rocky island on sea blue. Whose banner is that?"

Turning his head toward the flag, Jaerd grunted. "That is the banner of the Sarian Union. It has not really existed in many decades, having broken up into its separate members some time ago." He scratched his jaw. "Tarrak Goldmar says they have not sent a garrison here in a century, but their banner is flown out of tradition."

Remaining silent, Shaela began to tune her harp.

It sounded fine a moment ago.

Curling his cloak about his arms, Jaerd watched the few clouds in the sky scud across the newly risen sun. It slipped farther to the south with every quicker passage overhead. "You sing *Storm of my Heart* very well." He leaned against the parapet opposite her, after first scraping away a light dusting of snow. "The thing is, I've heard that song in Gavanor and in the Free Cities, and the words you use are different from either of those." Jaerd kept his gaze fixed on her. "In fact, the only other place I have heard the words sung like that is in the Barony of Dadric – in my home town."

Jaerd took a step toward her reaching out with his hand. The young woman dodged his grasp, but he clamped onto the corner of her cloak. Her hood fell away, and she met his eyes directly.

"Dawne?" Jaerd's heartbeat accelerated with excitement and fear.

The woman's face mirrored his own in more ways than one. Both excitement and fear played upon her features, which had the same defined chin and prominent cheekbones that he and Tallen both wore. Her eyes, however, were a blue-green match for his. This close, Jaerd could also see the honey color at the roots of her long tresses.

She nodded faintly, caught like a rabbit in his hand. "Surprise. It's me. I…I had no idea I would meet up with you. I—"

Jaerd lifted his hand palm out. "Stop right there. What in the Fiery Hells are you thinking joining a military expedition out here!" He smacked his palm against his forehead. "Mother is going to kill me when she finds out."

Dawne's lips quivered and wetness pooled in her eyes. "I'm sorry! I didn't know what was going on, it's just..." White knuckles formed on her fisted hands, and two rivulets ran across her cheekbones. "It's just that you left a long time ago on your great adventure. Then Tallen took off on his, and I had nothing left but the inn and boring Glynn! It was—"

Grabbing her in a giant bear hug, Jaerd spun her about on the rooftop of Highspur's bastion. He laughed aloud, the sound echoing off the mountain and out over the fortress. "Dawne! I can't believe it. I haven't seen you in five years. First, Tallen out in the world, now you too. This is just amazing. Wait a minute!" He set her down taking a step back. "You can't be here!" Jaerd took Dawne by the arm and dragged her back toward the steps. "No, no. This won't do. I'll have to send a squad to take you back with the next southern dispatch rider."

Dawne pulled back against his grip. "But I don't want to—"

The long, drawn out toll of a deep bell sounded out from far above. It rang again, rolling down the mountain from Farseer's Spire.

Jaerd knew it could mean only one thing. "Boris!"

Releasing his baby sister, Jaerd dashed down the steps into the bastion. He charged past dozens of others reacting to the alarm, intent only on finding a steed and riding out to meet the returning earl. He took the steps two at a time, his blue cloak fluttering behind him.

Within the stables, he found Khalem Shadar already mounted along with six other men.

"Hurry!" the Hadoner shouted. "We will escort you."

Jaerd leaped over the rump of an already saddled steed and kicked his feet into the stirrups. He put spur to horse, and they galloped out the wide front entrance. Both gates stood open, and Jaerd led the charge out to the defile, hundreds of others cheering them from the walls.

Once he cleared the front gate, Jaerd saw a group of blue-cloaked men riding ahead, already turning out of the defile and onto the hilly plain. He also noticed the red trim on those cloaks. A wolfhound, hardly shorter than the horses, loped along behind them.

Khalem Shadar pulled in beside him. "For a big man, Magus Britt was quick out the gate."

Jaerd nodded in agreement. "Then we must catch up." He spurred his horse again, slapping its withers with the reins.

Out on the plain, the ground rolled in the last few hills of the Dragon's Feet. They gradually leveled out toward the Norvus River. Pushing the horse and his companions, he rode hard over the recently emptied grain fields, until he crested a tall rise overlooking the river about a mile away.

Magus Britt and his four companions galloped down the far side, not two hundred yards ahead of Jaerd and his men. Brawny ripped the dirt with his claws alongside them. On the far banks of the Norvus River, a cluster of steel and blue clad cavalry struggled to cross. Shapes buzzed about them.

"By the Waters!" Jaerd reached into a belt pouch and pulled out the spyglass his father had given him years before. He held the brass device up to one eye. A curved, bat-like wing passed across his field of vision. He tried to follow it, but another orange and brown striped beast with hard horn and claws passed in front of it. The creature swooped down and tore a man from his saddle, sending his horse tumbling. The monster ripped the soldier in half, before tossing the pieces to the ground and climbing for altitude. "Dragons! Dragons assail them!"

Jaerd put his glass away and untied the curved horsebow attached to his saddle. Putting spurs to his mount, he held the bow in one hand, his reins in the other. They charged over the ground, as the lead soldiers of Boris' detachment splashed out onto the near riverbank.

Moments later, the first flash of lightning shot out from the mages. It danced about the wings of a green and red beast that dared to swoop upon the fleeing men. Hundreds of Bluecloaks now churned their way across the shallow water, leaving a wide brown smear in the snow on the banks. More lightning flew from the mages. A blue-white bolt leaped from one dragon to the other. A massive boulder shot up from the riverbank to crash into a maroon beast with cobalt ridges. It tumbled to the ground with the rock. The other dragons veered away, pounding their wings to gain air.

The mile passed quickly beneath galloping hooves. Jaerd picked out Earl Boris at the head of his men, with Lord Gael of the elves close behind. Hundreds more horsemen dashed by, some barely clinging to their blown mounts. The rumble of the cavalry left a heavy cloud of dust in its wake. Brawny dashed among them, herding the loose horses toward Highspur's gate. The wolfhound's eyes darted back and forth, searching for a particular beast.

Glancing at Khalem, Jaerd signaled toward Magus Britt and his men. "We'll give the mages cover and follow them in!"

The Hadoner nodded, and whistled to his warriors. They galloped in a wide arc to circle behind the mages. Jaerd signaled Magus Britt, and the Battlemage nodded from the saddle in return, his face set in the fierce knot of battle.

At the top of the ridgeline, Jaerd reined in his horse and scanned the horizon with his spyglass. He saw black dots receding into a gray distance. However, under the pallid sky a haze of dust drifted into the air. The hoof-churned track in the snow led directly toward the murky cloud. It grew larger, spreading along a strip of the horizon. Jaerd could not tell what it was, but the dragons flew directly for it.

He lowered the glass and looked at Khalem. "We should get back to the fortress. Now!"

Once inside, the front gates slammed shut behind Jaerd and Khalem, the crank of chains lowering the portcullises rattling within. Jaerd rode up the slope, scattered with dismounting, battered Bluecloaks – men tired and gray of face. Brawny glanced furtively among the returning soldiers, his steps nervous and quick. An occasional whine slipped from his throat. The officers and those with the most grievous wounds passed through the towering inner wall. Jaerd and Khalem followed.

"...once they killed Gaeric we were at their mercy." Earl Boris breathed steadily, and sipped from a fresh canteen. The elf lord Gael stood beside him in grim silence. "We were only three leagues from the Norvus River at the time."

Boris shook his head, turning away the healer who offered his services. The man then turned to Magus Britt, who stared at his blackened fingers.

"You discharged quite a bit of power out there, Magus." The doctor took hold of the Battlemage's fingers. "Let me heal them before they blister."

Britt relented, and in a few seconds, he appraised his healed hands. The doctor departed to examine others who had returned.

Patting the mage on his stout shoulder, Earl Boris grimaced. "Sergeant Hall lies out there with Gaeric. We were unable to keep the bodies of the dead once the dragons came upon us." He drew again upon the canteen. "However, Captain Vonstrass, Magus Stanton, and Doctor Forstra made it safely back, as did almost seven hundred of our men."

Lord Marshal Magdon joined them with an aide at his

shoulder. Earl Boris offered a formal salute. "My Lord Marshal. I must inform you of the dire situation our fortress faces." Boris scanned the officers gathered around him. Jaerd saw the somber expression the earl wore and knew in his sinking gut what must be coming. "I do not exaggerate when I say this host shook the ground with its passing. Attempts to count them could only be made at a distance. Those counts were incomplete, because we could not see the end of their horde."

Murmurs passed through the assembled commanders. General Vahn of the Free City men stood with his mouth gaping open. Jaerd heard Khalem Shadar draw in a sharp breath.

Marshal Magdon stroked his sword hilt. "What estimate can you make of their number, My Lord Earl?"

Boris worked his jaw, as if unwilling to divulge the number. At last, he looked directly at the marshal. "At least one hundred and fifty thousand."

Exclamations of fear and disbelief shot from most of those gathered around. Lord Marshal Magdon rubbed his temples, and General Vahn swore to each of the five Aspects in turn. Magus Britt stood solid and calm, his bushy eyebrows drawing together.

"What's more," Earl Boris said, "Gael and his scouts counted at least six different clan banners." He looked at Magus Britt, who lifted one craggy eyebrow. "Only Mammoth Clan was missing."

The Lord Marshal coughed, hacking up yellowish phlegm, which he spat upon the stone flags. "How far behind you are they?"

Turning his eyes northward, even though he could see nothing but the lofty wall and towers, Earl Boris folded his arms. "They pressed us hard. I would say that their vanguard will reach the Norvus before nightfall."

Jaerd slapped a fist into his hand. "Then we must get messages off to Gavanor and the Free Cities. We must warn the southern lands of this new horde massing on our doorstep." He looked toward the flow of men gathering upon the walls. "We must send for relief."

Lord Marshal Magdon nodded and shifted his blue cloak about him. "Captain Westar is correct." His gaze focused on Jaerd. "In the meantime, we will see to the defenses of this fortress. You will have command of the forward wall, Captain."

The marshal looked at Earl Boris and Darve Northtower, his face taking on a practiced aura of command. "The dwarves hold the inner gate, while Bluecloaks man its towers and walls." He lifted his thin finger toward the bulky structure above the caves. "I will command the bastion."

Magus Britt nudged Boris while eyeing Jaerd. "Captain Westar came up with an excellent new use for my enhanced Quickfire. Most of the mages will man the inner wall." He nodded toward Gael. "As will your elves. We'll need their bows up here." The Battlemage forestalled Boris' question. "I will explain all to you once you have eaten and rested." Looking at Gael, Magus Britt narrowed his gaze. "We have at least a few hours, correct?"

"Sundown," the elf lord replied, his one eye tracing to the north.

Jaerd ran his bare hand over the rough stone battlement, still warm from the sun now setting at the mouth of the defile. The solidity of the stone gave him courage. He knew how many centuries it had stood against that which came. *It will probably be this stone's last fight. Spirits of Water, I hope this works.*

A slow rumble crawled up the approach to Highspur. The heavy haze of dust that Jaerd had seen on the plain that morning now hung over the rocky walls of the defile. It rose above the corner of the Dragon's Feet that hid the Norvus River from Jaerd's view. A loud, growling bark met it from the peak of the inner gate towers. *I would swear that dog knows Hall didn't come back. I wish I had him down here.*

Behind Jaerd, a shout rang out, and a soldier came running down. The Bluecloak hurried up the stairs to Jaerd and offered a quick salute and a piece of paper. Jaerd noticed a gray cast to the man's face, even in the direct rays of the setting sun.

With the dragon-spangled blue banners snapping about him, he took a deep breath. Opening the folded letter, he scanned it quickly.

Enemy larger than original estimate. Rearguard still crossing Norvus. Trolls, dragons, and siege engines identified. Proceed with original plan if feasible.

He crumpled the note and tossed it into an iron-wrought fire pit, stoked high against the coming night. The dry parchment curled and blackened in a flash of red flame. His heart felt as if it burned with the note in a fire stoked by fear. "Lieutenant!"

Kent Varlan jumped to his side with a salute. "Sir!"

Nodding to the young man, Jaerd pointed down along the wall. "I want you to make a final pass of the turrets. Make certain every scorpion crew knows to concentrate on the biggest things first."

The lieutenant gulped, but nodded. "Yes, sir!" He dashed down the stairs.

Jaerd looked at the men operating the two catapults placed upon the gatehouse, the only large weapons on the front wall. He gave the soldiers a confident nod while warming his hands over the fire.

The boom of a large horn, a haunting, single note, resounded up the vale toward them. With it came a billows blast to the flame of fear burning inside Jaerd. He heard the loud roar of thousands and thousands of voices following it, filled with the hatred and rage of centuries of oppression. Far behind the roar, the fat, orange sun dipped into the purple haze of a distant sea. Its dying rays cast the defile into a crimson glow, as if blood already coated the rocks. Down in the vale below, pinpricks of red light popped through the dust. Thousands more appeared, as torches and campfires lit up the hills of the Dragon's Feet.

Jaerd leaned once more against the stone of the battlement, his heart turning to ash. The masonry felt colder and less substantial as he watched the fires spread into the coming night. *I never imagined this. I never believed this could be real. Now, here it is, stretching before me. By the Waters, why did I agree to come here?*

"Steady hearts, men!" Pounding out the flames of fear, Jaerd lifted his voice above the rumble of the orcish horde. "These walls have thrown back greater hosts than this." He grabbed a torch from the barrel, dipped it into the fire pit, and raised it on high, waving it about. "We are all that stands between the peace-loving nations of our homelands and the chaos that barks at us from the darkness. Do not let your fear overcome you! Embrace it! Feed from it! And cast it back at our enemies along with our steel!"

Jaerd joined the brave shouts ringing up from the gate tower and along the wall. He spied Lieutenant Varlan, who stalked among the defenders, taking up the huzzahs and passing them along. Soon the inner gate echoed the cheers as well. Their cries tumbled down the ravine, muting out much of the orcish noise clambering in his ears.

A thrill rippled through Jaerd, fortifying the seedlings of his courage. They rose from the ashes in his heart. The men around him fed off it, and soon shouts of "Bring them on!" and "They'll smash upon this wall!" echoed down the line.

Then the slow, tortuous creak of heavy wheels reached him from the ravine, followed by shouts of anger and bellows of pain. Fires moved in the darkened passage. Soon, Jaerd picked out heavy catapults, and the bulky, misshapen figures that pulled them. Orcs snapped long whips over the creatures' heads while they heaved their burdens forward.

Jaerd laid his torch along the edge of the fire pit and leaned out over the battlement. "So those are trolls...and to think Tallen killed one." He exchanged glances with the corporal next to him. "Guess I'll just have to one up my little brother today, eh?"

Two heavy thumps sounded behind Jaerd. He looked up to see a pair of faint yellow sparks tumbling through the sky overhead. The thumps sounded again, and two more sparks flew, this time from further to his sides. As the first two projectiles crashed into the oncoming enemy, they exploded in a burst of green-orange flame. The fire flowed like water, covering both the siege engines and the creatures that pulled them. Blood-curdling screams of agony and rage echoed toward the defenders. The smell of caustic chemicals and burning flesh seared Jaerd's nose.

He looked to the two catapult teams on the tower roof. Their sergeants held a torch to the payload until the fuse lit, then nodded in readiness. He sliced the air with his hand.

"Launch!"

The catapults heaved against their grounding chains, hurling the round pots full of enhanced Quickfire at the oncoming enemy. Explosions rocked the night, illuminating the walls and ravine with a flash of green light. The pot metal ripped apart, shredding the enemy with molten chunks of slag.

Screams of pain and death erupted again from the orcs and the trolls they drove. Their black catapults stopped moving forward, and a cheer rose from Jaerd's men. *The worst thing about the enemy entering your range is that it usually means you are within theirs.*

Jaerd ducked against the battlement. "Cover!"

Two dozen hollow thumps sounded in the night. The gate tower lit with the red light of burning pitch. Fiery balls rocketed toward the walls of Highspur. Just before they crashed into the defensive line, over half of them stopped in midair then hurtled back at the enemy. Only a few crashed into the battlements, taking out soldiers with each of them.

A cry lifted from the defenders. "The mages!"

Jaerd looked at the red-trimmed Bluecloak just a few yards away. The man's hands lifted in the air, and his eyes focused on the siege engines. Jaerd gave the mage a sharp nod. "Well done, Stanton."

The orc crews scrambled each time the trebuchets within the four inner towers launched, desperate to avoid the Quickfire. Shorter ranged catapults worked from the interior wall, pumping fiery death upon the orcs. Jaerd's own two crews scrambled to reload the buckets of their machines. He signaled the sergeants.

"Launch at will, gentlemen." The weapons heaved again, and the green inferno of death brightened within the vale. Those enemy engines still operable loaded and launched again and again, while the Bluecloak Battlemages held many of the orc missiles at bay. Magus Stanton stopped two balls of fire that would likely have found Jaerd and his men, forcing them to tumble back down the slope.

The exchange continued for several rounds, and with each launch, fewer orc weapons successfully fired. Jaerd noticed the strain on Stanton's face increase with every attack. More and more of the enemy missiles crashed into the forward wall, and Magus Stanton winced. "It is easier when they are not so close together."

Jaerd waved to his crew sergeants. "Concentrate on that cluster over there where their weapons are still firing."

The catapults launched toward the southern edge of the ravine, decimating the weapons. Jaerd smiled at the sound of orcs and trolls screaming. Some pulled what engines they could back out of range, and another volley of fire chased them down the defile.

Shouts of victory soared up from the walls. Elf, dwarf, Bluecloak, and Hadoner alike lifted voices and spears into the fire lit night. Jaerd clapped his men upon their shoulders, nodding and raising his fist as well, the fear in his heart little more than glowing embers.

A harsh blast from a sonorous horn cut short their moment of joy. An ocean roar of angry voices drowned out the southerners' cheers. With a heave of torches and glittering metal, a host of the enemy surged up the defile.

Jaerd cupped his hands around his mouth. "Ready!"

Fire flew down from the inner towers, both magical and mundane. The enemy died, but more rushed over and around their burning comrades. Hundreds of gargantuan trolls charged over the scattered remnants of broken siege engines, carrying bulky iron ladders.

Leaning back, Jaerd grabbed one of his runners. "Tell Varlan and the scorpion commanders to focus on the trolls!" He shoved the young man down the stairs and waved to his men. "Target the ladders and the trolls!"

Yard-long shafts flew out from the turrets on the walls, punching through armor and burying themselves in heavy hide. Some of the trolls fell, dropping their ladders and tripping their fellows. More followed, and Jaerd knew the fire and missiles could not stop them all. His hand rubbed Shar'leen's hilt, and the fear in his heart rekindled.

The clank of iron on stone rang across the battlefield as the ladders clattered against the wall. Orcs and trolls swarmed up to meet the plate-armored Bluecloaks at the top. The defenders pushed ladders away with hooked bills and pikes, only to see them lifted back into place again. The fire from the inner wall moved back to the horde's rear to avoid harming Jaerd and his men while they fought off the assault.

Sheer numbers won over, and scattered fights broke out along the wall as groups of orcs reached the top. Crossbowmen and archers in the turrets fired down on the enemy, while the armored billmen held the line. At Jaerd's signal, reserve units drew their swords and charged in to fill gaps when they opened.

A pair of trolls clambered onto the wall along his right, flinging both men and orcs aside. Scorpion shafts stuck out from both creatures' hides, yet they still cast soldiers about with vigor. Three billmen charged one together, getting their weapons firmly planted into the beast's hide. The creature toppled into its companion, and it crashed into one of the turrets, already weakened by catapult shots. The scorpion on it fired, its shafts sinking into the troll, but not before the new stone shifted under the weight. The entire structure tumbled to the ground behind the wall, crushing trolls and Jaerd's men alike.

Trying to drown the fires of dread with calm, Jaerd shouted down to the garrison house below. "Reserves to the right!"

A hundred Bluecloaks charged along the wall, pushing back the enemy advance to where the collapsed turret once stood. Just as they pushed the black-armored orcs off that battlement, another troll clambered up on Jaerd's left, wreaking havoc among the defenders and opening a hole for a large platoon of orcs to swarm behind it.

Jaerd shouted to the garrison house again. "Reserves left!" He turned to Magus Stanton. "Those men are my last reserve unit. It's probably time for Magus Britt to drive them back."

Stanton nodded and looked back toward the inner gate towers. He flicked his finger and a bright yellow spark flashed in the air above Jaerd. With the signal given, the mage fire that fell among the enemy intensified, highlighted by flashes of lightning. Heavy piles of boulders tumbled down along the front of the wall, crushing the enemy warriors while they burned. The entire force of Bluecloaks surged forward, pushing the orcs back into the wall of fire and electricity.

The horde wavered before it collapsed. Its lead battalions began to retreat, forcing those in their rear to first halt then begin a hasty withdrawal. In seconds, the retreat became a rout. Catapult and arrow fire chased them so long as they remained within range. A few paused to help wounded comrades who cried out for help as they passed. The magical fire stopped, and Jaerd ordered his crews to cease. He looked over the battlement, watching the enemy horde flee, his fear returned to low embers.

An eerie quiet settled over the ravine, as the attackers fled back to the safety of their main force. The creak of metal sounded behind Jaerd and horsemen trotted out from the inner fortress. Earl Boris and Magus Britt led them. Jaerd climbed down the inner stairs, past the triage of wounded soldiers.

"Captain Westar!" The earl saluted from his saddle. "Well done, sir. Your men are as staunch as any I have seen." He nudged his stallion closer. "They will come again…and soon."

Jaerd returned the salute, his face twisting in concern. "Aye, My Lord. If they come again like they just did, I don't think we can hold them."

Boris rubbed his mustache. "Then perhaps it is time to execute your plan?"

Magus Britt folded his arms. "Indeed."

Jaerd snapped another salute. "Will do, sir."

The earl traced his eyes along the wall. "We should bring back two-thirds of your force now, including the wounded. The rest will have to be enough to sell your plan."

Gripping his sheathed sword with one hand, Jaerd whipped it out and tipped it to his forehead. "Aye, My Lord Earl. We will do it." He looked at Magus Britt. "The boltholes are ready?"

The Battlemage nodded.

Lowering Shar'leen, Jaerd turned on his heel to pass out orders.

The inner gate opened to receive the wounded, along with half of his capable men. Jaerd cast his eyes along the scant defense of the wall, the flames in his heart leaping up when the dwarf-forged iron gates clanged shut behind him. The hollow sound billowed against the embers of his fear. He looked at Lieutenant Varlan, who stared at the starry sky with a soft smile on his face.

"Only a few hours until dawn." The noble born lieutenant turned to Jaerd, the smile remaining. "We will do better fighting in daylight."

Slapping the young man on the back, Jaerd nodded. "Indeed we will, Kent."

Soft words of music drifted down from the bastion on high. Jaerd could not quite pick out the words, but the trickling melody was unmistakable. *I cannot believe Dawne is here. I am going to kill her if she survives this!* Thoughts of his sister's bravery quenched the flames of fear in his chest. *If she can face this, then By the Waters, so can I!*

"She plays *The Stand of Eron's Rock*." Jaerd's eyes drifted up the torch-scattered mountain. "One verse for each night those Bluecloaks held the pass against the Hadonese Sunguard. They were more outnumbered than we."

Lieutenant Varlan chewed his lip. "Only four men survived, according to the song."

Jaerd slapped him on the back again. "Maybe you'll be one of us who do."

As Dawne reached the fourth verse, a thunderous horn blast, echoed by hundreds more, boomed up the defile. The roar of orc voices followed, washing over her beautiful, fragile song.

Jaerd waved a lit torch on high. "Steady! Bring them in."

The thump of trebuchet and catapult began again, its rhythm watering the shoots of courage sprouting in Jaerd's heart. They grew in strength as fires spread again below, joining the previous ones that had never died out. The enemy charged, heedless of their deaths. The trolls came, still carrying dozens of heavy ladders. With fewer bows under Jaerd's command, the enemy arrived at the wall more swiftly.

Dozens of orc warriors died, arrows through necks and eyes and hearts. But hundreds more scrambled up the iron scaffolds to leap, screaming, among the defenders. The Bluecloaks fought hard, but it was not long before they fell back toward the center of their line.

Signaling the station runners, Jaerd nodded his head. "Begin rolling up the wings."

The men dashed off, passing word down the frantic line. The soldiers within the farthest turrets abandoned their posts, fleeing to the gate tower. The blue line compressed toward its center, and black figures swarmed up behind them.

Jaerd pointed to his crew sergeants. "Begin the evacuation."

The Bluecloaks within the gatehouse fell back toward the inner wall. They flowed into the excavated boltholes, Jaerd counting every one as they entered.

"Sir!" Lieutenant Varlan stood along the northern parapet, watching the edge of their defenses. "The enemy has cut off our right flank's retreat!" The young noble drew his sword, waving it toward the two dozen troops he had kept in reserve. "Get the rest of the men through, sir! We will get them out!" The soldier lifted his sword on high and rushed into the surge of orcs. "Gavanor! Gavanor!"

The platoon charged with him, shouting and cutting their way into the orc warriors. The gap in the line closed for a moment, and the soldiers on the right flank retreated down the stairs to the boltholes.

Jaerd turned to Magus Stanton. "Now!"

At a wave of the mage's hand, a large red flash lit the interior courtyard. Jaerd and Stanton, the last to leave the rooftop, charged down the stairs of the gate tower. Magical fire rained down from on high, giving cover to the retreating Bluecloaks.

The screams of battle reached Jaerd's ears as they passed the doorway out onto the northern wall. He drew Shar'leen, her steel catching light from the floating ball of magic Stanton had created. He moved to join the fray where Kent Varlan and his men fought.

"Captain!" The mage grabbed his arm. "You must let your men do the fighting. Your responsibilities require your survival."

Knitting his brow in anger, Jaerd jerked his arm out of the mage's grip. Stanton's nod of acquiescence gave him pause.

He's right, blast it. "Come on," he said, sheathing Shar'leen and pulling the mage after him.

Jaerd waited at the entrance to the bolthole, pushing through every man he could. The orcs upon the wall surged through the magical storm, overtaking Lieutenant Varlan and his soldiers.

After letting a stab of regret hold him for one final moment, Jaerd squeezed through the tight passage of stone and dirt.

Earl Boris waited on the other side. "You are the last."

Jaerd shook his head, watching his men filter toward the barracks level of Highspur seeking aid and rest. "Lieutenant Varlan has a platoon still upon the wall to cover our retreat."

The grave frown on Boris' face answered before his words. "The enemy holds the wall. It is time to spring your trap."

Nodding to his superior, Jaerd faced Stanton. "Drop the supports. Collapse the boltholes."

The mage grimaced in sad sympathy, but stepped toward the holes. He closed his eyes, and a muffled rumble shook the ground. Dust and scree shot from the holes, wrapping Jaerd in a cloud of sorrow.

Earl Boris started up the stairs to the inner gatehouse. "If you would join us, Captain."

Steeling himself, Jaerd charged up the steps after the earl. The fresh face of Kent Varlan hovered in his memory, taunting Jaerd with shouts of valor. He forced the lieutenant's image away, filing him with the dozens – now hundreds – who had died under his command.

He stepped out onto the battlement over the gatehouse, surrounded by scurrying soldiers, elves, dwarves, and humans alike. The catapults along the wall fired continuously, as did the trebuchets in the tower tops above. He came to a halt next to Earl Boris and Magus Britt, staring down upon his former command.

The front wall swarmed with orcs and the scattered bulk of trolls. The enemy had already turned the scorpions to fire upon Highspur's inner defenses. Dozens more scurried to turn Jaerd's catapults and load them. Thousands of enemy warriors spread along the wall, and more surged forward to follow them.

Earl Boris scowled down upon the horde. The dimple in his chin quivered. "Do it, Joz."

Magus Britt closed his eyes and lifted his spread fingers in front of him. Jaerd felt nothing real, but imagined tiny tendrils of magical fire spreading out to the niches built under each turret. In his mind, he saw a large tentacle of flame reaching into the crates packed beneath the roof he had just abandoned. He envisioned a spark touching the fuses.

Britt opened his eyes. "In a moment."

The seconds crept by. *It's not going to work.*

Then he felt a rumble down below him. Beginning at the

300

outermost turret, green fire exploded from under the stone and oak structure. The blast ripped through the orc warriors, lifting broken stone and broken bodies alike. Jaerd watched each turret discharge in succession, like a line of soldiers saluting on parade.

The blasts ripped through the ranks of orcs and trolls. Those who survived the consuming inferno were shattered by wall fragments or crushed by collapsing turrets. Finally, the gate tower rocked with a yellowish flare. The concussion sent a wave of hot air that rushed over Jaerd's face, whipping back his hair. Stone crumbled, bringing down the entire rooftop, the catapults, and the forces commandeering them.

The earl waved his hand. "Now!"

Every weapon and mage along the inner gate began a vicious onslaught of arrows, lightning, and fire. Screams of pain and death peeked out from behind the racket of attack. Secondary explosions sounded along the wall, throwing more stone and fire into the horror-struck enemy. The conflagration threw up a cloud of dust and smoke, obscuring Jaerd's view. It continued for some time, before Boris signaled a halt.

Jaerd stood there, watching the green and orange fires burn through smoke and haze. Slowly it settled and the sun slipped up from behind the mountain. The dawn brought an eerie mix of light that spread down the defile before him, chasing back the shadows. A few scattered warriors fled, some carrying their wounded. The haze cleared, and the sun rose higher to expose a desolate hellscape of scorched earth, shattered stone, and the mixed bodies and entrails of thousands of orcs and trolls. *And men...*

The putrid stench of death drifted up to the defenders, as did the plaintive cries of the dying. The whelps of agony and despair, fear and pain, sounded no different than those Jaerd had heard on any battlefield before.

And the blood running down the ravine looks just as red in the light of dawn.

Earl Boris looked to him with a relieved smile. "Excellent plan, Captain. Well done."

Jaerd turned away from the scene before him, the sour taste of vomit burning the back of his throat.

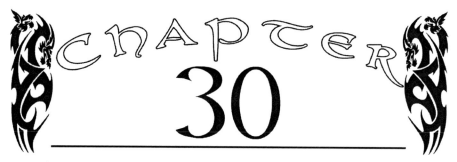

CHAPTER 30

Tear down the walls of humans.
Burn down the trees of elves.
Rip out the mines of dwarves.
Shatter them all to Fiery Hells.
– Common Northlands song

Slar stomped out of his command tent, the shouts of an army camp distant still to his mind. Even the stench of a two hundred thousand orcs living, eating, and shitting together barely touched his nose. He did notice the sun rising over the humans' mountain fortress. Dawn came later with every day of the siege. For weeks he had watched that sunrise move farther south.

We need to be on our way south too, or the winter snows will trap us here. Our only hope to crack this bone is Galdreth's plan.

Slar tightened his mammoth skin cloak, and the warriors saluted him as he passed. He barely acknowledged them, his eyes focused on the nearby tent shared by his two sons. *Likely they still sleep.* A guard outside the flap ushered him in.

Grindar stood strapping on his armor, while Sharrog finished tying his clan sash, sewn with a rampaging boar.

"Greetings, Father." Grindar bowed deeply with a fist over his heart. "We will visit with men from Ram Clan today. They were wounded in a feint on the northern tower."

Slar clapped his elder, larger son on the shoulder, but his eyes fixed on Sharrog. "Do you still refuse to speak to me?"

The younger orc met his gaze evenly. "I will answer any question put to me by my Warchief." He shifted his stance as if gathering courage. "But I will ask a question in turn. How long will we waste on this fortress? The fat lands of the south are within our grasp. Winter is here. We should be well on to the Free Cities by now."

Slar clenched a fist, anger rising in his throat. The burning pain returning to his gut reminded him that he agreed with his son. "Our Master does not wish to leave a force undefeated at our rear. We must destroy the southerners here before moving onward."

The younger orc laughed. "Ten thousand of our number could keep them bottled up. They are so few that only the strength of their fortress gives them any weight. The rest of us could be plundering Kirath and Dern by now."

Shaking his head, Slar placed his fists on his belt. "That is not our Master's plan, and until that plan can come to fruition, we must hold them here."

Sharrog lifted his hands to the sky. "What *is* this plan? Why does Galdreth not see it through already? We are dying here while we wait for a dark spirit's *plan* to come to fruition."

With anger rising again inside him, Slar lifted a single finger. "The plan requires Mammoth Clan be with us before we move south. Galdreth is still among them." He sighed, some of the rage slipping away. "Sargash balks at accepting me as his Warchief."

Slamming his wide hand down on a rough-hewn table, Grindar growled. "He has no choice. Galdreth will make him see."

"Sargash is unimportant other than that he distracts our Master." Slar turned back to Sharrog, lowering his voice to a conspiratorial tone. "Galdreth has...spies...among the enemy. Soon, very soon, our Master will order those spies into action. It will be up to us to be ready."

Grindar bowed at the waist. "It will be my honor to lead the vanguard when that time comes. The Boar Clan shall be the ones to finally break this mountain open."

Ignoring his eldest's words, Slar glanced at Sharrog. "Do you not wish this honor as well, my son?"

Sharrog stomped toward the tent flap. "Let us go visit those dying for our *Master*. Does Galdreth watch them slip away in pain like you do?"

The chirurgeon cried a shout of victory once he pulled the broken arrowhead from the side of a dazed warrior. Slar felt a piece of the same joy. *Every life saved is a warrior who will fight again or a father who may return to his home.*

He walked among the lines of pallets, stacked with the healing and the dying. Many wore scars from the humans' liquid fire – the stuff of demons. Other warriors had been pierced by sharp arrows, like the one Slar had just seen drawn out. Bear Clan lay next to Wolf Clan. Rams died with Snakes. *Is this our future? To die united?*

"Warchief Slar, it is an honor to have you visit our infirmary again." The chief healer wore a once white apron smeared with red. His hands left more crimson on an already bloody towel, and a splatter of scarlet dotted the tufts of white hair behind his ears. "It cheers the men to see that their Warchief cares about their sacrifice. Those that go on to the Halls of Fire are heartened for their journey when you are witness to their passing."

Slar clapped the orc healer upon the arm. "You are the hero here, Clayburn. You have saved hundreds from leaving for the Halls too soon."

Grindar tapped a fist to his heart. "Indeed, Doctor Clayburn, my father speaks the truth." He winced as he looked about the tent packed with wounded orcs. "Is there anything you need here? More assaults will be attempted later in the week."

The doctor stared at his folded hands. "If I may, my Warchief – there are many shamans here within the camp who have the power to aid in healing. None have responded to my call for their assistance." Groaning with age, he knelt upon a knee. "Warchief, could you please give orders for a few to aid us? So many more could be saved."

The prodigal knot in Slar's gut spiked up into his chest. He tasted blood and bile on the back of his burning tongue. The rage boiling in his mind drove it back down. "I will see to it, Doctor. You *will* have their aid if I have to drag them down here with a company of warriors."

He looked at Sharrog, who had not spoken since entering the tent, save a few gracious words to the wounded. The young warrior looked about, a grimace of sorrow covering his face. "Sharrog, take a polite message to Ortax and the other shamans that their Warchief requests that they minister to the needs of our army's wounded – both physically and spiritually."

Sharrog snorted. "Ortax is likely to laugh me out of his tent, telling me he has more important things to do."

Slar raised one eyebrow in an expression his son should know quite well. Sharrog bowed his head in submission. "If Ortax refuses this request, then let him know that I command it. If he refuses that, come get me with all haste." Slar pounded a fist into a thick, pine tent pole, sending shivers through the sewn and oiled hides. "I will throttle him myself." He pointed his sharp claw at his son. "You may tell him that."

Bowing from his waist with a hint of a smile, Sharrog turned and jogged out of the tent.

Slar turned to Doctor Clayburn. "They will treat you with respect as well, doctor, or I will know about it. Understood?"

The doctor tapped his fist over his heart twice. "Of course, Warchief."

Leading his elder son out of the tent with a few final, kind words to the injured warriors, Slar shifted the steel plate protecting his shoulders and breast. "Come, Grindar, let us review the front."

Slar and his son made their way to a stone outcrop at the mouth of the death-filled ravine. Blood soaked most of the rocky soil, and soot blackened the stone banks of the defile. In the distance, the crumbled front wall where so many Wolf Clan warriors died lay spread in every direction. *Those bodies will never be recovered for their pyre. At least most of them burned, as is their honor.*

"How shall we ever take this place, Father?" Grindar whispered into Slar's ear. He shifted the long scimitar slung over his shoulder. "That second wall is more formidable than the first by a magnitude of ten. We cannot move siege towers up this ravine. Nor can we maneuver a large enough ram to attack their outer gate."

Slar pursed his lips, his thoughts identical to his son's words. "Galdreth promises a plan. The Master's spies will move soon." He patted his son's shoulder, though he barely believed his own words. "You and your men must be ready with the largest ram you can haul up there." His eyes drifted back toward the granite fortress. "Galdreth will handle the rest."

CHAPTER 31

Midwinter, being the high holiday of Gannon, is the best time to visit Daynon. Warmed by the Bay of Hope, the season is usually still tolerable. Most importantly, the Midwinter Balls in the capital of the kingdom are events not to be missed.
— "A Traveler's Tour of Gannon" by H. M. Davana

Weariness sat heavy on Maddi's shoulders and forehead as she turned the key. The door had barely opened when gleeful shouts and claps of joy rang in her tired ears.

"Tonight is the Midwinter Ball!" Tanya threw her arms around Maddi's waist. "You are going to look so beautiful!"

Ami stood at the counter in the kitchen, making a cheese sandwich for Tanya's lunch. "She is right, you know. Also, you could meet the king to plead your case for the hospital…well, it might happen."

Maddi sighed and settled into a comfortable chair. "I just want to take a nap. I don't know if I'm more tired from working in the slums, or from arguing with students in class – especially Doctor Darilla. Why in the blazes he would sit in on a class where he thinks he knows more than the teacher, I will never understand."

Placing the plated sandwich on their table, Ami snapped her fingers. "Come on Tanya, eat your lunch. Maddi needs to rest a little before she gets ready." She curled a half smile at Maddi. "You take a nap and then we'll help you dress."

Maddi covered her face with her hands. "Do I have to?"

Ami laughed. "Of course you do. You're a part of the real world now. A king and one of his ministers have noticed you."

After an hour or two of tossing with no sleep, Maddi gave in. Tanya held up a fluffy cotton towel for her to wrap herself in when she stepped out of the copper tub. The little girl and Ami both helped her dry her hair and brush it out until it shined. When she slipped on the dark blue-almost-black velvet dress she had purchased for the evening, Tanya giggled with glee.

"It's the first gown I've ever bought." Maddi smoothed it over her hips while Ami hooked the buttons up the back. "I never thought I'd need such a thing."

Ami strained to get the last button in place. "Well, it's beautiful on you."

Tanya clapped. "Yes! Beautiful!" She ran over to Maddi's dresser and grabbed the small box there. "Now, the earrings."

The sapphire and diamonds wrapped in silver slipped easily into her lobes. They sparkled along her jaw line, drawing in the lamplight. She looked at herself in the cloudy mirror Tanya held and could not hold back a smile. "The neckline on this dress is low. It needs a necklace." She sighed. "To think of the jewels I left in Dern…"

Giggling all the way, Tanya ran into her room. Ami smiled knowingly and lifted an eyebrow when Maddi looked to her. The little girl charged back out, another small box in her hand. "Merry Midwinter!"

Shock dropped Maddi's jaw, turning it into a smile when she untied the package. It opened to reveal a white opal shot with pale blue, suspended on a thin silver chain. She lifted it around her neck, and Ami helped to fasten it.

Maddi shook her head. "How did you—"

Ami shifted Maddi's hair back in place. "We took up a collection among your friends."

Maddi frowned and turned her head. "Who?"

"I believe Doctor Darilla gave five marks, as did Doctor Gramm." Ami clucked her tongue. "Many of the students look up to you more than any teacher. They've learned more being a part of your mission than any class in the history of the College. Some are even talking about going back to their home cities to do the same thing there."

When Maddi shook her head, the earrings glittered in the mirror. "By the Talismans, I hope they aren't calling me Lifegiver."

A soft knock rapped at the door. Ami slipped over to open it, Tanya close on her heels.

A man in gray livery stood upon the porch, bowing formally. He gestured toward the street. "The Lady Doctor's carriage awaits her."

Taking one last look in the mirror, Maddi sighed. *I have to do this if I want to build the hospital.*

Tanya tackled her with a hug. "Have fun! I wish I could go."

Maddi tousled Tanya's red hair. "Maybe next year." She

looked at Ami, who dipped her chin. Steadying herself with a deep breath, Maddi glided out the door, resolute.

The footman bowed, gesturing toward a closed carriage with heavy curtains. A beautiful pair of matching black horses stood in its traces. One man sat on the driver's bench, while a second footman held the door open, his head inclined politely. Inside the carriage a bit of incense burned in a charcoal brazier to warm the coach against the evening chill. Thick black velvet upholstered the benches, and Maddi sank into the rear seat.

A startled jolt ripped through her at a pop from outside. The footman held an open bottle of sparkling white wine. "It is Urbanan, madam, if you would care for a glass during your ride to the palace."

Maddi nodded, and the man poured. The amber liquid bubbled to the rim of the flute, and it tickled her nose when she sipped. At her smile, the footman placed the bottle into a silver bucket of ice, set it inside the carriage, and then closed the door. Maddi sipped again from the sweet, fruity wine. A whip snapped and the carriage jerked forward, clattering over the cobblestones.

Peeking through the drawn curtains, she watched the streets of Daynon roll by while she sipped her wine. The incense carried the aroma of pine, bringing back memories of Midwinter festivals during her childhood. Images of her long dead father floated through her mind, followed closely by those of Renna. Buried emotions percolated to the surface of her soul, threatening to break into tears like the bubbles popping at the top of her wine. She fought them back with a deep breath, staring through her cloudy haze at the streets but seeing nothing.

When the carriage came to a halt, she realized that she had managed to stave off her tears, but only at the cost of neglecting her wine. She downed the remainder in a single gulp. The footman opened the door, and she stepped out onto the palace grounds.

The evening had arrived, the setting sun allowing only a faint blue cast to the sky. Multihued beams of magical light danced among the towers of the Ivory Palace. More played across the silver dome of the High Hall, creating the semblance of a dragon in flight. Every few seconds, a scatter of colored flares popped in the sky then tinkled to the ground in sparks of gold and silver. Maddi stood in awe, watching the display.

After refilling her glass, the second footman gestured toward the steel doors. "Madam, the Lord Doctor awaits you at the gates to the High Hall."

She strolled along the paths of the palace, sipping her newly refilled wine and watching the guests gather, while the footman followed at a respectful distance. The noblemen among the guests wore long, colorful tunics and coats, with puffy, feathered hats. Mages, clerics, and scribes dressed in flowing robes of wool and satin.

When Maddi looked at the women, however, she barely avoided a snicker. Not only did many wear elaborate dresses with tall, frilled collars, but their hairstyles grew more elaborate the closer Maddi came to the High Hall. Some styles climbed into the sky, pinecones and mistletoe nestling within. Others had woven evergreen branches into elaborate curls. *How will those fools ever get the sap out of their hair tomorrow?*

Others carried themselves with more dignity. Some women wore elegant gowns not much more elaborate than Maddi's. Their hair hung in simple curls, or lifted in diamond set caps of fine silver.

From one side of the grounds, a dozen dark cloaked figures passed through the crowd. As they came closer, Maddi noticed their masks each carried a different face. A scowling figure stomped around, lightly shoving the shoulders of good-humored guests, while another followed him with a smiling face passing out hugs. A shocked face danced around the crowd, cowering before people, and a blank mask walked steadily with arms folded.

Maddi finished her wine, dazzled by the spectacle around her. A servant appeared from nowhere, a silver platter carrying more bubbling flutes. She exchanged the empty glass for a new one.

They reached the steps of the High Hall, and she noticed two plays unfolding at each end of the stone terrace. One took place in front of a dark backdrop, the other white. The costumes somber at one end, more serene at the other.

She looked at the footman, pointing. "What is that?"

"They are the matching plays of Balance, Milady," he replied, "put on by the Temple every year. One follows the path of Order, one Chaos. Both have the same characters and ending, yet entirely different plot. It is meant to be a lesson, and many people compare notes at the ball within."

Maddi let the man lead her up the stairs. Before she could pay much attention to the dark play near her, shiny boots tapped against the stone. The Lord Doctor Tymin Marten emerged from the crowd. A dark satin cloak wrapped around a silver jacket and vest. Fine silk embroidery slipped out from his sleeves and collar. His chain of office dangled from his neck.

"Lady Maddi, it is so wonderful to see you here." He paused, a look of stunned surprise passing over his features. "You are more beautiful tonight than I could ever have imagined."

Wrinkling an eyebrow, Maddi folded her arms. "Spend much time imagining how beautiful I am, do you?"

The Lord Doctor grimaced. "No more than appropriate, I assure you." He waved the footman away and offered his arm to Maddi. "Come. There are many here tonight who wish to meet you."

Maddi took his arm, her eyes scanning the crowd. Most wore the jeweled sigils of noble houses, while others appeared to be wealthy commoners. Servants in blue and silver livery blazoned with the rampant dragon of Gannon bowed at their passing. Many held more trays of the sweet, white vintage, or a platter filled with a variety of canapés.

"The king has spared no expense on the ball this year." Marten took a proffered glass from a nearby servant, his silver rings clinking against the goblet. "This is real Urbanan white, from across the sea in Uria, not like the Avarosan copy Duke Ferric has his people make." Closing his eyes, he sipped the wine. A faint smile remained on his face when he lowered the glass. "The Avarosan stuff is good, but nothing like the real thing."

Rolling her eyes, Maddi downed the rest of her flute and handed it to Marten. "Get a lady another, would you?"

Marten laughed and took her empty glass. "Careful, my dear. The king has asked to meet you this evening, though he usually does not arrive for some time after the ball begins."

Maddi scoffed, despite the slight warming in her temples. "It takes a lot more than that to get a Free City girl drunk. I've seen the inside of more than a few taverns that you likely wouldn't set foot in."

Marten smiled and gestured to another servant bearing a tray.

The Lord Doctor led her to the entrance, past many of the nobles lined up, trying their best to look like they were not waiting. The guards there, the only armed men in the crowd, waved the doctor through.

Marten leaned in next to Maddi's ear. "Being a member of the High Council has its privileges."

Within, the crowd thinned and spread out through the vast domed space. The great room, lit by magical glowglobes bouncing colored lights from the ceiling, captured Maddi's first gaze. She looked about, her breath taken away by the wide array of sights. Dozens of exotic and mouth-watering scents mixed in her nose, while a cacophony of sound bounced from the high stone.

To Maddi's immediate left, stacked hay bales climbed into the air, with wagon wheels and aged farm implements scattered about them. Thin, reedy music rose from a fiddle, and the scent of roasted red meat floated toward them. She took a few steps toward it.

"The Western Realm is so overdone. We should go this way first." Marten led Maddi to the right, passing palm trees set into large wooden barrels and hung with paper lanterns. Servants in the white desert robes of Hadon passed out fiery peppers and meats on skewers. One offered her a flatbread smeared with a fragrant paste. Maddi chewed at the soft, warm bread, and the flavor of dates and cinnamon coated her tongue. A low drum and flute hovered among the palms. She felt the beat deep inside, unable to avoid a matching, rhythmic sway in her steps. Thoughts of spinning about in the Lord Doctor's firm grip danced into her mind.

Marten spread his hands wide. "Every part of the known world is represented here tonight. A dozen lands expressed in their food, drink, culture and music." He stretched his neck to look about the hall. "I am certain even the Free Cities rank a booth here."

Maddi left her vision of intricate dances, refocusing on the doctor's face. "The Free Cities are older than anything you Gannonites call civilization. Dern was founded in the Elder Days!"

Suppressing a smile, the doctor lowered his head in acquiescence. "I meant no disrespect, my dear. The Free Cities are indeed ancient and worthy of esteem."

Maddi sniffed. "I doubt we'll want to eat the food there, though."

The Lord Doctor chuckled. "This way. There are people you must meet."

Along the eastern side of the High Hall there clustered a few stone structures resembling castles. Maddi noticed when she approached that they were painted facades. A dozen different dishes were being served and devoured here, from light seafood in olive oil to heavy pastries filled with beef and cheese. Her mouth began to water.

Marten took a silver goblet filled with a deep red wine and tried a tentative sip. He nodded in approval. "Uria is a favorite of the Eastern Realm nobility. The food in this section is usually quite good." He cast his eyes back and forth among the revelers.

"Ah. My Lord Mayor." Marten reached out his hand toward a handsome man in fine clothes of silk, richly cut and at the creeping edge of fashion. "May I introduce the woman who has done so much to aid your fine city?" He gestured in Maddi's direction with a flourish. "Lord Mayor Callis Abreva, this is the Lady Doctor Maddi Conaleon, the woman your common folk now call Lifegiver."

The mayor fell into a deep bow, his blond hair bouncing about his head in waves. "Madam, may I thank you for the compassion you have shown my people." He gave Marten a sidelong look. "I have also heard of your wish to build a...how did you call it Tymin – a hospital?" Mayor Abreva spread his lips in a wide smile. "I only hope His Majesty approves so that we may begin construction immediately."

Maddi curtsied, entirely uncomfortable with the act. "Thank you, My Lord. I will make certain the people of your city know that you deserve praise for your strong support of my mission."

The mayor nodded with a grin. "You are indeed kind, my lady."

Giving the mayor a short nod, Marten took Maddi's elbow and led her out of the Urian section, and into a much different area. A soft mist only a few inches thick hung about the floor here, heavy enough to hide Maddi's feet. The doctor stepped over to a small booth that sparkled like quartz crystals grown together in a cluster. He returned with two drinks in stemmed glasses – one glowed a faint green, the other a faint red.

"Apple or strawberry? The mages of the Isle of Wizards make a fine drink either way."

Maddi took the red one, chancing a sip. The strawberries bloomed on her tongue.

"Delicious," she said with a smile.

"Lord Doctor Marten...is that her?"

The commanding voice of a woman, rusty at its edges but still with a heart of steel, rang out from a cluster of yellow and blue-coated men. Marten tensed, and Maddi caught the faintest glimpse of a wince upon his face. When he spun about, however, he turned on his gracious charm.

"Your Grace," the Lord Doctor said with a bow. "May the merriest of Midwinters come to you and to House Lindon."

The woman wore her gray hair pulled back in a tight bun, wrapped in a net of blue lacquered tulips. She wore a simple but elegant dress of yellow wool. Her piercing eyes examined Maddi from head to toe.

Maddi tried another curtsy.

"You show balance, if not courtly training." The woman narrowed her gaze further. "Yet you have the look of a Free City woman – a Derner if I'm not mistaken."

Maddi curtsied again. "Yes, Your Grace."

The Lord Doctor intervened with a gracious sweep of his hand. "Lady Doctor Maddi Conaleon, may I introduce Her Grace, the Duchess of Allanor."

The wrinkled woman took Maddi's hand in her firm grip. "You must bring your mission to my city. It is just across the delta." She scowled at the Lord Doctor. "It is good to see that someone from that college has finally done some good for the people."

The duchess turned her eyes back to Maddi, and her face softened with a matronly smile. "If the king fails to fund your hospital idea here in Daynon then rest assured I would do so in Allanor."

Maddi bowed her head, squeezing the woman's hand. "You honor me, Your Grace. Your people are lucky to have such a caring liege."

The duchess cackled a harsh laugh. "You'll do just fine in this court, my dear." She floated away to be engulfed by her retainers.

Marten set his drink upon the tray of a passing servant. "Too sweet. Let's visit the elvish island and see if they have anything stronger."

The next area still maintained the low mist, but a cluster of potted pine and spruce trees closed around a hidden cove of wicker tables and chairs. Only a few guests gathered here, most of them couples desirous of seclusion.

"Here." Marten picked up two small glasses of a clear liquid. "It is an elvish liquor – very strong." He knocked it back in one gulp then gasped for air. "Do it quick..." he said, his breath caught in his throat.

Maddi followed his lead. The ice-cold liquor hit the back of her throat like a ball of fire. It burned going down, eventually mellowing as the warm sensation sank all the way to her toes. A strong hint of juniper hung in her nose. "Good." Her voice came out far steadier than the doctor's.

Marten opened his mouth to speak, but then paused. Maddi followed the line of his gaze to a couple sitting at a nearby table. A man with a shaven head flipped a gold mark along the back of his fingers. His companion wore long tresses of wavy, golden hair, her eyes sharp. Marten walked over, hand outstretched. "Gwelan Whitehand, what a rare surprise to see you in Daynon...and at the Midwinter Ball of all places."

The man slipped the mark into his pocket, but hesitated before accepting Marten's grip. "Lord Doctor." He lifted a hand toward his companion. "May I introduce Jule Wynsor – a goldsmith in my employ."

Jule offered a bright smile along with her hand to Maddi. "And you are?"

Maddi took her hand gladly, returning the smile. "Maddi Conaleon – I teach at the Doctor's College."

"What do you teach?" the woman asked.

"Just one class in herbology," Maddi replied, seating herself in the chair Marten pulled out from the table. "I've really only been there a few months."

Marten placed his hand upon her wrist. "Nonsense." He waved a servant down with two glasses of sweet, elvish wine, handing one to Maddi. "You are one of our most promising new teachers, not to mention your work with the poor folk of Daynon."

"Really?" Jule lifted her own wine glass in toast. "Gwelan told me rumors of you. Your work is most gracious."

The man hoisted his clear liquor. "Indeed, it is."

All four drank, though Maddi found herself uncomfortable with the attention. She looked about the room, searching for any excuse to change the subject.

Jule obliged her. "You teach herbology, you say. You may have something in common with Gwelan. He often obtains rare herbs for alchemists, doctors, and the like."

The man nodded over his drink, keeping his arm wrapped around Jule's shoulders. "That is, in fact, how I met the Lord Doctor in the first place." He glanced at Marten. "What was it you were looking for, Marten? Sylipsis root?"

The Lord Doctor cleared his throat. "I do not remember. It was some time ago."

Gwelan leaned forward, a slight smile on his lips. "It was but a few years ago, and that wasn't the only time. What else has there been?"

Maddi curled a sly smile upon her lips. "Yes, Doctor. What else?" Her smile widened. "I'm familiar with a few purposes for sylipsis. Usually, elder nobles looking to make new sons seek it out."

The Lord Doctor spluttered his wine in spray across the table. He coughed, to the great joy of Maddi and Gwelan. Jule offered him a cloth napkin.

"I needed it for research..." Marten sipped again from his wine, a slight blush visible in his cheeks even in the dim light. "...not for personal use."

Reaching for his drink, Gwelan parted his lips to make another comment. Before he could speak, a plain faced man in severe, dark robes coalesced from the shadows behind Marten.

"My Lord Doctor, how good to see you. I had hoped we might have private words this evening."

The thick, gold chain around the man's neck looked familiar to Maddi. It held a pendant shaped like a quill pen with a sapphire-set feather. She also noticed the brief, acid glare from Gwelan Whitehand cast in the new arrival's direction.

"Lord Chancellor." Marten rose from his seat. "This is not the best of times for business."

The chancellor lifted his nose and stared down it. "Any time is a good time for the business of the kingdom. As a Lord Privy, you should understand that quite well."

Marten stared at the chancellor, before bowing his head in acquiescence. "Very well, My Lord." He turned to Maddi, a conflicted expression on his face. "I am sorry, my dear. This should not take long." Marten smiled at Gwelan and Jule. "I hope the two of you might offer the hospitality of your company while I deal with the needs of the realm."

"Of course." Jule patted Maddi's hand and smiled. "I like her."

The doctor snapped a sharp bow before he followed the chancellor off into the shadows behind the royal dais.

Maddi sat there for some time, laughing and talking with her new friends. First one glass of wine went down, then another of the juniper flavored shots. The next glass of sweet wine settled into her brain.

Gwelan stood up, downing the last of his own drink. "Come. Those roasted peppers in Hadon have been drifting to my nose all night. I would love one right now."

Jule reached over from her seat. "Would you join us, Maddi?"

Shaking her head, Maddi stared off at the gray curtains. "I believe I'll search for my escort." She clasped a hand from each. "It was wonderful meeting you. I hope we see more of each other soon."

She slipped away, careful with her steps. *I think I've had a few more to drink than I thought.* Maddi giggled then covered her lips with a hand. *Pull it together, girl. You've drunk more than this before.*

She drew in a few deep breaths and rubbed her face to clear her mind. A servant bearing a water pitcher passed, and Maddi stopped him for a cup.

Pouring a long draught down her throat helped her focus. "Thank you." She placed the cup on the tray, and the man bowed before returning to his rounds.

Scanning the crowd as she moved, Maddi made her way toward the rear of the hall. A few faces recognized her, including the Duchess of Allanor, who still maintained her gaggle of followers. She nodded politely to each person, but did not stop.

Peeking behind the curtain, Maddi saw long tables stacked with food and drink, dirty and clean dishes. Blue and silver liveried servants moved among them, dashing in and out to the floor. Along the far wall, an arched entryway opened, lit by glowglobes and guarded by a pair of billmen. *I don't see them among the servants, so that has to be where they went.*

Wending her way through the tables, Maddi averted her eyes from the few couples – nobles and common folk of both sexes – seeking privacy for more than just talk. The wet sounds of kisses floated to her ears, and the image of Lord Doctor Tymin Marten in far fewer clothes drifted into her mind. She had seen him in the slums without his shirt, when it had been splattered by blood. His smooth chest rippled when he moved, his shoulders thick with muscle. Marten had caught her looking that day, unable to shift her gaze quick enough. *Marten also surprised me with his heart. He works in the slums nearly as hard as I do.*

At the entryway, however, the guards crossed their bill pikes.

She giggled and covered her lips in fake surprise.

The one with the second bronze pip of a corporal raised his hand. "I am sorry, My Lady. No admittance for guests."

Maddi fanned her face with one hand, mocking the ladies she had seen in court. "Why my dear sirs, I do declare. I am the guest of the Lord Doctor Marten. I felt a little ill at the lack of his presence and have come to meet him." She looked past their crossed weapons. "He asked me to meet him in private here after giving him a few minutes head start."

The other guard moved his bill as if to let her through, but at a scowl from the corporal, he slammed it back into place. The guard softened his expression when he turned back to Maddi. "I am sorry, madam. The Lord Doctor did not command us to allow you through after him."

Fluttering her eyes, Maddi gave the men a wounded expression. "Well, he must have forgotten, so great was his haste to conduct business with the Lord Chancellor." Her gaze turned shy. "He hoped to find me awaiting him in his private office."

The corporal looked at his subordinate, who shrugged his shoulders. Suddenly a harsh call came from an older woman directing servants like a general on a battlefield.

"Now, Rigby, don't you know who this woman is? She's the Lifegiver." An element of awe crept into the servant's voice when she said the name Maddi had grown to despise. "Don't you owe her more respect?"

His face paling, the corporal lifted his bill. The other guard followed suit. "Excuse me, madam, I did not know." He gestured inward. "Please, go ahead."

Maddi nodded before taking a step into the entryway, but the soldier grabbed her hand first. It had to be the softest grip a guard had ever used on her.

"I have to say thank you, ma'am." The corporal lifted his brows in earnest. "You saved my brother. We lost the lad to alcohol down in the gutters of Daynon. You healed him, and he came home to us." He knelt down upon one knee. "He's cleaned up and joinin' the guard now. Thank you." The soldier kissed her hand. "Thank you."

A great discomfort crawled up Maddi's spine. She forced a near look of revulsion into a smile of gratitude. "Please, sir, stand. I am just sorry that I was the first person to care about him, other than you."

He nodded, and allowed Maddi to pull her hand away. She walked up the passage, hiding the mixed emotions that sought out her face. *Blast these people!*

At the far end of the tunnel, Maddi exited into a wide gallery with tall windows along its curved outer wall. Long red curtains hung between them as they curled their way around the rear of the High Hall. A thin blade of light shone underneath a side door, one of several along the inner curve of the gallery. Maddi crept up to it, listening at the crack.

"...you swore it was for him alone. I do not like you having such a powerful poison unused. I do not trust you, Sammin." The door muffled the voice of the Lord Doctor, but Maddi picked out his words. "You failed to give it to him when he visited the city, now it is time for you to return it to me. We will adjust our plan accordingly."

Poison?

Maddi heard the chancellor cluck his tongue. "You need not concern yourself with that part of the arrangement. You have your role." Something tinkled and thunked like a heavy purse tossed onto a desk. "That role has increased with this hospital idea of yours. I will keep the half of the money for use in the execution of our plan. The rest can go to your…pet project."

Another muffled clink passed through the wood to Maddi's pressed ear.

"Speaking of your pet project…" Maddi could almost hear the leer in the chancellor's voice. "…will you meet success with it tonight?"

Marten cackled a licentious laugh, one Maddi had never expected to hear from his lips. "Perhaps. That dirty urchin she adopted is cared for tonight. I intend on getting a few more drinks into her, get her in the carriage, and then get *into* her myself." The laugh sounded again, joined by a similarly salacious one from the chancellor. "Speaking of which, I should probably return, or I might lose my opportunity."

Fire burned in Maddi's chest, her breaths quick and insufficient. She backed away from the door casting her eyes about for a hiding place. The gallery, faintly lit by glowglobes, curved away in both directions, open to the ceiling. Her heart beat with anger, hurt, and fear. Her mind was unclear. She heard the latch lift on the office door.

The curtains! Maddi ducked behind the long, red drapes, holding her breath and straining to catch any sound. The creak of a door opening filled her ears.

"Allow me to go first." The chancellor's voice remained low. "We should not be seen returning together."

"I will wait here only a minute." Marten sounded frustrated.

Unmoving, Maddi kept still in her hiding place. A peek around the crimson fabric, and she watched the chancellor walking into the entryway of the main hall. When she stepped around the drapes, her jaw set in rage, Marten's eyes widened in surprise.

"You!" She fought to keep her voice in a fierce whisper. "You would use me and my hospital to further your poisonous schemes! Is that what you wanted the sylipsis root for? Poison?" She clenched her fists, fighting the urge to strike him. "How much of the king's money were you actually going to give to us? Or were you just going to keep half of it again?"

The Lord Doctor's face contorted from fear and surprise to a dark rage she had not imagined upon his handsome features. "You do not understand. I don't know why you thought to eavesdrop, but – whatever you heard – it's not what you think." He moved toward Maddi. She thought she sensed him embracing his Talent. "I—"

A bright halo preceded the rustle of conversation and movement down the gallery. Armed men in blue cloaks trotted down a set of steps, followed by mages holding globes of light. A cluster of festively dressed nobility followed the soldiers. Each eyed Maddi and the doctor with predatory gazes.

Marten backed away, lowering his head in a bow. Maddi retreated toward her curtain.

A girl and a boy in blue livery aided an old man dressed in pure white. The Opal Crown sat evenly on his head, though his brow drooped. King Arathan's steps were short and shallow as he descended the flight of stairs with a great deal of aid from his pages. The nobles surrounded him, fawning and pretending not to notice his infirmity.

At the bottom of the red-carpeted steps, Arathan lifted his head to gaze at Marten. "Ah, the Lord Doctor. Have you come to offer me healing before the ball, my old friend?" The king shifted his gaze toward Maddi. Despite the age wracking the rest of his body, the fierce blue eyes still held the steel of a boy who reunited his kingdom. "And you – ah, yes, you must be her. Tymin told me he would bring you tonight. I have so desired to meet the woman my people have named *Lifegiver*."

He tilted his head toward her. "In my great-grandfather's time, you would have been considered a threat to his power." Maddi furrowed her brow, and the king laughed, jovial and with some of that old, youthful strength. "Do not fear, my lady. I consider you an asset to our kingdom."

Maddi lowered herself into the deepest and most graceful curtsy she could produce. "It is an honor and a pleasure to serve, Your Majesty."

The king inclined his head toward her and raised a finger with a thought. "Perhaps, rather than Tymin fumbling around with my joints again, you could offer the use of your Talent upon me."

A few of the nobles encircling the king frowned, casting dubious stares in Maddi's direction.

Maddi curtsied once more. "It would be an even greater honor, Your Majesty."

She walked forward, the crowd of nobility begrudgingly parting for her. The king held out his arm, and Maddi took it, embracing her Talent.

The glitter of life forces surrounding Maddi sprang into her mind's eye – the nobles, the pages, the Lord Doctor Marten. King Arathan glowed with the energy of life. It throbbed with his pulse, outshining even that of Marten. The nobles faded within the brilliance of Arathan.

Maddi delved into the king, finding the places where age and wear had broken down his joints and ligaments. She rejuvenated them, strengthening the padding between the king's bones and repairing the tears in his muscles. Where she found weak points in organs and arteries, places worn thin by time, Maddi added a veneer of her own *psahn*, regenerating the deteriorated tissue.

The deeper she poked within the king's life force, the more she felt something odd about it. A shadow hung over it, different from that of normal disease. Maddi felt chaotic energies swirling within the shadow. It existed solely within the king's life force, not within his body. She reached for it, but drew back, fearful that she could not keep her own *psahn* safe. Maddi backed away, abandoning the king's life force with a swift exhale.

King Arathan straightened, shooing away the pages who reached to aid him. He took a few slow steps then skipped into the air, tottering slightly when he landed again. Half a dozen nobles reached for their king to steady his thin frame.

"Nay!" The king stood firm on his own, sweeping the air with a commanding hand. "Do not touch the royal person!" The nobles scattered back, dipping their heads in supplication.

King Arathan turned to Maddi, his wrinkled, narrow lips on the verge of quivering. "I have not felt this well in a decade. The name my people have given you is indeed justly deserved." He shifted his gaze to the Lord Doctor. "I will double my stipend for her hospital, Tymin. Chancellor Vyce will see to its distribution." The king gave Maddi a roguish smile. "No man has ever watched my coin so well as Sammin Vyce." The smile turned to a scowl when the king eyed his nobles. "Perhaps that is because he was born low. The man had to develop real talents to excel in this world."

Most of the nobles inclined their heads, though Maddi noticed a few who did not. Three golden trees set with emeralds as their leaves hung from one frowning noble's neck. Another bearded young man with amethyst and jade grape clusters on his pendant stared at the king, his face unreadable.

Arathan cast his regal smile upon Maddi once again. "I will dance at my Midwinter Ball for the first time in years. I hope that we pass each other in a turn upon the floor."

Maddi curtsied, and the king moved on. His retinue followed him, but not without some icicle-filled stares for Maddi. A moment later, she stood alone with the Lord Doctor again.

"Maddi," he whispered fiercely, his eyes darting about the hall. "I don't know what you thought you heard before, but you must let me…"

She did not hear his final words. Instead, she raced down the gallery, and out onto the grounds at the first exit she found. Walking stiffly, trying not to run, Maddi found a public coach pulled up outside the main gate. "Can you take me to the Doctor's College?"

The carriage driver knuckled his forehead. "That's a bit of a distance. It will cost a half mark, my lady."

Realizing she had brought no coin, Maddi pulled the sapphire earrings from her ears and folded one into the man's palm. "I would ask that you make all haste."

They pulled up at her house in less than half the time it took to arrive at the Palace. The driver knuckled his head and bowed several times to her from his bench, barely able to take his eyes from the jewels.

She opened the door, her hands numb against the keys. Tanya and Ami lay cuddled together asleep. Thankful that she did not have to face them now, Maddi drifted silently back to her own room. Her tears never slipped until she had buried her face into her pillow.

CHAPTER 32

Midwinter is usually considered the end of the oyster season in the Bay of Hope. It is also when their flavor is at their peak. Some cracked pepper and a squeeze of lemon is all one needs to perfect them.
– "A Culinary Guide" by Julinnia of Chiles.

Tallen wrapped his cloak tighter against the chill blowing in off the sea. The sky hung heavy and gray above him with a threat of winter weather. He hooked the bulging sack of lemons through his belt, tying them safely. His eyes drifted toward the white blot of the sun where it forced its way through the leaden clouds. It already dipped toward the horizon.

"Blast!" Tallen cursed at the wizard whose house he had just left. *The old bastard would not stop talking. I had hoped that only one or two stories about Hadon would be the price of a few lemons. Too bad he's the only wizard on the Isle who keeps lemon trees in his solarium.* "But those oysters that came in this morning would be naked without it," he admitted aloud. "I promised something special for the party tonight."

He jogged along the gravel path, his eyes watching the sun dip farther toward the sea. Darkness mulled about the trail by the time he reached the fork. One choice led around Walnut Hill, taking him miles out of his way. *I'll be lucky to make the party at all!* The other fork led into a thicket between the hills – the place Varana had quite clearly forbidden to students.

All she said was that it would interfere with touching my power. Tallen shrugged. *I don't see why I can't cut through. It will save me hours of running.* He made his choice and jogged into the thicket.

Breezes moved the pine trees, and birds chirped in their branches. A cardinal darted across his path, and a pair of rabbits, fat for winter, dashed into a patch of briars.

It took him a few minutes to realize that the strange fuzziness in his mind was nothing to do with his exertion. It increased gradually, slowly swamping his brain. His thoughts ran smooth, but someone or something had cast a blanket over his senses. He tested his power, reaching out to the force he could so easily call these days. Tallen could not find the Aspects. They hovered beyond a cloud of haze, distorted and intangible.

Tallen increased his pace, the sack of lemons slapping against his thigh. Trees loomed overhead, their shadows darkening the path while evening crept ever further into the sky. His steps slowed when an unexplained fear lifted the hairs on his neck. He cast his eyes about, noticing the now silent birds. He reached for his power, still hidden behind that hazy wall of interference.

"Now!" came the gruff shout from the trees. A dozen shapes darted out of cover, growling.

Desperate to make the cover of the forest, Tallen ran toward the trees. The attacker moved faster than he did, cutting off his escape. His heart pounded in his ears as he looked about for another route to freedom.

Four of the largest figures closed in from the circle surrounding him. One look at the red eyes and Tallen knew they were orcs. Suddenly, a rough net that spun around his head blinded him, cutting into his skin and pulling him to the ground. The orcs began to beat him, harsh kicks and punches bruising his ribs and arms. The pain drove out his breath, and he ended his meager struggles.

Rough hands forced a hood over his head. His arms were pinned to his sides by a heavy skin that wrapped around him, crushing the lemons against his thigh. He groaned in pain, receiving an extra kick to his ribs in response.

"I said he is not to be harmed!" Tallen heard the thump of steel on steel and a harsh grunt. "Anyone kicks him again and they lose their head!"

Tallen groaned as they hoisted him up. Pain sliced into his side with every difficult breath. The tarp squeezed his arms against his chest. The jostling motion exacerbated every pain and swelling bruise on his body. His mind danced in and out of consciousness, until he felt hard stone slam into his side.

"We'll keep him here until nightfall. Then I will dose him with the magebane, and we can sneak him back to the boats."

The words scudded along Tallen's mind, obscured by a fog of pain. Nowhere could he find his power. He could not even sense its presence.

His breath eased as the tarp came loose, reducing some of the pain in his chest and legs. Torchlight blinded him as the hood ripped away, taking a piece of his ear. The attackers unwrapped the net and bound his hands and feet with rough hemp ropes. Green hands ripped the sack of lemons from his belt. Tallen did not resist, remaining silent while they manhandled him.

"You'll do well to remain that compliant, Human." The orc doing all the talking wore a thick boarskin cloak, with a chain of tusks around his neck. "Our Master has great plans for you."

Tallen edged himself into a corner. His lip felt damp. He wiped it on his shoulder leaving a smear of blood on his shirt. Orcs huddled together not far from the cave entrance, waiting for the last of the dying day to slip from the sky. Tallen watched them from the corner of his eye, the fear welling inside threatening to overwhelm him. Some of his pain had ebbed, but his side still ached with every breath. *They are so many, and I don't even have a dagger.*

He stretched for his power, pounding on the foggy haze with his will. Nothing would give. His mind collapsed in despair, the nervous quiver of panic gathering in his stomach. The bindings tore against his hands as he struggled.

The sound of a dislodged rock drifted to him from deep within the cave. A strange clicking sound followed it, echoing faintly along the stone walls. The orcs, busy mumbling among themselves, did not notice. Another rock tumbled and one of the warriors turned his head.

"Did you hear that?"

The others pointed their ears toward the tunnel leading farther into the cave. Their boar-cloaked leader stepped toward it. "Scarvin, take four men and find out what's down there."

Half of the orc warriors drew their scimitars. Each lit a fresh torch from the one set into a wall niche. Tallen watched them advance into the cave. Their light still hung on the walls for some time after the orcs disappeared.

The torchlight flickered. Screams of fear and pain filled the cave. The crack of metal on some chitinous substance clattered to Tallen's ears. The shouts and screams abruptly died.

Silence reigned again. The remaining orcs, mumbling in fear, drew their weapons and huddled near the tunnel entrance.

Their leader's lips curled around his fangs. "All of you – down there! I will watch the vessel. Find out what happened!"

None moved, their wide eyes darting about in fear.

"Go! Or I will see to it that your skin is flayed from your bodies!"

The orcs shifted their feet before grabbing a set of torches and making their way down the tunnel. Their screams started far sooner than the last set of warriors, though they lasted no longer. Tallen pushed himself back into the corner, while the orc leader took two steps closer to the tunnel's entrance.

A bundle of leather and metal crashed into the orc leader, throwing him hard against the stone. He lay still, dark red gore oozing from a dent on the side of his head where it had hit the wall. Tallen realized the bundle that had crashed into him was the upper half of one of the warriors, ripped from his legs and still gasping for air. The warrior's red eyes died, and the death grip on his scimitar gave way. The weapon clanged to the floor of the cave.

Tallen scrambled closer to the sword, hurrying to cut his bindings along the sharp edge. Blood and gore from the torn warrior's body made the blade slick. Pain sliced along his wrist, and Tallen knew some of the blood was now his.

The clicking sound returned from the deep, much louder and closer this time. A bulky shuffle and the drag of metal on stone followed.

His heart pounding in his ears, his mind barely treading water in a sea of panic, Tallen scraped the rough rope along the sword. The threads popped, just as a loud thump sounded behind him. Another orc body landed in the cave, its head and one arm and shoulder missing.

Tallen's wrists came free. Blood rushed back to his fingers. The tingle of pain made them almost as useless as they had been numb. He fumbled with the orc blade, frantic to free his legs. The last strand parted, and he scrambled to his feet, his eyes on the back of the cave.

A long, bladelike leg peeked out of the tunnel, tapping the stone and making a distinct click on the rock. A second appeared, and both braced against the floor. The legs heaved, and from behind them, squeezing out from the narrow opening, a heavy carapace flopped into the room. Spindly antennae searched the cave, while a dozen beady eyes reflected the light of the torch. Four more hard legs followed, and the creature heaved its bulk around to stare at Tallen. A gaping, razor-beaked mouth opened, and stinking slime leaked out – the foul stench of rot and bile stinging his nose.

Tallen looked into the tar-like eyes, staring back at him with his own death. The maw closed in on him, the slather dripping in yellow globs. He scrambled back toward the mouth of the cave, desperate to keep the sword between him and the beast. It crawled closer, tapping the stone with its legs and sniffing the air with its antennae. Tallen drew short, rapid breaths. The hot press of panic muffled his thoughts.

The giant, carapace-covered creature thrust out a single appendage, piercing and pinning Tallen's right leg to the ground. Dropping the scimitar, he screamed in pain as a hot lance of agony shot through him. The world spun, and he flailed his arms about. One of his hands touched the bag of lemons he had carried. They tumbled out onto the floor, a few of them split open and leaking juice. The monster paused, moving back a half step from the rolling citrus. The leg stuck in Tallen's calf dragged him across the floor, and he screamed again in agony.

In desperation, he grabbed a lemon, the juice stinging the cuts on his hands. He threw it at the creature, hitting it in the face. The monster withdrew its leg from Tallen, squealing and wiping its eyes with antennae. A gush of red blood shot out of Tallen's wound. Another scream burst from his lungs, as his own blood sprayed across his face. The world spun. He flailed, struggling to get away. His hand touched a second lemon.

He forced his mind to focus.

Grabbing the scimitar, Tallen pulled the lemon along its sharp edge. The fruit cut with ease. Before he could turn the weapon toward the creature, it flung its appendage out, knocking the sword away. It ricocheted down into the tunnel.

The giant insect lunged forward. Tallen dodged its outstretched leg, his mind sharpened by the pain racing through his body. He took the two halves of lemon in both hands and squeezed them in a wide spray of acidic juice. The fluid splattered across the monster's dozen eyes. The creature roared a guttural scream and skittered backward, crashing its fattened rear end into the far wall of the cavern. It flailed about blindly, rubbing its black eyes with its antennae. Tallen edged toward the cave entrance, his one leg numb and useless.

The creature shook itself. The antennae rubbed the eyes again, and it found Tallen. The beast opened its maw and roared, splattering slather across the cave. It charged forward, and Tallen grasped with awful certainty that it was his death coming for him. This time those pincers would rip him apart, just as they had the orcs. He took a deep breath and embraced his end.

A sudden bundle of black feathers and razor sharp talons burst into the cave, throwing itself at the creature's eyes. An obsidian beak thrust itself in and out, destroying a black, liquid globe with each stab. When the monster swung at it, the bird dashed away, and the legs struck its own face. A ferocious light filled the cave, and a roaring man hurled himself at the beast.

Tallen's heart leaped into his throat and the threat of tears pressed against his forehead. "Tomas! Merl!"

The paladin swung his burning sword in swift, decisive arcs. The creature's spindle legs were sliced from it in a swirl of blue-white flame. The bulky body came crashing down to the cave floor, the remaining legs flailing about. Tomas took a step back, and with a sudden speed, thrust Steelsheen deep within the monster's head and thorax, burying it to the hilt. He ripped the sword away, eviscerating the front half of the creature. Slime and entrails splattered about the cave, leaving the body quivering on the stone.

The paladin turned his fierce face toward Tallen as he slumped down the cave wall onto the gore drenched floor. He gasped for air and his vision danced with stars and blackness.

"Tallen!" Dorias held him, the familiar smell of pipe smoke in the wizard's cloak bringing a half-smile to Tallen's face. His eyes wanted to roll back in his skull. His mind ached to drift away and rest.

"Tallen, stay awake. You must not sleep." The oaken baritone seemed familiar. "Let me touch him, Dorias. He needs healing. He lost a great deal of blood, and who knows what poisons linger on that *skittering*'s claws."

His friends jostled him, but it felt as if it were another body in another time. A warm tingle flushed through him, focusing on his lower leg and the side of his chest. He felt a dull pain there, like a bruise that had knitted over time. Soon the pain became an itch, one that spread to other parts of his body.

Tallen sat up with a wordless shout.

"Easy, lad," the paladin whispered. "I've cured most of your ills. That thing roughed you up pretty bad."

"The orcs did their part, too," Tallen winced. The dull pain in his side remained, especially when he spoke. "How did you find me?"

Tomas frowned at him. "I told you I would use my skills to watch over you. This area interferes with my abilities enough to prevent my sensing the orcs, but it could not hide your emotions once they attacked you. We've been running for nearly an hour to get here." He stared at the wizard. "I told you we should have brought the horses to the Isle."

Dorias nudged the boarskin-cloaked body of the orc leader with his boot. "This one is a shaman. I hope he was as uncomfortable here without his power as I am." The wizard fixed his sharp gaze on Tallen. "I know Varana warned you about coming near here." He leaned over, digging around in the shaman's pockets until he pulled out a smooth, dark stone. He flipped it in his hand. "This is just like the one Joslyn Britt gave us."

Merl cawed, his squawks resolving into what sounded like words to Tallen's ears. "Deeper! Deeper!" The raven's warm breath left puffs of vapor in the cold air of the cavern.

Stuffing the tracing stone in his pocket, Dorias nodded his head. "I agree, but your sword will have to lead Tomas. I cannot create a light. No mage could so much as sense their power in this cave. Amazing…"

Tallen heaved against the wall to stand upright. Tomas offered a hand to help, but he waved the paladin away with a grateful smile. "You told me your healing skills were minimal." He took a tentative step. "I feel like I could walk for miles."

Tomas grinned. "Your wound was not much more than minimal."

"Good," muttered Dorias, his attention focused on the tunnel. "Then we won't have to leave you here alone." He glanced at Tomas. "I have a feeling something important is hiding down here."

"I know to trust your feelings on these matters." The paladin drew his sword. Ardent flame leapt up its shining steel blade and banished the shadows within the cave, but did nothing to help the stench. The deeper they went, the fouler it became. They passed two piles of mangled orc bodies. Dorias stopped to search each.

"Boar and Ram clan warriors, I think. It is hard to be certain." The wizard wiped his hands on his vest. "You can still make out some of their tattoos."

The drip of water echoed up the shaft. Tallen made out a faint, green glow farther down the tunnel. Whatever the source of the light, it hid behind a sharp turn. Tomas held up his free hand. "I sense nothing alive. The *skittering* had no mate or brood. Surprising for one so large."

Dorias nodded, a fear Tallen had never seen in his eyes.

I know the feeling. It's as if a wall of mud stands between me and my power.

"I've never heard of one growing anywhere near that size," the wizard said. "They are attracted to magical power and objects." He put his hand Tallen's shoulder. "You are probably why it came up out of its nest. The orcs must have been in this cave for some time." The wizard pointed at the green glow ahead. "Whatever that is, it's the object that interferes with our power. It almost certainly drew the *skittering* and mutated it to such a large size."

Tomas began to advance then paused to look back. "Shall we?"

Pulling out his dagger, the Ravenhawke nodded.

The paladin, sword held at the ready, led them around the corner.

A bright emerald glow almost blinded Tallen. A stalagmite rose from the floor of the cave. It served as a natural pedestal for a stone that looked like a piece of jade about the size of the hayball he used to kick around the yard of the inn as a child. Light coruscated over its surface. In the presence of the stone, Tallen's power disappeared entirely from his perception. He felt as he had before first entering the Dreamrealm. Plain. Ordinary. Helpless. *What is this thing?!*

Dorias stepped closer. "By the Waters and the Earth...a Viridian Stone. None were thought to survive the Cataclysm." He stretched his hand over it, casting odd shadows in the green rays of light. They hung about his face, giving him an almost orcish complexion. "They were created for mage prisons."

Tomas lowered his sword. "Does Varana really know what is down here?"

Nodding his head caused the emerald beams to dance on Dorias' face. "She has to." He turned his eyes from the stone to look at the other corners of the chamber. Tallen followed his gaze and saw a large chest set in a recess, covered in stinking filth from the creature that had made its nest here. "What have we now?"

The wizard knelt over the chest, wiping away some of the filth with his dagger. Tomas moved closer, bringing the brighter light of his sword to bear. Dorias stepped back. "I cannot touch my power here, so you'll have to do this the hard way."

A single blow of Tomas' gauntleted fist, and the ancient wood shattered. He carefully brushed away the splinters, and Dorias leaned in closer to look.

"Scrolls and papers..." The wizard hurriedly assisted the paladin in getting at the contents. He brought out a short, parchment scroll with faded golden tassels. He unrolled a few lines, scanning them with swift eyes. "By all the Aspects! And the Talismans, too!" He pulled a few more lines out. "It's called *The Dragonsoul Paradox*!" The wizard's face glowed with more than the light of sword and stone. He drew out another scroll, scouring its first few words. *The Spirit Trap*! By the bloody Balance, Tomas, this is it!" Dorias replaced the scrolls and hoisted the chest. "Come. Let us be away. I must begin reading this at once."

Tallen followed the paladin's light out of the cave, the wizard reading while they walked. His eyes did not stray anywhere near the chest or its documents, nor did his scattered thoughts. Mostly, he just thought of Maddi and how much he wanted to see her – how much he wished he could hold her hand. The engrossed heroes leading the way back to the Academy made a poor substitute.

Tallen awoke to a flap of wings rustling at his window. A light dusting of snow lay along the sill, but the sun reigned over a blue sky. His leg itched, though only a pinkish scar of new, hairless skin remained to tell of his encounter with the *skittering*. Merl cawed a greeting.

"Good morning." Tallen's throat burned, dry and raw. He sipped from a cup of water next to his bed. His throat cooled, Tallen looked up at the raven. "You saved my life. Thanks."

Merl bobbed his head before proceeding to clean his feathers with his beak. A knock at the door preceded its opening by only a bare moment. Tomas entered, his sword sheathed at his side.

"I'm glad you have awakened." The paladin reached up to scratch Merl's beak. "Dorias has been awake with those scrolls all night, while Merl and I guarded you." He handed Tallen a clean shirt. "He insisted we join him the moment you awoke – if you feel able."

Tallen eased his legs over the side of the bed and stood up. Both his legs felt strong, though he still felt a tightness along his chest. "Some breakfast would be nice, but other than that I am fine."

Tomas placed an apple in his hand. "I thought you might be hungry. We'll get something more substantial soon."

Once he was dressed, Tallen followed the paladin out of the

dormitory. Passing across the academy grounds, he noticed a few odd stares and a scurrying pace to the residents. "Is it just me, or is everyone a little jumpy today?"

"I informed Varana of the orc incursion." Tomas shifted his sword belt. "The mages have increased security on the Isle."

They found Dorias at a corner table in the library, the broken, musty chest at his feet. The scrolls and other documents lay carefully placed around the tabletop. The wizard held a magnifying glass to his eye, as if he examined every pen stroke. Only when Tomas tapped his finger on the table did Dorias look up.

"Ah, Tallen!" He laid the glass down. Standing up, he clapped him on the shoulder. "How good it is to see you up and well. Tomas' healing skills are far greater than he ever gives himself credit for."

Bending to scratch the scar on his leg, Tallen nodded his head. "I would agree."

Tomas folded his arms. "Rather than wasting your time rubbing my ego, perhaps you could tell the lad what you've found."

The wizard walked to the window and opened it just as Merl fluttered to land on its ledge. The dusting of snow that had come with the night had disappeared, and the fresh breeze invigorated Tallen, sweetening the stuffy room. "There is much that I have yet to discover, but what I have found thus far is bleak." He turned to face Tallen, wrinkles of concern creasing his forehead. "One of these scrolls is written by the hand of Leolan Calais himself, the last lord of Lond and the father of Varana. He is the one who led the elves to Valen. He was in regular contact with the Dragonsoul Gan during the Elder Days." The wizard stared at one of the ancient parchments. "Imagine…the last Elf king held these very pages. That is *his* handwriting." The wizard fell silent.

Tomas cleared his throat. Dorias jerked his head upright, as if escaping a trance. "Sorry." He took a seat, gesturing for the others to do likewise. "So Leolan claims that Gan understood the destruction being wrought upon the world by the Dragon Wars. The spirit knew that they would continue until Galdreth destroyed everything. Even the dwarves switching to side with the forces of Order was not enough to stop the madness." Dorias sighed. "Therefore, Gan created a trap. Only it required that both Dragonsouls be imprisoned, so their powers might cancel each other out." The wizard stared out the window at the distant harbor. "The unintended repercussions of magic...how they have haunted our species from the dawn of time..."

He leaned back in his seat. "The trap worked. Both Dragonsouls were sealed away. But the reaction to that much magic cut off from the universe – the reaction to the power it took to do the sealing – it broke the continent. The Cataclysm changed many things. And much of it was unforeseen, even by the Elves of Lond."

Tallen processed the wizard's words. *Thankfully, I already learned at least some of this history since being on the Isle. Otherwise he would have lost me.*

Dorias kept his eyes on the harbor beyond the window. "The Elves tried to stop the Cataclysm. A great shield of magic, cast by thousands of elf mages, protected the lost kingdom of Lond from the earthly, physical destruction of the Cataclysm." He rubbed the day old beard on his cheek. "But again, unintended consequences..." The wizard turned his raptor gaze on Tallen. "Learn well, for it was the reaction of that much magic striking the protective shield that poisoned their land, or so Leolan believed."

Pulling a chair out from the nearest table, Tallen sat down. "But what does all of this have to do with me? Why do Galdreth and his orcs want me?"

A dark shadow passed over the wizard's features. He looked away from Tallen. Merl cawed softly. "It has to do with their prison. It was permanent, or so Gan believed. It seems, however, that the trap did not close as tight as Leolan and Gan hoped. The Elf king writes of a crack, a way for Galdreth to escape. It only requires one thing." Empathetic eyes turned in Tallen's direction. "He must possess a Dreamer."

"Possess?" Tomas spoke up for the dumbstruck Tallen. "Like a *psahn* wraith – a demon as the common folk call them?"

A deep sadness hanging about his lips and eyes, the wizard nodded. "Almost exactly so."

Tallen's heart sank, tumbling down to the bottom of his soul, where only fear and tortuous anxiety dwelt. He leaned forward, elbows on knees, cradling his head in his hand. Tomas and Dorias both approached him, but their movements were lost in his swirl of emotions. It was as if all the events of the last half year gathered into one heavy swell of heartbreak – a swell trapped solely behind the dam of his will. He struggled to fortify that wall with faith in newfound friends, and with hope that, together, they would defeat those who sought him out.

A Dragonsoul wants me? The very beings that caused the Dragon Wars and the Cataclysm? They destroyed the world once in their wake. What do they care about me and those I love? We are just pawns in their millennia old game.

He searched for words, but his mouth remained dry and silent. He clenched his fist, waiting for the dam to break.

The anger took him by surprise, swelling in an instant to burning rage. The deaths of those he loved, the terror to which they had been subjected, scoured his mind and remolded his emotions. As quickly as it had flared, the hot anger cooled into an icy resolve. Tallen's eyes narrowed, and his fists unclenched. He looked toward his friends. "What do we do?"

He saw the smiles that crept on their faces. Their expressions of anxious sympathy faded away, replaced by resolve that matched his own.

"I have a gift for you," Dorias said with a proud nod. "More than scrolls hid in that chest." He pulled a small piece of folded, yellow linen from his pocket, handling it with reverent care. The wizard opened the aged fabric to expose a twisted amulet. "It is made of four metals, copper for Fire, gold for Air, iron for Earth, and silver for Water." The four metals twisted around the edges, a wire of each meeting in the middle. "The diamond set in the center is like nothing I have ever seen. As you can probably tell, it radiates with the Psoul Aspect."

The diamond drew in Tallen's perception, its crystal clarity catching light in every facet. He felt what Dorias described, but not just Psoul. The whole amulet radiated with all the Aspects of magic.

He held out a hand in refusal. "I cannot take this. It is too powerful and precious."

"You must." Dorias folded it into his hand. "You are the only man I have ever met who can put it to its full use. I promise I will help you discover its secrets." He dropped his voice to a whisper. "It's value is immeasurable. Keep it hidden."

Tallen clenched his hand around the medallion. It felt warm in his palm. He tucked it away in his pocket.

The wizard tapped a thoughtful finger against his bare upper lip. "As for our actions, not retreating is the first step. I say we head out to meet up with Boris at Highspur. He is one to…"

The door to the library opened with a rush of air. Within the doorframe stood Varana Calais, her face contorted from its normal, peaceful beauty into a snarl of anger. The men rose.

"You have found works in my father's own hand and you did not tell me?" She stormed over to the table Dorias used.

Her anger gone in a flash, she danced her fingers lovingly over the script. A luminosity sparkled in her gaze that Tallen had never noticed before. "I have not seen his script in years. I remember it as if I were a girl again."

Dorias spoke in a soft tone. "I did not know as much when we came to you this morning. If I had, I would not have hidden it."

Varana's face reclaimed some of its earlier glare. "So you say."

The wizard bowed his head. "Please, Varana. On the memory of the friendship we once shared, I would not have hidden your father's works from you." He lifted his eyes and narrowed his gaze. "Which begs the question, who hid them in the first place?"

The elf sorceress returned her eyes to the scrolls. She examined each one in turn. "I would chance that it was my father himself. These others are written by mages close to him at the time of the Cataclysm, men who came with our people to Valen." Varana paused a moment on one page in particular. "All of whom are long passed, as producing children was the first goal of those who survived."

Tomas leaned in to get a better look. "Why would King Leolan have hidden these scrolls?"

Varana continued to read the parchments as she spoke. "My father visited the Isle many times before he died. The Viridian Stone was almost certainly his. At the time, mages who still followed the cult of Galdreth sought to resurrect their master. These scrolls point to a way to do just that." She moved one parchment to scan another. "Undoubtedly, my father sought to keep these works from their hands." Varana offered the slightest of smiles to Dorias. "No wizard in his right mind would ever willingly approach a Viridian Stone, especially without knowing what it protected."

Dorias shrugged. "So you understand now what is happening to Tallen? Why he is not safe here?"

Straightening from her examination of the documents, Varana stared pointedly at Dorias. "The Isle is as safe as anywhere in this world. Tallen is surrounded by mages, and now we know what to watch for." An icy glaze covered her features. "And he would be close enough to handle should the Dragonsoul take him."

Rising to his full height, Dorias wrapped his cloak about himself and folded his arms beneath it. "Tomas and I have taken an oath to protect this young man. His powers have grown so that he can also protect himself, Viridian Stones notwithstanding." He leaned toward her. "We can no longer hide from this challenge. We must face it."

Varana laughed. The darkness tinting it changed the entire demeanor of her crystalline voice. "That is always your counsel, Ravenhawke."

Tomas bowed his head. "It is counsel that usually rings true, My Lady."

Dorias did not soften his tone. "I will brook no harm to the lad. Killing him would not stop Galdreth. It would simply seek another vessel, even if it were one less powerful." He eyed Tomas. "I would hazard a guess that Talented healers could also suffice the Dragonsoul's purpose if necessary, though I cannot say if it knows that." He looked back to Varana. "Besides, we need the boy. His power could be a mighty weapon against the enemy."

The long white hair hung still on Varana's shoulders. She stared at Dorias, her violet eyes just as unmoving. A beam of sunlight cut through the library window, setting her flaxen hair aglow. She folded her fine fingers together.

"Tell me, Tallen." Her voice remained even as she shifted her amaranthine gaze upon him. "You know what we have to offer you here, yet you are still a free person. I, too, care for your well-being. What would be your choice?"

Tallen dropped to one knee. "Lady Varana, you have taught me more than anyone about my power. You are a gracious lady, and I would hope to someday count you among my friends." He lifted his gaze to meet hers evenly. "I would take a hand in my destiny, rather than hide from it. This power will not leave me be. It has chased me a thousand miles from my home. It has killed and harmed those that I love."

Varana frowned. "I do not think you understand the rarity of your power, young man. For near a thousand years I have trained mages upon this Isle. Few have walked into my presence radiating your strength. I also do not think you understand that you have only waded into the tidal pools of your power. The great sea that awaits you might well be beyond your control."

Tallen remained focused on her, willing his certainty to leap across the gap between their eyes. "I will not leave Dorias' side." He noticed the wince on the wizard's lips from the corner of his eye.

"Ha!" Varana jerked her head. "As if that were a reason for me to agree."

Tallen spread his hands before her. "I can only do what I can, My Lady. This power intends to have me, and it has gotten closer each time it has tried. If Tomas and Dorias plan on heading west to face it, then I will go with them." He looked up to meet her frown. "I will be safest on the move."

His bearded chin held in his hand, Tomas nodded. "That is true, in my opinion."

Varana frowned.

"I will teach him." Dorias clasped his hands together, pleading with her. "He is a Dreamer above all of his other powers – one greater even than I. That is where he needs the most guidance."

Varana shook her head. "You Dreamers are always a great pain. Caladrius was one of the worst." She chuckled. "You, Dorias, are very close." Varana turned to Tallen. A severe expression masked her features. "If you return with the spirit of a Dragonsoul imbedded in your mind, young man, know that I will do all I can to destroy you."

Tallen bowed his head. "And if I return victorious?"

She laughed again, this time laced with mirth. "You humans are ever hopeful. It must be a result of your short, bright lives." Varana looked at Dorias. "You have taken many things from this Isle, Ravenhawke. I hope this adventure turns out better than the last."

She returned the full force of her gaze on Tallen. For a moment he felt her fear, her pride, and her hope. She reached out a hand and brushed cool fingers against his cheek. "Go. Find your destiny, young man. May it be merciful to you…and to the rest of us."

CHAPTER 33

The nights did pass in lonely fear,
And the days in stabs of terror.
Men wondered if their choice to fight
Had been made in grievous error.
— The Stand of Eron's Rock, Sixth Verse

Captain Jaerd Westar stood upon the gatehouse battlement, watching the orcish camp in the distance. The mist of his breath hung in front of his face, before being ripped away by the dry, cool breeze. The enemy swarmed like ants upon their hill, but none made the long, deadly approach up the defile to the ruined pile of stone that was once Jaerd's command.

Maester Darve Northtower slapped his hand upon the stone parapet. "They have tried to assault us a dozen times – they have no weapons that can take this fortress. All we have to do is outlast them." He stroked his long, gray-streaked beard. "We stripped the surrounding land bare before they came. If they did not bring their own food with them, they are doomed."

Bran Northtower and his twin Brax stood at their uncle's shoulder. Bran nodded his head at Darve's statement. "They are also living in their own crap. That cannot be healthy, even for an orc."

The elder dwarf laughed. His dark eyes, as rare among dwarves as the sword over his shoulder, sparkled in the midmorning sun. "Indeed, my nephew." He nodded at Jaerd. "I fought alongside the Bluecloaks at the siege of Shazrel. That was in the desert." Darve chuckled. "Dry crap is much easier to deal with than wet crap."

Clutching his sides, Bran broke into peals of laughter. Jaerd could not help but join him with a smile. Once the dwarf regained his breath, he wiped a happy tear from his eye. "Have they even made it past the front wall since the good captain here blew it up?"

His smile fading, Jaerd looked down upon the destruction he had wrought. The foundations stood, unblemished by the explosions. The stones of the wall itself were still stacked in a few

337

places. However, other sections had huge chunks ripped away, as if a giant had taken great bites out of it. The gatehouse lay there, little more than a pile of tumbled stone. Both towers had crumbled completely. The iron gates and portcullis stuck out at random angles.

The edges of Jaerd's lips dipped even farther, and his stomach twisted in knots when he focused on the dark crimson remains of hundreds of orcs scattered through the wreckage. Though their bodies were half-frozen, the stench assailed his nostrils, even at this height above the field. *It would be the stench of thousands if the orcs didn't risk their lives to recover their comrades' bodies.* Curling his lips into a snarl, Jaerd pointed at the gatehouse. "They held that pile for a few minutes yesterday. That's about it. I counted over three hundred that we killed in the process."

Bran laughed again, but Darve sensed Jaerd's mood. Brax, who had remained stoic all morning, shook his head. "Any fortress can be broken." He turned and walked away, fists clenched at his sides.

His more cheery brother nudged Jaerd's ribs. "Don't mind him. He tends toward dark moods. He's been that way ever since he was a child." Bran chuckled and followed Brax's steps. "A good punch in the arm will solve this one."

Jaerd twisted his gaze back to the shattered wall. Darve stood at his shoulder, stout and still. Jaerd was glad for the company, but grateful that the dwarf chose to keep silent.

"It haunts me, Maester Northtower. The destruction I have dealt."

The old dwarf nodded, his eyes fixed upon the same scattered carnage. "Aye, lad. It always haunts the best of us. But you must remember that we would not live today if you had not done what was required." He clapped Jaerd's arm. "Always remember those you are here to protect. That's what I do. That's what I did when I served here long before you were born. Remember those you love who stand far behind you." He swung his free hand out at the orc camp. "Would you rather that horde found them?"

Jaerd laid his hand upon the battlement, the rough texture of granite cool under his fingertips. It offered the same strength he remembered from the obliterated front wall, yet more ancient, more reassuring.

"Over seven thousand men – Humans, Dwarves, and Elves – can be upon this wall in an instant." Darve's voice remained soft, lilting. "Our defensive spread is less than a third of what you had out there, and we are twice as high above them."

Squeezing his hand into a fist, Jaerd gritted his teeth. "We will hold."

Darve patted his arm again. "We will hold."

Tapping the glowglobe twice, Khalem Shadar brightened it to illuminate the hewn stone cavern of the storeroom. Jaerd and Boris both stared in wonder at the wide expanse. A dozen piles of barley grain spread out before them, each three times as tall as a man. A gray cat hopped out from between the piles, curling her tail around Khalem's legs. He clucked his tongue, and she loped over to Boris, who reached down to scratch her ears.

"We have two more such rooms full of wheat." Khalem Shadar tapped the other side of the globe to dim it one shade. "Three more hold hay and other animal fodder."

Boris cradled his dimpled chin with one hand. "How do you keep it from spoiling?"

Khalem pointed to the cat. She leaped upon a barrel and proceeded to clean her paws. "Well, there are our friends down here, who watch out for many things. The rest the mages keep an eye upon." The Hadoner lifted a sharp, black eyebrow. "Especially Magus Britt. He checks on the food stores regularly, though I am not certain whether he or the pests would consume more."

Boris laughed. Jaerd smiled, but his mind concentrated on the food stores. *How long will this last seven thousand men?*

"And we have dozens of dairy animals, both goats and a few cows." Khalem sighed. "They go through fodder fast when we cannot let them graze in the grasslands. Luckily most of the garrison horses were in herd out upon the Norvus plain when the enemy arrived."

Boris nodded his head. "Slaughter the dairy animals for food after your next fodder storeroom empties. Keep the rest for the horses we have." He made a wretched face. "I hope it does not come to this, but begin slaughtering the horses when only one storeroom remains." The earl held up a warning finger. "Do not slaughter mine."

Khalem smiled. "We are months away from that, My Lord. Even the dispatch riders I sent to Hadon could reach the Empire and return with an army of spears to aid us by then."

Boris shook the Hadoner's hand. "Your men will be welcome, but let us hope Gavanor and Daynon can answer before then."

Jaerd looked one last time at the barley, before Khalem again dimmed the glowglobe. They walked back up the crate and barrel stacked passageway leading to the stable level. "So you say that water is no problem either."

Nodding his head in the yellow light, Khalem pointed to a cross tunnel. "That leads to the cistern. Deep springs and mountain rains feed it. It could sustain this garrison for an elf's lifetime and is well beyond our enemy's reach."

"I have also seen the meat stores," Boris said as they walked, the cat trailing not far behind. "Your hunters have been busy. I believe we could eat for a week and not eat the same animal twice." He narrowed his gaze at Khalem. "What about vegetables? Elves do not live so well as Dwarves and Humans on bread and meat alone."

Khalem twirled his fine beard. "I have spoken with Lord Gael at length about this. We have a large store of apples and pears from the orchards along the riverbanks. Magus Britt has seen to it that they are kept in tight spells of preservation." He smiled. "We also took your advice and began a vegetable garden in terraced steps up the mountain. Our first harvest has been secured by the mages as well."

The earl returned the smile. "Something I learned about while visiting your people."

The smile on Khalem's face faded. "I suggested as much to the Earl Farseer two years ago when I arrived." He chuckled and shook his head. "Earl Brandon did not think it such a logical idea when it came from my mouth."

At the entrance, the cat abandoned them, at last convinced they carried no treats. Jaerd trudged along behind the earl, and Khalem kept pace. Only when they passed the mess level did Boris speak. "Aid from Gavanor should arrive within a month, six weeks at latest, depending on how long it takes to muster a sufficient force."

Jaerd paused. The earl's troubled face sent anxious fingers up his back. "Then our stores should be no problem."

"No." Boris wrinkled his eyes in uncertainty. "Stores are not our problem."

"Then what is, My Lord?"

Earl Boris shook his head. "I don't know."

Looking to Khalem, who shrugged, Jaerd searched for a change of subject. "It is two days until Midwinter."

The earl raised a thick, dark eyebrow. "And?"

340

"And we were thinking that it might be an opportune time to rid ourselves of most of the hog stock." Jaerd gave the quartermaster a significant look.

"Ah, yes, My Lord Earl." The Hadoner shifted his sword belt. "Fresh roasted pork for weary defenders to celebrate the turn of the season. The days will at last begin to lengthen again. It will remind the men that all dark times must end."

Searching for further arguments, Jaerd lifted his hands. "And it will fill the garrison's bellies with hot fat to ready them for the cold nights still ahead. Plus the pigs eat a great deal of fodder without anything but their meat to offer in return."

Folding his cloak behind his back, the earl came to a stop, his eyes fixed on the entrance to the top level carved out of the mountain. Jaerd had yet to enter the temple dedicated to all five Aspects and the Balance. Boris nodded. "Yes. That sounds good. We will also have a service – not mandatory, but recommended." He passed his gaze between Jaerd and Khalem. "Then a feast."

Jaerd stood behind a group of officers, waiting for Boris to begin. He looked about the temple, his eyes drifting over the five walls. Artisans had carved representations of each of the magical Aspects upon them. Blue-painted, wavy lines marked Water. In the middle of the room stood a tall pedestal, on which rested the split, pearl and onyx circle of the Balance.

Jaerd gazed at the graceful waves of Water. *The Westars keep true to Water, while most folk in Dadric pray to the Balance – most of the entire kingdom, I suppose. I guess we're just old fashioned.*

Over a hundred noblemen, officers, and sergeants crowded within the pentagonal, carved space. More than a thousand enlisted men of all three races stood upon the shoulders and terraces of Highspur. The wall of the Psoul Aspect, directly across from the entrance, stood at Jaerd's back. He could almost reach out and touch the silver-painted ankh carved into it.

Pervading everything, however, was the distant, herb-crusted aroma of roasting pork. More than one stomach growled as they waited for the service to begin.

Darting his eyes about the room, Jaerd noticed Lord Gael standing close to Khalem Shadar. The elf's one eye focused on Earl Boris. Lord Marshal Magdon leaned on a cane close by. Tilli

Broadoak hovered in another corner, the only dwarf within the temple. Even Dawne, wrapped in her dark cloak, stood just a few yards away.

I will help her maintain her ruse…for now. I suppose I'm the only one who would care anyway.

Boris lifted his hands, bowing his head in thanks to those who gathered. "Welcome, friends, on this Midwinter evening. I asked everyone to gather so that we may remember that there is more to life than battle and death. That there are things worth fighting for." He took a step into the center of the temple. "Our struggle and sacrifice are not in vain, no matter their outcome. No matter our race, we, the men of Highspur—"

"And women," piped in Dawne, and Tilli nodded her agreement. Jaerd could not help but smile at his baby sister.

The earl smiled, nodding his head. "Men *and* women of Highspur – which reminds me…it is the women in our lives we fight for the most. We stand here to protect our mothers and wives and daughters, our sisters and childhood sweethearts." He lifted a finger. "In fact, why don't we—"

A loud popping noise ripped through the entryway of the temple. Jaerd slapped his hands over his ears, but ran toward the source of the racket. Just as he exited the temple, pushing his way through the startled soldiers, the popping ceased. A great clang rang from the front of the gatehouse, followed by a heavy thump. Gray dust billowed up from the far side of the wall.

Jaerd understood with horror. "No!"

He dashed for the gatehouse. Boris followed close on his heels, as did Khalem and Gael. Up the stairs Jaerd charged, pulling Shar'leen from her sheath. The blade offered a moment of reassurance to tamp down the dread that surged through his spine. The clang of steel on steel sounded from above, along with the whoosh of rushing flame. Jaerd took the last three steps in one leap, screaming without words as he charged into the winch room.

The calm surprised him. The heavy stench of burned hair and flesh assaulted his nose, followed by the acrid, metallic scent of blood, which coated his tongue.

Darve Northtower knelt, holding the body of his nephew Brax. The young dwarf's beard had melted away, leaving the red welt of fresh burns and the black of charred skin and hair behind. Tears dripped from the older dwarf's face. Sergeant Redarm hovered over him, his axe dripping crimson. Bran Northtower, always the happier of the two, lay dead, his empty eyes staring at his brother's axe imbedded in his skull. A bald, pointy-bearded head lay tucked in the arm of a velvet robed dwarf's body.

"I'm sorry, Uncle," Brax croaked, a spray of blood foaming at the corner of his mouth. "I told him not to...not to get involved with them." His one good hand gripped Darve's shoulder. "I swear to you I quit, and never looked at the Cult again."

Darve stroked his nephew's still smoking hair. "Easy, my boy. I believe you. I know you did not betray us. Rest now." He caressed Brax's one smooth cheek. "The Halls of Earth will house you alongside our ancestors, until they spit you out to be born again."

"I...I..." Brax's breath rattled one last time, and his uncle closed his eyes.

Boris grabbed Darve's shoulder. "By the Fires, man, what happened?"

The dwarf knelt there, his eyes focused on his dead nephew. "Again a dwarf is a traitor. This time back to the powers we first betrayed." He pinched the bridge of his nose. "Yrik and Bran relieved Brax and Sergeant Redarm on guard in here. Brax returned to tell his brother something, I know not what, that was when the racket up here began." Darve rose, gently releasing his hold on Brax. "Marrax and I rushed in to find the twins battling each other. Brax won. Then Yrik burned him. My sergeant took care of that traitor quite deftly you can see." He shook his head, eyes filled with grief. "But not before he cut through the master chain and hinge pins on the front gate."

Sergeant Redarm knelt down beside the robed body. He picked up a long, crystal rod. "He used this."

Darve nodded, his face deep in a frown. "Yes. It is a charged magical tool for just such a purpose. It is very rare, even among my people."

Earl Boris gritted his teeth. "You brought traitors among us! From within your own house!"

Sadly shaking his head, the old dwarf dropped to his knees. Sorrow hung heavy on his face. He lifted his hands and opened his mouth to speak.

An ominous horn blast echoing up the defile cut off his words.

Lord Gael dashed to an arrow slit and scanned the distance. "They come! It looks like they have a ram."

Leaving Darve on his knees, Earl Boris dashed over beside Gael. "Is it large enough to break the portcullis and inner gate?"

The elf nodded. "The gate hinges inward into the courtyard. Their ram looks stout enough." He searched a moment longer. "The entire horde must be on the move this time. They bring taller ladders as well."

With a sudden fierce scowl upon his face, Darve Northtower rose to his feet. He looked to the Lord Marshal Magdon, who had hobbled up the last step as the horn sounded. "Then it is time to implement our plan."

Boris looked confused. "What plan is that?" the earl asked.

The Lord Marshal placed one hand gently on the earl's shoulder. "A plan to get you out."

Before Boris could protest, Magus Joslyn Britt trotted up the stairs, huffing. Brawny stalked beside him, as he had since Sergeant Hall had not returned. "Yes, Boris," the mage said between gasps for breath. "You must listen to us. The outer gate lies flat upon the ground below us. Highspur has fallen; it is just a matter of time."

A frown clouded Boris' features. "Gentlemen, I do not know exactly what it is you have planned here, but I will not flee just when things begin to look dark."

Magus Britt barked a harsh laugh, and Jaerd was shocked to hear the hopelessness in his voice. "*Begin* to look dark?"

Marshal Magdon held up a placating hand. "Someone has to get out and get our last messages back to the king. You are the best one to carry those messages."

The earl raised a black eyebrow. "Why would you say that?"

Magus Britt stomped forward, his own bushy, gray brows drawn down in anger. "Blast it, Boris! You know damn well why. Bastard or no, you are Arathan's only son. You are the only one he might listen to through all the murk of his council!"

Boris opened his mouth to protest, but that only seemed to infuriate the Battlemage. "You have been hiding from this your entire life. Arathan is practically on his deathbed, and you should not die up here. You would leave our entire kingdom's future at risk to prove a point of honor."

Boris took a step backward under the onslaught. Marshal Magdon put his hand on the mage's shoulder to placate him.

Magus Britt brushed the hand off, but kept silent. He backed away and looked at Magdon. "I apologize, Lord Marshal. However, the enemy comes, and we will not hold them for long. We must act."

Jaerd watched in stunned silence.

Boris eyed each of the officers around him. "You are all agreed upon this?"

Magdon nodded. His grandfatherly appearance reminded Jaerd that the man must have faced down sons older and more stubborn than Earl Boris. "Lord Gael will lead you through the secret route. Several others have been chosen to join you, a representative from each nation here." He pointed to Khalem Shadar. "If Your Grace would join this group as well, so that you may take word to Hadon of the enemy's strength."

Khalem bowed deeply. "Were your words not so true, I might insist upon my staying to die with my comrades." He straightened with a flourish of his arm. "I will bring back fifty thousand Sunguard to aid in retaking Highspur. We will march all the way to Dragonsclaw itself if needs be."

Darve adjusted the grip on his sword. "Tilli will go for the dwarves. I've already told her." He turned to his sergeant. "Come. We must see to what defense we can muster." The dwarves bolted from the winch room, shouting orders to the soldiers who scrambled about.

"Come with me." Gael took Boris' elbow. "We must get to the passage."

The earl balked. "I have not agreed to this yet. I will not leave my command."

"This is *my* command, *General* Mourne," Lord Marshal Magdon said, his voice cold steel. "I order you to take witness of events here back to the kingdom." He adjusted his collar with its four silver stars. "This was the king's final order to me before I left Daynon. He gave me specific command to forbid you to sacrifice yourself out here in a dire end."

Lord Gael looked at Boris with his one sharp eye. "Do not be so quick to sacrifice yourself. Even when life is long, that does not make it any less precious at its end." He pointed at the black falcon stitched on Boris' tunic. "Your people need you alive far more than any man in Gannon."

Shouts echoed up from the approaching enemy below. The thump of trebuchets shook the gatehouse. Brawny growled at the windows.

Khalem dashed to the slit to peek out. "They approach the front wall." He looked back at the others, an anxious scowl clouding his forehead. "Lord Gael is right. Our remaining gate will not stand against their rams."

Jaerd stood in silence. *I'm better off saying nothing when nobles argue, but we need to act soon!*

Boris' eyes drifted over the dead dwarf bodies in the room. He lifted his gaze to the Lord Marshal then offered a sharp salute. "Forgive me, sir. I will do as you command." He looked at Magus Britt. "You instigated this situation as much as anyone, I am certain. You are coming with me." Boris turned his steely blue gaze on Jaerd, who had the impression that several thoughts passed through his commander's mind. "You as well, Captain. I will need you in Gavanor."

"I am not leaving without Dawne." Jaerd said the words before he realized he had opened his mouth.

The thump of trebuchets and catapults filled the moment of silence before Boris asked, "Who?"

"You know her as Shaela, the bard. She is my sister." Jaerd planted his feet. "If we are leaving, then I will not leave her to the mercy of these orcs."

Shouts rang from the walls outside the winch room, the twang and hiss of bows providing melody to the rhythm of the catapults.

"Then let us go." Boris nodded to Gael, and the entire group dashed down the stairwell.

Outside, the shouts of imminent battle bounced across the courtyard. Men rushed about, arming themselves. The delicious scent of roasting pork hung over the entire fortress, as if mocking those who would soon die hungry.

Ignoring it, Jaerd ran with the others up the switchback staircase between each entry into the mountain. At the fifth level, standing just outside the temple, he found Dawne. She clutched her harp, her face filled with fear. Tilli leaned on her bow, a pack on her shoulders.

Marshal Magdon nodded to the dwarf huntress. "Mistress Tilli. You are to—"

The blond haired woman raised her gloved hand. "Darve told me of his plan. I tried arguing, but in the end, we Dwarves must follow our orders just as you Humans."

"Good." The marshal eyed Boris. "At least your people know to argue in private." He looked back at the other officers. "Your horses await you. The passage is inside the bastion."

Within the box of stone, Magdon led them down a long hallway not far from the one leading to the main stairwell of the fortress. It sloped downward past packed storerooms, before ending in a large cellar. Magus Eldester waited there with Tarrak Goldmar, his stout body covered in its usual soot. Eight horses stood along the wall, including Boris' stallion and Khalem's Hadonese stepper. They had saddled a pony for Tilli, and one horse carried a large bundle of supplies strapped to its back.

Tarrak stroked the packhorse on its shoulder. "There are enough supplies to last several weeks, though it should not take that long for you to get through to the Free Cities if you press." He walked to the wall and pushed it. The mortared stones swung open on a pivot, revealing a dark cavern.

Jaerd reached out to clasp the old dwarf's hand. "Goodbye, my friend. I..."

The stout old dwarf gave him a nod and patted his elbow. Jaerd had difficulty meeting his kind eyes.

Gael and Khalem led their horses into the passage. Magus Britt nodded to Magus Eldester, and followed, creating a globe of magical light upon entering the darkness. He whistled to Brawny, who trotted into the cavern after him. Jaerd gestured at Dawne, who led a horse through. Tilli pulled her pony behind.

Earl Boris saluted the marshal a final time. "Hold the bastion as long as you can. Then flee through this passage yourselves." He dropped his chin to focus on Marshal Magdon. "Do not stand to the last man just to cover our escape. Use the tunnel at the end."

Magdon nodded, returning the earl's salute. "Get through to Gavanor. Once Highspur has fallen, there is nothing to protect the Free Cities or the Western Realm from this horde." He clasped Boris' hand, a sad smile on his face. "And do not forget that your kingdom needs you more than any other man."

The earl said nothing. He grabbed the marshal's hand with both of his. He let go reluctantly, then took the reins of his black stallion. He offered a salute to Tarrak and Eldester before marching into the passage. Jaerd followed close behind him, his mind awhirl. He focused on Magus Britt's light, following it around a corner.

The hollow boom of a heavy ram on iron echoed through the stone. Jaerd caught a glimpse of the door to the passage sealing behind them. When darkness descended, only the distant echo of ram on steel remained, haunting their steps into the deep.

CHAPTER 34

Victory's taste is bitter sweet. Count your dead before you relish it.
— Boar Clan maxim

Slar shoved the messenger out of his way and charged up the ravine toward the smoking hulk of the southerner's fortress. Cave entrances bellowed black fumes and vapors, fired by defenders who knew they were doomed. His warriors scrambled over the mountainside, mopping up what little resistance remained. Others moved in the opposite direction from Slar, carrying wounded friends back to the camp for aid.

By the Fires! A shaman had best be aiding him or someone will be flayed! He scrambled up the heavy, plank staircase built hastily over the shattered front wall of the fortress. Hopping down to the devastated courtyard on the other side, Slar pushed his way through startled orcs, most dropping to one knee when they realized it was their Warchief who muscled past them.

One door of the huge inner gate lay flat upon the ground. Slar jogged over it, raising dry dust with every step. Inside the gateway, the portcullis lay to one side, ripped apart by his trolls and their ram. The inner doors splayed open, leading to the smoking heart of the fortress.

Within the courtyard lay thousands of stacked bodies, most wrapped in their precious blue cloaks. Piles of armor and weapons lay scattered about, pulled from the corpses of the dead southerners by the clan warriors roaming through the ruins. Slar ignored the debris of battle and searched for the sight he dreaded to find.

A bellow of pain rose up from a small cluster of orcs kneeling near the entrance to the gatehouse. Slar recognized Grindar's lieutenant and Brother Ortax hovering over them. He ran forward, heedless of anything else.

Grindar lay upon his back, one entire side of his body burned black, his left arm charred to a stump. His one unruined eye darted back and forth, focusing on nothing. His lips, where they could still move, curled in unmitigated pain.

Slar threw himself down next to his eldest son, grasping his remaining hand and holding it to his chest. "My son...my son. I am here."

"Father!" The eye did not focus, but at least the ear could hear. "We took the fortress." Grindar's words tumbled out one side of his mouth. "We took it!" He clamped onto Slar's hand.

"*You* took it, my son." Slar brushed a lock of black hair from Grindar's wandering eye. "You are the greatest warrior the Boar Clan has ever known. Our ancestors will welcome you to the Halls of Fire with a banquet like none you have ever seen."

Grindar scrambled with his hand to grasp Slar's mail hauberk and pull him closer. "Forgive Sharrog, Father. Find and forgive Nalan. He..." The wide-chested orc spat up blood in a coughing fit. He gasped for air, finding only enough to squeeze out the final words. "He loves you..."

The red eye, a mirror for Slar's own, stopped its relentless roving and stared at the long, black cloud of smoke that leaned over the Dragonscales. Slar brushed it closed with his finger and fell back on his haunches. Hurried steps sounded from behind him. Slar turned to see Sharrog come running up, a dismayed look on his face. He paused and Slar shook his head at the question in his younger son's eyes. Sharrog's face collapsed, and he stumbled forward to kneel over his dead brother.

Slar watched one son mourn the other for only a second before his slow boiling wrath burst free. "Why did you not offer him aid, Ortax?" He grabbed the shaman by his boar pelt and slammed him against the granite wall. Ortax lifted his hands, but not before Slar held a knife to his throat. "Even the greatest of shamans could not summon their power swiftly enough to stop my stroke." Slar growled. "Is this some further plot of yours to weaken me?"

Ortax held his magic. "Forgive me, my Warchief. I seek no such thing." His words came out tight, strangled by Slar's grip. "Your son was far beyond my ability to aid. My loyalty to the Boar Clan is greater than any conflict of council between us. I would have done anything to save him. He was the future of our clan."

Sharrog placed one hand upon Slar's, the other on his own dagger. "He's right, Father. No shaman could have saved Grindar."

Letting go, Slar shoved his knife back into its sheath. Ortax adjusted his boar skin cowl. Squinting one eye at his son, Slar gazed at Sharrog's hand still on his weapon. "Would you have used that on me to prove your point?"

His chin dropping in dismay, Sharrog moved his hand. "I intended to plant it in Ortax's eye the moment he started to use his magic."

Slar stopped in his tracks and turned to face Sharrog. He placed one hand upon the young orc's shoulder. "Please see to it that your brother finds a place of honor upon today's pyre." He looked at a cluster of clan warriors emerging from the human keep. "I have other responsibilities." Slar looked to Ortax. "I am sorry, Brother. Please forgive the rage of a grieving father."

Not waiting for a response, Slar climbed the stairs past smoke billowing from the caves. Sergeant Radgred leaned against his axe where the steps met the terrace in front of the keep.

"The only southerners to escape seem to be those madmen who charged out the front gate near the end." Radgred spit upon the stone. "They lit everything afire before they left, and took all the remaining horses with them. Hundreds tried to hold their keep, but we crushed them." Radgred pointed to the distant tower near the peak of the mountain. "Only there do they still hold. We cannot get to it, and they have a mage or two up there, so no dragon is willing to dare the assault."

Slar frowned at the black and gold banner fluttering on high. "We will get them. They are of no consequence now."

Slar's old companion shifted his axe to point at the gatehouse. "We also found the bodies of the Master's servants. They have been taken away as you commanded.

Unable to look at the fortification where his son fell, Slar focused on Radgred. "What about prisoners?"

"So far, only a few dozen have surrendered. However, we did catch some of their officers in a deep passage. They were collapsing what we believe to be an escape route."

Radgred waved at some of his warriors, who then proceeded to drag three captives over to Slar. One lay on the ground unconscious, the red fringe of human mages upon his cloak. The other two stared at Slar in defiance. A dwarf covered in black soot wrestled with his captors, while the old human in blue marched with a great deal of dignity.

Slar gazed at the human. *Four stars upon his collar. A prize indeed.* "I would guess you to be the highest rank here. I know those stars are important to your people." He folded his arms. "I will not insult you by asking you questions. There is no information you could give me that I might find useful, and I do not find torture to be an honorable pastime." Slar nodded to Radgred, who pulled a dagger. Two of his warriors did the same. "Were I free to choose, My Lords, I would release you to meet again on another battleground. I consider you enemies defeated in combat, not through cowardice, but by betrayal." He shook his head. "However, we all have our orders, and mine were to leave none alive."

Not taking his eyes from those of his prisoners, Slar signaled Radgred and the others. "Honor them as warriors."

The orcs lifted their daggers and, as one, drove them into the necks of their captives. The aged human died quickly, but the dwarf gazed at him through his spouting blood for several moments before he fell. Radgred wiped his dagger on the human's blue cloak.

Slar stared at the dead men. *There is no honor in this...*

He thrust his hands in rage at the sky, the knot in his gut burning with ferocity.

My son!

Epilogue

"When the winds of Chaos blow, all lands feel their wrath."
— Caladrius Dreamwalker

Elyl Falana squinted against the glint of the setting sun where it peeked through the emerald leaves. His arms strained against his bow, drawn to full. The steel head of the nocked arrow lined with the heart of the doe. He held his breath. *May the Spirits of Air return your psahn in the next generation of your kind.*

A sudden rustle in the trees spooked the doe, whose head lifted only a fraction of a second before she darted off into the underbrush, white tail flashing. Elyl cursed and relaxed his bow. A large horse crashed into the clearing beneath his perch, its dark haired rider haunting Elyl with his few glimpsed memories of his father.

"I know you are here, brother." The rider shouted, dancing his black-fetlocked horse in a circle. "Mother calls us in. She wants you to take command of the rangers again."

His movements full of grace, Elyl swung down from the tree, landing lightly next to his brother's horse. "So…Celedra has decided to return to the world?"

Garon shook his head, the dark locks separating around his pointed ears. "No. Our people will stay within the Blue Mountains, as we always have. Only we will set stronger guard upon the borders." He frowned at Elyl, his cobalt eyes almost glowing in the dusk light. "We must keep the Chaos in the outlands at bay."

"Ha!" Elyl shook his head as he took his brother's proffered hand. He leaped up behind Garon onto the horse's rear haunches. "Such things are not held back by shields and arrows, dear brother. Chaos has its way of seeping through the thinnest of cracks, and hiding from it does us little good."

Garon said nothing, giving his horse a kick once Elyl had settled in. Elyl clutched his brother's cloak when the steed leaped forward.

But I have no doubts, hiding is all we will do…

Tahrad Shannai peeked over the eastern parapet of the Tower of Malad. The sun glittered off the Clarion Ocean. He looked to the north, where, beyond the life giving waters of the Al'ahrad River, the Shining Sands spread like a rippled, golden version of the ocean. *I suppose the sand moves much like the water, only slower.*

To the west of the tower, Tahrad saw the great imperial city of Baladesh spreading along the river, set above the green patchwork of farms within the floodplain. The city grew out southward as well, stretching toward the fertile Plain of Moab where the heart of the Empire of Hadon lay.

This is amazing! No wonder the imperial family forbids it to all but their favorite servants. I should find a way to sneak Selina up here. He cast his eyes about the terrace, scattered with divans and canvas chairs. A small fountain shot up in the center, while a few date and palm trees in large pots and leveled platforms gave shade. Flowers of every conceivable color and shape grew in more pots and hanging containers, giving an element of lush splendor to the desert palace of the emperors. Tahrad breathed in their many scents, reminiscent of sweetness and honey.

A sudden jingle of metal threw Tahrad's heart into his throat. He leaped behind a pair of tall, potted palms and hid within their fronds, clasping his hands in prayer. *Please, Mistress Krina, see me safely from this tower. I swear I will never walk in forbidden gardens again.*

Two men strolled out onto the terrace. One wore the elegant robes of household royalty, the other a simple soldier's tunic. Tahrad did not recognize the second man, but the markings of armor still creased his clothes. The man in silk with his oily, pointed beard could only be the emperor's nephew, Prince Faroud.

"I have been waiting for you, Malohm. It is not wise to keep a prince waiting." He plucked a flower and held it to his sharp nose. "You have made the appropriate payments?"

The soldier bowed his head. "I have all the captains and lieutenants in our purses, and soon I'll have the boatswains too. Only Prince Sharam's ship in the flotilla remains untouched."

Faroud raised a finger. "Just remember, my friend, every man you pay now is another we must dispose of before the end." He laughed a cruel cackle that echoed over the terrace. "At least my royal cousin's men will tell no tales from the bottom of the sea."

Folding his arms, the soldier lifted an eyebrow. "Will that eventually include me, my Prince?"

Laughing again, this time with less rancor, the prince threw his arm about the soldier's back. "Of course not, my friend. I will need an admiral for my navy when the scepter is mine." He leaned back and poked the soldier with his finger. "That is – if you remain loyal." The prince laughed, echoing the cruelty Tahrad had heard before. "I can always hire an assassin for a traitor then kill that assassin too."

The soldier frowned at the laughter washing over him. "I will remain your eternal servant. I care not who is emperor. I only desire a chance for my revenge." He ground one fist into the other hand. "Sharam allowed my family to burn at Persus. I will watch his family drown before me."

When his laughter faded, the prince examined the leaves of a small jasmine bush. "Yes. Too bad about the children, but they stand as much in my way as Sharam does."

The soldier stood rooted to the ground, his empty gaze focused on the prince. "We shall also have the war with the barbarians in the north. We shall retake what was rightfully ours." He thumped his chest. "We shall retake our honor."

The prince waved his hand. "Yes, yes. We will blame Gannon for the deed with claims of magical assault. I will make certain my uncle invades out of revenge. The plump fields of Avaros will once again make the empire rich."

Dropping to one knee, the soldier lifted his hand. "With the grace of High Madrahn looking upon us, we may even go farther."

Faroud took the offered hand, lifting the man from his position in the old way of fealty. "Then let us embark upon this voyage together, my friend. And may the treasure at its end be enough to fill both our ships."

A bee bounced against Tahrad's neck. He swiped at it in a moment of startled tension, and his hand caught the edge of a palm. It rustled against its neighbor.

The soldier jumped over a low divan and threw the palms aside. Iron-hard fists grabbed Tahrad by the scruff of his neck and drug him out onto the terrace. The graying man held him down, one knee upon his neck. Breath became hard to find. Blackness began to swallow Tahrad's consciousness.

"Easy, Malohm. My friend, let the boy breathe. He is near to passing out."

Tahrad bounced back into consciousness, his head throbbing in pain. He blinked to focus his vision upon his captors.

Pushing the larger man aside, the prince smiled at Tahrad in a kind fashion and lifted him to his feet. He clucked at Mahlom's scowl. "Well, my boy, you truly chose the wrong day to sneak out onto the forbidden terrace." He brushed Tahrad's chest and held him up straight, wrapping an arm around Tahrad's shoulders. The prince walked him toward the door. "You must be certain not to tell anyone of our words. You can make that promise, can't you?"

Tahrad nodded his head profusely, his quaking hands lifted in praise. "I promise, my holy Prince. I swear by High Madrahn, and the goddess of my mother's people, Mistress Krina. I will say nothing of what I heard here today."

The prince looked over his shoulder. "See, Malohm. That did not have to be so hard." He picked up the speed of his steps. "Now, let us help our young friend down from the tower."

Missing the doorway into the tower did not surprise Tahrad so much as the speed with which the stone streets rushed to greet him.

lord Chancellor Sammin Vyce breathed steadily, his feet stepping in rhythm as he climbed the Paladin's Spire. *He denies it, but that fat bastard must have a lift in here somewhere. There is no way he makes this climb on those flabby legs.*

Once he reached the top landing, at least a hundred yards above the grounds of the Ivory Palace, Sammin paused to calm his breath. He patted his forehead dry with a lavender scented cloth, and then tucked it away up his charcoal sleeve. Pulling the lace of his shirt straight from his jacket cuff, he reached to tap on the carved whitewood door.

"Come in, Sammin, my friend, no need to knock."

Sammin heard the High Elder's lips smacking through the door. He pushed it open with a grimace.

The air inside felt sultry, and it smelled of sweat and gamy roast meat. The elder sat on a thickly padded chair, a far-too-thin robe of black and white silk strained around his bulk. A slight sheen of sweat covered his brow. A side door of the chamber closed shut, hiding a soft giggle.

"Welcome, Sammin," the elder said with a fraudulent smile. "It is so rare I have visitors in my high chambers." He gestured toward a silver platter set on a side table. A headless, roasted carcass rested upon it, about the size of a small goat. "You should try a taste. It is quite fantastic." The elder pulled a long strip of meat from the haunch and stuck it in his mouth, before sucking the grease from each finger.

If it will shut him up…it does not smell too bad. Sammin reached for the meat with pale fingers, his hand halting, frozen in horror. *Those are paws, not hooves!*

The elder spread his smug smile even wider. "Sad that so few appreciate a delicacy when it sits before them." He stripped a long piece from the back. "The hardest part is finding a chef in Daynon who knows how to cook canine properly."

Refusing to be too startled by the elder's purposeful show, Sammin plowed on to business. "The papers…you claim to have them?"

Sighing, the elder picked up a small satchel leaning against his chair. "Always so direct, Sammin. You must learn to enjoy the blessings of life, not just its trials." He peaked into the leather bundle. "The paper is a century old, as is the ink. The beeswax seal is the same as has been used around Lake Iyar for far longer. The monk who wrote it is deaf and mute, and he knows the legal wordings for the time of the Gavanor Rebellion." The elder handed the satchel to Sammin. "You will find it impeccable."

Looking at the small sheaf of aged parchment within, Sammin frowned. "It must be, or you had better learn to eat without your head attached to your gut."

High Elder Varon Hastrian waved a thick hand at Sammin. "Do not fear, my friend. It will pass even the most scrutinous eye."

Eager to be gone, Sammin folded the flap back over the satchel and tucked it under his arm. "Let us hope so, Elder." His steps quickened with each one until he was out the door, and it closed behind him. Sammin heard fat fingers snap and another boyish giggle. He descended the steps two at a time. *It will all be worth it when I stand behind a new, more pliant king…*

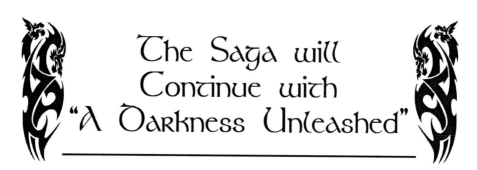

The Saga will Continue with "A Darkness Unleashed"

About The Author

Photograph by Bradley Daniels

It is well known that J. T. slew several dragons in the pasture near the farm where he grew up. He found the hidden Waterfall of Life deep in his grandfather's woods, with only his little brother and their dog, Pongo, to aid him. Many other quests, often borne from the classic books of fantasy literature, consumed his days and nights.

After a long dark quest through a much feared land known as "Q'orp'orate Qubicle", J.T. Hartke was cast out to find his own way. He spent a short time cooking for a mad master and another stint as a fool. He learned many lessons during his exile, the greatest of which led to his muse. At last, J. T. took it upon himself to create his own quest—and thus was born The Dragonsoul Saga.

A Message From The I.I.I. Staff

We here at I.I.I. would like to take a moment to thank all of the fans of The Dragonsoul Saga. It has absolutely blown us away that this series has been embraced so fast and with such loyalty by so many of those who have been with us over the past few years.

But, our company slogan, "Built by Fantasy Fans for Fantasy Fans" is more than just a catchy tagline. It is a call to action, and my friends, we still need your help.

We have all been victims, my friends. Victims of having a favorite T.V. show canceled. We ask ourselves, "Why? It was well written. I know lots of people who enjoyed it. Why was it canceled?" The answer is simple – the fans did not get involved.

We live in a new world, my friends. A world of information. You, the fans, now have more power than you can possibly know. The power to propel something that you enjoy. The power to help it thrive and grow.

Sure, it is our job to put out quality products. Give the fans an interesting and thought-provoking story to sink their mental teeth into. But, it is you who will decide if this series continues. And it takes very little time or effort on your part to do this.

If you liked this book, please, tell a friend. If you tell even one person who picks up this series, you have done your part to ensure you will get the opportunity to read this series to its completion. I am willing to bet, without straining too hard, you can think of someone you know, just one person who would enjoy reading this story as much as you just did. They may have not even heard of it. Why not tell them? Let them know how much you enjoyed it. Give them the opportunity to enjoy it as well.

If you are feeling energetic, write one or two lines about this book on your Facebook page. Or My Space, or Good Reads, or whatever you use. We know you have one of them, we see it in your "favorites" folder. Send out an email to a few people you know who are fantasy fans. Just a line that says, "Hey, I just read this book. You should check it out." And that is just the beginning of what you can do, my friends! (Queue the patriotic music and let the flags wave in the breeze) Amazon.com or BarnesandNoble.com are wonderful places to let the world know how you felt about this book. With just a few minutes of your time, you could write a review. You can blog about it. Sffword.com, goodreads.com, librarything.com are all wonderful places to connect with other readers. Let them know you enjoyed this book!

My fellow fans, I stand before you today to let you know that you have the power to ensure this series does not go gentle into that good night! We have a dream... that The Dragonsoul Saga will continue to entertain people for years to come. So, ask not what a good fantasy saga can do for you. Ask what you can do for a good fantasy saga!

Thank you,
The I.I.I. Staff

"Hi. My name is J.T. Hartke, and I approve of this message."

CPSIA information can be obtained at www.ICGtesting.com
Printed in the USA
BVOW012011290712

295605BV00002BA/2/P